HOUSE *of* MASKS

DEANNA KNIPPLING

WONDERLAND PRESS

Contents

The House of Masks

A Space Opera

Book the First

La fin est proche

Chapter I

Thomàon

IT WAS A TIME that had come untethered from time itself, a time which reflected a hundred other times that had come before it, and a thousand more that would surely come after. It was a place of such deception that one's lies revealed one's secrets more than they hid them, and of such decadence as to corrupt one's very flesh, or to refine it—to immortality.

We called it Thomàon, a blue jewel of a world amongst the diamond stars of the black velvet night. We did not recall the origin of the name. In fact, so much time had passed since we had contact with the other gems of the sky that we had all but forgotten that they existed. We told tales of other worlds as though they were fantasies or myths. And every year we gathered together for the Great Masquerade in the Silver City, and sealed ourselves within the Great Dome, while storms and madness reigned without.

Now the Great Masquerade has come to an end, the Masks are removed, all has been revealed—and all lies in ruins.

But once Thomàon was a paradise.

Its fields were green, its oceans blue. Across the world rose the elegant cities of the Grillons, fantastic whimsies of architecture, miraculously created by a savage, stupid, and maddened race. Their cousin race the Scarabées rooted through the earth, bringing forth such minerals as we desired: shining metals, iron, corundum, diamonds, and that most precious material of them all: the golden elixir, which granted immortality. Other creatures may have existed, but we did not much notice them. Machines worked the fields, and brought in the harvests, and carried us across the waves to our private islands, our far castles, our laboratories, our fortresses.

On the world of Thomàon lay but a single great city of humankind, the Silver City. The Silver City could hold at the height of the Season the entire human population of Thomàon, that is, a million human inhabitants. And in the Silver City there was a single great castle, the Castle of the Silver Spire, home of a hundred fountains, reflecting pools, and towers, and a thousand balconies. At the heart of the castle was the Silver Spire itself, an enormous, graceful tower, high enough to bathe itself in the clouds during any weather. It was the only piece of the Silver City which protruded from the Great Dome when it was sealed, and whose tip held such devices as to inform the Silver City when the Season had finished and it was time for our revelries to come to an end.

The Season was a midsummer storm so severe as to require the sealing up of the entire Silver City under the Great Dome. During it, the Silver Spire was projected with images, which illuminated the city in a disorienting maze of light. Dancers in their gowns became like gods while projected upon the Silver Spire. Roses became impenetrable briars; fireworks became conflagrations; sunsets, holocausts. Everywhere in the Silver City would be bathed in that enchanted light, from the castle to the labyrinth of streets, to the navigable wonderland of roofs, steeples, balconies, widow's walks, temples, gardens, pathways, and cables that stretched everywhere between them.

All of which was nothing, compared to the music.

Viewed by airship, when the Silver City was not sealed by the Great Dome, the castle appeared to be an enormous sundial: the Silver Spire in the center threw such a shadow across the other rooftops as to mark time itself. The inhabitants followed the hours in its shadow: the cafés to the west, in the morning; the sleeping-bowers of the north, for noontide's lull in the heat; the teahouses and restaurants of the east for one's repast; and then a return to the castle for one's entertainments: singers and operas, acrobats and circuses; fortunes told by the Scarabées; assignations; assassinations. Then, throughout the night, a slow ebb to return to one's apartments in the south, to sup, and to sleep.

When the shadow stood so perfectly straight at noon that the Silver Spire cast no shadow, then it was the time for the Season to begin: prisoners were released from their prisons; miners sealed their mines and caught the last trundling ore-carriers back to the city, always arriving in thousands at the last minute, laughing at the danger of it; artists sighed and cursed the gods for not giving them more talent as their latest paintings, and statues, and other oeuvres were wrapped and brought to the castle to replace last cycle's decor; bakers and cooks wiped the sweat from their brows against their arms, with no time to take out a handkerchief as they prepared to feed the horde soon to descend upon them; gamesmen rattled their dice and nicked the edges of their cards with their thumbnails, in preparation of their great feasting upon the foolish; beggars and thieves squabbled over streetcorners, rooftops, doorways, and disguises; nobles awaited deliveries of clothing, jewels, and perfumes, in terror lest their illusions be outdone by their fellows; assassins collected the first halves of their fees, and bided their time, sharpening their knives and mixing their potions. Underneath the streets, where in the great, cavernous reservoirs they lay in safety, the gondoliers practiced their songs: tales of lovers, of betrayals, of ironies, of cruel deaths or kind ones, of killers who lived amongst the innocent, of the innocents who so charmed the wicked that their lives were spared for just *one* more night.

King Corentin and Queen Delphine ruled the Silver City and awaited the raising of the Great Dome against the storms soon to be arriving, and saw that their preparations were good. The Council of Masks, under whom the king and queen served, and which ruled the rest of Thomàon from amongst the populace, speaking for the poor, the lame, the blind, the night-dancers, the beggars, the bakers and cooks, the prisoners, the gondoliers, and even the nobility—their eyes looked out from behind their masks, and also saw that the preparations were good.

To the powerful, all turns of fate are, in the end, good.

But the gondoliers sang gloomily, the Scarabée fortune-tellers cast their shells and hummed dire songs of vengeance, and the hawks wheeled in the sky, and whispered to their hawk-masters of doom and damnation.

Chapter 2

The Prison Ship

IT WAS THE LAST flight to Thomàon from Shakes Prison, a dire island fortress that was little more than bare rock, the high stone walls of the fortress, and an inner stronghold that rose within them. Atop the inner stronghold was a landing pad, and upon the pad was the *Sésame*, a seed-shaped brown airship, small and quick—and better armed than its appearance would suggest.

Shakes Island was located in the center of the Mer de Tempêtes, on the opposite side of the world. When there was daylight in the Silver City, there was only darkness at Shakes Prison.

Some said, and not incorrectly, that it was *always* dark at Shakes Prison.

It had come to the last moment to leave for the *Sésame* to arrive in time to land within the airfields outside the Silver City, and its cargo and passengers unloaded before the city was sealed within its dome. To wait an instant later was to risk attack—but to have left an instant earlier would have brought its own dangers.

The storms of the Season were already rising, as they rose all across Thomàon, and the skies had turned to deep shades of purple and gray. The winds tore at the *Sésame*, making it shiver upon its landing pad. The stones of the stronghold groaned under the rising winds. Bursts of rain and hail tossed desperately against every surface, as if begging for shelter. The wind and sea roared and dashed themselves against the high stone walls of the fortress, knowing that if not today, then someday they would erode the very stones into sand and ruin. The sound was deafening, and reminded those who remained upon the little island that to fear the waves was wise.

Of those remaining, there were only two.

The prisoners and guards and servants had been sent ahead, on an aerial pleasure-barge full of silks, courtesans, and other luxuries: the prisoners' sentences had finished, and all were free to return to the Silver City, their various debts paid in full. But that had been an earlier flight.

This flight was the one that carried that which the prisoners had retrieved from beneath the sea surrounding the prison during the year previous, work so painstaking, deadly, and delicate that to perform it was to be forgiven rape, betrayal, or murder. To survive a term at Shakes Prison was considered to be forgiven by the gods themselves—a blessing given this year to only a lucky few.

The treasures themselves were few, and sealed within cases that were to be delivered directly to King Corentin and Queen Delphine, and no others, and held in trust for the Council of Masks. They were such treasures as one might never encounter in a hundred lifetimes, the last remnants of a substance which had once been plentiful upon Thomàon—and the very existence of which was a terrible secret. The air upon the pleasure-barge, piloted by electronic ordinateurs rather than men, was such that all who traveled upon it found themselves having forgotten the last year—prisoners, guards, courtesans, and servants all. None of them were to be trusted with any hint of the secret.

The only one who knew the secret was the warden of the prison, one Marks Lemure, the chief warden of Thomàon. He was a thick-jawed man, with thinning, dull blond hair and wind-reddened skin. His eyes were narrow, his shoulders broad, and his muscles like iron. He was a stern man, but as changeable as the sea, with a smile that was as quick to amusement as authority.

The secret of the treasures of Shakes Prison—the fact that there *was* a secret—had never been betrayed, not by Marks Lemure, and, at his assurance, nor by anyone else. Of such men there have ever been few.

Atop the stronghold was an enclosed elevator, for loading and unloading materials and passengers from the ships at the landing pad, a stone enclosure with two heavy sliding doors made of an untarnished silvery material.

The doors slid open, and Warden Lemure stepped onto the roof of the stronghold and into the bitter storm. Within his arms was the last of the three treasure-cases. He walked with small and careful steps, head down against the rain and wind-lashed waves. The case was gray, and flat, and the size of a courtesan's diary: neither large nor noticeable, nor heavy to hold.

Nevertheless, the Warden felt its weight within the heaviness of his heart: it contained the last of what had once been found in such plenitude beneath the waves of the Mer de Tempêtes. Within the small case was the last of the sand of an hourglass which had once seemed to run endlessly, and he knew that only a miracle could save Thomàon now.

He placed the case within a small and hidden hatch on the side of the airship, where it fastened itself to the underside of the passenger deck above it. Lemure stretched his fingers through the slim hatch and felt the touch of the two other cases fastened next to it. Once, the secret compartment had held dozens of cases—but now, only three.

The last three.

He withdrew his hand. The hatch sealed itself, seamless and secret against the rest of the ship's hull.

The other luggage had already been loaded by the guards, before they had left on the pleasure-barge, to revel and oubliate. The *Sésame* was already fueled, and the storms were rising.

Only one last thing remained—a single passenger to be escorted to the ship, his daughter Ammaline.

She knew nothing of the treasures, or of any other secrets; she was only a young woman, not to be burdened with such things. As beautiful as a goddess, yet still as sweet-natured as a babe, she had been orphaned as a young girl at the tragic death of her mother.

Lemure returned to the elevator and commanded it to descend, not to the depths of the fortress from which he had retrieved the treasure, but to the upper levels of the stronghold, where he kept his daughter.

He unlocked the steel door and let himself inside the apartment, calling, "Ammaline! It's time."

"Coming!"

The hallway itself was little more than bare stone, lit by bulbs sealed beneath thick glass reinforced with heavy wire. Ammaline's rooms were to the right, her door open, and warm light shining from within.

The light extinguished itself, and a thump echoed from within the room.

"Are you all right?"

"Coming!"

Ammaline appeared in her doorway. She was wrapped from head to foot for the storm, a gray waterproof cloak that closed around her so that the wind would not tear it open. She wore a gray hat like an overturned bucket, and carried a small, lumpy bag with her—one that he knew would contain a ragged scrap of blanket, given to her by her long-dead mother. She tucked a viewscreen inside it. Her long, curly black hair had been pulled back into a braid, but more than a few strands had escaped, and jutted unruly from under the eaves of her ungainly hat. She had to tip her head back to peer out at him, her mother's violet eyes viewing him softly, with love and trust.

She limped a few steps, then disciplined herself to even her gait. She took his arm. "I'm ready, Papa."

"Nervous?" he teased her.

Her eyes widened and she pulled away from him. "Why did you have to remind me! I'm terrified!"

Ammaline had passed other Masquerades within the Silver City, but this year would be different: she had been invited to sing upon the stage of the Opéra du Mendicant, the magnificent theatre housed within the Silver Spire itself.

Her voice, all agreed, would be one for the ages, if only her father would let her loose from Shakes Prison more often, to have her heart broken a few times at court. As yet, her perfect but innocent voice could not support a tragic opera without raising eyebrows, although she was a delightful soprano for an operetta or two.

Her father acknowledged the truth of this: and yet he could not open her cage, and set her free.

Not yet—not *this* year.

He touched a gloved fingertip to her nose. "You'll be fine. Let's go."

They entered the elevator together, Ammaline turning her face as he typed in the security code. They rose up together, Lemure standing steady without support, and Ammaline holding the rail at the edge of the compartment.

The doors opened onto a barrage of small, stinging pieces of sleet, and roared in rage at the two of them—at the fortress, at the ship, at the heavens themselves.

Ammaline gasped and clutched her father's arm again. "Why do you always have to wait until the last minute?"

He laughed and pulled her along with him into the storm, toward the *Sésame*. "It's more fun that way!"

"Oh, Papa!"

They dashed across the stone to the landing pad, the large side hatch opening as they approached, and a short, study ramp descending for them. Ammaline skipped up the hatch, ducking and hunching her shoulders, clutching her bag to her chest. Lemure followed her, more dignified in his steps but no less quick for that.

The hatch sealed behind them, admitting them to a small compartment with a pilot's seat and passenger cradles. Ammaline stripped off her coat and stowed it in a compartment under a cradle.

"Would you like to sleep?"

She pulled her viewscreen out of her bag and held it up for him to see. "But I want to watch Océan LaFerme sing!"

Her father laughed. "And if I don't want to listen to her sing for six hours? All the way to the North pole and back down again?"

"I will wear my casquettes!" she promised. "You will only hear it if I sing along with her."

"I would like nothing better," he told her, and began his last set of flight checks—one that ended with ensuring his daughter was secure in her cradle.

She was still wearing her ugly hat: he tugged it from her head and stowed it in the compartment below. Already she had the casquettes tucked into her ears and was humming along with the great diva's latest concert.

He kissed her on the forehead.

She smiled. "I love you, Papa."

"I love you, too. Ammaline. Sing for me a little, will you?"

"Of course."

She began to sing along with the diva, *Les beaux rêves*—an old song indeed, said to come from the Vieux Monde, la Terre herself.

Lemure settled himself into the pilot's seat, fastening himself tightly into place. Despite the lateness of the hour, he ran one more set of flight checks, for the storm would forgive no mistakes.

Then he lifted the *Sésame* from the landing pad. The wind caught the ship in a moment, and swept it tumbling out over the ocean.

There was a hitch in Ammaline's voice as she s-sang…

Then the *Sésame* righted itself, and Lemure lifted it higher, above the tumult of the waves, and righted its direction. The wind still struggled to upset them, but the ship declined to be again overturned. Soon they were flying toward the pole.

Ammaline continued to sing.

The next two and a half hours were peaceful, without incident. The little *Sésame* hummed through the air, as if contented to be aloft. Ammaline spent much of her time singing. At one moment she would sing phrases from the song she was to sing at the Opéra du Mendicant, little variations of a melody she had practiced already endlessly. At the next moment, she would sing a familiar old tune in the style of Océan LaFerme, then sing it again, in a new fashion, to see if it better suited her own manner. Like many artistes that Lemure had known over the years, she had yet to discover her signature of voice—but such a discovery seemed to be near at hand. Lemure had no skill in music, yet even he could hear a pattern to the changes his daughter was making to those old, long-familiar songs. Then again, Ammaline would sing an entirely new song, hesitantly at first, and then with more confidence: new songs that the Diva, unbeknownst to that famed lady, was teaching to her.

It was a method for passing the time as to lighten one's cares, to unburden one's soul—if for a few moments only.

Then, less than half an hour from the pole, the lights within the cabin began to flash red, and an alarm rang. Lemure frowned at his viewscreen, which showed the icône of a radio dish flashing.

An emergency distress signal—one that he should not answer, with such treasures on board his ship.

"What is it, Papa?"

Ammaline knew as well as anyone what the flashing red lights in the cabin meant; if he lied to her about the signal, she would likely remain silent about it—but the knowledge of it would poison her, just a little, against him. He could not stop to answer the call, no matter how desperate—and yet he *must* stop to answer the call.

Caught between love and duty, he weighed the time and the knowledge that he carried a slim pistolet à aiguille secreted under his coat. He flipped open the communications channel for the signal.

"This is the *Sésame*. Who calls?"

"Lemure. Thank the gods that you are coming. It is I, Paquet. I am alone, and I am desperate."

Paquet was one of Lemure's assistants, who sometimes worked among the police at the North Pole.

"What is it?"

Paquet coughed, a terrible sound full of wetness and pain. "It cannot be said over the radio, Lemure. You must land."

"Are you hurt?"

"I am dying, Lemure. My body you may leave for the Grillons. But my words, you must carry with you."

"I am coming," Lemure told him. "It will be twenty minutes."

"Pray that I live that long, or we are doomed. I am in the dining hall of Building One. *La fin est proche.*"

With a sigh, Lemure answered him in kind. "*La fin est proche.*"

The end is near. It was a statement that was not unexpected, particularly in that Lemure had himself made it many times, over the years. But it is an entirely different circumstance to acknowledge the truth, than to find oneself laboring under its burdens.

As soon as Lemure had signed off on the channel, he glanced over his shoulder to see what Ammaline had made of the conversation. She seemed to have been ignorant of the entire matter, a recording of the diva's programme shimmering on the shield above her eyes. Her body twitched in time to the faint music coming from the casquettes over her ears.

She only pretended not to have heard, Lemure knew. But it was a fiction that would save him having to explain that which he could not. He flew onward, accelerating faster than was safe. The ship accepted the challenge coolly, as if not even the storms of the Season could shake it—not after that first moment of worry on take-off.

Soon the ice of the continente du nord was passing below them, blue and white and green, with stark black shadows cast away from the hovering sun. He slowed the ship as they approached Pelletier Station. The ugly gray buildings stood on stilts that could raise or lower the buildings as the ice encroached. They had been raised to their highest reach for the Season, in the hopes that the Grillons would not do so much damage. Each year, it proved to be a vain hope.

Lemure landed the ship atop one of the buildings without waiting for authorization—the only authority left on the station was Paquet. Nevertheless, Lemure touched the pistolet under his coat as he stood.

"You will wait here for me," he told Ammaline, as he unsealed her from the cradle. "If I come alone, or bearing one other man, you may unlock the door. Otherwise, you are to touch this button—" He indicated the pilote automatique. "—and leave me behind."

"Never, Papa!"

"You must, my dear. The north is dangerous. Who knows what traitors or thieves lie in wait? If you do not leave me, then you will be dead—and word will not reach King Corentin or Queen Delphine." When she hesitated to answer, he added, "If you will not agree to this, then I shall continue to the Silver City, and leave this man to die."

Her voice hitched in her throat, and her hands flew to her cheeks, like a little girl. "Oh, Papa! I promise I will do as you say."

He pressed her hand to his heart, then opened the hatch and stepped out onto the icy rooftop. Looking back only to ensure that the hatch of the *Sésame* had closed, he ran toward the elevator, whose doors opened at his approach.

Chapter 3

Visions of the Opéra

AMMALINE WAITED WITH BATED breath for the return of Papa from the depths of the polar outpost, Pelletier Station. Although the little *Sésame* was perfectly warm and comfortable on the inside, the entire ship shivered from the strong winds that buffeted it from the outside.

The Season's storms were rising, even at the North Pole. The screens of the ship showed the view outside the ship, of an endless series of snow-dunes, sculpted by the wind into strange architectures of green and blue ice—ice that was rapidly deepening in color, as the clouds overtook the horizon, then dropped the station into shadow.

How long was she to wait for Papa?

How long was it safe to wait? Before the storm was so severe that it would crash the ship, or keep it grounded—and exposed to the Grillons when they inevitably arrived to gnaw, and shatter, and kill?

Papa had not said. She had not even the knowledge of whether the ship would automatically take itself to safety, if the storm rose too high.

Ammaline had been raised as a sort of hothouse flower, honored more for her delicacy than any ruder, more tenacious virtue. In a way it had been necessary. Her mama refused to leave her papa; he had to serve most of his year among the prisons, as Chief Warden. Ammaline and her mama had to be protected from the prisoners, both because of their ill-nature, and because of their desperation. The situation left Ammaline and her mama as little more than prisoners themselves. Although they were not required to dive under the waves and into the caves under the prisons, to dig for Papa's treasure, they had not the prospect of having their sentences end at the start of the Season, either.

Papa had agreed, however, to allow Ammaline a taste of freedom: she was to be allowed to ask the great diva, Océan LaFerme, if she would take her on as an apprentice.

It was clear that Papa put no great emphasis on the possibility. He expected the diva, who had a reputation for fickleness, to say no. Perhaps he had already spoken to her—either directly or through a friend of a friend, for Papa had many friends—and ascertained that *this* year at least, the answer would be in the negative.

But Ammaline intended to make Océan LaFerme twist in agony over such an answer. She would sing so well, so purely, and with such emotion, that madame would be unable to deny her request.

If Ammaline and her papa reached the Silver City alive, that was.

The storm grew ever darker, and the ship shivered ever the harder, but when Ammaline checked the ship's readouts, only a few minutes had passed.

Five minutes—seven—eleven minutes—

And then the elevator doors opened, and Papa was returning, leaning against the wind as he walked, his dark flight suit rippling over his skin. He was alone. The knees of his flight suit were dark and wet, but soon turned white—and red—from the clinging sleet and snow that had risen with the storm. White flakes clung to the ends of his sleeves, and to a large patch across his chest, and turned dark as the fluid that covered him soaked into it. His face was dotted with blood, and itself held darker storms than did the sky itself.

It was at that moment that Ammaline took her visions of childhood, and, without looking too closely at them, set them to the side.

She did not press the pilot automatique button; she sat in the pilot's seat and began a set of flight checks, making sure that the ship would be ready to leave immediately when her father arrived. He had not taught her how to fly—but it was simple enough to discover such things, on one's viewscreen, if one were curious.

And Ammaline had *always* been curious.

When he reached the ship, she opened its door to admit him, closed it behind him, then stood to return to her cradle.

His sharp eyes narrowed as they ran over the readouts on the screen, which she had put up for him to view, so that he could see at a glance that there was no reason for further delay. He waved a hand toward the controls. "Take over for me. I am sick at heart and will sleep. Wake me if there is trouble."

A thousand times she had dreamed of him giving her permission to fly, but never had she dreamed the taste of her victory would taste like chewing a piece of metal foil. She sat down in the pilot's seat and ran over the flight checks again—and again—until her father was safely ensconced in the other cradle, and she could see the readouts of his heartbeat fluttering on her screen, at first racing dangerously, then slowing as the medicine he had requested took effect.

As he was sinking into a drugged sleep, her father murmured in the ancient language, "En fin de course...la fin est proche."

And then, according to her readouts, he was asleep, even before the *Sésame* had lifted off. Ammaline bit her lip and pressed the button of the pilot automatique, which was large and red, in order that it could not be mistaken during such emergencies as this. In any other weather, the ship would have lifted off smoothly and safely, and followed its pre-programmed course.

But today?

Ammaline, strapped into position, could barely move more than would be required to pilot the ship. She waited, hands at the ready to interrupt the pilot automatique. She had flown a thousand ships in simulation, but never with the true wind pulling at the controls—and yet something within her told her she must be ready to follow her own instincts over those of the ship.

And yet—she hesitated.

As her hands hovered doubtfully, the ship lifted according to its programme, and was taken by the winds, dashed from the top of Pelletier Station, and into the icy ridges that had built up around the station.

The ship shrieked with the impact, but did not smash or shatter, only complained—loudly.

Papa stirred—then sank back into sleep.

Ammaline nudged the thrust direction the tiniest amount, angling the ship's nose upward

The next time the ship skipped off an ice ridge, it angled upward until it was caught by the wind and dragged far off course—but without turning end over end or spinning.

Further and further upward the ship rose, as it was swept further and further away from its destination—until the pilot automatique was able to succeed in its struggle against the wind, and turn the ship in the correct direction.

Ammaline watched the ordinateur run its calculations and recalculations, its margins of error and safety both reducing quickly. Soon it was established that the *Sésame* would arrive at the Silver City intact—but whether it would be able to land safely, or in time to be admitted before the dome was sealed, was another matter.

Ammaline set up a distress signal, unsure of what else to do. There soon came a response:

May the Gods save you and your daughter, Lemure.

Which message Ammaline took as notification that even by the engineers of the Silver City, nothing else could be done.

At first, terror gripped her. She could only just see her papa in his cradle past her shoulder—she had strapped herself in so tight that she could not turn so far as to see him clearly. She watched him, straining out of the corner of her eye, until she had convinced herself a dozen times that he was still breathing. To look at the readouts upon the screen in front of her did nothing to ease her heart.

But he breathed, and she saw him breathe, and again she saw it. The ship flew from the continente du nord over the great ocean, la mer, which stretched from pole to pole, and all across the world. It would be hours before she once again was over land.

She watched the numbers and calculations shift slowly, a pendulum that one moment swung closer to salvation, and the next moment closer toward doom. The range between hope and despair was a slender one, and, dissolving into exhaustion, she began to imagine—without ever quite falling herself asleep—that she had safely arrived at the Silver City, and was being escorted to a room where she would be allowed to prepare herself for the even greater ordeal of her presentation at the Opéra du Mendicant, and to Madame LaFerme.

Madame LaFerme would sweep into Ammaline's humble room, trailing shimmering cloth and exotic scents. "Come with me, for you must replace me at the opéra this night. You must appear to be me—you must act like me—you must sing like me—we have only a few moments—you are ready?"

And Ammaline would answer, "I am ready, Madame."

They would go through shadowed back corridors, to dressing-rooms, down stairs, through mirrors that became secret doors, and finally descend ladders into darkness. She could smell the damp, and hear water splashing and dripping, the rhythmic, secret sound of someone trying to row silently.

Instead of the stage, they had gone beneath the Castle of the Silver Spire to the reservoirs below it, which at least in stories were the forbidden territory of gondoliers and pirates—and often it was impossible to determine which was which.

Madame reached a platform and stepped away from the ladder. As Ammaline followed her, Madame lifted one hand over her head, lighting a bright torch.

The surface of the reservoir was only just below them, and it was filled with nearly as many beautifully carved gondolas as it could hold, as far as the eye could see.

"You must sing," announced Madame LaFerme. "You must sing as well as I, or they will kill you, and all of Thomàon will be destroyed as well. You must sing."

And then Madame threw her head back and began to howl, a ghastly sound.

Ammaline's head jerked upright. The landing alarm had sounded; they had arrived; her father was disengaging himself from his cradle; they had arrived in time, and were safe.

Chapter 4

Preparations

THE SILVER CITY WAS a paradise of white limestone buildings faced with promenades of tall columns, a city of temperate weather (except during the Season, a time entirely lacking in temperance), clear blue skies, and fountains topped with weathered bronze angels, unlikely creatures said to be from the Vieux Monde. Here and there were erected monuments to conquests whose victories now seemed unlikely and unnecessary—*when* had the Scarabées been so naughty as to require a booted foot upon their necks?—temples to gods who were more remembered for their feast days than their divinity, labyrinthine gardens, old mansions filled with the work of a single artist, towering Grillon architecture re-erected within the city at great expense, open-air markets supplying every delicacy and indelicacy, modern sculpture-gardens that danced at the slightest breeze, and solemn memorials to times past when injustice prevailed.

Whether those memorials condemned, or celebrated, was often to Ammaline less than clear.

And yet the sights of the Silver City itself were only one-half of the whole, for above the city itself was the underside of the Great Dome, which reflected the city a second time. In daytime it softly glowed a bright, cloudless blue with the hazy image of the city floating overhead, a castle in the clouds. At night, the dome was speckled with artificial stars and the reflected lights of the city like a dark mirror, a fortune-teller's scrying dish filled with ink.

In Ammaline's imagination, there were *two* cities: and often she felt that the one *above* was the true city, casting as its distorted reflection the one *below*.

The *Sésame* slowed as it approached the Silver City.

The dome over the Silver City was in the process of being erected, and would soon be sealed. The separate sections of the geodesic dome rose into place, hovering until it locked itself to its fellows. Each irregularly shaped section was its own shining, pilotless ship, and each reflected the deep colors of the storm as it fitted itself slowly, and grandly, into place. Only the last few sections remained to be sealed. The hum of them was a song, so low in pitch that it was impossible to follow the melody. One could only sense the sound of it when the chords themselves changed.

Sounding half-asleep, her father mumbled, "Don't touch the controls," nearly scaring Ammaline out of her wits.

Quickly, she tried to turn to see him, but she was still fastened tightly in her seat, and only managed to wrench her neck against the restraints. Just then, a trail of lightning raced over the outside of the dome, making her squeak with fright.

"It is all right, my darling...we are safe...you have brought us here safely..."

She eased herself into a state of relaxation, and turned slowly this time, until she could see her father out of the corner of her eye. "Are you all right?"

"You have stopped the bleeding...I will live..."

Ammaline blinked in startlement: *she* had not been bleeding at all. And it had not been her father's blood that had covered him, when he had returned to the ship, but the man Paquet's. She turned back to her screens, to confirm that her father was injured, whole in body, if not in mind.

Did he dream?

But even in dreaming, she trusted his instincts, and so, as the *Sésame* flew straight toward the Great Dome rather than the landing pads that the ship had used on previous trips, she did not lift a finger to nudge the controls.

The little ship flew directly toward the geodesic plates. At the last moment, Ammaline closed her eyes—but there was no impact. The plates, which had appeared to be sealed, parted before the little ship, allowing it to slide between them.

Ammaline touched one of the control, to adjust a viewscreen. Behind them, a geodesic plate was just fitting itself back into place. It was a miracle: the plates had not yet been sealed, or it would have been impossible to move them, until the end of the Season.

Although the clouds outside the Silver City hung dark and threatening above them, the inside of the dome was shrouded even deeper in darkness. Until the plates were all in place, it was not safe to have them lit.

The *Sésame* moved steadily toward the center of the city, toward the Castle of the Silver Spire itself. Gently flew the ship as the dome finished sealing itself above them, the ship's engines humming soft and contentedly, as though it had been an entirely uneventful trip.

The ship selected one of the roofs at the outer edges of the castle, hovered for a moment as permission codes flashed across the screen, then lowered itself on top of the roof as gently as a leaf settling on the forest floor on a still afternoon.

When the ship had stopped moving, Ammaline's restraints released her, and she gasped for breath that she had not known she needed. She sagged forward in the seat, every muscle stiff and suddenly cramping.

Her father had wakened more fully; when the cradle released him, he sat up easily and smoothly. He gave her a sympathetic glance as he approached the screen, looking over the readouts.

He dropped a hand onto her shoulder. "You have done well."

She rolled her head on her neck. "I did not do much of anything, to tell the truth. Only a little nudge at the beginning...and then nothing. But I am so stiff!"

He squeezed her shoulder gently. "It's difficult to relax when you're in the piloting restraints. As you come to trust your instincts, it becomes easier."

"It must become easier, or no one could bear it!" She shook her head at how unusually the day had gone. "How could we pass through the dome, Papa? Wasn't it sealed already? And why have we landed here, on top of the castle? I did not know there were landing pads on the roofs!"

He patted her shoulder again. "I must report to their majesties as soon as possible, darling Ammaline. A servant is being sent to escort you; I will return to you as soon as I am able. We can talk then."

She lifted her cheek to him, and he kissed it, then dashed out of the ship. A moment later, he was holding several small cases in his arms, striding toward an elevator booth whose door was already opening, revealing the presence of a Scarabée servant.

Her papa and the Scarabée each hesitated at the sight of the other, her father turning pale, and the Scarabée lifting a single pair of shivering central arms, then lowering them. Then the two of them did a sort of circular dance that ended with her father inside the elevator, and the Scarabée outside it. The two of them stared at each other until the doors closed; then the Scarabée turned, heavily and slowly, toward the ship.

The Scarabée was small for its kind. A few small islands lay somewhat near Shakes Prison, and on occasion her father would have to inspect them, taking Ammaline to visit them as the whim took him. The Scarabée villages there were small and meagre, but the Scarabées themselves were much larger and denser, of a deep bronze color. Their shells contained large air sponges that allowed them to stay under water for several hours at a time, maintaining their underwater farms, and allowing them to dig through the rock and silt along the sea floor, searching for treasures to offer her father.

The city Scarabées were smaller, in general, their beautiful shells less dense. This one's shell was mirrorlike in places, shimmering and opalescent.

Over the ship's speakers, the Scarabée greeted her in a lilting, feminine voice—feminine for a Scarabée, that was. Its voice was like the plucking of a musical instrument with such long strings that one could not but feel the thrum of them, deep in one's chest. "I offer you my salutations, Miss Ammaline. My name is Madame Opale."

"You have a lovely name," Ammaline said, as the Scarabée trundled across the rooftop, its leg-stalks seeming too frail to support it.

"As do you," Madame Opale replied. It reached the door of the ship, which it was too broad to enter. Its face peeked through the open hatch, antennae politely waving. Its face was round and friendly, with two enormous black eyelets, a rounded snout, and stubby mouth-parts. A bit of gold scrollwork had been added around the curves of its eyes—just as a human woman would apply makeup to add allure to her glance. "You may leave your luggage on the ship; I will discuss the matter with the mechaniques to ensure they do not send anything amiss, just to tease you. They have been rather mischievous lately."

Madame Opale's voice was so low, yet powerful, that it seemed to caress Ammaline from within the depths of her chest. A strange ache blossomed within her, and she coughed.

"Do you feel well?" Madame Opale's antennae curled the question.

Ammaline could not bear to tell the Scarabée that the sound of its voice had caused the reaction. She stood from her seat on wobbling legs. "Do you know, I have never flown a real ship before, or for so long, or through a storm! I am afraid that I am stiff and sore, and I feel as though I was not able to breathe well for so long, that my lungs ache!"

Madame Opale's antennae straightened to their very tips. "It was *you* who flew the ship? Was that not dangerous?"

Ammaline laughed nervously. "I suppose it must have been. But I should not talk about that—it touches on Papa's business."

The Scarabée lowered its head. "Warden Lemure's business is no business of mine, of course. May I take you to your room? I will have the mechaniques draw you a hot bath on the way and bring a bottle of lavender salts, so you can have at least a short soak for your stiffness before..."

Madame Opale had to back away from the door, for at the words *hot bath*, Ammaline fairly sprang toward her.

"Oh, a bath!" she exclaimed. "Madame Opale, you are a saint!"

A Scarabée could not laugh—or, rather, the sound of a Scarabée's laughter was such that it would drive anyone with a sense of pitch out of the room, for it was an ugly sound. Instead, Madame Opale rubbed two of her leg stalks together, making a purring sound that approximated a chuckle.

"A saint? No. But I have raised so many egglings that you could not count them, and they are not so different than the children of humankind, and I know that most of you like baths, and all of you like a little something sweet."

"Chocolate?" Ammaline asked.

Madame Opale's antennae twitched. "I will ask. But the mechaniques..." She sighed, another rasp of leg-stalk against leg-stalk. "...as I say, they are mischievous. Be sure to smell anything they bring you, before you eat it."

The two of them crossed the roof toward the elevator doors. Above them, the last of the dome-plates had settled into place, and they were beginning, very softly, to glow.

ALL THE WAY THROUGH the carpeted, elegant hallways, Madame Opale complained in her low, thrumming voice that the rooms were small and meagre, and that Miss Ammaline would have received better, if it had been any time other than the Season.

It rattled its mouthparts like the clucking of a tongue as they stopped before the wide door, then touched its antennae to the lock-plate. "They were the best that I could arrange, this close to the Opéra du Mendicant. There is hardly a dressing room to be mentioned. And the view! It is nothing but rooftops, I am afraid."

The door was decorated with a shallow silver repoussé showing a Grillon city, surrounded by dancing human figures. Ammaline caught only a glimpse of the door before it swept itself out of the way, revealing a sitting room that was hardly to be imagined, let alone described.

For one thing, the room was pink, with white and gold trim upon every surface. The carpet was of such deep pile that Ammaline wondered how one might walk upon it in heels without falling and breaking an ankle; the walls were decorated with lavish paintings in oils of castles, ruins, and nobility upon the strange, great beasts from the Vieux Monde that had been called *horses*. Gilded curlicues decorated the corners of each frame.

The room contained enough furniture to fill Ammaline's entire apartment at the prison; there were several large pink-and-gold armchairs, footstools, side tables, a pair of escritoires on either side of the room, and an enormous divan large enough to support at least three gossiping Scarabées, all in a row.

Several doors led from the room, as well as a pair of glass doors that led onto a balcony with a bronze railing. The view was indeed mainly of rooftops, which seemed to be crushed together so closely that one might leap from roof to roof—if one had the legs of a Grillon.

"The doors lead to your bedroom, to the dressing room—in the middle—and to the bath." Madame Opale swept its way into the third room and flung open the door, its antennae twitching. "Ah! At least the mechaniques have followed their instructions *so* far."

A cloud of lavender steam wafted from the door, which led into darkness and shadow until Madame Opale waved a leg-stalk into the room, activating the motion-sensor. The bathroom filled with such light that Ammaline nearly raised a hand to shade her eyes.

Within was glass, and gold, and porcelain, and towels nearly as thick as the carpets, and silk drapes that opened onto no windows, but which billowed as Madame Opale turned on an invisible, humming fan, to take up the steam.

Ammaline allowed the Scarabée to help undress her out of her cloak, hat, and flight suit; the ways of the Silver City were not the ways of Shakes Prison, and the Scarabée, with its delicate antennae, would be searching for those little mechaniques clinging to Ammaline's clothing that might allow a spy access to the inner court. Whether to spy for political reasons or simply to record the singers as they performed mattered little; all must submit to a search upon entering the castle, a fact to which Ammaline had long been accustomed.

After the search was discreetly done, Ammaline lowered herself into the bath with gratitude. It was perfectly hot, the sort of near-scalding water that made one's skin flush red, as if with a fever, and that seemed to draw out all thought, memory, and other discomforts as it cooled.

Ammaline lay back against the angled back to the porcelain tub, closing her eyes in bliss. She barely started when the Scarabée began running its antennae through her hair. The lavender salts—and the temperature of the bath—would destroy any mechaniques that clung to her skin, and Madame Opale would go through Ammaline's bags at a discreet moment, unpacking them and placing items within the frequency-blocked drawers, in case of a passive receiver missing its close attention.

But with the gentleness of Madame Opale's touch, it was easy to forget that the antennae stroking her hair meant anything other than *love* and *comfort*.

It was all very ordinary—except for the luxuriousness of the rooms. Ordinarily, Ammaline stayed in the same rooms as her father, in a discreet back corner of some outdated mansion. The last thing that the warden of Shakes Prison wished to do was attract attention.

But a diva-in-training had higher aspirations: to be seen was to be given the breath which with to sing. At least, that was what Madame LaFerme liked to say, during her programmes and interviews.

Madame Opale, finished with her search of Ammaline's locks, began to tentatively stroke her hair with her antennae. "I should not ask, but—Miss Ammaline, would you sing for me? I have heard all of your public programmes that have been recorded, but I should like to hear you sing to me, very much."

Ammaline began to rise, the water sluicing off of her.

Madame Opale put a foot-stalk upon her shoulder. "But no! You need not stand. I do not wish for an opera—only a little tune, if you would, for an old Scarabée such as myself, a faithful servant."

Ammaline settled back in the tub. "I will not be at my best," she warned, then ran through a short exercise, to make sure that her throat was not strained from her trip in the *Sésame*. But even if the rest of her body had resisted the restraints, Ammaline's training had kept her from tensing her throat, and she was soon ready to sing.

The bathroom had a delicious echo, the sort of sound that made one's voice sound better than it truly was. Ammaline gently warmed her voice with another exercise or two, then began to sing the same song she had been practicing on the ship, *Les beaux rêves*. Madame Opale continued to stroke her hair, and even thrummed along with her, like a bass violin adding its murmur to Ammaline's tune.

"That was lovely," the Scarabée announced. "You quite have my gratitude! I shall tell the others that it is true, how lovely your voice is. It is beyond everything the gossips say of it."

Embarrassed, Ammaline ran a hand through her hair; the Scarabée had left it perfectly combed, but she still wanted to give it a wash. "The gossips all say that I need to have my heart broken, if I am to sing properly."

Madame Opale rattled her leg-stalks. "Or break someone *else's* heart for them. But the gossips never think of that, do they?"

Ammaline dunked her head under the water. Under the surface, she could pretend the heat in her cheeks was due to the hot water, and not to blushing.

After her bath, she emerged, wrapped in a silken robe, into the dressing-room, where Madame Opale had set out a grand gown, one that Ammaline was sure her father had not ordered for her—it was too expensive, and *much* too daring. It hung on a free-standing rack in the center of the dressing room, a pair of gold slippers underneath it. It was made of a deep rose-colored silk with a large floral print, lace undersleeves, and a neckline that showed nothing but invited everything.

Most intimidating of all, the waist was *tiny*.

Ammaline cried in despair, "I shall never fit!"

"Nonsense!" A voice rang out from behind her, at once so familiar and surprising that Ammaline gasped in surprise: *it was Madame LaFerme!*

It was impossible! Ammaline pinched herself, certain that she had fallen asleep in the bath, that it was all a dream. And yet, would a dream fill the room with such a presence? Madame LaFerme brought with her the scent of white musk and warm amber, spiced incense and a melange of flowers—a woman's scent, and the rustle of layer upon layer of fabric.

Ammaline turned, her skin sparking with terror and excitement. She had known that she might see Madame LaFerme in person, finally, after all her years of admiration, but that it should be *now*, and so privately, she had not imagined!

And yet she *had* imagined it, in a dream, and she was not entirely certain that this moment, this glorious, overfilled moment, was not the continuation of it!

Madame LaFerme was tall—clothed in a shimmer of baby-blue silk that was not a court gown—wore a silvery wig—a black beauty-mark on one cheek—and then Ammaline was performing the deepest curtsy she could achieve, her head lowered in humility before her Goddess, her Muse of Song.

Madame LaFerme giggled. "My goodness, darling child. It's only *me*."

But there was a twinkle in her voice, as she said it. Madame had known, and had expected, the effect that she had had upon the backward daughter of a prison warden, who spent most of her life lost in programmes, trapped on an isolated island in the center of a stormy sea.

A curled finger hooked underneath Ammaline's chin, lifting it.

Ammaline raised her eyes to those of the great diva. "Madame, it is my greatest pleasure to meet you."

Madame LaFerme's mouth, tinted a dark rose, twitched at one corner. This close to her, it was possible to see small wrinkles in her skin, not of age, but of movement: laugh lines, frown lines, faint lines of worry pinched between her perfect brows—but, more than these things, the faintest lines of sadness. Every smile that Madame LaFerme made, must be made through the faintest suggestion of grief overcome, of sorrow set aside for the moment: of bravery, in the face of ruin.

If only I could feel as intensely as she must feel! Then no one should say that I could not sustain a tragic opera!

"But no," said Madame, the lines of sorrow deepening around the corners of her mouth, and under her eyes. "You have many pleasures ahead of you, do you not? Let us instead say, when they ask us—and they *will*, darling child, they are *so* intrusive—that it was a moment that felt weighty, yet mobile, as if an entire world pivoted upon it."

"Madame?"

Madame sniffed and straightened, taking her finger from under Ammaline's chin. "*Do* stand up, child. We must have you ready and dressed in good time for supper, and I fear that it will take every moment we have, for you have not learned the little tricks of how to appear as one must, if one is to survive in the public eye. Madame Opale?"

The Scarabée rested in a corner, its friendly face turned toward them, but its antennae politely curled up and waiting to be addressed. Slowly, they uncurled. "Yes, Madame LaFerme?"

"We have an hour."

The antennae stood at shocked attention. "Madame!"

"We are to attend an early supper with several notable personages that should be of great assistance in gaining the attention necessary to launch Miss Ammaline's career. It is of the essence that she be well-presented—" Madame LaFerme swept an arm dripping with lace toward the gown. "—but not *too* well presented. Let her look a little childish and vulnerable tonight, so that men of power can imagine themselves in power over her, as one would be in power over a beloved niece. They can be taught otherwise at a later time—but let us not allow them to assemble an idea that Miss Ammaline is so strong or resolute that she cannot be taken advantage of."

The Scarabée rubbed its front leg-stalks together with a thought-ful-sounding purr. "I believe I understand what you are getting at, Madame. When one plans to turn a pawn into a queen, one does not start out with the piece behaving with the strength and directness that it will someday possess, but with humility and vulnerability, which only just manages to evade every attack."

Madame LaFerme smiled a thin smile, with her lips pressed together, and the lines under her eyes still resonant with sorrow. "Just so."

While one end of the dressing room was taken up by an enormous vanity, with silvered mirror and gilded trim upon the pale, painted wood, the other was taken up by clothing: racks and racks of it, stored so that each of the racks must be pulled out like a book from a shelf before the dresses upon it could be perused.

Madame Opale, ignoring the dark rose dress, dropped to the floor and paced back and forth before the racks of clothing. So many of her leg-stalks emerged from the depths of her shimmering, opalescent carapace, that they blurred and whispered as she turned back and forth upon the carpet. "The ivory? No, too innocent—it looks like a wedding-dress, and they already complain of how her innocence keeps her from singing to her potential.

The red is too simple, and too direct. Those choices are clear. But the others? The others?"

Madame LaFerme bent at the waist, and laid one pale and elegant hand against the Scarabée's carapace. "My darling, you must contain yourself. I shall pick something for her."

She tugged at the handle at the end of one of the racks, and slid it outward. Perforce, Madame Opale had to stop her pacing, lest she charge into the delicate, precious dresses.

Madame LaFerme ran her hand along the row of dresses, touching this one, then that, her hand finally hesitating between a light pink one, and one of deep blue.

Ammaline, in a shy voice, managed to say, "May I see the blue one?"

Madame LaFerme's mouth and brow twisted in annoyance. "But it is too dark for one so young...no, let us see." She pulled the dress from the rack and held it out.

It was not a court dress, that much was clear—there were no broad panniers to hold out the fabric and display it, or to create a space around the woman wearing it, so that she might not be approached except by those she allowed to do so. The skirts were not full enough for that. The fabric was dark blue embossed velvet, with a subtle floral pattern on it. The square neck needed no fichu, for it was already tousled with delicate ivory lace, as were the ends of the half-sleeves. A row of gold buttons closed the front, and a dark blue belt held the waist tight—but not as tightly as the court dress.

Madame LaFerme held the dress up in front of Ammaline, pursing her lips. "Sing. Something informal, something a little old-fashioned."

Ammaline's mouth opened in surprise—but quickly she gathered her wits, and began to sing *Les beaux rêves*.

After the first few notes, Madame LaFerme handed the dress to Madame Opale, who had risen to stand upright once more. "Perfect. Madame Opale, dress her. I will prepare the paints. We must not be late."

Chapter 5

Across the Rooftops

Unseen by Ammaline and Madame LaFerme, a shadowy figure passed outside the balcony of the sitting room, on its way from one shadowy errand to another. It was dressed completely in dark gray, a tough and featureless fabric that had little in common with the delicate fripperies only a little distant.

Because of the energy it took to light, and cool, and protect the city-wide dome, nights during the Season were longer than was natural, and sunset had come early.

The figure glanced toward the window, saw that one-half of the pair of glass doors was a little ajar, and moved onward through the darkness.—Some other time, perhaps.

A gap of a dozen feet lay between the figure and its next rooftop destination; without hesitation, the figure dashed silently toward the edge of the rooftop and flung itself across.

As if it were a long-limbed Grillon, the figure arched gracefully, and quite impossibly, through the air, and landed on the other rooftop, nearly as silently as it had jumped off the first. It continued onward, its gray clothing soon a soft blur in the distance to anyone who might be watching it—but there was only a single mechanique on a distant balcony, emptying its small dustbin into the wind.

In the ordinary way of the city, the figure would have been spotted by a hundred different security systems, their microphones hearing what the human ear could not, their motion-sensors and cameras seeing clearly through the befuddling darkness. But the figure was invisible and silent to those sentinels, too; a nice trick that would have fetched a pretty penny, if the figure had ever chosen to reveal how it was done.

The figure was of a personage both infamous, even legendary—and entirely unknown. The dark gray shadow that flitted so unnaturally from rooftop to rooftop was none other than the Easer of Ways, an assassin who had either blessed or plagued the Silver City for a dozen years—depending on whether one was paying the assassin to do someone in, or receiving the service more personally, as it were. That so skilled an assassin was never found, identified, or punished, was a subject for much rumor and discussion. Who protected the Easer of Ways? What sinister political purposes did the assassin serve?

And how, *how* did the assassin move so silently, so swiftly, so invisibly?

The celebrations of the Masquerade had begun with the sealing of the Great Dome, and already a long parade filled with floating platforms snaked through the streets, following no predetermined pattern, only the whims of the floats at the head of the procession, here turning down a broad avenue, there piling up to snake down an alleyway behind a mansion, where the pressure of bodies and floats building to such that the parade must split into two pathways of light and revelry, then reuniting on the other side of the mansion, leaving behind broken glass, beads, feathers, footprints—that is, little more than memories.

The dancers wore no more than the barest shimmers of paint upon their skins and the masks upon their faces; musicians played until their clothing was soaked in sweat at their effort to drown out the crowds cheering them; acrobats climbed wrought-iron gates and leapt from them in swan-dives, to be caught by their fellows; children, forbidden from descending to the streets, threw lit fireworks down on the celebrants from overhead; figures out of myth and legend topped the floating platforms, decorated in mirrors, sequins, glass jewels, feathers, and flowers—everywhere, thousands and thousands of blooms. Everywhere the parade went, it was both followed and anticipated by the crowds: ordinary folk who had traveled from all across Thomàon for sanctuary and celebration.

And yet there was still the possibility of shame and restraint, for the Season was fresh and new, and its drunken, addled celebrations had not yet had time to compound themselves with surfeit and exhaustion. The revels were loud and merry but they were not yet terrifying with their wantonness.

The shadowy figure hesitated as it landed on a rooftop just above the parade. It thought it had seen something that it should not have, not then.

It peered down at the chaotic, surging movement of the crowd below it.

Among the merry-makers was a knot of folk whose movement was not of gay abandon, and whose cries were not cheers, but shouts of pain and fear. They were surrounded by figures dressed in black—not the soft gray that hides from the eye, but the black edged with gold trim that announces itself as the hands of Authority itself, well-prepared to crush anything it should catch in its deadly grip: in other words, the police.

These officers in black, whose faces were concealed by featureless gold helmets, worked to capture various members of the crowd, with some success. The captured butterflies, glittering and winged with silks, were dragged to small crafts marked with large gold stars.

What crimes had these merry-makers committed?

It could not be the crime of public drunkenness—that was no crime, not during the Season. It could not be for fighting or attacking other members of the crowd, for until the black-and-gold figures swept in, there had been no disturbance. It was the *Season*, and generally any crime short of murder was not pursued or punished, only, later, reimbursed.

But wait! The figure in gray leaned closer toward the edge of the roof. Did not the ones who were being removed all wear a certain symbol: that of an eye, looking out from within half a mask?

Only the Easer of Ways could have picked out such a detail among the chaos, having eyes that were as sharp as its legs were unnaturally nimble and strong. The merry-makers wore the charm among cheap strings of beads, or had it stamped upon their sweating skin, or shaved into the roots of their brightly dyed hair, as casual as any other element of a Masquerade costume.

But the police selected those celebrants without error, even going so far as to pull one of them, a musician, from one of the floating platforms.

The surrounding folk began to notice the disturbance, and cry out in protest: these were no mere satirical costumes, no mere celebrants who wished to see a uniform torn and plundered, but dark and secret figures—neither often seen, nor spoken of.

The music stopped, leaving behind the sound of shouting: "To the left, to the left! Behind you!" A bright flash filled the air, with the sound of a heavy bang that was louder than any firework echoed down the street.

A panic arose among the merry-makers, and they began to scream and disperse in their several directions. However, the police had prepared for such a thing, for they had blocked the streets around the head of the parade, cutting it off from the rest of its body: a blockade had been placed in the street, and the latter half of the merry-makers were being directed away from the disturbance.

Suddenly, the air was heavy with tainted, stinking smoke, and the celebrants wept bitter tears from it, coughing and spitting and sneezing at it, struggling to cover their faces and eyes. The police behind their gold helms were silent and grim, and redoubled their efforts. They were less selective now, as if they had achieved their main aims, and now merely wished to sow deceit and chaos, to cover what they had done. The participants who had been earlier removed—those bearing the symbol of the eye in the half-mask—were no longer present, even within the small police craft into which they had been loaded. The craft had slipped away silently, replaced with identical others.

Over speakers which seemed to call from every direction came orders to disperse. But was that not what the revelers were attempting to do, and being turned back from every direction, by the gold-masked police?

In what seemed but a few moments, the street was empty: the police had removed themselves, the civilians had been removed, and the balconies above the street were empty, with all curtains drawn and all lights extinguished. The air drifted with smoke, an eerie fog lit by the last few twinkling lights of the abandoned floats.

The mechaniques emerged from their small ports in the streets, along the sides of the buildings, examined the wreckage, and summoned larger trucks to dismantle and remove the larger obstructions. They began to sweep up the smaller bits and pieces, to the tune of tinkling glass. As suddenly as the disturbance had begun, it was over.

The shadowy figure continued on its way, greatly troubled.

But the way across the rooftops to the palace was clear, as promised, and there were no further disturbances to be seen—not even by the eyes of the Easer of Ways, and eventually the shadowy figure arrived at its destination: the Castle of the Silver Spire.

It did not arrive at the spire or at the Opéra du Mendicant at the heart of the castle, but at a small, oft-unnoticed building that looked to house servants, or stores, or a repair-shop, or some such unimportant detail of the constant scurry that attended all bureaucratic functions—for what one *sees* of a bureaucracy is often but the tip of the greater iceberg of bureaucracy which lies beneath it—but which housed a small, but important, meeting-room, one with twelve chairs, lead-lined walls, and no access to servants, mechaniques, or other intrusions, so that those who entered must serve themselves.

There were no windows, no water, no drains, and no electrical conduits in the room, which was perforce lit by a generator that lay within.

However, there *must* be air. The ducts were well guarded—but not against one who possessed certain talents.

The shadowy figure steeled itself for the final jump, for it was a particularly long one, as this dull and drab building rose several stories above its fellows, and had walls that were guarded by all sorts of traps, several of which, it had been reported, were changed recently. Perforce, the figure must leap nearly three hundred feet to reach its roof, and land with perfect silence when it did so.

The figure stood atop the gayer, more fanciful building nearest the plain one—roofed with silver-blue tiles and a dozen mobile sculptures that stood still only during the Season—adjusted a few straps here and there, gathered its strength, focused all its mental and physical energies, paused a moment to chew its tongue in annoyance, ran—and leapt.

The shadowy figure spread its arms as it sailed, and the shadowy gray fabric stretched, and spread, and became stubbed webs that caught the air, and helped the figure to glide through it.

If anyone had looked up, they would have seen a shadow, and perhaps heard the sound of the fabric rippling as first it caught the breeze. But no-one was looking up; the Masquerade's revels began this night on the ground below, not the dome above. The mechaniques could not sense the figure at all, at the moment; the Grillons were outside the Great Dome, swarming and raging in their breeding madness; and the Scarabées were either underground, or contentedly doing that domestic work of hearth and home that seemed to be their true calling.

In short, the shadowy figure went unseen.

It aimed past its target, then—at the last moment—ripped the cords that held the flaps of its suit in place, and dropped fifty feet out of darkness, and onto the roof, landing with the sound of a whispered hush on its strange-made legs.

It froze in place, hoping against hope that it had not been heard, and struggling not to giggle with delight.

Made it!

And no one seemed to have heard, or seen, a thing. The shadowy figure breathed hard for a moment, then put its hands over its mouth as it yawned—a habit that had long been with it, that after a moment of excitement, it should always feel a wave of exhaustion, albeit one that soon passed. It pinched its nose and yawned again, behind a featureless gray mask, then squatted up and down on its haunches, to make sure that it had strained nothing upon landing. It crossed its arms over its chest, yawned again, then shook itself all over, and stretched out its neck.

Then, to work: it pulled at a pair of straps on its chest, loosening a flat bag therefrom, and unsealed it, withdrawing out several items: two small wheels, a neat coil of wires, two pieces of rigid plate, a battery, an antenna, a small motor—all made of some matte material that the figure handled with some delicacy. The items were quickly assembled into a small, primitive, ugly mechanique, no larger than the stretch of the figure's palm between thumb and forefinger. Also the figure withdrew a small, hooded nozzle from a pocket on its elongated thigh, and withdrew a length of tubing with it. Attaching the two, a small torch was soon lit and burning its way through a latch on a filtered air-grate. The filter was cut, the mechanique inserted, and the grate replaced. The figure rewound the nozzle and tube, searched for any loose materials, then tucked the pouch back against its chest, strapping it once again into place.

A shadowy nook soon found itself with an even more shadowy occupant, as the figure folded itself into a small, compact shape and closed its eyes.

Within the air duct, the little mechanique, entirely without its own intelligence, rolled through the pitch-dark maze of tunnels unerringly, coming to rest against another filter, one that was designed to hinder sound more than it did dust. The mechanique turned so that its antenna nestled into the filter, not quite breaking through it into the other room, one end collecting the speech that occurred within—it was a microphone as well as an antenna—and the other transmitting it to the figure that had gone motionless above.

The slight delay that had been caused by watching the interruption of the parade above, revealed its consequences—for the conversation that the figure wished to overhear had already begun.

A deep, gruff male voice said, "That is it, I tell you. The last of the elixir. One case only."

A woman's voice answered him: "Cannot they make more? We might raid their nests and take it for ourselves."

The male voice replied, sarcastically: "And what would that make of you, if you took it so soon? What would it change in your genes? You might find yourself with wings."

The woman's voice responded crossly, "Take it, find a way to artificially age it. I'm not stupid."

A long, frustrated breath. "Have you heard a word I am saying? His research has done nothing more than use up what remaining supplies we had—and, at any rate, we have not the time for it now."

"He's only one man. Surely he can be spared. They are not so threatening, after all."

"He will not find anything in time, and what the uprising means is that the young elixir will be destroyed."

"Destroyed? Why?"

"They're not stupid. They'll wreck their stores to prevent us from taking them."

Another male voice, this one smooth and placating, said, "Why should they? They have not only cooperated with our taking their cured stores, but serve us without complaint."

There was a slap, but not protest—as if one of the speakers had slapped themselves on the forehead, or slapped a table.

The rough voice spoke again: "Stop interrupting. The Scarabées didn't butcher Paquet. It was men. No one else was reported missing from the city. So who was it?"

The smoother male voice snapped, "So you say. But what proof do you have it wasn't the Grillons?"

Another male voice, this one clipped and nasal: "Paquet was not without political sympathies in a certain direction. I knew the man. He was a child, nothing but drama and delusion. This would not be the first time that he deceived us with rumors."

The small noises in the room went still, as though everyone had frozen, and held their breath.

The smooth male voice nearly gasped with shock. "Deceived? You think the incident with...you think he said those things on *purpose*?"

The clipped voice said, "No. I do not think he spoke with ill intent. But his naïveté led to tragedy, no one can deny *that*."

The woman's voice sighed. "He meant well."

The rough male voice had become even rougher, almost hoarse with strain. "Paquet's wounds, when I found him, were consistent with his story."

Sharply, the smoother voice interrupted him: "You destroyed the evidence of them? You left behind no trace?"

Through gritted teeth, the rougher voice answered: "Yes."

The woman said, "Very well, Monsieur, let us say that you are correct, and Paquet was killed by men, or something *like* men. Nevertheless, it seems that no more elixir will be forthcoming at any time soon, until it can be reliably produced. I wish to protest the necessity of saying such, but...let us say that it is so. For now. Let us also say that there is the possibility that they are uprising, or at least, they are plotting something that is beyond what we know."

Cloth rustled.

The woman's voice continued, "If all of that is true, it is bad news, but there is worse. Général?"

The clipped voice snarled, "We have word that there has been a cluster of Les Yeux in the city. They infiltrated one of the parades and were headed toward the palace. Several of the members were caught with explosives on their persons. The plot was foiled this time, but it may not be, the next."

The rough voice asked, with deadly enunciation: "This incident was not manufactured by your police, Général? We all know how you like to allow the dramatic rise and fall of rebellious groups."

The clipped voice answered, "I do not understand what you are speaking about."

"Don't lie!" The rough voice became louder. "Do you not understand that it is our petty foibles—and our ability to deny the proof that they exist—that has brought us to this pass? We *knew* this moment would come, and did little to prevent it. We dove ever deeper into these unnatural practices, thinking nothing of consequences. I warned you, but you were unwilling to see—"

The milder male voice interrupted him. "Warden, you overstep yourself. *You* signed the accords, just as the rest of us did, and agreed—"

His voice was, in turn, interrupted—by the man with the clipped voice.

"It's the woman. I told you that he should never have been allowed to have a child with her. We agreed—but no—he *must* have a child to give to this woman. And now look at him! Aged, gray at the temples, soft around the middle—mortal. He thinks to himself, 'But what about my—'"

"Enough!" roared the Warden, for it was he that spoke, and Ammaline to which the clipped voice referred.

The woman's voice said, "I must attend to something near the opéra. Let us stop now, cool our tempers, and return to the matter in the morning."

The Warden growled, "Nothing will have changed."

There was a single clap, and the woman's voice said, "Just so."

Cloth rustled, chairs scraped—and the figure in the shadows bit its lips in frustration. It, too, had other places it must be, and soon, but to have the meeting cut off so soon! It would not be able to travel the city in such a manner, in daylight.

But there was nothing else to be done—for now. It left the little mechanique in place in case of future opportunities, stood up, stretched and yawned like a cat, then turned and ran to the edge of the rooftop—leapt—

And disappeared once more into the night.

When next the shadowy figure was to be seen, it was no longer shadowy, but had found its way to a secret cache, and into a different suit of clothing: deep rose-colored satin breeches trimmed with gold cord, a white silk vest embroidered with a thousand gold leaves and vines, a satin coat, embroidered likewise, the color of a maiden's blush. Lace cuffs emerged immaculately from the sleeves of the coat, while silk hose from the bottoms of the breeches, and silk pumps decorated with pieces of gold-colored Scarabée shell at the ends of the legs that filled them. Above the tumbling lace cravat that emerged from the neck of the coat rose a powdered, pale face, its cheeks touched barely with the lightest blush, its lips painted a tantalizing peach color, and eyes of a clear, bright green. A wry smile touched the lips as what appeared to be a young nobleman adjusted his cuffs. While his dress spoke of opulence and extravagance, his wig was but a humble one, bouffant on top and with only two rolls on the sides of his head, with the remainder of the wig pulled back into a scarlet ribbon.

His appearance was such that he seemed to be someone that everyone knew, but yet could not put a name to—or could put two or three names to. There are certain faces that seem attractive, individual, and interesting, and of course one knows them, has known them well for some time—could never mistake them for anyone else. And yet, in a crowd, as soon as one comes to think of that person, one sees them everywhere. Across a crowded room, one catches their eye—waves—approaches—discovers that the person that one greeted was a complete stranger, after all.

Attractive young noblemen in brightly colored clothes all look alike; it is the aged and the ugly who have acquired their own characters.

Our new-made nobleman showed a pass-ring at one of the doors and entered into the complex of buildings at the heart of the Castle of the Silver Spire, that were supposed to be the heart of the government on Thomàon, but that served only as centers of public entertainment. He nodded to those who nodded to him, but pressed onward. His clothing was seen everywhere—tasteful, expensive, *pink*—and his face was familiar. "Ah, it is Christophe," said many of those who noted even that much. But there were a dozen handsome young Christophes who it might have been, and none of those who noted him, noted him with the same surname.

A Christophe indeed. But which?

The young man soon found himself, as he had intended, on the opposite side of the crush on the floor of the opéra, and entered, neither conspicuously nor inconspicuously, into a hallway with small side-rooms along it. He bypassed them all and took a turn at the end, where the hallway narrowed and became shabby-looking: it was now part of the servants' domain. It was empty. He squatted near a low half-door, and, using a pass-card, opened a small sliding panel to an elevator used by mechaniques carrying food and drink for the human servants to take up, and serve.

He scooted himself in, grimacing at the strain on his hips and knees—they *had* rather taken some punishment, that evening—and crawled inside.

He rose, then emerged into another servants' corridor, this one also empty of the ubiquitous presence of servants and mechaniques, during a party—the first night of the Season. It was more than unusual; it was unprecedented.

And yet—no coincidence, then, that the young nobleman passed unseen—it had happened twice.

The young nobleman took a back door into a room filled with the laughter of young people. They were just rising from a supper-table, an enormous one that held at least fifty guests. The servants waited respectfully to clear the table—but the floor was filled with tittering voices, embraces, pastel silks, powdered wigs, black beauty spots that dotted the pale cheeks of faces with empty eyes.

The young nobleman produced a napkin from somewhere and dabbed his lips as he threaded his way through clusters of bright silk flowers—pink, aquamarine, daffodil—and just as artificial as the figures who wore them. A man in white nodded to the young nobleman, saying, "Ah, Christophe! You must stay a moment, and speak to me about the latest compositions of Master Prévoyance!"

"Alas," said the young nobleman, waggling his eyebrows, "some other time."

The man in white winked broadly, and was left behind.

At the far end of the room was a figure dressed in baby-blue silk, with the tallest of wigs, and the starkest of beauty-marks upon her cheek: Madame LaFerme, the Great Diva!

Beside her was an absurd figure in dark blue, the dress of a middle-class woman, whom the young nobleman had expected, but whose presence still unnerved him, with a chill and a fleeting numbness: Ammaline Lemure, daughter of Warden Lemure.

Next to Madame LaFerme, dressed in immaculate silvery white, was Queen Delphine, lady of the Castle of the Silver Spire.

The young nobleman attempted to pass by the women with a nod, but their skirts were so large that he was forced to brush them as he passed. "Excuse me! Your pardon." He bowed, then straightened, moving onward, turning his head so that they could not study it. He had caught a glimpse of Ammaline pinching her eyebrows together, and frowning.

But by then it was too late: one touch of his hand against skin, and it was done. He slipped from the room at the far end, left the dining-room through a large set of double-doors, then activated the tiny mechanique he had left behind.

A gasp, a rustle, the sound of a body falling to the floor.

And then screams.

"An assassin! The Easer of Ways! Stop him! The man in pink!"

The young nobleman smiled as he ducked through another low half-door into another elevator for mechaniques. The tiny cube descended, more or less, to its original level, the same narrow corridor he had left just a few moments before.

The uproar had not yet reached this level; or, rather, it had not yet joined its chaos to the already-existing jumble of faces, bodies, smells, and sounds on the opéra floor.

The young nobleman in pink smiled at those who smiled at him, waved, and headed upstairs in another direction, toward the mezzanines over-looking the ballroom below—and the balconies overlooking the rest of the castle roofs.

A woman in a peach-colored gown squinted blearily at him as he stepped outside. He smiled, wondering what the woman would make of what he was about to do, stripped off his coat, vest, breeches, and wig—then stepped up onto the railing in his deep rose-colored breeches, kicked off his heels, and leapt to another balcony twenty feet away.

"Christophe?" she called after him, as though she had noticed nothing out of the ordinary. "Is that you?"

Chapter 6

The Ingenue

AMMALINE WAS RUSHED FROM the dining-room at full speed, whisked away from Madame LaFerme's side by a pair of guards in the charcoal-silver uniforms of the castle. Their shirts and hose and wigs were all a dull gray, and their long vests moved stiffly from the armored plates that shifted inside, but made no sound. She was moved along the narrow back servants' corridors so swiftly, that she had barely time to wonder what had happened, or what, if anything, she should do about it. Call her father? She was being rushed along too quickly for that. Ask the guards if they had seen whether Madame LaFerme had been hurt? Ask whether she would still be expected to perform later that evening?

She opened her mouth to speak, when both guards stopped at once, both of them taking her by the arms to halt her from moving forward.

It occurred to her that if anyone wished to do Ammaline the slightest bit of harm, the present moment was an ideal one. She had no idea whether the two guards were who they seemed to be; it was only that they were dressed as such that made her trust their identities.

"Who—? What—?"

She began to ask to see their identification cards, then realized that the cards would be just as useless as the uniforms. The only way for her to trust them was to have her Papa appear, and tell her that they were to be trusted.

But before she could shake herself free of them, they turned her to the side, rushing her in a different direction, down an even more narrow corridor, so that they were forced to rearrange themselves and walk single-file, one guard ahead of her, and one behind.

"Where are we *going*?"

"Hush, Mademoiselle," said one of the guards in a low tone. "The assassin has escaped the opéra and is moving about the rooftops. When last he was seen, he was moving this way."

From above, there came the sound of footsteps. The two guards nodded to each other, and one of them left the corridor at a run, footsteps as soft as the padding of a cat.

Then again, perhaps the guards *were* trustworthy, and Ammaline was to be separated from them, one by one.

"We are almost there," the remaining guard whispered.

"I do not recognize this place at all."

"We move through the servants' corridors."

"It hardly seems wide enough."

"The Scarabées walk more easily sideways, Mademoiselle." The guard stopped at an unmarked panel on the wall, and took out a small view-screen and held it against the door. A latch clicked and the panel slid open a fraction of an inch. The guard opened the panel by shoving it open with hip and fingers—it was stiff in its tracks. He ducked inside a moment, then reappeared, waving her forward.

She was in the back of her own wardrobe; she recognized the elegant dress she had abandoned earlier, pastel and shimmering.

Her face turned hot as she looked at it, remembering how the others had looked at her, in their pastel and shimmering ensembles. The gown that had been laid out for her would have allowed Ammaline to become invisible; as it was, every eye was turned upon her with amusement, at the backwater girl who had worn sombre, outmoded tones to a pastel feast.

And Madame LaFerme had let her.

Ammaline's eyes narrowed. Had Madame LaFerme played her for a fool?

While Ammaline had contemplated this possibility, the guard had searched the rest of the rooms. "You are alone, mademoiselle. I have checked that the door is locked. Make sure the panel locks behind me when I am gone. I must help search for the Easer of Ways. Allow no-one into your rooms except your father."

"Not Madame LaFerme? Not Madame Opale? Am I still to *sing*?"

The guard shook his head grimly, and slipped away through the secret panel, which closed first with a click, and then with a heavy, sliding noise as heavy bolts built into the door slid home.

Ammaline paced back and forth across the wardrobe, her arms crossed over her chest. Why had Madame LaFerme let her make such a fool of herself? Her chest burnt with hurt, acid and bright, a hurt that roiled her stomach at first, then slowly drained her of all energy. Her head began to hang, her eyelids to droop: it was as though she had taken a sleeping-draught. But she had not; the bitter cup from which she had drunk was one of humiliation and betrayal, a weary brew indeed.

She turned toward one of the mirrors, and saw that her face, lightly powdered, was streaked with black eye-paint and had left stripes of soot and flesh across her face. Her tears had, in fact, nearly rolled off her chin and onto the dark blue dress.

Behind her in the glass, the room was a shimmer of silk and satin, pale ivories and pinks and lavenders, flourishes of lace, thin edgings of gold and silver. The eye was brought forward, inevitably, toward her own central figure, in dark blue.

Ammaline found a towel and wiped her face before she could damage her dress, then looked through the clothing until she found what she was looking for: a piece of nearly invisible, spider-webbed tulle, dotted with silver thread. She tore it from the dress it adorned—a vapid piece of pink silk—and lifted the cloth over her head, making it into a veil. Then she dashed to the paint-box and underlined her eyes, so that they were dark and haunted.

The dress was of an outmoded fashion, was it? Why not make it even less fashionable, then?

With a sudden tearing of cloth, she tore away most of the lace on the dress, removed the belt, and tore free several over-panels of the skirt. Then she tried to tear free the wig that Madame LaFerme had selected for her—one that Ammaline now knew was just as outdated as the dress she wore—and quickly learnt that the wig was more firmly attached than she had realized.

After once again ruining her eye-paint with her tears, she carefully un-picked the pins holding the wig in place, and undid her own brown curls from underneath it. The hated wig was replaced on its stand, no doubt carrying a dot of blood in its silver waves and rolls. Ammaline put her hair up with a silver clip in a simple twist, then dropped the silver netting over her head.

There. She looked sophisticated and mysterious. Her heart squeezed in her chest, and burned brighter, this time with the roar of a furnace: one that burned fuel, and produced heat.

For a moment, Ammaline did not care the least what anyone thought of her, not the insipid courtiers in pastel, not Madame LaFerme—not even her father.

She would ask Madame Opale to help her, when tonight was over, to remake the blue gown. She would wear it—and make all the others jealous. To be a diva was to be shameless, after all. *Eccentric.*

To celebrate, she went into the front rooms, and threw open the glass doors that overlooked her little balcony with its bronze railing. If she was not to perform that evening for the small concert she had been scheduled to sing, then she would hold her own. She began to sing, not the *Les beaux rêves* that she had been singing all day and evening, what with one thing and another, but *Pense à moi.*

It was another of the songs of the Vieux Monde, part of a dramatic performance that had involved three lovers: a madman who had taken on the aspect of a monster, a young ingenue, and a more sensible human lover. The madman had worn a mask, in order to hide the scarred visage beneath it. The young ingenue had found herself just as enchanted by the scarred man as the mask, finding herself drawn to his very monstrosity. Ammaline had always found herself drawn to the character of the monster as well—and not the sensible young man, whom the ingenue had known from childhood. But in the end, it was the man the ingenue had turned to, and not the monster: for he *was* a monster, scarred not only in face but in soul.

Or so the story said. Madame LaFerme was famed for the role of the ingenue. As Ammaline's voice echoed back to her across the rooftops, she entertained the fantasy that the role would become *hers.*

And that Madame LaFerme herself would become jealous.

She sang with her heart burning with anger and resentment in her chest, yet with her vocal chords at ease, in perfect form, until she reached the lines where her opposite was to join her: the voice of the young man who was human, who was *not* a monster.

Ah, well. She should have picked a song that was not a duet.

But faintly, in the distance, there came a voice:

"C'est inouï! Ne Christine pas? Bravo!"

Ammaline hopped on her slippered toes, then put her hands on the railing, to listen for the next line.

But it did not come. Either the singer had not thought to continue the song, or had not cared to, or…or could not remember the next line, or had become embarrassed.

There were shouts from below, in the direction of the castle. A loud crashing sound echoed through the streets, then the sound of shattering glass, falling to the street. An alarm shrieked. A voice shouted, "Get out!"

And, in the darkness of the dome's evening, she saw a shadow moving across the rooftop. It was not human—it moved too suddenly and strangely to be human. It was almost—it was almost the silhouette of a Grillon! Had one of them broken through the dome? Had thousands? Were they all under attack?

Ammaline backed away from the balcony.

A voice softly called, "Christine! Have you forgotten me?"

The voice, it was not familiar. But neither was it unfamiliar, either. The flames of anger in Ammaline's heart went silent, as she questioned her memories.

Before she could remember, the shadow became a silhouette, and then a figure dressed in pastel tatters, perched upon the bronze railing of her balcony, dripping blood that was not red—but a dark blue-green, such as the Grillons had—panting, tired, limbs twisted inside the clothing to seem other than human.

The light caught the figure's face.

If the voice had been on the edge of Ammaline's memory, the face, so long unseen, was firmly across memory's threshold. Ammaline dashed forward as the figure swayed on the rail, and nearly toppled backward. She pulled the figure forward and into her arms, thinking, *How light they are!* and exclaiming, in a hushed whisper that strained her well-trained throat,

"Manon!"

The beloved face turned toward Ammaline's, eyes wide, and whispered in terror, "You are not my little Ammaline! You are La Voisine! I have come to the wrong room! I am doomed!"

And then the young personne, Ammaline's oldest friend, fainted in her arms, sagging against Ammaline's shoulder, and making her stagger backward. It was not their weight that was troublesome as much as their height—for Manon had grown uncommon tall, with a tangle of arms and legs.

Ammaline might have been raised like a princess at the top of a tall tower—but she had been raised by Warden Lemure, a man who believed that a trained body led to a trained mind. She heaved Manon up so that their weight rested more solidly on her shoulder, then dragged them backward into her rooms.

It was awkward work, Manon sliding down in her arms, every second wondering if the guards would burst in—or, worse, her father!

The facts had struck her at once. The figure before her—Manon—was dressed as a nobleman with powdered hair and clothing of various shades of pink and deep rose. A curl of deep red caught her eye as she dragged Manon across the floor, cursing the thickness of the carpet the whole while, and she suddenly realized: it was the man with his hair tied back with a scarlet ribbon!

She had seen him pass through the room just before everything had been upset, politely making his way through the crush. Amongst an entire roomful of pastel courtiers, he had dressed in darker hues, with breeches of a deep rose, and a scarlet ribbon in his hair. It was as though he had wished to have his appearance remarked upon. Ammaline, at the time, had only felt the hot embarrassment that he had worn the deeper hues and attracted the eye of the others without a single blush or moment of shame, all the while he had begged pardon across the room.

It had all happened in a flash.

The man with the scarlet ribbon, having just passed by the young woman standing next to Ammaline, had bowed to Madame LaFerme and Queen Delphine, and said, "Excuse me, your pardon," as he had been forced to brush very nearly by Queen Delphine's silver-white skirts. Ammaline had not been a part of the conversation between Madame LaFerme and the queen, but had been but a short distance away, being snubbed by two of the queen's ladies-in-waiting, and had seen and heard everything. He slipped out of the room and disappeared.

Then, suddenly, the lady-in-waiting next to Ammaline gasped, lifting her arm. The back of her hand was beaded with blood. Even more startlingly, there was a small movement under the skin of her arm, a bump that raced up to her elbow, then disappeared under a bunch of lace. In its wake, it left a crimson pathway, where it had torn through the flesh under the skin. The miniature mechanique implanted under her skin had moved quickly.

Ammaline had grabbed the young woman's arm above the elbow, gripping as hard as she could.

She felt the bump against her hand as whatever had crawled under the young woman's skin had come against Ammaline's grip. The young woman locked eyes with Ammaline, her face slack and horrified under her white makeup.

Ammaline pressed down with both hands, weaving her thumbs against each other, as the machine or creature tried to crawl this way, then that.

"Help," the young woman gasped.

Madame LaFerme exclaimed, "Ammaline! What are you doing?"

"Help me," the young woman begged Ammaline in a hoarse whisper. "Oh, the Twelve! Please help me, I did not mean to become a traitor—but the Roi—"

And then Ammaline was roughly pulled free of the young woman by two guards in gray, and the young woman whimpered. Her eyes widened, then went blank, as Ammaline tried to explain that there was something crawling under her skin, and her dress must be removed at once—

And then the young woman choked, fell, and lay on the floor, twitching, as blood ran from her mouth.

Madame LaFerme, despite having foolishly behaved with tragic consequence the moment before, grasped the situation immediately, and shouted, her powerful voice carrying clearly above the screams of the crowd,

"An assassin! The Easer of Ways! Stop him! The man in pink!"

The chaos, if anything, had worsened, and the assassin had escaped. The Queen and Madame LaFerme had been swept away immediately, and Ammaline only a moment later.

Now, Ammaline heaved Manon onto the enormous divan. Manon was unconscious, breathing shallowly but clearly. An ear pressed onto their chest revealed a steadily beating heart. A search about Manon's limbs proved that they had a deep gash which had pierced through the rose-colored breeches, soaked with a dark blue-green that oozed through the wound.

How Manon's blood had come to be of such an unusual color, Ammaline could only guess. But she pressed down upon the wound, hissing in annoyance. She could not call for help; Manon was wanted by one and all, and in great danger. And, in fact, the guards were no doubt marching toward her room at this moment—for everyone and everything in Thomàon was watched at every moment.

Except, somehow, for the Easer of Ways, who always seemed to be able to escape detection.

Ammaline suddenly remembered that many of the baths in the Castle of the Silver Spire were equipped with medical mechaniques, in order that their residents might receive treatment with all discretion.

If there was such a mechanique in the room, and *if* it was able to treat Manon's changed physique, and *if* the Easer of Ways truly had methods in which to escape detection, *then* perhaps her friend might be saved.

Ammaline tore the silver netting from her head and used it to tie a small silk pillow against Manon's thigh. Then she heaved the personne across her shoulders, again amazed at Manon's lightness, and staggered with them to the bath.

The medical mechanique slid from the wall as Ammaline entered, a solid, sterile plastic tray cushioned with gel pads. Ammaline lowered her friend onto it. The mechanique beeped at her until she put one of Manon's hands, dangling over the side, onto their chest, and then closed over them with an opaque cover, concealing them entirely and making Ammaline's heart leap up into her throat.

The tray began to emit whirring, buzzing sounds, went silent, jerked, buzzed again.

Ammaline paced back and forth in front of it, waiting.

She had immediately grasped the truth of the matter, or at least *a* truth of the matter, that her friend Manon, her little playfellow on the streets of the city, was none other than the assassin, the Easer of Ways, for whom the guards searched.

When they were ten years old, on the cusp of saying farewell to their childhoods, Manon had disappeared without a trace, and Ammaline's father had taken her aside, and explained that Manon was well, but that she, Ammaline, must never try to find them or even to speak of them again, if she held her friend with any affection whatsoever. When Ammaline had asked the reason why, her father had only shaken his head and said, "I do not approve of it. But they have chosen to risk themself at a chance for making their fortune, and I cannot speak against it."

Manon was an orphan who had grown up on the streets, but had the sort of curious mind that restlessly searched for something more, and so knew more about history and science that Ammaline ever wanted to learn. Ammaline had tried to convince her father to adopt Manon, and raise them like siblings. She had almost convinced him—when Manon had disappeared.

Everyone knew her father was on good terms with King Corentin and Queen Delphine, the rulers of the Silver City, but only Ammaline knew that her father spoke directly with the members of the Twelve, the true and secret rulers of Thomàon, chosen from among the people, each one serving under the name of one of the Twelve Gods.

Had Manon been selected as one of the Twelve? Had Manon come to the Twelve's attentions through Ammaline telling her father about her friend?

She did not know. She could not ask.

The tray beeped again, and the cover rolled back.

Manon's clothes had been cut away from their thigh, the pillow removed. The wound had been sewn closed, the skin painted brown with antiseptic.

Their eyes were open, showing a sparkling green—not Manon's lovely, large brown eyes at all.

Had Ammaline been mistaken? Was this some stranger? No. No matter how changed, Manon was still Manon. That which was Manon could not become unrecognizable; if there was no recognition, it was because Ammaline had changed. It shamed her that she had not recognized the man with the scarlet ribbon, and that she had not been able to identify her friend from their voice.

She had not *thought* of her friend in years; and yet she had never stopped dreaming of them.

Manon lifted a shaky arm, wrapped it around Ammaline's neck, and pulled her close, so that their foreheads touched. "It *is* you. I thought you were La Voisine, the mystic."

"It is I."

Manon giggled, then coughed. Their voice was a deep contralto. "Help me...help me sit up."

Ammaline helped them upright, then to their feet. "What happened, Manon?"

"It's too much to explain. And I have to get out of here, before...did you recognize me? From the party?"

Ammaline nodded. "The man with the scarlet ribbon. I tried to save her, the woman you killed. But they pulled me away, and—whatever it was—it killed her."

"You are very brave. And I am sorry you had to see that."

Ammaline stepped under Manon's shoulder. They were tall, very tall even for a man, and yet so very light. "What happened to you? Where have you been all these years?"

They walked together toward the balcony. Manon put a foot upon the rail, then swayed. "I don't know if I can do this."

Ammaline put a hand on their arm. "Stay. For a little while."

"They will come. Sooner or later, someone will have told the police they have seen me, and they will search here. They will search every-where."

"But until then?"

"Why put you in danger?" Manon asked, bitterly. "You saved my life. And now I must tear myself away from you again. Do you know, Ammaline, that not a day—"

They both froze as one as they heard the soft whisper of a door opening across the thick pile of carpet.

Manon grasped the rail again. "I must go."

Ammaline leaned toward their cheek, to plant a kiss there, only to meet Manon's lips, which were cool and dry. A hand touched the back of Ammaline's head, pressing it close, then lowered itself to the back of her neck, where a sharp pinch made her suddenly dizzy.

She had been giving a fast-acting drug, she knew.

She sank to the floor of the balcony, her dark blue skirts puffing, then sinking, around her. Gray fog closed around the edges of her vision.

Her last sight was of Manon climbing onto her bronze railing, then leaping into the sky, elegant and alien in motion.

"The Twelve! She has been attacked!" cried Madame LaFerme, from a distance. "And this blood! It is the blood of the Easer of Ways! That is why I have been unable to reach her!"

Sinking into blessed unconsciousness—Ammaline had no desire to speak to Madame LaFerme at the moment—her lips still tingled.

From the meaning. From the possibility.

Of that kiss.

Book the Second

L'elixir d'or

Chapter 1

An Errand in the City

THE ROOMS OF MADAME LaFerme in the Silver City were similar to those of Ammaline Lemure: a sitting room, a balcony, a bath, a dressing-room, a bedroom, all opulently decorated. The main difference was that the rooms of Madame Océan LaFerme were decorated with seashells and painted in the blue shades of the sea. She rolled her eyes every time she entered them.

However, she did not have to *live* there, except during the Season. She had her own country-house away from the city, but it was sealed up and abandoned at the moment, for when the Grillons overwhelmed it. When—*if*—she returned, it would likely be a mess of shattered glass, cast-off Grillon shells, and damage from the storm. Some years, she returned to find her house untouched; others were less lucky. This Season felt as though it would prove to be one of the less fortunate ones.

The queen had often pleaded with her to take permanent rooms within the city, but Madame LaFerme valued her independence—which she should never have had, if she had stayed within the walls of the castle.

It was not as though living in the Castle of the Silver Spire had kept safe her assistant, Mademoiselle Coty Bourge.

The guards had demanded to know why anyone should wish to kill Mademoiselle Bourge, age seventeen, and Madame LaFerme had wept that no one could have wished her little Coty any harm, and that the assassin must have been attempting to take her, that is, Madame LaFerme's, life instead, but missed.

She had thrown herself upon the shoulder of one of the guards and confessed that she had been receiving threatening letters of late, and led the guards to the file where she kept her correspondence, showing him the letters. He had demanded copies, and she had sent them to him with the touch of a few buttons.

The guard had asked a few more questions about Mademoiselle Bourge, about the letters, and about Madame LaFerme's recent activities. She had answered them all. Then the guards had left, promising to soon return. She reminded them that she must likely perform later that evening, then reminded them of where they might find her, at the Opéra du Mendicant.

As soon as Madame LaFerme was left to her own devices, she entered her dressing-room in order to repair her dress, in case her performance was not to be canceled.

She was interrupted by a knock upon the rear door of her dressing-room, the one hidden behind the racks of clothing. Lost in thought, she would not have noticed it, except that a small light flashed on the side of her dressing-mirror.

Startled, she adjusted the controls of the mirror to see who required her attention. Standing in the narrow corridor by her back door was one of the castle pages, who often brought unofficial—and unrecorded—messages from the king and queen and other notable personages.

In other words, not a person to be ignored, at such a moment as this.

Madame LaFerme let out a mild curse and threw down her black eyeliner upon the vanity. Her appearance, no matter how essential to her profession, would have to wait. It would all have to be redone before her performance, at any rate; she only wished to make sure she was presentable, in case anyone saw her as she moved through the halls.

She placed a mask over her face, one that looked like an ordinary mask of the Season, covered with glitter and feathers, but that would protect her eyes, nose, and mouth from anything being sprayed in her face. She set the latch to catch the door if it were shoved, and opened the secret door a slim crack, holding a pistolet à aiguille out of sight around the corner.

"Yes?"

All she could see of the page was a slim line in the dim hallway. "A message."

"From whom?"

But the page only shrugged, slipped her a folded piece of paper, and trotted away.

Madame LaFerme closed and barred the door once more, hanging the mask back in place. The paper was smudged around the edges and sealed with red confirmation wax. She brought the envelope back with her to her vanity, where she searched through her drawers until she found her signet-ring, and held it over the red wax until it released the edge of the paper. She tossed the little circle into her drawer for the mechaniques to clean up later, then sat upon the edge of the vanity stool and read the note—which occupied but a moment, it was so short:

We must meet.

It was followed by the sign—scrawled in pen rather than stamped—of a little black paw.

Madame LaFerme made a most inelegant sound, crumpling the paper in her fist as she did so. There was no time left for meetings and assignations, not tonight.

And yet, it must be done. She could not afford any trouble—not tonight.

She pawed through the drawer again and retrieved the confirmation seal, pressed it onto the paper, and set it into a metal tray. Then she held her signet ring over the message until the red wax bubbled and began to dissolve the paper.

Soon the message was nothing more than a dark smudge at the bottom of the tray, and finally nothing more than a sour smell in the air. Meanwhile, Madame LaFerme had removed her makeup, revealing a face which seemed younger than it had but a moment previous. She sprayed perfume to cover the odor of the dissolved letter, then stripped herself out of her gown. It was splattered with blood, so she dropped it on the floor, along with her underthings, for the mechaniques to clean or dispose of, she cared not which. She had laid out another gown to change into, after she had finished her makeup.

A brief glance in the mirror revealed a body apparently in the prime of its youth but possessing quite unusual features, especially about the joints of her legs. She crouched a little, bending her knees backward, then forward again. They popped a little, stiff from holding themselves to a singular direction.

The queen had said that the effects of the lack of the elixir would not show so soon, perhaps not ever. But Madame LaFerme had known her friend for a long time, and knew that although Delphine rarely lied, she sometimes said what she *wished* were true, rather than what was likely to be so.

Well, then. If Madame LaFerme wished to secure a future supply of the elixir, she could brook no delay in this meeting, even if it meant she were late to her performance—or she missed it altogether.

She pulled a suit made of tough, featureless, dark gray fabric from underneath the skirts of a pale yellow silk dress, and donned it, pulling the hood up over her head so that all but her eyes were covered by it. Then she checked the back door of the dressing-room, to see if she might slip out that way, and ascend to the roof, or if she must leave via her balcony—which she always disliked doing.

The corridors were clear.

She slipped out, locked the door behind her, edged quickly along the corridor, and silently ascended a narrow spiral stair that led onto the roof. By the time she emerged into the claustrophobic night under the Great Dome, Ammaline had finished singing, so that Madame LaFerme heard nothing of her protégée, not even a final echo. Instead what she heard was the song of the Silver City, an ever-shifting tune that contained the sound of music, of laughter, of cheering—and one faint, discordant element that she was not expecting.

She turned one ear toward it, then the other, then even pulled back her hood to make sure she was hearing what she supposed: silence.

It is much more difficult to sense something which is *not*, than something which *is*.

In a direction that should have contained the most riotous of celebrations—one of the main parades—there were none of the sounds that she ought to have heard, and only the soft reverberations of celebration from other directions.

It was the same direction that she was to meet—the one whom she was called upon to meet.

Madame LaFerme took several deep breaths, then relaxed herself, closing her eyes, stopping her breath, and even slowing her heartbeat, while letting her sense of hearing extend to its utmost.

There *was* a sound coming from that direction. Not the sounds that she feared—sounds that would indicate that the dome had been breached, and that they were about to be overwhelmed—but ones that might prove worse.

If Madame LaFerme's voice was remarkable, her hearing was even more so.

What she heard was the sound of whispers. What they whispered, not even *she* could make out. Not at this distance.

She must go, and go quickly: she took a deep breath, and her heart began to beat firmly once again. She pulled up her hood, shaking her head to clear it of the ominous silence. The others, they had their plans and machinations, their wheels within wheels, poised to transform the world—or destroy it, for none could anticipate the consequences of their actions with perfection.

She herself had her own plans and machinations, but they mainly served to keep her poised to escape any trap.

Had she positioned herself foolishly this time? Her casual promise to launch Mademoiselle Ammaline Lemure into society had already had curious repercussions.

And her meeting tonight—!

It was very nearly a commitment of a permanent nature to one side, if she were discovered. And yet, Madame LaFerme had always been of such a nature that her pleasures often overtook her intentions. This assignation, which had begun with the lure of the forbidden, had become dangerous...risky...exciting. She did not *believe*, precisely, in the cause that her lover had espoused.

Quite literally, her passions compelled her.

And yet her instincts to caution had not been abandoned entirely.

She stepped backward to the edge of the roof, then ran forward, leaping into the night sky, invisible from below—and to the many mechaniques that watched from every direction, even from the great dome above.

She leapt from rooftop to rooftop, alighting as silently as an insect.

The whispers stilled themselves, leaving behind a silence so profound that she could not but hear it echoing back to her from every direction. Then soft sounds began to emanate from within that silence: soft, stealthy movements interrupted by the sound of metal being snapped, glass swept, heavy cobblestones dragged...

She came to a stop atop a tall building overlooking the erstwhile parade route, and looked over the edge.

The street below was as empty as though there had never been a parade, and never would be again. And yet the evidence of what had happened had not been entirely erased: the mechaniques were hard at their work. Hundreds of the small ones, too many slim legs surrounding a central body made of dull gray metal, crawled to and fro, picking up small, twinkling bits of glass as though they were insects fighting over crumbs. Larger ones were replacing the balcony railing, patching the gouged white concrete of the streets, and fitting glass back into windows.

As she watched, one of the largest ones squatted over a red stain on the street, and she heard the sound of whirring, as a brush descended from its belly, to clean off the blood.

"Océan."

The voice startled her, despite its familiarity, or perhaps because of it. She turned, her body tensing as if for flight.

"Armand! You startled me."

The man who stood before her was tall and dressed in gray, just as she was. He pulled back his hood, revealing his face and allowing his dark hair to fall loose about his shoulders in waves. His eyes were dark, so *very* dark, and set deep into his brow; his lips were broad, and full, and as easily bursting into a smile as a predatory frown. His eyes, they swallowed up anyone who allowed themselves to return his gaze, and, more than once, Madame LaFerme had seen that gaze pierce the souls of women, making them vulnerable to his seduction—and their consequent, inevitable destruction. More often, she had seen those eyes pierce his enemies, causing them to become nervous, uncomfortable, too talkative, too defensive, too revealing.

Tonight, those eyes seemed distracted, and she felt herself relax with relief.

How had it come to this? How had he made her betray herself? Did she hate him more, or want him?

He pleased her; even so, she should have been able to discard him as an inconvenience, and refuse his summons.

"I was about to go to the place where we were to meet," he said, "but stopped out of curiosity, to see...but of course I should find you here, Océan. Your curiosity..." He shook his head, as if unable to find the words to describe her foolishness. "It boggles the mind."

She pressed her lips together. He was in a sardonic mood tonight, which never boded well. She did not have time to soothe his moods. If *that* was the reason he had brought her here—!

"Armand. I must prepare for my performance. What do you want?"

He chuckled. "So direct. Are you tiring of me, my pet?"

She thought of how long she had held him at arm's length. A *long* time. She knew what kind of man he was; she had known it from the start. But—suddenly, almost against her will—it had seemed as though he were a risk worth taking. He was *so* very delicious, and always had been, and she had always been attracted to him, playfully but unconquerably flirtatious.

Then Delphine had whispered to her that the supplies of the elixir had become low—"but surely we will learn to create it ourselves!"—and it had, almost by coincidence, seemed that the time had finally come to take a taste of the man who had made so many of his enemies dance to his tune.

She smiled thinly at him. "The Easer of Ways struck at supper. My assistant, Mademoiselle Bourge, has been assassinated, while the warden's little innocent daughter, who is to be my protégée, looked on. The elixir is all but gone, and I must perform in little less than an hour's time. I am not tiring of you, Armand; I am merely *tired*. I am tired of all the games that we must play with each other."

"When you tire of the games we play, you tire of life."

Madame LaFerme felt her nostrils flare. "Then it is well that we have little Ammaline to take my place."

In an instant, he had swept from the edge of the roof to her side, and held his hand under her chin. His scent was subtle, half musk and half a drug whose name lay at the tip of her tongue, but that she was too distracted to remember. "Océan, my darling, you must not say such things. Ammaline? She is useless to anyone, except as a pawn. What realm could she possibly rule? She is no Great Diva, and never will be. You must not fade. No-one can take your place."

"She will take *mine*," Madame LaFerme said stubbornly, irrationally. "I can already feel it, the stiffness in my joints, the fragility of my bones."

Really, why not just agree with Armand? It would be easier, as it always was, to subsume her irritation, her irrationality, her discomfort, and allow his plans to carry her along.

His hand moved from her chin to encircle the back of her head. He pulled her forehead to his, then lifted his face, and kissed her on it, like a father apologizing for chastising his child. "You will live forever. I promise it. Soon, all of this will be over, and we will go to your country-house, and repair it, and escape from the city forever."

It was a lie; she *knew* it was a lie; and yet it comforted her.

"Armand," she insisted pettishly, "why have you called me here?"

"There was a second death, at the supper you attended."

"What?"

He licked his lips. "A man in white was seen leaving the dinner, as the guards ran in pursuit of the Easer of Ways."

"And?"

"And the body was indeed drained of blood. You must take care, Océan, lest you be hurt—and all our plans be torn asunder."

"And who was *killed*, Armand?"

"Oh, a nobody. It hardly signifies." He gave a name; she did not recognize it. "And there is more."

Madame LaFerme's head was already spinning from the suggestion that the White Gentleman had returned after having been absent for more than twenty years. She had thought—everyone had thought—him dead.

"Is it him? Or an impostor?" she asked.

Armand waved a hand. "It is unknown. No one saw him leave. It only happened that the Easer of Ways, posing as a young nobleman, spoke to a man dressed in white for an instant, before the assassin destroyed your Mademoiselle Bourge. And then the body was found, bloodless. It is suggestive, is it not? But you have not asked what about the letter."

She felt the skin on the backs of her hands prickle. "What letter?"

He reached into a pocket of the gray suit and pulled out a letter, not sealed but merely folded. When she did not take it, he waggled it at her.

Had she written something indiscreet? Surely, she had—but what? What could she have written, that he might confront her about *now*?

Reluctantly, she took it from him and unfolded it, and began reading it in the darkness:

Madame LaFerme will be visited by an old sin later tonight.

"How did you get this?" she asked.

"I spotted a Scarabée on her way to your rooms and took it. What old sin, do you think?"

He asked as though he knew that she knew the answer, knew it very well; he asked it suggestively, as though she were betraying him with another.

There was a flutter in Madame LaFerme's chest, of impatience, of outrage. She suppressed it. Now was hardly the time to start a lovers' quarrel. "Very well."

She tucked the letter into a pocket of her own, and turned to go.

Armand's hand locked onto her arm, twisting it painfully. "What old sin, Océan? One of...us?"

"I don't *know*, Armand. I must go. Delphine will be coming to wish me well before the performance."

She tried to wrest her arm away from him; he held it until she understood that there was no escaping him, and then released her, raising his eyebrows, stepping away from her, and lifting both hands, palm out. "Go, then. I am not stopping you."

She did not like to leave like this; he would punish her later with his silence, with foul moods, with belittling words that would cut her to the quick.

"Armand..."

Whatever showed on her face seemed to soften him a little. He smiled at her. "I am done playing now, I promise. Go! And good luck with your performance. Although you never need it. I will see you soon, my love."

He swept her up again, wrapping his arms around her, kissing her, swallowing her. She hardly knew it when she had returned to her own rooftop, he left her so light-headed.

She slipped downstairs to her room, and in through the back passage to her wardrobe. It was time to change into her second gown of the evening. She stripped off the gray suit, hung it under the skirts of another of the dresses—she hardly cared which—and threw on the dress she had laid out earlier.

Before she twisted her arms around and buttoned it up in back, she paused.

The dress smelled of a nobleman's perfume, sandalwood, jasmine, and musk.

And—it was warm. There was no time to wonder: she buttoned herself all the way up the back, positioned her wig without pinning it—it would soon have to come off—and off she went, to sing at the Feast of Fools.

Chapter 2

A Public Performance

Madame LaFerme fled along the back corridors toward Opéra du Mendicant. Within moments, without time to warm up her voice privately, so that she must sing scales as she ran, she would face her most terrible, most discriminating critics: the People themselves!

The People could not be persuaded by artisanship or the illusion of good taste: they demanded amusement. They had no appetite for arias, could not tolerate tragedies, and viewed as merely out-of-date the old songs of the Vieux Monde. They liked nothing better than pratfalls, dropped trousers, lifted skirts, a rough hand planted firmly about someone else's bottom followed by a silk slipper planted firmly in the fork of a crotch, putting nobles through mock trials and burning them in effigy, throwing rotten fruit from the stalls, and howling bawdy songs full of double entendres.

The Great Diva must hold herself with great dignity in front of the public, except on one occasion: the Feast of Fools, at which she must debase herself with all the power of her considerable ingenuity.

Some said that Madame LaFerme showed her true face at the feast, that she was a harlot and a wanton who liked nothing better than to be pelted with rotten tomatoes, that she picked lovers of all sorts—more than one at a time!—from among the crowd, use them hard, then banished them from her bed; that someone else did all the singing for her and she used secret microphones and speakers to manage her performances, that she was not merely the Great Diva, the greatest living soprano of her time, but the Great Diva *herself*, the goddess—or at least one of the Twelve Masks, one of the not-so-secret rulers of Thomàon.

If Madame LaFerme *were* a goddess, she certainly did not feel like one. She felt put upon, both by her obligations to her public, and by her obligations to her lover. Worse, she felt hot, she felt bloated about her hands and feet, the joints of her knees and hips hurt from all the leaping around she had done, she felt great black circles swelling under her eyes, the mark of several sleepless nights, and—she was convinced—lack of the elixir.

With her enormous skirts, she could not move through the corridors used by the Scarabées, not even if she moved sideways. She was forced to rush through the public corridors, almost as if it had been decreed she must do so. As she ran, the thick-piled carpet, marble tiles, and expensive rugs changed the sound of her court-shoes from a hushed whisper, to the tattoo of a rolling drum beat, to a muffled, furtive knocking sound. She passed golden lanterns, recessed lighting, crystal chandeliers, vaulted ceilings, frescoes, silver-backed mirrors, carved wood paneling that was so ornate that it seemed more an encrustation of coral, gilded plaster, more than a few portraits in heavy frames hanging from gold chains, white marble angels, colonnades, delicate vases, busts of the King wearing a mustache and metal armor, and of the Queen with a nipple bared, wearing only a diaphanous scarf like a nymph from the Vieux Monde, fountains, tapestries—and crowds, everywhere the crowds of the People!

Behind her the words echoed everywhere she went: "Madame LaFerme, she is late for her curtain! Make way, make way!"

But finally, inevitably, she was stopped.

It was in the Hall of the Masks, which served as the entrance hall to the Opéra du Mendicant. Before any ordinary performance, the hall was filled with sellers of food and drink, of souvenirs, of programmes, of clever little cheap mechaniques like dolls, which enacted the scenes of the opera about to be performed.

On the day of the Feast of Fools, there were no sellers: everything must be given away as largesse to the crowds, and the Twelve help them all if the crowd could not satisfy its every whim! A fountain in the center of the Hall ran red with wine; enormous wheels of cheese lay on tables, and the crowd cut off slices with their knives; mechaniques bearing trays of champagne, or beer, or canapés, or drugs, were kicked aside and crushed underfoot. All was madness: all was the will of the People!

Above them in the hall hung representations of the Twelve Masks, the gods of Thomàon, who were embodied within the People themselves, chosen at random from the People themselves at a young age, and brought up as heirs to power—reminding the People that even upon this day, they were watched—watched from within.

Primary among the masks were the King and the Queen, white masks with golden crowns—the King's with a gold mustache, and the Queen's with gilded hair. The identities of those who wore *those* two masks were, of course, known to all: that the rulers of the Silver City were placed at the highest rank among the ruling council came as no surprise. Their masks were placed above the doors to the Opéra du Mendicant itself.

The Archaeologist's mask was hung on the wall to the right of the King, and was slightly smaller, with a pair of crossed shovels that half-looked like keys, with filigree at the ends and teeth cut into the blade. To the left of the Queen hung Océan's own mask: that of the Great Diva, whose mask was simple but entirely gilded, the mouth opened. Someone had thrown a great wad of tinsel up to the mask, and it hung suggestively from her lips.

The People *knew* that Madame LaFerme was the Great Diva, that was, one of the council. The face of the woman who wore the mask changed, but always it was such: the greatest living singer played the rôle of the Great Diva. It was traditional. And, for the greater part of the year, Madame LaFerme was treated with all deference. But the respect she was given only seemed to make the Feast of Fools more vicious, more violent every year.

It was as though the People could sense what was coming: Thomàon was about to sink into madness. Océan could feel their final doom thrumming underfoot, as if the entire planet resonated with some mechanical flaw that would tear it apart. She felt it the way she could feel her own body failing—and when she had asked Delphine whether she thought an answer to that doom might not be found, even *she*, that great denier, could not deny it.

The other masks were out of her line of sight, but she could feel their presence staring down at her back. The Player's mask bore a chess-piece on its cheek; the Assassin's, a pair of crossed knives. The Puppet-Master's mask had white gloves to go with it, gold threads leading from its fingertips. The White Gentleman had two gilded teeth that rested upon his lower lip, the very picture of the infamous monster of the Vieux Monde. The Hawkmistress's mask bore an enormous papillon de nuit, its scent-glands extended, clinging to the side of her mask.

Grandpère's mask hung beside hers, his mask speckled with coins. La Voisine, the Seer, had a mask made unlike the others—not made of white plaster with gold trimmings, but crystal-clear, and rippled with silver specks.

Last but not least was the Madman, half of whose mask was shaped like that of the silvery crescent moon. Madame LaFerme did not like to face the mask of the Madman, and was glad that it lay at her back, for all that she felt it staring down at her, making her guts writhe with guilt.

Madame LaFerme had *very* remarkable ears. Even for one of the Twelve, she knew too much.

Perhaps that was why the King and Queen allowed her to be used so ill, on the day of the Feast of Fools, when they themselves would not face the crowds.

The crush within the Hall of Masks was thicker than anywhere else, prey-birds being after all drawn to fresh meat. The people around her wore costumes of the cheapest sort, easily torn. The air reeked of bodies, drug-haze, and alcohol. The parades that had wound through the city all met in the entrance halls surrounding the Opéra du Mendicant, and entered together.

All but *one* of the parades, that was: the one that Armand had showed her, the one that had disappeared.

Madame LaFerme was caught by an army of arms, stopped in the center of the hall, and laid hands upon. A personne wearing a dog's snout grabbed her from behind and rubbed their crotch against her, grabbing her breasts. She kicked them off her, and they rolled on the marble floor, laughing as they were pulled to their feet.

"Get out of my *fucking* way, you indecent, filth-covered drunken pigs!" she roared, applying the power of her voice behind the sound in order to fill the room. "I'm going to be late, you shits!"

The crowd roared with laughter.

The dog-faced personne called jeeringly, "Who's a drunken pig, then?"

A thousand voices called back, "I am!"

"Then get out of the way for the lady, you drunken pigs!" the personne called mockingly.

"Never!"

On all sides around her, the citizens locked arms against Madame LaFerme, leering and sticking out their tongues.

If they only knew how she could leap!

She made a grand gesture with one arm, then placed the back of her wrist against her forehead. "Let me go! I must perform for my public!"

"We are your public!"

Amongst the crowd, she caught sight of a face she knew: not her lover, not the man known on the streets as the Roi du Rats, who weaved his tangled webs of lies and manipulations in order to make the People dance—but very nearly, one of his adjutants. The personne wore a white half-mask, concealing half their face, with one peering eye that glowed red from behind it.

Madame LaFerme only recognized the personne from their voice, whose mocking laughter her own skillful ears picked out from the crowd, even as she shouted and spat and clawed for release from the circle surrounding her. She carefully allowed her eyes to slide away from them; their glances had not met, and she did not think they knew that she had seen them.

But she knew, now, why her lover had summoned her: not for accusations, not to witness the absent parade, but to arrange for her delay on the way to her performance.

Why?

There was a reason; there were a thousand reasons, with Armand, all of them in service of plans delicately balanced once against the other, so that one of them fell, it would fall in such a way as to support the success of the others.

She grabbed the man in front of her by the glittering straps of his dress, and forced him to trip over her ankle, so that he fell on the marble tiles of the floor. He rolled out of her way, and came at her from behind, grabbing her around her middle, and swinging her off the floor in a great, skirt-swirling circle.

She twisted in his arms and clawed at his face, leaving three careful scratches down the side of his rouged cheek, three red stripes more of smeared rouge than of blood. He shouted and dropped her, putting his hands to his face.

The crowd swallowed him. She turned back toward the doors of the opéra and confronted a woman who stood tall upon platform sandals made with mechaniques that lifted and lowered her. The woman rose up, swinging a feathered baton; Madame LaFerme leaned forward and bit the woman's breast, not hard, only to make the appearance of it.

The woman screamed, and Madame LaFerme snatched the feathered baton from her, twirling her out of the way, then slapping her on the ass with the baton, and kicking her with her court-shoe as she fell. The woman was caught by the crowd—and also disappeared.

Next, as if by chance, Madame LaFerme caught hold of the personne upon whom she had remarked earlier, the one with the white half-mask. She raised a fist in their face as if to give them a blow, then caught the back of the mask and pulled their head toward her, kissing them with a mock-kiss such as those in the theatre use, while placing the baton between their thighs and making suggestive movements with it. The personne moaned with pleasure, then sank in Madame LaFerme's arms, fainting almost convincingly—a nice touch.

Battle after battle, Madame LaFerme fought with the crowd, a complex dance without injury or offense, but only the appearance of it, although certainly her dress suffered, soon turning to a collection of tatters. Slowly, she worked her way toward the door that would permit her to enter the Opéra du Mendicant.

But her performance had already begun.

And, really, when had it ever stopped?

Suddenly, the great double doors of the opéra opened, not the humble side door she had planned to use, but the ones for the use of the crowds. Out poured a wave of uniformed people dressed in white silk pajamas that covered them from neck to ankle, and matching white half-masks. Upon their shoulders they bore a platform, and upon the platform stood a jester, half in red, half in blue and gold, with the painted mask of a human face, so hideous that it could not be true to life, wearing a three-pointed cap-and-bells and carrying a baton topped with a miniature of the mask.

The jester roared, "Where is my wench? Give her up to me, you fribbles! you blasphemers! you fools!"

It was Armand.

Océan LaFerme was grabbed around her middle, and swung up onto the platform beside her lover.

Armand grabbed her and kissed her, a real kiss that left the taste of his salty lips and alcohol-soaked tongue within her mouth. It was a bad whiskey he had been drinking, which made her nostrils flare from the smell of rancid yeast.

She began to pull away from him, but his arm tightened around her waist. She struggled; he kissed her again, mashing his lips to her and smearing her makeup as she wrenched her face away.

"Stop, you mangy ass!"

Laughing at her, he released her, and she stumbled backward and nearly off the platform, only to be caught and pushed forward again by the crowd. She shrieked in mock-outrage and charged toward him, as any maiden might whose virtue had been insulted, slapping him in the way of actors, so that it was more sound than sting.

His return, however, was far more serious: a real blow that knocked her onto her rump, legs spread out in a vee in front of her, and leaving her stunned and ill with the sudden pain.

He sneered down at her, his upper lip dancing with the tension of his contempt. He did not dissemble at that moment, of that she was sure: his breath came hard and fast, his hands clenched and trembling with emotion.

He loathed her. For nearly a year she had made love to him in the secrets and the dark, wondering at the foolish caution that had kept her from him for so long, giving herself to him in passion.

Her "foolish caution" had been nothing more than wisdom; his seduction, a calculated lie.

It almost seemed that the lie had been calculated that he might achieve his plans for this very moment.

She rubbed her pained cheek with the back of her hand. The taste of blood might fill her mouth, but he had not broken the outer skin. It was just as well; if she had begun to bleed in public, the color of it would surely have caused comment.

She climbed to her feet, nearly to be thrown back down again as the platform tilted, and turned toward her lover. All around the platform surged the throng of white-pajama'd fools, all of them wearing—she now noticed it—white half-masks with the one red and glowing eye.

She was in the middle of a sea of fools, fools every one, and she did not leave herself out of their number. A fool for trusting Armand the man, for trusting the Roi du Rats, the demagogue who ruled the streets of the Silver City, always eluding the police; for trusting the Puppet-Master himself, one of the Twelve Masks who ruled the Thomàon, for trusting a man with blood as dark blue as her own!

The platform lurched as the Puppet-Master's agents carried it toward the double doors.

Armand hardly seemed to notice her. He had conquered her, for the amusement of the crowd; it seemed as if his purpose for her was over. He spread his arms wide and leapt into the air, kicking his heels together and setting his bells a-jingle:

"Let the Feast of Fools begin!"

Chapter 3

The Feast of Fools

Inside the Opéra du Mendicant, the stalls had been removed and the musicians' pit covered with a platform, so that the floor was a slope that led downward from the doors to the stage, which was shrouded by enormous red velvet curtains. Above the floor rose four balconies, each fronted with white porcelain panels decorated with various instances of the Masks, and each with its own gilt railing. Behind the railings of the first balcony were the private boxes. The rest of the balconies were lined with rows and rows and rows of seats, like smooth red velvet teeth.

Overhead rose the strong gilded ribs of a great dome, a dome that was, tonight, opened to the artificial sky. With the Great Dome protecting the entire city from the storms of the Season, it was unnecessary for additional protection from the weather.

So when the Diva, the Puppet-Master, and all his bootlickers entered the opéra, above them rose the slim needle of the Silver Spire, bathed in a succession of images, all of them depicting Madame LaFerme this night, amongst the crowd: fighting, kissing, groping—but, in particular, being knocked down on her ass.

Madame LaFerme turned her eyes away, annoyed that she had allowed her gaze to linger.

The platform and its bearers began their headlong journey down the slope of the floor toward the stage, picking up speed, even as several of their number tripped, fell, and were trampled. She swayed this way and that from the leaning of the platform, but now she was ready for the movement, and no longer stumbled—although she pretended to, lurching this way, then that, while sobbing her eyes out and begging for help.

If Armand had long been playing his rôle, so had she hers. She would play it double, tonight.

The platform reached the edge of the stage, the feet of its bearers drumming on the hollow platform that covered the pit as they crossed it, a thunder that promised one of them was sure to fall through.

Armand, wearing his jester's clothes, stepped off the platform and onto the stage—he tripped, rolled, and turned, springing to his feet with his back to the curtains.

Madame LaFerme ran to the edge of the platform, and tried to climb down off it and escape. She was caught immediately, then handed up to Armand on the stage. Once again, she struggled against him.

And, once again, he hit her, this time on the other cheek.

It *hurt*.

She fell loose-limbed to the stage, going limp as she sobbed noisily.

Once again, Armand released his contempt at her, a contempt so enormous that it overspilled the noise of the entering crowds:

"Take that, wench! They call you an artist? They call you the Great Diva? I call you my *bitch!*"

She did not answer the insult, but remained sobbing. The surest way to become enmeshed in the schemes of the Puppet-Master was to resist them: to argue, to debate, was to become the fly that struggled in the web, tightening the threads.

Armand's attention turned away from her; she felt it shift, like a spotlight being aimed in another direction.

"Did you know?" he asked the crowd. "Did you *know* that they asked someone else to lead the festivities tonight? To be paired with this slut?"

The People were still pushing their way in. Madame LaFerme risked a look to the floor, and saw that the platform she had been carried in upon had disappeared. Even the gang of white-pajama'd bearers had disappeared—or taken off their outer costumes, rather, for among the crowd were the red-glowing eyes of the masks Armand's assistants had worn.

It was going to be an ugly night, even for the Feast of Fools, unlike any other. At least Ammaline was not present, and would not be required to see Madame LaFerme's debasement, or join into it. But what did Armand hope to accomplish this night? What was worth alienating her forever?

What plans did he have? Did he have *any*? Or had his mind finally snapped, so that the awful truths of his soul must bubble up, and reveal themselves to all, without control or calculation?

Tucking her chin to her breast, Madame LaFerme snorted. Armand? Lose control? Cease to play games?

She felt a hand on her arm drag her roughly to her feet. Then she was pushed toward a pair of Armand's assistants, caught by them, and spun to face the crowd.

Armand was in front of her, his jester's jacket open now, the gold buttons hanging limp. He gestured toward her. "And look! Why anyone would want her is beyond me. Any other night, her flaws would be clothed in satin and lace and diamonds. But now, look at her! She is just another wench, another *bitch*, another king's harlot crying her eyes out—but you know she loves it rough!"

The crowd exploded into laughter.

Armand waved an arm, and they fell silent.

"But it is not Madame LaFerme we despise. No." He wheeled around in a pirouette, and caught Madame LaFerme around the waist, still holding her roughly, but this time without overt malice. "She is but a symbol, a symbol for Thomàon itself. A wench covered in glitter and gems, a harlot available to the highest bidder. But she is *our* harlot, and we love her, despite her flaws."

Armand's arm gave way behind her, and Madame LaFerme leaned back, thinking it was about half likely that he would snatch his arm away and let her pratfall to the floor.

Let him! She knew how to take a fall.

But he did not. He dipped her, elegantly, then pulled her back onto her feet and gave her a rough kiss, one that would have charmed her, had she still believed in him.

When he pulled back from her, she dissembled into a rueful smile.

"Darling," he purred at her, touching her face, then spun her round and round, so that the rags of her gown came scandalously close to her knees. "You know how fond I am of you."

"Armand," she whispered, feigning desire, and was not shocked to hear her voice carry, amplified, throughout the hall.

"You know how much I adore you," he said, aiming her toward the front of the platform, so that the lights caught at her. "How much we all adore you."

A puff of air blew toward her from below. One of the Puppet-Master's minions was lowering a sparkling pipette from his lips. She glanced down at herself without allowing the angle of her head to shift, and saw that her rags now twinkled in the light.

She felt, without seeing, that behind her the stage had fallen into the focused darkness of the stage, a blank canvas upon which to write the tragedies of the bedroom, the melodramas of the universe.

The lights over the audience turned golden, then began to dim through the colors of a natural sunset. The faces of the audience vanished, all but the first few rows, whose faces became hollow and ghostlike. A faint memory, nearly erased by time, clutched at her heart: she remembered—she thought she remembered—faces that were ugly, old, damaged—different shades of flesh—faces that showed the evidence of an ongoing existence.

She felt the pain of the memory, but had neither the time nor the will to examine why, why it should pain her that the people before her were so similar, so easily categorized.

If she did not focus on her danger at this moment, if she did not play the game according to, yet undermining, the Puppet-Master's rules, she would be punished. She might even get herself killed.

"Armand," she sighed breathily, stretching out her hands toward him.

"My darling, my lovely, it is time."

"Time for what?"

"To sing!"

For a moment she was in free fall. There was no music to cue her as to what to sing, only silence.

Then the low thrumming of *Les beaux rêves* began, and the spotlights shining down upon her began to flash, pink and green. Although Madame LaFerme could not have counted the number of times she had sung the song, she felt the hair upon her arms and across the back of her neck to rise.

She folded her hands in front of her in a gesture of pleading, looked toward the heavens—toward the technological wonder of the dome, that was—and began to sing of bittersweet, evil old dreams.

The crowd made a sound which was halfway between a cheer and a jeer, the sound of a crowd that hears the first bars of its state anthem, as it were, and began to sing along with her. Their voices rose, a susurration of sound that was both powerful and unfocused. They were out of tune, they had no rhythm, they missed their timing—but they were the People, and although they sang badly, the badness of their singing expressed a sort of truth about their power.

It did not matter whether the People were educated, intelligent, or correct. Their voices carried an almost kinetic force.

And yet...Madame LaFerme's voice led them. Even as their volume rose, so did hers. Armand could not control the volume of the People, but he could ensure the message he wished them to hear, was heard.

She reached the first chorus, belting out the lyrics with passionate cynicism, dashing about here and there on the stage, breaking into dance, and finding herself supported by her own voice, recorded, in harmony.

Her voice was rough in tone, no longer the light and lyric voice that once she had possessed, but a truly dramatic one. How she would have been jealous of her own voice, as a girl! How she would have delighted to sing such songs as were now forbidden her, that now were all but forgotten as well.

What if she were to begin singing one of them now?

She sobbed her lines of the beginning of the bridge, then resumed dancing. The glitter upon her skin had begun to itch, and a line of sweat was running down the small of her back. The lights overhead were not the old stage lights that used to be so hot—another memory that clutched at her chest—but her body, her body remembered their heat.

Barefoot, ragged, the itch of glitter and makeup melting under the lights, the smell of the old pancake makeup, the *wigs*. Back when she was young in truth, before she had decided that she could no longer face the criticisms of the stage, when she must take on the mantle of her other passion, flight…

Harmonizing with her own past self, Madame LaFerme knew that she had not the strength to resist. She would fall in. She would be transformed to others' desires. She would play whatever rôle had been assigned her.

Les beaux rêves led her to its bittersweet conclusion. She repeated the chorus…repeated it again…and again…and again…as her former self's voice danced through its own cycles.

The song faded, the lights dimmed, and she lowered herself to the floor, cursing her aching, backwards knees, and Armand for making her almost reveal them. The spotlights tightened to a single point of light, then vanished.

She felt the floor sink under her as she was lowered from a trapdoor. She stayed perfectly still, lest a fragment of light catch her costume, and did not shudder when she felt a piece of cheap, tacky black velvet drop over her.

A soft sound dragged above her as the sounds around her changed in acoustics from the great, open echoes of the opéra, to the close, yet hollow, underbelly of the stage. The black velvet cloth was removed from her head—the area under the stage was nearly as dark without the cloth as with it.

From above her, she heard Armand announce, "And now for the elections of the fools!" The tone of the music changed, becoming both more complex in its rhythms, and less rich in its tone. It was one of the newer popular songs, she recognized it, but it had not attracted her attention. There was a mixture of the voice of a dulcet, breathy tenor and the chanting of a countertenor, whose voice had been layered with a mechanical roughness.

Madame LaFerme made a face. To have her song followed by this one cheapened it, turned it from a hymn celebrating the opportunistic decay that Thomàon had become, to just another pop song.

She turned her face toward her shoulder.

A soft red light swung across the floor in front of her. She sighed and swung her legs off the platform. Although Armand's chaos seemed random, it was carefully planned. More performances were lined up.

And she was in the way.

She rose to her feet, clenching her teeth at the pain of standing up, which ran through her knees and up to her hips. A hand clasped hers before she could stumble and fall, holding her steady for a moment, then slowly leading her through the darkness toward the small red flashlight.

The figure beside her accompanied her under the length of the outcropping of the temporary stage, then into the warren of dressing rooms and prop rooms under the stage proper. The red flashlight stayed aimed at the floor, helping them navigate through the props, which waited upon their trap doors for their moment to rise upward, and into the light.

Abruptly, the figure beside her pulled her to the side. A trap opened above them, and a platform next to her began to rise, holding a female shape upon it, larger than life, a stylized statue of one of the Twelve. She hadn't been paying attention; it might have even been the statue that represented herself, but younger and larger, without the modifications that were failing her now: her aspect as a goddess.

She stumbled over a cable, and the figure next to her supported her again. The hand was smooth but strong, and she caught herself half-hoping that it would be Armand next to her in the shadows, telling her that his performance had not been a cruel joke, but a necessary step in a larger plan.

But that was a foolish wish. The gods did not play fair with each other. They did not love each other, but only betrayed.

The figure next to her squeezed her hand and pressed it, signaling her to wait. Then it circled round her and she heard the opening of a door. A dim line of dull red light followed, and then the figure beside her pushed her through the doorway, closing the door behind her.

She was alone, in a long corridor leading into a sharp turn and darkness. The smell was more of mildew here, old paint, plastic, grime, sweat, tarnish, and damp.

The makeup smelled different on Thomàon, but the rest of the scents were the same.

Another door opened along the corridor, spilling out a welcome clean white light, and a young personne stepped out, dressed in a light yellow costume, wearing a white wig: a courtier, or an actor pretending to be one. They gestured her close. "Madame? This way, if you please. There is another gown for you, more suitable."

She straightened her back, brushed her hands across the shreds of her dress, and walked toward the open door, which the personne closed firmly behind her, leaning on it when it would not at first quite shut.

The room was small, hardly the room of a diva, but at the moment she could have cared less about its plain cement bricks studded with dusty gray acoustic foam, its bare, stained poured floor with carpet cut from larger pieces, or spotted ceiling tiles: in the center of the room was a dress, suitable for wearing in court.

Not a stage costume—those were often lighter, to save the singers and actors the weight—but a piece of couture. The dress was taffeta in fabric, wisteria in hue, and trimmed with light blue silk roses, green silk embroidery, and light blue ribbon. The panniers were large, the front panel of the dress styled to show a broad expanse of shimmering, unwrinkled taffeta.

A bank of mirrors blazed with light. The table was scattered with makeup and a wig in a pale cream hue, dotted with tiny silk flowers in light blue.

The dresser clucked their tongue at the sound the door made as it closed, then turned to Madame LaFerme. "Strip, if you please, Madame."

She reached around to her back to begin undoing what was left of the dress's fastenings, but the personne had already begun to do it. She rolled her shoulders and stretched her back as the dress came off her, her spine crackling.

Her rags fell upon the floor at her feet, and her hoops and corset soon followed. Soon she was nude, her cold sweat making her shiver. The personne handed her a towelette. She wiped her face as they began wiping the sweat from her back, the cleanser on the towelette making a thousand small cuts sting as they were cleaned. If the dresser thought anything of the unusual articulation of her joints, they said nothing about it.

Soon she was shivering, but clean. The personne pulled at the rags of her dress, and she raised one foot, then the other, as they slid it out from under her.

Then it was on with her chemise, stockings, shoes, drawers, stays—her lungs squashed like a sponge as the dresser pulled the laces tight enough for court, which was *far* tighter than needed for the stage, which meant that she was done singing for the night. Then she was pushed onto a stool for the dresser to airbrush a few light layers of contouring onto her skin, then dust her with a light layer of powder. They darkened her brows and eyes, tinted her lips, colored her cheeks lightly with blush, brushed a little blush between her breasts.

Panniers, petticoat, stomacher all tied and tightened into place, then the fastest professional placement of a wig that she had ever had painful pleasure to experience: pin curls, wig cap, adhesive, pins, wig, more pins, a quick styling—it could not have been more than fifteen minutes altogether before she was back on her feet and following the dresser through the dim corridor, the door of the dressing room closing behind them.

She was used to quick changes for the stage, in clothes and wigs particularly built for that purpose. But not for court: and yet she looked perfectly well-dressed, if one did not look too closely. The dresser's pace was rapid, but nothing like her run earlier that evening across the castle. She breathed slowly, keeping her temperature low, so that she would not ruin all the dresser's good work by presuming to sweat.

At the end of the corridor was a turn, and then stairs, and at the top of the stairs, everything foreign about the area under the stage was left behind. She was back in her own territory, backstage behind the dozens of heavy velvet curtains, the intricate rigging of the cables, some of them slim enough to slice skin, but stronger than steel.

Through the gaps in the curtains, she could see a mock-trial. The Puppet-Master had been dressed in a barrister's robes and wearing a white peruke on his head, the powdered curls and tail nearly bounding off his head as he narrated.

Madame LaFerme did not see who was on trial. The dresser was leading her toward the door to the boxes. They stepped through a door, and the world changed again: from darkest shadows to dimmed lights, from bare floor to deep-piled carpet, from lack of ornamentation to ostentation, from backstage to the public areas of the Opéra du Mendicant.

The backstage door closed on noiseless hinges behind her. The dresser climbed the set of narrow carpeted stairs leading to the boxes, slowing in pace, assuming an air of dignity that belied their status as a mere dresser. Madame LaFerme followed at a much slower pace, struggling to navigate the stairs without disturbing the set of her panniers.

At the top of the stairs, the personne waited for her, stood in front of her as Madame LaFerme straightened herself, then puffed out their chest like a proud hawk preening upon a mistress's leather glove.

A sound caught the personne's attention, and they turned their head with a slow, predatorial movement—it was as if the personne had let fall their rôle for a moment. Then it was resumed, and the dresser was only impatient, beckoning for her to hurry.

Madame LaFerme's eyes narrowed. Who *was* this dresser?

The corridor behind the boxes was all luxury and low lighting, chandeliers with live flames burning low, red patterned carpets, sideboards waiting with sparkling wines, immense vases filled to overflowing with roses.

The People could have whatever they wanted this night—but those who used the boxes were those who provided their largesse. The personne led her to the door of the box nearest the stage, and opened it with a touch of a ring to a lock-plate, a ring that Madame LaFerme had not previously noted. The personne opened the door for her, and let her into a curtained area, pitch black.

Before closing the door for her, the personne bounced on their toes, almost like a child jumping with excitement, then pressed a finger against their lips and closed the door.

Madame LaFerme's mouth had opened with a click. She made herself close it again: as the dresser had jumped, their knees had turned themselves backward, in the same manner as her own.

One of the Twelve!

She had been dressed by none other than the Assassin.

Madame LaFerme took a deep breath, set the mystery aside—did this mean the Assassin working for, or against, the Puppet Master to-night?—and let herself through the dark curtains and into the opera box in front of her.

In front of her was a row of wigs and powdered hair, pale faces staring down at the stage, some of them holding opera glasses to their eyes, others leaning toward each other to gossip.

There was one head that was not decorated with wig or powder, but remained its resolute dishwater color, streaked with gray: the Warden himself. Madame LaFerme felt the hair go up on her arms, remembering things which it would be better not to bring to mind at the moment, lest their reflection appear upon her face. Beside him was his daughter, his Ammaline, a monstrous child—a naïve innocent—a gorgeous voice that would likely never come to its fruition.

She was dressed in a simple chemise gown of deep blue velvet that had been tied with silver cord, the same color that she had chosen earlier, but a different dress. Her wig had been removed and she wore her natural hair up in a twist, tied with silver cord and with silver netting over her head, and across her shoulders. She had added light-gray gloves, and a silver chain—what hung pendant from it, Madame LaFerme could not tell from behind.

She seemed—older. Transformed.

Neither father nor daughter had noticed Madame LaFerme's entrance. Next to the girl sat the royal historian, her slight figure leaning forward, leaning her elbows on the seat in front of her. She held a set of opera glasses and wore a brown-and-gold brocade coat over an ivory silk dress, even more completely against the current fashion than Ammaline's simple dress—but then, Yvonne la Gorge had never been one to move with the times; she had more than once declared herself, arrogantly, as time's enemy. Ammaline glanced at her on occasion, finding the historian more interesting than the histrionic performance happening in front of her.

Madame LaFerme sensed the presence of other figures in the box, saw a few additional powdered wigs, but did not stop to worry them out: her eye was then caught by the events of the stage, and she had to suppress herself from groaning.

On the stage was a trial, the trial of the king and queen.

Not the real ones, thank the Twelve, but two of the Puppet-Master's toadies, still wearing their half-masks under their false crowns, red eyes glowing from the half that was complete. They stood in the dock, side by side, with red velvet robes thrown over their shoulders, and carnival costumes underneath, ragged, cheap, and sparkling. Their crowns were ill-fitting, too large, and slid down to catch their ears, having to be pushed up over and over again. The crowns were cardboard badly covered with gilding, and embedded with twinkling fairy lights. The half-masks concealed their features somewhat, and Madame LaFerme did not recognize them.

A dozen masked "witnesses" watched from the witness box, holding up scorecards, shoving each other, guzzling champagne from buckets—no glasses or bottles necessary—while the magistrate was played by another masked man wearing a full wig that had a stuffed bird on top, which mechanically spread its wings, squawked loudly, and shat down the side of the magistrate's wig. The lawyer for the defense was lying on the table in a state of undress, her breasts exposed, and was snoring in unmistakable squeaks. A pair of court officers groped her in her sleep.

Being dressed had given Madame LaFerme time to calm herself somewhat, and for a moment she almost forgot her danger, not to mention her outrage: her stomach tightened at the thought of how much trouble Armand would be in, after the performance.

Then she thought, *Let him burn.*

He strode back and forth across the stage, declaiming.

"Who shall take responsibility for these crimes, which have happened before us?" roared Armand, striding back and forth across the stage.

The king and queen turned their masks toward each other, shrugged, and spread their hands.

"First there is the charge of sending citizens to the foul, inhumane prisons of the Warden Lemure, with no just charge!"

In the box, Ammaline's head turned toward her father, who sat stiff and unmoving with his arms crossed before him.

"Our citizens are slaughtered there, and for what? For what? When they return at all, they return unable to recall what it is they have done during their little visit to the prison!"

Warden Lemure scratched his cheek, but otherwise made no response. Ammaline turned her head away from her father, then lowered it, then twisted around in her seat. Her face was in shadow. Madame LaFerme saw the girl startle.

Madame LaFerme held a finger to her lips, and Ammaline turned back round in her seat, facing the stage. Yvonne turned her head slowly toward the back of the box. Her face, too, was a shadow, but its expression easier to imagine: eyes narrowed, lips pressed together, chin lifted.

But she, too, turned back toward the stage.

"But if only the guilty were sent to prison, that would be still a crime. If the dead were not buried at sea, or burned, or otherwise destroyed, then we could mound their corpses upon the stage, and discover that a new mountain had been added to the geography of Thomàon!"

Armand sank to his knees before the magistrate, turned in profile, clasping his hands in front of him. The spotlights tightened upon him, throwing the rest of the stage into darkness.

"But I beg you, dear magistrate, tell me—why is it that the arrest and abduction of so many innocent people never remarked upon? The Gold Stars take them, and they disappear, and if their friends and families complain too much, they disappear, too!"

It had not often been said out loud before—it had *never* been said in so public a forum.

But Armand was not done.

The horrible grotesquerie of a mask that he wore almost radiated sainthood as the spotlight tightened still further.

"And who else is responsible for such monstrosities, if not the government itself?"

Warden Lemure cleared his throat, not for attention, but simply to clear it, in the space after Armand's roared question, and Ammaline glanced toward him again. Very slightly, she was leaning away from him now.

Damn Armand!

They had all agreed to keep the girl out of this, to leave her in a state of naïveté. She should not be called upon to bear the truth of her father.

Although Madame LaFerme was not surprised, she still felt a flush of outrage, hot across her chest, not so much for Ammaline's sake as for the knowledge that she had believed a promise by Armand—again. She had been fooled—again.

From behind her, Madame LaFerme heard the soft sound of the door opening. She had not yet crossed the threshold of the curtains, had not yet allowed them to fall shut behind her, and so she was able to turn, to look, to *see*.

Behind her stood the personne who had escorted her to the box but a few moments before, the dresser. Their face had once again changed, losing its aspect of bland competence, becoming sharper and deadlier.

Madame LaFerme felt herself respond to the change, and leaned forward to meet the intruder—with deadly force, if necessary.

The dresser was no dresser, but the Assassin indeed.

Had they been sent to kill her? To kill the Warden? Ammaline?

There was a spot of blood upon their face. They raised a finger to their lips, then closed the door behind them. They beckoned Madame LaFerme to come closer.

She shook her head.

The personne rolled their eyes, slightly shaking their head, then said in a low voice that no one might have heard, but for Madame LaFerme and her preternatural hearing:

"Gold Stars coming. Take Ammaline and get out."

So Armand had finally crossed what rules there were left among the Twelve, and Lemure's arrest had been ordered. She frowned. She could see that she herself was in danger of arrest—having only just participated in the travesty upon the stage—but—

"Why Ammaline?" she murmured, in a similarly low voice, one that only the Assassin might hear.

The Assassin stared at her, as if only just realizing the depth of Madame LaFerme's ignorance. Their expression shifted: eyebrows down, frowning, then a slight widening of the eyes, a parting of lips—then pity.

"Did you not know it? They are the Puppet Master's soldiers now."

The Assassin dipped a hand into the dresser's coat they wore, and swiftly flung something toward Ammaline. Madame LaFerme reached to intercept it, but missed—it struck the back of Ammaline's head with a papery sound.

Ammaline twisted 'round in her seat, saw Madame LaFerme again, then strained to peer into the darkness behind the curtains.

"Ammaline," the Assassin called. "Come."

The Assassin's tone was not imperious. It was hushed, but—desperate. It seemed to fly straight to Ammaline's ears, or, because *she* had not the ears of one of the Twelve, to her soul.

Her face, in silhouette, was impossible to read. She stood.

The Warden glanced back toward them, then did a double-take. His daughter walked past Madame LaFerme, silver threads in her dark blue gown twinkling, then reached her hands out to the Assassin, who took them.

A brief clasping, and then the Assassin let Ammaline's hands drop, and walked past Madame LaFerme to take the chair that Ammaline had just vacated. The Warden's head turned forward, and the two began to speak.

Ammaline watched the Assassin sit. Madame LaFerme took a deep breath, assembling what she had been told, and what she had just seen, and evaluating it. Her judgment was swift.

She clasped Ammaline upon her shoulder. "We must go now. Come with me."

Ammaline leaned away from her, as if to pull away.

Madame LaFerme's grip tightened, her fingers digging into the fabric of the dress. "The Assassin has asked it of us. If you care for them, go with me *now*."

Ammaline took a breath, as if to assemble her own knowledge. She gave a nod. Madame LaFerme opened the door to the corridor, heard the sound of footsteps approaching but saw no one—not yet—and pulled Ammaline from the room, gripping her hand tightly, and walking swiftly toward the back stairs she had only just ascended.

She was no fool. She did not run.

And she did not look back.

Chapter 4

In the Royal Box

THE FEAST OF FOOLS had never been the Warden's favorite social event—he was not a social man. The lights, the sounds, the crude sentiments had never attracted him. He always felt as though he were watching the maggots on a corpse as each writhing worm commented on how delicious the taste, even as they ate themselves out of house and home.

The People capered, the People danced, the People sang—were they not entertained? Why, then, must they also blaspheme?

But this year was different, as he had known it would be.

The great double doors of the opera had burst open, filling the stalls with the People. At their head, they had carried a platform, upon which were Madame LaFerme—the Great Diva herself—and the Fool, dressed in jester's motley and wearing a grotesque mask, its face stupid and belligerent.

The Warden wondered whether any but he remembered the identity of the man portrayed by the mask: balding head, receding dark hairline, jowls, pig eyes, bulbous nose, overlarge white teeth.—He corrected himself. Of course Yvonne would remember Old World history. She probably had entire files of trivia that she quizzed herself on every year.

She probably knew how many years had passed since the masked figure had been president, a fact that even the Warden had allowed to slip from his memory. He wasn't a soft man, but he had to be able to function.

The Warden had recognized the Puppet Master—that fucker, Armand—at first glance, even before he had opened his poisonous mouth. What could Thomàon have been, if not for him?

What was he planning?

Lemure had begun to worry that Armand didn't just want to jerk around a single planet by its strings. He wanted to expand. But how? The lightship was dead, communications had been cut off with the rest of the galaxy, and they had been suppressing the development of the relevant technology for...

The Warden's shoulders sank.

For at least a thousand years.

He sighed. Océan LaFerme was being abused on stage, her eyes flashing, but submitting to the outrages that Armand performed upon her. She had held him off for a long time, but recently they had become lovers—or, rather, Armand had only recently decided to seduce her. It was disgusting. Océan *knew* what Armand was like. But she'd still succumbed like the moonstruck heroine in an opera.

She sang her signature song, *Les beaux rêves*, and then sank from the stage on a platform. For her sake, Lemure hoped that Armand was done with her.

Probably he wasn't.

Lemure watched as Armand insulted the "gods," in the forms of plaster statues of the Twelve. He seemed to take particular pleasure in humping the leg of the Puppet Master—himself. Of course he mimed jacking off all over the Great Diva, and he spat upon the faces of the King and Queen. His minions performed a well-rehearsed dance scene, switching outfits at least five times.

Then a mock trial started, in which the Puppet Master was the prosecutor of the king and queen, played by two of his minions dressed up in cheap, badly fitting crowns.

A sense of unease passed over Lemure, and he glanced over at Corentin and Delphine, sitting off to his left.

They were not dressed for court, but in more ordinary clothing, if garish outfits from Old World history so ancient that it had been ancient even before they had left the planet could be called *ordinary*. They wore masks, Corentin wearing a white cat's mask with gilded details, and Delphine wearing a matching rabbit mask, with tall ears. They were rolling their eyes and making jokes to each other in low voices.

Along the right-hand end of the box sat Yvonne, the Historian. She had taken off her mask and was leaning on the chair in front of her on both elbows, staring at the performance intently and motionlessly with a pair of opera glasses—recording the travesty, no doubt, in case the official recording had all the juicy bits edited out.

But, even closer, there was Ammaline.

What would happen to her?

Lemure had never given her any of the elixir. Her mother had begged him not to, and he had agreed. At the time he had thought of it as meaning that Ammaline would grow old and die someday, but that at least she would die human. He had had mixed feelings. When he had first arrived on Thomàon, the possibility of immortality and "superpowers" had thrilled him. Now his feelings had changed. Would the world have remained a paradise, if they had never found the secret of the elixir?

Lemure snorted, the sound lost under a mocking *wah wah wah* from the stage.

Humanity had not been exiled from Paradise. They had shit all over their home planet, then left because of the smell.

The door opened behind them, then closed. Someone had come into the foyer behind the black velvet curtains, someone who rustled with the sound of expensive fabric and who smelled like musk and amber, spice and flowers as sweet as jasmine, but more alien.

Madame LaFerme. She had been released from the stage, then, if not her performance.

A moment, and she parted the velvet curtains behind the seats. Lemure looked away from her. She had been ragged and bruised, up on stage, and he had seen her knees several times as Armand dragged her around—she hated to have her mutations exposed. He remembered when she had first agreed to take the elixir. She had screamed when she learned what it had done to her body...

She stood motionless at the curtains for a few moments.

Ammaline shifted in her seat, looked back, then forward again. Yvonne also shifted in her seat. Madame LaFerme had been noticed. But not by Corentin and Delphine. They were sniggering and elbowing each other at their own mock-representations on stage.

On stage, Armand was accusing the king and queen of being behind all the unrest and upset. He wasn't leaving the Warden out of the picture, either.

His voice rolled through the theater:

"And who else is responsible for such monstrosities, if not the government itself?"

Bold words for a man who was part of that same government, who set many of its policies, and who, in fact, paid a large percentage of his income every year to perpetuate it.

Lemure felt his throat tighten as he tried to hold back his rage. He was normally a phlegmatic man, able to adapt to almost any hardship with a stoic calm.

But Armand had always gotten under his skin.

Lemure cleared his throat and tried to force himself to relax his fists. Ah, but to be able to put those fists around Armand's neck and snap it, once and for all...it would almost be worth dying permanently, in order to do it.

But snapping Armand's neck would be a temporary pleasure. The fucker would...

Lemure lost himself for a moment in the realization that he *could* snap Armand's neck and make it stick.

Once the elixir ran out.

The door of the box opened again. Lemure glanced back. He could not see who else had come into the box—they stayed behind the velvet curtain—but whoever it was had captured Madame LaFerme's attention. She stiffened. Lemure looked back toward the stage. It was some lover of hers—or someone calling her back to the performance.

Armand would not have simply *let her go.*

Then she murmured, "Why Ammaline?" and Lemure's mind went white, one eye twitching in tune with his suddenly elevated heartbeat.

Armand would not simply *let Ammaline go.*

Why hadn't he seen it before? He *knew* Armand. But the agreement to leave the girl out of the machinations of the Twelve had held for her entire life...

But Lemure had been a fucking idiot. Of course Armand would have planned something horrific to do to Ammaline. She wasn't just an innocent, a non-participant.

She was a way to hurt Lemure.

A piece of paper flew out of the darkness and biffed Ammaline in the back of her head. She turned around in her seat. Lemure turned too, and did a double-take to see the Assassin standing behind Madame LaFerme.

The Assassin whispered, "Ammaline. Come."

They had been childhood friends, before the personne had been given the elixir and had their memories brought up to speed. *Manon*, that was this one's name.

Ammaline hesitated, then stood, walking back into the darkness to join her friend—but no, the Assassin did not stay with her, but came to sit beside Lemure himself. Lemure hardly gave them a glance: his eyes were on his daughter and Madame LaFerme, who were whispering together, the woman's hand on the girl's shoulder, in a grip so tight that it made the silver threads woven into the midnight blue dress shimmer.

Ammaline nodded, and the two women turned and left through the back of the box.

The Assassin waited until they both heard the click of the door, then leaned close to Lemure. "The Gold Stars are coming. The Puppet Master plans to execute the three of you on stage."

"Ammaline?"

"I have put her under the Diva's care for now. But the soldiers are already in the halls. I think LaFerme will take them below."

Below meant not just to the theater's basement, but down into the reservoir under the city. It would be dangerous—but not as dangerous as confronting a coup.

Reluctantly, Lemure nodded. "And the elixir?"

"I don't know. I don't know where it's usually kept."

Lemure snorted. "I do. But so does Armand. It's somewhere else now, though. I did manage to convince them to move it. But I have to assume that Armand has found out where it is now, regardless. What is your plan?"

The Assassin, old eyes in a young face, shrugged. "I'm no strategic genius. I disrupt plans, I don't make them. I bought Ammaline a chance to get out. I don't have a plan, other than to be disruptive—"

They both froze in place.

A soft rhythm had picked up underneath the cacophony on the stage. Footsteps.

Not the discipline of military footsteps. But footsteps. *Many* of them. Someone was coming.

The Gold Stars.

Lemure tilted his head back, breathing noisily and slowly—triggering some autonomic nervous responses, shifting others from subconscious to conscious control. It was a mental discipline, one that most of the Twelve hadn't bothered to master. He used it when he knew he needed to kill.

He reached down to the knees of his trousers and pulled the rip cords that held his braces in place. They came loose and slid down his legs; he kicked them away from his feet as he slipped off his shoes, unfolding and stretching his toes.

Corentin glanced over at him just as Lemure was pulling out a few of his weapons from their resting places in his coat. One glance of Lemure preparing for a fight with the Assassin beside him, then a cocking of his head as he picked up the marching footsteps, then a glance down at the stage.

Then Corentin, too, was bending forward and pulling the cords at his knees.

Delphine took a deep breath and her skirts began rustling as she moved. But by then, Lemure had glanced toward the Historian, the odd little la Gorge.

She was gone.

The Assassin had set aside their wig, but made no other apparent changes to their costume. Since Madame LaFerme had entered the box, perhaps three or four minutes had passed.

But when one has lived—if one could call what they did *living*—for thousands of years, one learns not to be surprised by surprises.

Below them, the stage had gone silent. Armand was down on one knee and gesturing dramatically, ending with a finger pointed into the audience—toward their box.

Spotlights flared, lighting the box from above. Corentin's and Delphine's masks shimmered in the spotlight. They stood slowly.

From behind them, magnified by the speakers all around the hall, came the sound of someone pounding on the door behind them:

"Open up! By order of the People's Government!"

Revolution.

Behind his mask, the Warden found himself grinning, baring his teeth. For once, the Assassin was right: here, a plan was not needed.

Only disruption.

The Assassin walked to the forward edge of the box, putting their hands on the shining rail. The light caught them, a courtier in a simple half-mask. They glanced back at the Warden.

The two of them had never *liked* each other. But over the years, they had always worked well together: silently, swiftly, ruthlessly.

The Warden took a position next to the door of the box.

The pounding upon it grew louder. "Open up! In the name of the People's Government!"

"Little pig, little pig, let me in," said the Warden, strapping a répulseur on his left hand, then tightening the strap with his teeth. He held the little pistolet à aiguille in his right; it had been loaded with acid darts. Not fatal, but more of a distraction than most humans could handle.

"Open the door or we'll break it down!"

The Warden glanced toward the stage for one final assessment, saw the Assassin standing on the railing of the box, perfectly balanced on their extended toes, knees folded backward for a long jump.

Eyebrows raised.

The Warden nodded.

The Assassin leapt out into the hall, directly toward the glittering, low-dimmed chandelier.

Cue the gasps from below.

The Warden put his left palm on the door of the box, braced himself, and activated the répulseur. The door, old-growth wood reinforced with a steel core, exploded into flinders and shards.

Cue the screams from the Gold Stars.

Cue the arrival of Death.

Chapter 5

The Man Who Was Loved

A MAN—IF ONE COULD call the Puppet Master a man—who holds the strings of a puppet had better have nimble fingers; a man who holds the puppet strings of an entire world, had better have more agility than even countless fingers can provide. He must perforce be more than a master of puppets, for he cannot tug every string himself, but must employ sub-puppeteers, ambitious manipulators in their own right, who perforce tug in turn at the strings that are used to control their movements.

The Puppet Master must be a man who delights in such things: who is able to turn the tugs against him to his own purposes. Even more so, he must be a man who finds the ways in which each of us tugs our own strings, and uses our own habits to control us.

An addict tugs their own strings, thrumming bass strings with only a few notes, but powerful ones—it is well known. A scrupulously honest person is a harpsichord, waiting only for a skillful player. Lovers are violins that sing with happiness or sadness, equally fine. Power is a lyre—wealth, also. The arts require so much bowing and scraping and drumming and blowing that they form of themselves an entire orchestra.

Each of us has our threads, ropes, chains—and would rather bleed than cut them. No virtue cannot be turned against itself; no vice cannot be but a gift to the gods themselves.

What, then, bound the Puppet Master? He who had set himself above all other manipulators, politicians, connivers, con artists, and sycophants? What tied *him*?

Rather than answer that question, let us pause for a moment to consider another: how did the Puppet Master see himself?

There was a tale of the Vieux Monde, of le Terre itself, that may answer, or at least demonstrate, the answers to both questions.

The Man Who Was Loved

Once upon a time, there was a man from a small and isolated island, who found himself in a foreign land, asking for the safety of his people. He was well-spoken and intelligent, and everyone could see the nobility of his spirit.

He was brought before the King and the Queen of this foreign land, which had invaded his island, and begged for them to spare his home. They told him that his home had already been spared as much as could be allowed, for the island was of such strategic importance that it must either be annexed, or broken down into bare stones and flung into the sea.

But, they said, the young man could earn renown and honor for his island, and give it greater influence among the rest of the districts of the nation, by serving them, and serving them well.

The young man bowed his head, and served. With his intellect and determination, he rose rapidly through the ranks of the army under the King and Queen—until one day, they were cast down, as kings and queens are apt to be treated, when one's subjects are enslaved rather than ruled.

The People arose in anger and blood, possessed by madness and want.

The young man by then was a superior strategist, and saw that the Strong must always serve the interests of the Weak, in one way or another, for ever the name of Weak was given to those who must not know their strength. He, too, turned away from kings and queens, and bowed his head to those who controlled the People.

He served them well, and was lifted up by them, in the name of the People, leading them to victory after victory in war, in science, and in the law. His head, although low-born among the people of the island that had once been his home, now rose above the People themselves, and even above those who controlled the People.

It was an ecstasy of freedom that the man felt, standing upon the shoulders of the People.

Or, as the man, named now Empereur, cried, "Il n'y a pas de cordes sur moi!" For he felt there to be no chains that now could bind him.

Alas, there were innumerable chains upon the Empereur, strings that bound him more surely than they bound ordinary man, men of no consequence or note: for they came from within him.

He was an Empereur bound by Pride.

And, in his pride, he began to disdain the People. He threw aside the common woman he had married, and espoused a noble wife. He spent enormous sums that were desperately needed elsewhere, to feed and clothe the soldiers whose battles fed the machine of war, that all-consuming beast. He became, as had other Empereurs before him, more a king than the fallen King himself.

However, the People loved him still. He had done a great thing for them, such that they must hold dominion over all lands for all time to come. His fame would be immortal, and all honors rendered him were rendered unto the People themselves.

They raised this man upon a throne, even though this throne had been dashed down and spat upon when the King and the Queen had fallen, and the People worshiped him as they would a god.

But such a man is, alas, no god, but stands only so high as those whose shoulders he stands upon. Although the People had not forgotten him, he had forgotten the People, and as they fell beneath him, one by one, to starvation and nakedness and hunger, to the attacks of evil men who lay outside the Empire, he began to sink, and the Empire to sink with him, until finally he was defeated and imprisoned, and his Empire dismantled, such that it would never again rise to such heights, and the People starved even worse than they had under the King and the Queen, and froze in the winters, too.

But, unlike the names of the King and the Queen, his name was never dishonored among the People, but instead whispered down the generations, in a reverent tone:

Almost we conquered!

An old tale, one oft-repeated: always there is a homeland that is oppressed, and always there is a man who begs a favor, who is favored above others, and who rises beyond all expectation, to conquer, and leave behind him a trail of blood.

In the ears of ordinary men, the tale ends in death: death of the man, those who favored him, those who supported and opposed him, those who were his allies and enemies. Always the thrones of these men are built of bone—the bones of the innocent.

The dynasty might continue, or it might not; but the tale of the Empereur always ends in solitude, abandoned, perhaps disgraced or imprisoned—but always alone.

In the ears of men corrupted in heart and in soul by the lust for power, however, the tale ends another way: in glory.

As Armand stretched his arm toward the Royal Box and the spotlight swiveled from him toward Corentin and Delphine and—the fucker—Lemure, he panted for breath. His lungs were struggling to get enough air. But that wasn't surprising, after the amount of effort that had gone into his performance.

Every eye in the audience followed the spotlights up to the box, and to the pale faces of the King and the Queen, who froze in place for a moment. They had taken off their masks. They had been joking with each other, still smiling in the blinding spotlights, but their smiles faded. Their faces went blank.

Lemure bent forward for a moment, then straightened up again: his face was already itself a mask, a disguise.

Who are you today, Lemure? Which one of you are you?

Lemure's abomination of a daughter had already left; Yvonne la Gorge stood and slipped backward and to the side, so that only her face was visible, ghostly pale in the reflected glow of the spotlights. Océan had either not arrived, or had left already—perhaps to take her protégée off to a quiet corner to rage and weep.

No matter.

Corentin and Delphine were the two moths he wished pinned to the velvet curtains behind them, tonight.

The pounding on the door of the box was picked up by the sound system, and echoed throughout the hall:

"Open up! By order of the People's Government!"

Corentin and Delphine made small movements, adjustments, their heads jerking forward and looking down toward the floor. Good! They were going to fight. Fucking Marks Lemure stood up, cracked his neck with a roll of his head, then walked up the stairs to the back of the box, his elbows flexing.

Whoever was directly on the other side of *that* door was going to regret having followed orders—but not for long.

The floor shifted underneath Armand, throwing him slightly off balance for a moment, he dragged his knee back toward him and stood slowly as he sank through the trapdoor, pulling his arm back toward his chest so it wouldn't knock against the stage as he was drawn downward.

A face appeared from the shadows of the box above him: a powered, white face above a servant's vest, wigless, humble. Armand frowned: the face wasn't familiar.

And yet.

The figure skipped down the steps of the box to the front rail. The spotlights shivered, then pulled slightly away from Corentin and Delphine, to follow instead the figure at the front of the box, the figure who was climbing up to the top of the brass rail.

Shoeless, the figure's feet gripped the rail. The figure crouched—the knees bending backward—and leapt! stretching forth their arms and soaring out across the audience.

Armand snorted.

It had to be the young Assassin, a clone so fresh that Armand couldn't remember their current name.

The damn personne was pulling attention away from Corentin and Delphine, who would surely use the opportunity to get up to some mischief. Would they flee? Or fight?

It didn't matter.

They had no other options; he had planned for both.

The pounding of fists on the door of the Royal Box continued, the dim glow of the stage above Armand becoming a distant square overhead, the roar of the crowd softening. He was now under the stage, in another world.

A hand touched his arm. "Monseigneur? If you will take my hand, I will serve as your eyes for the moment."

Armand recognized the voice: one of his familiars, his henchmen, his peons. He held out his arm and it was taken, and he was guided expertly through the darkness.

Here was where Corentin and Delphine should have been waiting for him, if they had any intention of stopping him from overthrowing them. They should have known what he was planning, and they should have been waiting for him under the stage.

They should have turned the loyalty of his serviteurs, one by one, and left him with a traitor in the dark, a poisoned needle or a pistolet à aiguille, swift and sure.

It was moments like this that thrilled him, the moments in which he had to rely not on his own planning or skills, but on the thin thread of faith that his enemies and allies had not, finally, outwitted him.

They never did. But the moment of terror that they *might* was what fueled him, turned the prickling of his skin to both ice and burning flame.

Armand's earpiece said, "They have the Warden."

He did not respond. There was a curse, a splash, the sound of something falling on the floor, and another curse. "He's got away again. He's killing—"

The voice paused, while Armand was led through the darkness. The guiding arm tightened for a moment, bringing them to a stop, and then a door was opened, and a dull red light poured forth, revealing a corridor full of dressing rooms and storage; at the far end, stairs.

Armand entered. The figure who had led him was left behind, closing the door softly. He found his breath was shallow, his heart racing. The thrill of his plans almost having been defeated had not yet left him. It would, soon. He brushed his arm where the other had touched it, to brush away the feel of the other hand upon his jester's costume.

A door opened in the corridor. Inside was another of his faithful, a woman dressed as a doll, her limbs made up to look mechanical.

The voice over the earpiece said, "As instructed, we're letting K and Q escape, and we're following the Warden. He's leaving a trail of blood."

Armand looked upward for a moment. The woman began undressing him dispassionately. The jester's clothing was abandoned, the grotesque mask also. Wipes removed the rest of the makeup from his skin. He tolerated her touch, although it made his skin prickle and his fingers itch.

If only Océan had known how many times his hands had almost closed upon her throat, while they were making love!

She would ask him, "Your eyes are always so distant...where are your thoughts, love?"

If he had told her the truth, how she would have shuddered! "Why, darling, they are with my other lover, who awaits me in the tunnels below the city, in a place that you do not know, a place where one cannot see lights, cannot hear screams, and cannot find the dead!"

How he would have loved to tell her so: but the timing hadn't worked out. Oh, well.

The doll-woman finished cleaning him, then handed him the black suit. It was too tight for her to put on him; it was faster to do it himself. He shrugged into the pieces of it, putting it on like old-fashioned armor, fastening it together. When it was on, she handed him a scarlet suit of velvet to put over it, with puffed sleeves and breeches.

"They have him cornered," the voice reported over the earpiece. "In the fourth-floor washroom on the East side—" Another curse. "He's gone through the wall. They're following. There are...tunnels back there. None of the team has any idea where they go."

The doll-woman tightened the laces on Armand's sleeves, handed him a floppy velvet hat and a white mask, one eye surrounded with a ring of red lights to make it appear as if the eye itself were glowing.

Then, carefully, she handed him the sheath of his poisoned knife. It was plain steel, a Bowie knife. Coated with one of the Madman's brilliant neurotoxins.

He strapped it around his thigh, also taking care.

The voice made a startled squeak. "Oh, that's...he's gone again. We're down to two men, Monseigneur."

Armand stretched forward with his hands locked behind his back, making sure the hat and mask and sheath were secure. They were. He nodded toward the doll-woman, then let himself out of the room, closing the door behind him. He crossed the hall and opened a door to one of the store-rooms.

"Regrettable," he said, loud enough for the earpiece to pick up. "But tell them to continue. We *must* drive him onward."

"They do not hesitate, Monseigneur. If there was a moment of weakness, it was mine only."

Armand did not answer, but moved soundlessly across the room, pulling a light out of the pocket of the velvet suit. He swung it toward the far wall and caught a shimmer of light from a stage mirror at an abandoned makeup table. His fingers found the switch under the table and pressed it; he climbed onto the table and pushed the mirror inward, crawling through it, and dropping down to the other side.

He extinguished the light, stood to the side of the tunnel, drew the blade, and crouched down upon his thighs.

And waited.

It was less than a whisper, less than the memory of a whisper.

He *knew* his prey. But still, he almost missed.

Marks Lemure bounded down the secret passage, the only noise of movement that of his pursuit. Armand flicked out the knife, felt nothing but air, and stretched forward, losing his balance—

But scratching Lemure all down his side.

He tossed the knife desperately away. Lemure clawed at him, gouging his claws through the puffed velvet sleeves, going for Armand's throat. It was everything that Armand could do to keep the monster from killing him.

But Lemure's reactions were slowing. If the toxin on the blade had scratched any other, they would have screamed in pain—screamed until they could no longer inhale for breath, then died slowly, muscles locked and contorted.

But members of the Twelve always died harder than any others.

Lemure finally got his claws around Armand's throat. His hands tightened suddenly.

"You'll never have it!"

Armand gargled through his throat. He could hardly breathe, but it mattered little—Lemure's hands were loosening in their grip.

Lemure keened through his teeth. He knew what was coming. In a tight, high-pitched voice, he cried, "You'll die, and you'll die with me!"

Armand giggled.

Lemure tried to squeeze tighter, but his hands were twitching and shuddering. It was easy enough to push his hands away.

Armand pushed the Warden off him. He always loved it, when circumstances allowed him to kill the fucker.

Lemure's throat had almost closed. He hissed, "There is no more!"

Armand sat up, brushing at the rags of his velvet suit, wiping at his neck. "There *is*, Lemure. I saw you bring it in from Shakes Prison, when you flew in at the last minute with your daughter. I know where you put it. And I already have it."

"No."

It was a breath—Lemure's last. Armand switched on his flashlight and looked down at the man, his court finery in rags, his body lying in a puddle of blood. Unable to move, but his eyes glistening and alive.

Armand sighed in pleasure, reached down, and grabbed one of Lemure's feet, dragging the man through the secret corridor toward the two men who had chased him there, and who had frozen, their mouths agape, to see their leader having dispatched the monster who had killed so many of them.

Armand waved at them with the light. "You may go. Use the mirror at the end of the corridor. It'll take you into a storeroom just off the corridor under the stage. Report back upstairs."

The voice over the earpiece said, "Uh...Monseigneur?"

"Keep recording," Armand said. "I want to savor this moment later."

"Got it."

Armand dragged Lemure through the corridors. Upstairs was chaos, movement, change. Transformation. Even as he dragged the fucker along the floor, he, Armand, was being raised up upon the shoulders of his people, his rebellion.

They were already hunting the rest of the Twelve, such as they were in these decadent late days of their rule over Thomàon. Soon, their rule would be overturned.

And the universe would open up again before him.

Thomàon had been a game to them, a prison to him. A world that should have been joined to the Great Empire that spanned across the stars, had instead been hidden, removed from sight.

Soon, that would change.

But for now, he would take pleasure in the simple things, like the sound of Lemure's head banging on the concrete as he was dragged into a small side-corridor, the stickiness at the back of his skull as Armand dropped his leg, and lifted his old, dear friend onto his shoulder, holding his head steady with one hand, the stiffness of Lemure's limbs as he was shoved into the alcove on the side of the corridor.

Armand aimed the light into his eyes. Lemure was still alive, his eyes still moist. Armand bent down and picked up the cinder block stacked along the corridor. It was self-sealing, no mortar necessary. He set the light on the floor and began stacking the blocks quickly.

As much as he hated Marks Lemure, he had little time to spend on this indulgence. But it was worth it.

When he had all but one of the blocks in place, he said, "Since you cannot speak, I will say your line for you, Lemure."

He picked up the last block in one hand, the flashlight in the other, and watched with satisfaction at Marks Lemure, the man who had sabotaged the production of the elixir that made them gods, that made them practically immortal—and said:

"For the love of God, Montresor!"

And then set the last block in place, watching until it sealed itself to the others. Then he added,

"In pace requiescat!"

Chapter 6

Let the Choir Sing!

AMMALINE WAS PULLED ALONG the luxurious corridor behind the Royal Box by Madame LaFerme, the gold trim, elegant vases, and red velvet paper on the walls flying past in a blur.

Madame suddenly shoved Ammaline in front of her, so quickly that she almost fell headlong down a set of narrow stairs. She would have, but Madame caught the back of her dress, and pulled her back onto the landing, just as her arms flung themselves forward to try to catch herself.

"Go!" hissed Madame LaFerme.

Ammaline skipped down half a dozen steps, then hesitated. "But I can't leave you!"

Madame LaFerme was following Ammaline down the stairs, after all; she had only stopped to turn her skirts to the side, for they were too broad to fit down the narrow steps without turning.

Behind them came the sound of pounding on the door of the Royal Box, men shouting that the door must be opened, and without delay.

Ammaline took a step upward. "Papa!"

Madame LaFerme released her skirts with one hand, and held it out palm-first, stopping Ammaline where she stood. "Your papa sent us away. You will *not* shriek and weep over his fate. It would only slow him down." She made a face. "He does not want you to see him. He means to commit butchery."

Ammaline felt her skin come all over with gooseflesh. "Butchery?"

Madame hissed through clenched teeth, "Go! I will tell you all about his sins later. If we find a place to rest, we will discuss *all* sorts of things. Yes? Now go!"

She grabbed her skirts again, wrenching them around to the side, and began descending the steps, an unstoppable wall of fine silk and delicate embroidery.

Ammaline took several steps backward, felt a slipper slide off the end of the stair, then turned around and ran down the narrow steps, clinging to the rail, which carried the touch of a thousand hands upon it, tacky to the touch.

She stopped at a landing to look back, but Madame's pressed lips drove her onward, down and down the narrow stairs, to the main level of the Opéra du Mendicant. Another hallway to the left, this one clearly more public, and a doorway in front of them marked *Entrée des artistes*. She tugged on the handle, but it was locked.

"It's locked!"

Madame ignored her, ignored the door, ignored the hallway, and pushed Ammaline by the shoulder out of the way as she addressed a hanging drapery and a short pillar before it.

"What are you doing?"

"Watch the hallway and the stairs. Let me know when anyone comes."

A slithering, rattling sound followed, as Madame LaFerme dragged a small purse from a slit in her skirts, then concealed it from view.

Ammaline stood at the bottom of the stairs, glancing back and forth between the stairs and the hallway. Footsteps approached—multiple sets of them—but she did not know from which direction they came. The roar coming from the hall itself had not lessened, but had increased.

Manon!

The last Ammaline had seen her friend, they had been leaping off the rail of the Royal Box, and into the air—toward death or freedom, Ammaline could not know. Only the knowledge that Manon was the Assassin comforted Ammaline now: for the Assassin had never been caught, and had never been killed.

Ammaline glanced up the stairs, and saw no-one; she watched the hallway, and saw movement.

She whispered, "They are coming, from the hall, I think."

There was a click.

"Quickly!"

Ammaline turned and saw Madame holding the drapery aside, the pillar moved slightly, and a panel in the wall which opened onto darkness. Ammaline moved into the darkness, easily passing into the corridor behind.

Madame did not find it so easy.

She turned to the side and stepped sideways, but her skirts were too large to pass through the narrow panel, and became jammed, catching against the bolt-plates.

"Go!" Madame ordered her.

But Ammaline could not leave Madame LaFerme behind: she was neither so ruthless, nor so foolish, as to leave someone jammed in a doorway which therefore could not be closed.

She ignored the flapping of Madame's hand, and instead grabbed onto the hoops of her skirt, under the silk fabric. She pulled; when that did not work, she pushed—Madame unhooked herself from the bolt-plates—and she pulled again.

The corridor went dark, as Madame released the heavy draperies: but there were footsteps in the corridor, and shouts of alarm.

"Follow them!"

Madame stepped backward and would have fallen, but Ammaline pushed her back upright.

There was a flare of light as the draperies were jerked aside—

And then Madame LaFerme slammed the door. A bolt latched, and then another.

Both women stood and panted, as their pursuers banged and crashed into the door, howling.

After a few moments, Madame breathed, "It will hold for now." They had been plunged in the deepest darkness, but Ammaline had hardly noticed it at the time, gripped by fear.

She whispered, "Where are we?"

A dull red light appeared, hardly enough to see by, and a cool hand sought hers. "We are going under the opéra, down to the reservoirs under the city, to see if we can find help."

"Help?"

"Someone," Madame LaFerme snarled as she pulled Ammaline forward again, and at not much less speed than she had before, "who is not in the thrall of the Puppet Master."

Madame's skirts bumped into Ammaline as they jogged forward. The floor under their feet was solid plastic, hard, but not so hard that their footsteps clattered. Ammaline put a hand out to help steady herself, and found a wall, also of plastic, with a strange, honeycombed texture to it.

"The Puppet Master? The man in the mask who was so cruel to you?"

"You saw it, then? That *performance*?" Madame LaFerme did not wait for a response. "That bastard. I loved him—no, he *told* me I loved him."

"Who is he?"

"Stairs," Madame warned.

Ammaline seemed to feel the floor fall out from under her feet before she caught herself. The rail was one of cold metal. Ammaline kept her hand on it, hoping it would warn her more than Madame had. Their footsteps echoed now, when before they had not.

The air took on a breath of wetness. It cooled, not cold enough to freeze, but cold enough to make Ammaline's skin crawl.

"Who the Puppet Master is," Madame said, "is a long story. And your father should have been the one to tell it to you."

They reached the bottom of the stairs, and Madame lifted the dull light. Ammaline could see now that the light came from one of the rings on Madame's hand, a clever hidden device.

"To the right," Madame announced. "But your papa thought he had more time, I suppose—or he was too cowardly to do it himself. Brave before any danger, a coward before his conscience."

Ammaline tightened her grip on Madame's hand as she pulled her onward. The sound in the room changed, filling with echoes, echoes on top of echoes, and the distant sound of water running, splashing. The scent of the air was still mostly one of cleanness, however, and not the sucking green rot of water caught in pools along a coast.

Madame LaFerme stopped again, then turned leftward and down another set of stairs.

"We," she began, "are the gods. I am the Diva, Corentin is the King, Delphine is the Queen, yes? The Assassin, your friend I believe, is *the* Assassin. Each of the masks, well, it is complicated. But for now let us say that each of the masks is a person, and they are one of the gods."

Ammaline had known that the Madame LaFerme was the Diva; it was no great secret. Whoever was chosen as the greatest voice of her time, also inherited the Mask and the position on the Council of the Twelve. The current king wore the King's mask; the current queen wore the Queen's.

And that Manon had become *the* Assassin? The Easer of Ways? It was a strange thought, but not an impossible one. But why was Madame LaFerme telling her what everyone already knew?

They skipped down the stairs, then reached another landing, where Madame paused, held up her ring, and peered into the darkness for a moment. She inhaled deeply, raising her nose in the ring's dull red glow. Her nostrils flared.

Ammaline sniffed the air, but smelled...nothing.

Madame LaFerme snorted abruptly. "We are not where I thought we were. My memories are not the best these days, I suppose. How long has it been this time? It feels too short for this to be happening already."

"Pardon?" Ammaline asked.

"Never mind for now. I think—"

The ring flashed, and Madame LaFerme turned slowly in a circle, stopping when the ring flashed again, to the right—directly toward a dull silver wall, without feature.

"Ahhh," Madame LaFerme breathed, almost as if in awe. "We are *there*. I thought *that* way was lost forever."

She took one tentative step toward the metal wall, then another. The ring brightened, not enough to blind them, but as though to whisper, *Warmer, warmer, you are getting warmer...* Madame LaFerme put her left hand upon the silver wall, caressing it.

"How long, o *Téméraire*, has it been since last I have felt you thrumming beneath me, o my lover?" she said, in a tender, choking voice. "My darling! I did not forget you!"

And then she leaned forward and kissed the wall.

Ammaline stayed silent, unsure of what occurred, only that it was a sacred moment to Madame, and must not be interrupted—for any reason. But she did flinch, when she heard the sound of footsteps in the distance.

Fortunately, Madame heard them too. She turned her head to the side, trying to find the direction of the sound, then sniffed, and held her ring upon the wall, rolling the flat stone palm-ward with her thumb.

A hiss, and the wall became—a door, perfectly circular, drawing itself inward, then to the side. Madame pushed forward with her palm until the door drew itself away, then ducked to enter.

Once again, her skirts caught at her. With a snarl, she tore them free, then ripped loose the cage that had supported them, shoving them through the circular doorway before her. When she had done so, she held a hand back and snapped her fingers for Ammaline to take her hand.

Ammaline followed Madame through the odd doorway, hiking her skirts—far less cumbersome than Madame's—and climbing through. As soon as she had passed within, the metal panel slid closed behind them, sealing itself in silence.

Madame reached past her to the reverse of the odd door, and turned something upon it; there was a soft click. Madame's expression, in the dull red glow of the ring, melted from one of stern determination, to one of utmost pleasure, almost childlike—very nearly divine.

She kicked her skirts aside and began humming a song that Ammaline did not know, and put her hands along the wall next to the door, patting around. Another click, and there was light, the sort of light that one can see and be seen by.

What was revealed was a small sort of chamber, filled with white panels of heavy recycled plastic, tubes, cords, ordinateurs and their keyboards, small squares marked here and there with odd patterns, and another round door at the far end.

"Where are we?"

Ammaline's voice seemed to be swallowed by the small chamber. The air smelled…it smelled of something not unpleasant, but not something that Ammaline had ever smelled before. It was fresh enough to breathe, however—it suddenly occurred to her that the room was meant to be sealed, and they might have come into it, only to smother.

Madame LaFerme had gone to the far door. A turning handle that Ammaline had not noticed before was upon it, and Madame was turning it, then pushing it open onto darkness, smelling the air on the other side.

"It is safe," she declared after a moment. "Shall we?"

She did not wait for Ammaline's answer—or answer her own question herself—but instead climbed through the second round door, and out of view.

Ammaline found herself out of breath, her heart pounding at breakneck speed in her chest: *were* they to smother to death, after all, for lack of good air? She could not see Madame on the other side of the door; she could not see anything. She crept slowly to the door, picking her way around Madame's ruined skirts, until she was standing beside the door, which had half-closed itself. She put her hand on it; it was quite heavy, but moved when she increased the pressure.

Of the room or passage beyond the door, Ammaline could see only a sort of rough carpet on the floor.

Her voice was painfully tight. "Madame?"

There was no answer, although she could hear small sounds of Madame moving about on the other side.

"Madame?"

A rough noise filled the room, filled with static, but almost—music? A bang, then the sound of a choir, and a woman's voice singing in a language which Ammaline did not quite understand. A drum rattled, and then the woman sang in tune with it, an inelegant little song that might have been popular in the streets, if anyone could have understood it.

The choir stopped, and were replaced by the drums. Still the woman sang. Was it a religious song, or one meant for dancing?

The lights came on abruptly. The room was the same on the other side of the round door, more or less, but with more signs of use: black scuffs on the panels, grunge here and there where hands must have touched the same surfaces, over and over, worn parts of the carpet, silver tape on some of the cords and hoses. All about were black rails or handholds, on the ceiling, on the floor, on the walls.

Madame was nowhere to be seen, but her voice sang along to the music.

The music continued. Ammaline climbed through the second doorway, but did not close it behind her; it did not close of its own accord, for which she was grateful. She already felt as though she were trapped in the odd white room.

Ammaline followed the sound of Madame's voice to a black ladder that led upward. She put her hands on the rungs. Above her was a narrow tunnel, well-lit, leading up to another round door. If they had not been under the Silver City, Ammaline would have thought that they were in an airship, or a submarine. Perhaps the rooms were sealed against poisonous gas. But if so, why was Madame so cavalier about moving around them?

Ammaline swallowed, then tied up her skirts, and began climbing.

When she emerged at the upper end of the ladder—a long climb that left her feeling weak in the knees—she emerged into another small, sealed room of white panels, ordinateurs, and tubes.

And Madame, dancing.

The music was louder at the top of the tunnel, enough to drown out all other sound.

Madame had removed her wig and taken down her hair, and cast the pins down around her. She had torn the sleeves off her gown, and left them on the floor as well. She danced in time to the music, not elegantly, but as though she were a young girl, eyes closed in bliss, clapping her hands in time to the music. Her legs...they were misshapen, and bent where they should not, in directions they should not.

Abruptly, she dropped to her knees on the floor, but continued dancing, her hair swinging wildly. Now her elbows revealed that they, too, had powers of movement beyond that of any other soul that Ammaline had met—but yet seemed familiar.

The song came to a close, and Madame straightened up, and climbed to her feet, bracing herself on an ordinateur. Another song began itself, an electric violin drawing out a note, with thrumming chords beneath it. Madame smiled and lifted her hands beside her face, then lowered them and struck a key on one of the keyboards, lowering the volume of the music. Fingers snapped and a drum tapped out a rhythm. A bass line entered the song, then all sorts of electronic sounds. A woman's voice chanted, again in a language that Ammaline did not understand.

Madame sighed happily. "But we do not have time to dance all night, to songs from the Vieux Monde."

"They...do not sound like they come from the View Monde?" Ammaline said. "The language, I do not know it?"

Madame laughed. "There was more than one language, back in the View Monde. We agreed to only remember French."

Ammaline shook her head. Now that she seemed about to have her curiosity satisfied, she wondered if it would not prove to be a surfeit—if satisfaction would not make her sick.

Madame took Ammaline's hands and turned them palm upwards. "My child. I had begun trying to tell you earlier. Do you understand what I am saying, when I say I am the Diva?"

"That you wear the mask of the Diva," Ammaline said. "Chosen by the people. Everyone knows it."

—She wished to add that *that* was as much as she wished to understand. But then she remembered that above them, the Puppet Master, the Roi du Rats, had begun a revolution, attacking everything she knew: attacking her father.

It was her duty to hear this awful truth, and—well—far better to hear it from Madame LaFerme, she supposed, than from her father.

She felt her shoulders sink. She added, "But that is not the whole story, is it?"

As she spoke, her voice nearly cracked with the strain.

Madame smiled kindly at her, not with the stiff kindness that Ammaline had previously seen upon her face, but a warm smile, twisted a little with regrets. "No. It's not. Not by a long shot."

"A what?" Ammaline had never heard the phrase before.

"Never mind—a phrase from the Vieux Monde. The Old World." Madame looked around, then pulled Ammaline further into the little room, kicking backward with one foot at a panel, which popped open, revealing two folded seats. Madame unfolded them and turned them toward the center of the room. She pressed Ammaline into one of them, then sat lightly in the other.

"I was not named to the rôle of Diva because I am the finest singer on Thomàon," she said. "I *am* the Diva. I am the being, the creature, the god, the original person known as the Diva. I have lived on Thomàon for thousands of years, moving from body to body like a flame passed from candle to candle. I am...I *was* immortal."

Ammaline could not contain the sense of what Madame had just said. "What?"

Madame took Ammaline's hands again, then clicked her tongue and released them. She extended her fingers, stretching them far past their natural extension, then bent them so that they no longer seemed to belong to human hands any longer, but to one of the Grillons.

Ammaline shuddered.

Madame, barefoot, extended one leg, and bent it backward, rotating her ankle so that it bent the wrong way as well.

Ammaline turned her head, but Madame took her head and turned it gently back toward her, the cool fingers now feeling alien in their touch.

"Are you—who *are* you?" Ammaline asked.

"I am so old that my name no longer exists," Madame LaFerme said, lowering her hand. "It was Jenny."

Ammaline wrinkled her nose, unable to stop herself. *Jenny* seemed a name for animals, for pets, for cattle.

Madame laughed. Then her face fell into a more serious expression. "Those who wear the masks are not chosen by the people. They are not chosen by their successors, either—if you have heard those rumors. No! We are the same souls, the same people that we were when we first arrived here on our ship. The *Téméraire*. *This* ship."

Ammaline looked around her. This was the oddest airship she had ever encountered, if so. "And you came here from...the Vieux Monde?"

"Yes. Across light years. In cryogenic sleep." When Madame realized that Ammaline did not understand what she was saying, she added, "From another world, across the stars. In a starship. *This* starship."

Ammaline shook her head slowly from side to side. "But—"

"But *yes*," Madame said. "I am the original pilot of the ship. When we landed her and awakened the rest of the passengers, we...decided to make a few changes. The original crew and a couple of the most important passengers. We decided that we didn't want Thomàon to become like the world we had left behind. We ruined it, Ammaline. We ruined that planet, and here we were, headed off to ruin a new one, too. A colony world, to be stripped bare and sold to the highest bidder. What would we care? We would be rich."

She sighed and swung from side to side in the chair, her odd knees bending in impossible ways as she moved.

"But it didn't have to be like that, we decided. We all agreed to release a virus into the cryogenic maintenance system, one that would cause the rest of the passengers' minds to...to forget a few things. A few people died. It wasn't what we intended. But most of them just...forgot. Those who remembered were easy to manipulate, to convince that they had gone a little mad, like the rest of the passengers. They all looked toward us, like children. So we...we took charge."

She chewed on the inside of her cheek. "There were twelve of us. A nice number, we all thought. Twelve sane, intelligent people. What could possibly go wrong?"

She stopped speaking, staring into the distance. In the silence, Ammaline realized that another song had begun playing. A voice yelped, and suddenly Ammaline recognized the song. It was "La fille matérialiste," another of the songs from the Vieux Monde, but this time sung in that other language, that dead language from another world.

She began singing along with it softly, the words not the same, but falling into the same rhythms.

Madame smiled. "I translated that. I translated all the Vieux Monde songs." They sang together, Madame in the original tongue, Ammaline in the language she had thought the only one remaining from the Vieux Monde. Both of them rocked from side to side as they sang.

The song finished; Madame sighed, then wiped her eyes, which had gone sparkling and wet.

"I have to finish telling you now, I suppose. What went wrong was that—one of us—discovered something. A mineral, we thought, with interesting properties. The Scarabées seemed to be searching for it constantly, mining for it, digging it up and consuming it. We tested it."

Ammaline said, "The elixir? The golden elixir?" She had heard her father speak of it in hushed whispers.

Her *father.*

Was he one of them? One of the Twelve?

But there was no Warden among the Twelve Masks. He couldn't be.

But he must. This was part of the secret that Madame had threatened to tell her, up on the stairs.

"The golden elixir," Madame confirmed. "Of course. You are his daughter. You must have heard the whispers with which he surrounds himself at some point."

Ammaline's skin turned to ice. She shivered, crossing her arms around her and hugging herself.

Madame touched her chin, lifting it slightly. "You must be brave, child. This is an ugly truth. We tested the elixir on…on animals from the Vieux Monde. They *changed.* They…became something not quite themselves. And then." She closed her eyes. "God help us, we tested it on ourselves. The Madman went first, of course. He was always a fucking addict. Anything that could help him escape from normality, he'd taken it. Well, he took the elixir. And changed."

She waved toward her knees, stretching them in the wrong direction, extending her toes to bend them the wrong way round, too.

"His body changed. All our bodies have changed. But that's only part of it. Our minds changed, too. The cryo system on the *Téméraire* works as a sort of backup of one's memories—an inaccurate backup, for human minds. Mostly it only worked just well enough to help people who had been frozen to death and brought back to life—that is what I mean by cryogenic sleep, child—remember who they had once been, and convince themselves they were still. But with the golden elixir, the recording was perfect, with no loss of memory or awareness. We could leap from body to body without interruption—without *much* interruption."

Ammaline stared at her. She did not understand, but what was more important, she could feel herself willing herself not to understand.

She thought of her father—she thought of Manon.

The Assassin.

Her childhood friend, who seemed both her old self, and not her old self. Manon, who had disappeared.

For Manon's sake. For my father's sake. I will hear this. I will know the truth.

Ammaline took a deep breath, allowed the poison of forgetting to pour out of her blood and into her exhalation, and released it.

"Like Manon," she said.

Madame's face, already serious, softened into heartbreak. Tears filled her eyes again. "Oh, you poor thing. Yes. Like the Assassin. That is the third secret. The colonists...we tested the elixir on a few of them, the ones who could not return to awareness. They never did return to themselves. When we need to move from body to body, we...at first, at least...we moved into their bodies. We took them. That is the secret of our immortality. We use other people's bodies. We use the elixir to make the bodies stronger, more viable, longer lasting...and then we move our minds into them."

"And Manon?"

"Shh, let me tell it. The Madman. He found a way to use other bodies, ones that weren't ruined and old. Hard to use. Children. Their minds remain, and become…part of us, I suppose. We inoculate them with the elixir early on. Then…more, when they are older. There are several other bodies for each of us, ready at all times. Most of them are never used. The Puppet Master, he has hundreds of them. His entourage."

Ammaline's lips felt like ice, her hands as well. Her feet seemed so far away from her as to be unreal, illusory. She felt herself swaying.

Madame put a hand upon her shoulder. "Do you feel faint?"

Ammaline nodded.

"Bend over, put your head between your knees. Breathe only shallow breaths."

Ammaline did so, but felt no better. It was her soul that was dizzy, not her body. She felt ill.

Madam put a hand on her back and rubbed it gently. "I shall finish it quickly. Your father is one of us, the Architect. He was the one who found the elixir. In his role as the Warden, he mines it. But the world is almost out of it. It is almost gone: our twisted, horrible immortality—one that I cannot deny I have chosen for myself, again and again, is almost at an end."

"What about me?" Ammaline murmured. The idea had suddenly struck her. "What about me? Am I…am I meant to become the Great Diva? Are you going to take over my body, and move into my mind?"

The hand on her back stopped, shuddered. "You? No. You are…something different."

"What do you mean?"

Madame inhaled, inhaled so deeply that it was as if she did not intend to exhale ever again. But in the end, even *she* must do so. She breathed, "Now, *that* is a secret that is not mine to tell." She sighed out the rest of her held air. "Oh, child. I am so sorry. You were always meant for something else, something I do not agree with at all. But that is no fault of your own."

"What about my mother?"

The hand on her back tensed, and Madame's nails dug into Ammaline's skin. "That…is another secret that I cannot tell. What happened to her…I cannot."

Ammaline sat upright, her face suddenly wet with tears. She rubbed her face on her sleeve, and saw it come away with smears of face paint.

"She did something wrong, didn't she?"

But Madame would only shake her head, lips pressed together. "You will have to ask your father. If he lives."

"Who else are the Twelve?" Ammaline asked.

Madame opened her mouth—but the music stopped abruptly, a bright light flashed on one of the ordinateurs, and a low buzz filled the room. She tapped on one of the keyboards.

After a moment, she looked at Ammaline in horror.

"Someone else has entered the ship."

Chapter 7

Grandpère Overlooking the Jardin

OUTSIDE THE SILVER CITY were a number of châteaux, great houses owned by the wealthiest citizens of Thomàon. Madame LaFerme owned one, and a grand and extensive house it was indeed, of gold and white and blue. Warden Lemure did not own one, but then he had control over Shakes Prison and the rest of the palaces of correction across the world, built here and there—wherever the concentration of the material that became, with a little help, the elixir—was greatest.

Besides, he took little pleasure in the current fashion for the most grandiose elements of the Vieux Monde; he was known to say, in an ominous tone, that such excesses of architecture always boded ill for those who owned them.

He would then invariably draw a finger across his neck and make a hissing sound, but then, the Warden had always had an ill sense of humor.

Corentin and Delphine resided within the royal residence, the Castle of the Silver Spire, and had several smaller châteaux about Thomàon, where they used to meet with various folk when it was not the Season. The Assassin had no châteaux, but possessed instead an underground lair, or rather several, each of which was a closely hidden secret. The Puppet Master, the Roi du Rats, had for himself a rather luxurious château to the far north, which he himself only used in the hottest part of the year, but otherwise was filled with at least a hundred people, outside of the Season, of course, all of them spying on various targets, as well as upon each other.

The rest of the Twelve had their own dominions as well. The Player held la Tour de Défense, an impregnable fastness that he destroyed on a regular basis, only to rebuild it elsewhere soon after. The Madman had a crumbling, old-fashioned castle deep within a forested mountain range, a castle that lay half in ruins, filled with gadgets that had never been operable, but were only for show. It was called—for some reason—Castle Frankenstein. He did not live there; he was held elsewhere, to keep him from harming himself. Instead, the Hawkmistress lived there. Castle Frankenstein was quite comfortable, having been ruined only for show. She raised her hawk-moths there. The Hawkmistress's own château had been sealed one Season, and she had never returned to it. La Voisine, the Seer, either had possessed no château or had forgotten its existence, but was given succor amongst the Scarabées, wherever she should find herself.

The White Gentleman had had built a château at the south pole, a fastness of ice and snow, and created, as if by magic, a fortress made of diamond, shaped to resemble the ice that surrounded it, but with an enormous blood-red gem at its heart—or, perhaps, he had not. The château was only told of in old legends, mothers warning their naughty children to beware the White Gentleman, or he would steal them away and take them to the Fortress of Dorakyura, where he would murder them, drain them of blood, and hang them in a secret room, replacing them with identical copies, soulless but well-behaved. When finally the White Gentleman (it was considered unlucky to say his name) collected enough naughty children, he was to raise them as demons, to take his vengeance upon mankind, who had killed the only creature he had ever loved: a Grillon hatchling that he had raised as his own. It was said that the Season marked the anniversary of the hatchling's death, amongst that maddened race.

The last of the Twelve, Grandpère, was said to own Thomàon itself, to have purchased it with a gem so rich that it was worth more than the planet itself. How such a thing could be, well, it was not known; it was only a story. But the truth of the matter was that he lived very well, in a châteaux just outside the Silver City, named Versailles.

Versailles was itself a city of its own, although it was not called so. There were palaces, administrative buildings, natural hot springs and spas, shops, merchants, domes, cafés, cleaning women, guards, and so on. Anyone who could afford to do so, spent at least a week there, at one of the guest houses. A great medical research center was housed there, the Miséricorde.

Versailles thrummed with activity.

Not only was the château respected among the race of men, but it was also honored by the Scarabée, who graced it with their service. Scarabée servants were much in demand, as a mark of privilege and of culture: the strange, bumbling creatures seemed to soothe all those who lived around them as though by sorcery, pouring balm upon troubled souls, easing conflict, and bringing a sense of peace and harmony all about them.

They were particular whom they served; they served in the Castle of the Silver Spire, and they served at Versailles. A pair of them kept the Hawkmistress company, and a small cadre of them attended the Madman, in a vain attempt to return him to sanity. But the Player they shunned, and the Puppet Master; they came or went from Madame LaFerme's château depending upon her moods; they certainly knew of where the Assassin kept their lairs, but never revealed a single one.

There was only one domain they were forbidden: and that was Shakes Prison, and the other prisons over which Warden Lemure held responsibility. Once he had welcomed them, but after the death of his wife they had become an anathema to him, and he was said to be unable to endure their presence.

Many things were said of Versailles. It was said that the king and queen were mere figureheads, and that Grandpère ran the planet from a hidden bunker underneath the main palace. It was said that a third race of semi-intelligent creatures from Thomàon was imprisoned there, as hostages against the behavior of the Scarabées. It was said that a giant statue of a great beast, placed within one of the courtyards, had risen up and murdered its sculptor one night, and that it would rise again, to murder the king and queen and replace them with their bastard twin children.

It was even said that there was a tunnel which ran from beneath the Silver City to Versailles, so that Grandpère could be moved back and forth secretly during the Season. But that would have been madness, for Versailles was not protected by a dome, and was as vulnerable to the destruction from the violent weather and the attacks of the maddened Grillons as anywhere else.

In the Season, indeed, Grandpère was seen in his palace in the Silver City, which was not a palace at all, but a museum containing the entire history of the world of Thomàon, a place that was open to all, at every time of the year: the Louvre.

The Louvre was built around a central court. On one side were administration buildings—grand in appearance, a dull but busy hive of bureaucracy otherwise. On the other, was Grandpère's residence, the greatest museum on all of Thomàon.

It was built like a funnel, as if to lure in everyone who came near it, with two wide-spread limestone colonnaded wings that stretched broadly on either side of the central court. From there, the funnel narrowed, becoming two side-palaces, each of which held its own courtyards and fountains. At the back of the funnel was a square fortress, holding within its massive central courtyard not a sundial or fountain, but a suspended pendulum of shimmering silver, which marked of the hours of the day and the night as it swung back and forth over the marked tiles below it. The pendulum was said to illuminate principles of planetary rotation, although some of the citizens of Thomàon worshiped it as proof of the hand of the Twelve upon them. Below the pendulum was a pool of water, tasting of salt, that one might reach into and dip one's hand in, for the blessing of the Twelve.

During the Season, and whenever else the whim took him, Grandpère lived within a series of rooms at the top of the palace at the back of the funnel, which overlooked the pendulum in the courtyard in one direction, and, at the other side of the building (the rooms were extensive), the long stretch of gardens at the rear of the Louvre. The Jardin Botanique, with its mazes, hothouses, and nurseries, was one of the most beautiful sights of the Silver City, famed across all Thomàon.

That night, the first night of the Season—or rather, by then, early in the morning of the second—Grandpère was in his rooms, nearly as far away from the Castle of the Silver Spire as it was possible to reside, without leaving the safety of the city.

It was impossible for Grandpère to hold his ordinary fortnightly reception, during the course of the first night of the Season, and all but a few of his guards had been dismissed to attend the festivities. The Louvre itself had been closed up when the dome had been sealed, so that the crowds, maddened and drugged as they often were that first night, would not cause damage to the precious objects kept there. Within the Castle of the Silver Spire, they could do with as they willed—but not the Louvre.

And so the Louvre, unlike much of the rest of the city, was preserved from the violence of the merry-makers and the revolutionaries.

Grandpère sat in front of an enormous row of windows at the rear of his rooms, looking down onto this beloved Jardin. The gardens stretched all the way from the rear of the Louvre to the edge of the dome itself. Ancient, alien trees rose on either side of a long, straight path whose branches led one to exhibits celebrating the tropics, or the polar areas, or the long, dry plains, or the oceans. Small lights glimmered among branches. At the center of the garden, topiaries depicting the Twelve were lit, limestone arches above them.

He could imagine the scents of the flowers—some of them from the Vieux Monde, and others from the new one—and the feel of the sunlight on his skin as he walked under the ancient trees. How long had it been since he had walked in his garden?

How long had it been since he had walked at all?

He would not walk in them again.

Above the garden, the tiles of the Great Dome were black and dull. They had begun the evening styled to show a starry expanse of the night sky, but had abruptly gone dark, all but for a series of flashes that Grandpère could not interpret.

Code.

Grandpère's ancient hands tightened on the arms of his chaise roulant, and it rose into the air a little, preparing to move. He extended his fingers, watching the ancient skin wrinkle, and the roulant sank again.

His lungs felt tight, as if he were coming down with something. This body was becoming old—far too old. He should have moved into a new one ages ago. But to tell the truth—it was no illness that made him wish to cough, but the sight of smoke rising into the air. Great black billowing clouds rose above the lights of the city, disappearing against the sealed dome.

The nano-cleaners which should have whisked away the particles, had not.

Grandpère had known of the Puppet Master's plans to foment rebellion, but then, Armand always had some sort of plan or other to stir up chaos. It was beyond the fool to do anything else: he followed his nature, as he must. Armand was caught in rebellion; for thousands of years, he had been unable to do anything else, even though each successive incarnation of the government was his own creation—from some previous rebellion.

What would the fashion be, after this? Communism? Anarchy?

It didn't matter. At any other time, after a few hundred years of chaos and destruction, Corentin and Delphine would have sickened of Armand's rule—of which Armand also would have tired—toppled it, installed themselves as monarchs, and put everything back in its place. They had proven to be surprisingly effective monarchs, across their incarnations.

But now?

It was too late for Armand's little games, or for Corentin and Delphine to clean up after them.

Grandpère winced as he saw the fire's orange glow begin to light a few of the dome's tiles overhead, making them appear as low, overhanging clouds. A second fire soon appeared, and a third.

The crowds were burning things.

How he hated them, the descendants of the colonists that had been loaded onto the *Téméraire*. Stupid people, made stupider by the virus that had been used to erase their minds. Why had he ever agreed to such a thing, to bring them at all? Or to reawaken them? Why had he not had them all killed? They were less than human.

"Sir."

The familiar voice made Grandpère startle from his dark reverie. Next to him stood a man, middle-aged now, dressed in a pearl-gray suit and wearing white gloves. He was tall and elegant, his joints not yet wrecked by use of the elixir, and his face not yet distorted by wrinkles. Grandpère was so used to looking at his own ancient face that it was hard to recognize himself in the younger man beside him now.

Pierre Delunay, his clone, was holding a silver platter with a cup of cocoa on it, in a sturdy mug with cartoon owls on it.

Grandpère inhaled deeply. He could barely smell the cocoa, but at least he could still smell it—the taste, when he drank it, would be bland. He took it more for the comfortable warmth and the ritual of it than for the taste.

"Yes, my son?"

Unlike the others of the Twelve, Grandpère preferred to use his own clones to change bodies, allowing each of them to live lives independent of his own, then bringing them into his service when they had raised their children, became bored of the lives they had chosen for themselves, and longed for something bigger than themselves. None of them were surprised to discover that they were the double of the man who controlled the planet; none of them were dismayed to learn that they would be asked to give up their individuality in order to inherit the power he held.

Pierre said, "Armand has made his move at the Opéra du Mendicant. It appears as though he is making use of the Général's Gold Stars."

"And Corentin and Delphine?"

"Disappeared."

"The others?"

"The Warden disappeared in a trail of bodies; his daughter followed Océan down into the passages leading to the aquifer. Yvonne made it out of the castle and has sent us a recording of the performance for our records. Armand has also disappeared, but does not appear to have gone far. Paul is still inside his quarters. Jacques is on his way here, and asks to speak to you."

"Come to rattle his saber," Grandpère noted.

Pierre nodded, handing him the mug. They both ignored the way that Grandpère's hand shook as he took it.

"What will you do, sir?"

Grandpère sighed. More of the tiles over the city were turning orange. Red lights flashed through the streets.

He sipped at the cocoa. He could feel the texture of the cream that had been used to make it on his tongue; he felt the astringency of the cocoa's bitterness. It tasted more sweet than anything else. His taste buds were dying.

He liked to be old, but not *this* old.

"Would you be shocked if I told you to drop everything and take the both of us to the regeneration chamber?" he asked.

Pierre tucked the silver platter under his arm. "I'm ready. I have no hesitation; you know that. Let us go."

Grandpère shook his head. His chest had tightened again. He remembered back in his final days of the Vieux Monde, when pandemic after pandemic had spread across the planet, turning every minor illness into a terrifying wait for a diagnosis. "I cannot."

"Why?"

Ignoring the question, Grandpère said, "I have registered all but the last few days of memories, Pierre. They are yours, if you want them. You have already taken on the greatest part of the burden of them, along with my personality—if it differs at all between us. I am already a part of you."

"But what about you? Are you trying to save the last dregs of the elixir? For what? To buy me another lifetime that neither of us really wants?"

Grandpère looked over the burning city. "This isn't about Armand, or about us. It is about..." He fell silent, and the two of them watched as shooting sparks rose into the air at the far end of the Jardin.

They did not speak further on the subject.

The fire began to spread.

Pierre stiffened, touching one ear. "Jacques is here and wishes to speak to you. Will you see him?"

Grandpère glanced away from the window. His rooms were as spacious and open as he could make them, with only a few offices and bedrooms and therapy chambers walled off and kept separate. The rest of the area was of a piece with the rest of the museum, with hundreds of displays and objects about the area, still subtly lit for display.

The history kept in the Louvre, like all official museums, was only a part of the story. Yvonne couldn't stand the place, called it a living lie—but still sent him her records.

Grandpère took as full a breath as he could. His heart struggled in his chest, an old-fashioned clock that was once again winding down.

"What time is it?"

"One in the morning, nearly. Sir."

"And now he wants to see me?" Grandpère snorted. "Why not? Let him in."

Pierre pressed his lips together lightly, but his throat bobbed as if he were speaking. After a moment, he said, "Shall I bring a late supper for the two of you?"

"Has Jacques eaten?"

"No."

"Then bring something simple. Jacques couldn't care less whether or not he eats, but I dislike sending a man away unfed."

Without waiting to be dismissed, Pierre strode across the floor toward the entry doors. When Grandpère was away, the hall was opened up like any other part of the Louvre, for the children and sight-seers to view the history of their world, this little collection of arts and sciences.

Grandpère recalled the man who had made their existence here possible, who had given them all their power.

Paul.

Poor Paul. So brilliant. When he had modified the airships to repulse gravity, Grandpère had known the man was a genius. When he had saved them all from death using the elixir, Grandpère had known that he had written his own doom.

As ever, power demanded on Thomàon that no one else be allowed to share it. And therefore Paul had gone "mad," a state that Grandpère had not caused, but had done nothing to prevent.

He finished the cocoa and tucked the mug against his side, under a soft blanket that covered his lap—and the equipment that helped absolve him of his body's betrayals and indiscretions. Then he stretched his hands out again, the joints crackling as he stretched them to their full range in one direction, then the other.

Let it end, then. Let this strange existence, with all its monstrosities and mutations, come to an end. He was tired. He was ready.

Let Pierre do the dirty work. A little pain, and it would be over. He would no longer have to take up the rôle for which he had been born.

The entry doors flew open, and Jacques marched across the floor, his head snapping back and forth as he searched the room for threats, points of vulnerability, and traps. His hand hovered near a pistole at his side.

"Jacques," Grandpère called. "It is late. What could you possibly require at this hour?"

Jacques changed direction, aiming himself toward Grandpère's roulant. For a moment it seemed as though the man were about to shove the chaise toward the window, smashing it through the glass and shoving the old man seven stories downward to crash into the bushes at the base of the museum. But at the last second he swerved, and came to stand beside Grandpère.

Jacques was tall, slender, and walked with a bounce to his step, even after all these years. He simply could not shorten his stride enough to walk with real dignity. His cheeks were thin and hollow, and he needed a haircut. His shaggy mouse-brown hair was hanging into his eyes. Again.

"You know what Armand is up to this time?" he demanded.

Grandpère waved a hand toward the fires on the other side of the window, long fingers moving like spider legs. "Another revolution."

Jacques grabbed the side of the roulant and leaned his face close to Grandpère's.

"It's not that. He's stolen the last supplies of the elixir!"

Grandpère let his mouth fall open; he was surprised that the theft had been discovered, so soon.

Let Jacques think that Armand had taken the last of the elixir, if he wished. But Grandpère had always been one step ahead—one step ahead of them all.

For the Warden had not brought only *one* case of the elixir with him to the Silver City, but *three*.

Chapter 8

Grandpère on His Way to the Stars

PETE JOHNSON HAD RETIRED young. After spending most of his life building up a world-spanning computer software empire, he had taken a look at his life and found himself unhappy.

He was happily married—that wasn't the problem. He was rich—also not a problem.

But he was bored.

When you've conquered a field so thoroughly that no matter which direction you move you come up against anti-trust laws, it may be time to move on. Other people might have found themselves content with their lots in life.

But not Pete.

Either he was fighting incredible odds, or he was chewing his own arm off.

He took some of his money and did some research: what project could he take on that was "impossible," but that, if beat, would improve people's lives the most? In other words, what was the cost-benefit analysis of taking on the problems of humanity?

His projects included developing vaccines, cracking the genetic code, developing batteries that actually held a charge on the level humanity would need if it planned to go solar.

Distributing birth control. Dear god, the problems that could be solved by letting women choose when, and how many, kids to have—instead of overbreeding them like cows.

Pete didn't consider himself a philanthropist. He was a ruthless businessman who had screwed over some of the wealthiest people in the world to get where he was. His biggest spiritual achievement—by his own admission, but only to his wife—was that he wasn't as bad as he could have been.

It took a certain type of man to claw his way to the top of the heap. The fact that *he* had down the clawing had prevented someone else, far worse, from taking that spot. Statistically, just the fact that he had succeeded meant that he had done more good for planet Earth than, say, Mother Theresa.

By a long shot.

But, in his heart of hearts, Pete knew that he wasn't a great guy. Just not a worse one.

So when Joel Govender came out to Pete's redwood compound along the northern California coast with the promise that he had "something great" to show him, something that could save humanity as they knew it, Pete's ears pricked up.

He was starting to get bored again. His wife had gone on an extended visit to her mother—never a good sign. He needed a new project before he went off the rails.

Enter Joel Govender.

Joel had texted him just before he pulled into the driveway in front of the main building as his self-driving car navigated the gravel road faultlessly.

The door popped upward and Joel ducked out, the setting sun catching the shine on the top of his balding head. Nobody had followed him; nobody got out of the passenger seat. The trunk popped open, and Joel took out a battered leather satchel, throwing the strap over his shoulder, texting again.

Pete checked his phone. Joel must be texting someone else this time.

If Pete was number one on the planet, Joel was number two. The fact that he was driving north from Silicon Valley to visit was a big deal.

The fact that he was coming out alone was...bad.

Whatever Joel was up to, he didn't want his team to know about it. A secret meeting between the two wealthiest men on the planet.

Joel wasn't as bad as he could have been, either. But he was also one of the guys that Pete was glad that he'd beat out on his way to the top.

For now, at least.

Joel took the cedar steps up to the house two at a time. The car closed its own trunk and door, and drove itself off to the garage, where Pete's car guy was waiting for it to arrive, dressed in overalls and wiping his hands on a rag. He was eager to take a look at Joel's latest model.

Pete walked over to the door and opened it just as Joel reached it.

Joel put one hand on his satchel to keep it from swinging around and held out his other hand. "Pete! Good to see you. How's it going?"

They shook heartily, Joel squeezing his hand a little too tight, pumping it a little too long.

"Come in, come in! Angie's not here. She's off with her mom again. So it's just the two of us."

Joel chuckled. "Just the two of us, and about a million smart gadgets. You're never really alone these days, are you?"

Pete gave him a flat smile. "Angie keeps getting after me to update the house, but I like it the way it is. Unless the FBI has us bugged, we should be clean."

Joel's eyes stretched, bulging a little. "No automation? Seriously?"

Pete backed away from the door, and Joel stepped in far enough for Pete to close the door behind him. Pete waved his hand toward the kitchen, and Joel started walking alongside him, looking around at the rustic wood paneling of the interior of the house, the wide windows, the cases full of antiques and ephemera.

Pete pulled out one of the kitchen chairs for Joel. "No gadgets. Good dealers don't snort their product. Coffee?"

Joel laughed politely, sat, and started pulling paperwork out of his satchel. "Obviously, this is just a preliminary meeting. I didn't bring the, uh, product with me, and the inventor isn't here to speak for himself. Do you have somewhere I can put my electronics?"

"The microwave."

Joel laughed again, a little harder this time, and unstrapped his smart watch, laying it on the table. Pete was wearing an old Rolex, nothing more than gears and springs and jewels under a crystal case. He rummaged around in the kitchen drawers until he found Angie's junk drawer; there was still a Faraday bag shoved under a pair of busted garden shears and some ketchup packets.

He handed the bag to Joel. "This do?"

Joel packed his phone and watch inside the bag, folded the top shut, and shoved it into his satchel. "That should do it. Forgot mine, sorry."

"No worries."

The electric teakettle rumbled on the counter, then switched itself off. Pete set up a pair of stoneware drip coffee makers over the mugs.

Joel was half-turned in his seat. "Now, *that* is old-school. Are you that worried about surveillance?"

"No?" Pete said. "Cream? Sugar? I mean, I'm worried about surveillance. People like us have to be. But mainly it's a case of having worked on that stuff for so long that I'm disenchanted by it."

Joel made an *ah!* face, nodding. "That I get. Jesus Christ, there's nothing so interesting that it can't get old after a while." He slapped a hand on top of the small sheaf of papers in front of him. "Except this. Uh, nothing in mine. Thanks."

"This? What is *this*?" Pete checked the mugs; they were almost full. He gave Joel's another few seconds while he added cream and sugar to his cup. If Joel hadn't been there, he would have had cocoa instead. But this was a business meeting.

"It's incredible."

Pete carried the cups over to the kitchen table. It looked out over the back of the house, toward the boat docks and the sailboats. Pete had once taken up flying as a hobby but had hated it. A ship on the water felt more like flying to him than flying did.

He could have bought and sold countries. Instead he had a sailboat collection.

Joel slurped noisily at his coffee. "Good stuff. Thanks."

Pete repressed a smile. Now the man was just screwing around. "What *is* it, Joel? Don't drag this out."

Joel's expression softened. He looked out the window, set his mug down, and balled up his fists. "Space."

Pete shook his head. "You're already into space." Joel had the biggest privately owned space venture on the planet; he was making good strides, but it came in awkward lurches.

"Not like this."

Joel's hand moved toward the paper on the top of the pile. He picked it up without looking at it. His hand was shaking and his voice had tightened. "Take a look at this."

Pete took the paper. It was handwritten, a bunch of scrawled notes written in blue ballpoint pen on a sheet of legal paper, full of circles, lines, arrows, and formulas. "I don't know enough about physics to understand this. If it's not C++, I can't speak it."

Joel didn't bother to smile. He was still staring out the window. "It's a formula for a faster-than-light drive."

A shock passed through Pete, as serious as a heart attack. "No."

"Yes. It shouldn't work. It doesn't work. But it doesn't work in a way that made me cough up a billion dollars in funding."

"Shit." Pete picked up his mug of coffee and tried to drink it, felt hot liquid splash onto his shirt.

"Exactly. This kid, Paul Hong, he's a fucking genius, Pete. He can do it. Even if he doesn't do it, it looks like we'll have anti-gravity flight within five years."

Pete's skin crawled. His stomach lurched.

He felt sick.

"How...how does it work? By moving us into an alternate dimension?"

Joel looked away from the window, his pale blue eyes blank and unseeing. "It works by recoding this specific pseudo-metal so that gravity can't 'find' it. He's only been able to make a small amount of it, a milligram or so, from the one time he was able to piggyback some of his stuff on the LHC. He keeps it in a stainless steel pill container on his keychain, Pete. He just walks around with it."

"And...it moves faster than light?"

"It doesn't. But when he shakes that container for a couple of seconds, it floats in the air. It just...hangs there. I've seen it. I've had my *hands* on it.

He says that he wants to make a bullet out of it around a core of normal matter to see if the normal matter is affected by the acceleration or not."

Pete blinked. He tried to imagine a bullet made out of material that wasn't affected by gravity: what would happen when it hit? What if the casing fragmented?

What happened when it *didn't* hit something?

Pete handed him back the sheet of paper. "I have to admit, Joel, that it's going to take a while for me to wrap my head around this. I believe you, that this kid, Paul...?"

"Paul Hong."

"Paul Hong is on to something, whether or not it takes us into deep space. But what do you need me for? You're the second-richest man in the world, Joel. You don't need me to help you fund this."

Joel's jaw moved by itself, voiceless, for a few seconds. He picked up his coffee and slurped it again, put it down, held out his fingers. They were shaking. His skin was pale.

In a hoarse voice, he said, "I can't do it, Pete."

"What?"

"I can't do this alone. I can't be trusted."

Pete felt the hair on his arms stand up.

"I want you to go in with me on this so I don't abuse it. I mean, we're gonna abuse it. That's what we do. But I could own the planet with this stuff, Pete. Fuck, I could own the universe. And I *want* to. I can see the possibilities laid out ahead of me, and I want them. I want to be the most famous man who ever lived. I want to be the first thing kids read about in history books on Betelgeuse. I am who I am, Pete. I'm not gonna change."

Pete wanted to strangle the man. In fact, he was seriously considering it. "You want me to take responsibility for how this comes out."

Joel laughed and ran a hand over his bald spot. "I want you to be the asshole who develops the technology and screws over half the planet doing it. I want to be the guy whose hands are clean. So I can be on that first ship out. And build an empire...somewhere else."

Something snapped inside Pete's chest. *Oh, shit. It's the big one, a heart attack.* But it wasn't. His heart kept beating inside his chest.

He wanted to be the one on the first ship out. *He* wanted to build an empire, soaked in blood and corpses, strip-mining the universe for human-friendly habitation and water.

But he knew he wouldn't. He wasn't that guy; he never had ended up as bad as he could have been.

But Joel?

Pete picked up the paper again, studied it. "How much are we talking?"

"Billions. Trillions, if need be. Everything you got. Everything I got. We'll expand it if we have to—charity drives, collecting quarters from orphans if we have to. Humanity can't stay on Earth, Pete. We'll destroy ourselves. The only chance is for people like me to get the fuck off the planet, use ourselves up on conquering the rest of the universe. Taking risks, getting ourselves killed. Leave the caretakers behind, the wise men, the people who like to bake. They can stay here. But people like me, we have to do what we were bred to do. We need someone to take advantage of. We can't help it. We're fucked in the head. You know what I mean."

Pete knew exactly what Joel meant.

And it meant a death sentence.

Six months later, Joel Govender was dead, killed by the same kind of radioactive isotope that had been used to kill a few Russian assets, polonium-210. Pete came out of retirement to take over Joel's space program, and within five years, the *Téméraire* was ready to launch for real, after a series of successful short-distance flights out to Pluto and back.

It was sudden, so sudden that Pete had acted out of instinct, not out of planning. Paul Hong, supplied with enough funding to make his dreams come true, did so...and more. Pete's life was consumed. He sold the house, sold the boats. Angie divorced him, but that was for the best. He no longer had any room in his heart for anything else. He was headed out with the *Téméraire*. With him were Paul Hong and his partner Simon Poulin, the practical physicist and engineer who tested the ideas that seemed to slam Paul constantly, as if from outer space. A biologist, a linguist and archivist, a crack test pilot, several programmers, a mathematician, an engineer, a geologist—without the constraints of escaping Earth's gravity well, they could afford to be generous with their personnel.

And Joel's son Armand.

On their way to the stars.

Had Pete done the right thing in destroying all of Paul Hong's research back on Earth, just before the flight of the *Téméraire*? He never thought he had.

But at least, he told himself as they crossed the stars, he hadn't done worse, and left it in humanity's hands.

Chapter 9

An Exchange of Messages

Général Jacques Saveur-Chasse—the man who had been Jack Pearlman, engineer and programmer, back on Earth—was still breathing into Grandpère's face when he shook himself free of his last truly human memories.

"Are you listening to me?" Jacques demanded.

"No," Grandpère admitted. "My mind is going. I was remembering the day that Joel Grovender came to me with Paul's invention. He had a page of Paul's handwritten notes. He expected me to understand them at a glance."

Jacques straightened up, brushing the hair out of his eyes. "Jesus, Pete. Why don't you just move bodies already? Or are you in love with being the wise old man after all these years? Don't *any* of you ever change?"

It would have been a good question—and a fair one, if Jacques had been the sort of man to have ever changed, himself. But from Jacques, it hardly deserved a response.

Grandpère shrugged. "I don't have time to get used to a new body right now. I'll take care of it next week. Besides, I hardly need to leave my rooms. It's not as though I need tax myself physically."

Jacques sneered at him. "You're taxing yourself mentally, old man. The elixir? It's missing?"

Jacques was an intelligent man, but also a complete piece of shit, a morceau de merde. It had been Jacques's idea to take up French culture, three or four hundred years after they landed. They had all picked up the language onboard the *Téméraire*. Armand's mother had been French, and he would invariably switch languages whenever he wanted to curse at someone: and so they had all learned it, just to spite him.

Or had it been Armand's idea, the thing with making Thomàon French? It was hard to say, now.

He, Grandpère, should not have had the passengers killed; he should have had *Armand* killed. The Assassin would have done it, with pleasure. But although Grandpère had considered it many times over the years, it had always seemed expedient to put it off until later.

If they needed someone to hate, let them hate Armand. That had been his thought.

Jacques snapped his fingers in front of Grandpère's face. In a disgusted tone, he said, "You're not listening again."

"I am not listening, because I am making connections. I am *thinking*."

"Your thinking takes too long."

Jacques crossed his arms over his chest. He was wearing a pseudo-military uniform. Thomàon had no military; his title was more or less only a courtesy. What they had was a police force—the Gold Stars.

Grandpère coughed a little; the tightness in his chest had increased. "Tell me, Jacques. How is it that the Gold Stars are being used as part of Armand's little revolution? Are the two of you working together now? Or have your forces been subsumed?"

"The *elixir*, old man!" Jacques shouted. "Have you nothing to say about it? I have been asking you all evening for an answer."

"Indulge an old man. Answer my question first."

Jacques rolled his eyes. "The Gold Stars are against the revolution. I have set them to bringing in Armand's tools, in the half-masks with the one red eye. Why?"

"They were seen at the Opéra du Mendicant, attacking Corentin and Delphine at their royal box. I believe Marks took it into his head to slaughter all of them he could get his hands on."

"That fucker," Jacques said. "He hates me—but no, I didn't send them. I have nothing to do with Armand, and never had."

That statement was less than true; Grandpère could have named a dozen instances of their collaboration. But it hardly befitted the moment.

Grandpère took a deep breath, testing the limits of his tightening breath. Did he imagine it, or was there the scent of smoke in the air? "Then they have been suborned?"

"Or there are impostors dressed up in their uniforms."

Grandpère shook his head sadly. "Oh, Jacques. How can I believe that? How can you expect me to believe that you and Armand are not working together?"

"What do you mean?"

"You demand to tell me that the elixir is missing, Jacques. But it is *not* missing. It is simply not where you thought it was. *I* have it."

"You? Where?"

Outside, the flames had spread further; they were burning through the driest parts of the Jardin, the desert terrain. He could see the flames, the smoke. The tiles above the garden were turning orange. The fires were no longer limited to the city outside, but had made their way into the places that he held most dear.

The layers of smoke were lower than they had been before; the nano-cleaners on the tiles still were not working.

"Why should I tell you?" Grandpère asked. "When I cannot know whether you have betrayed us all to Armand?"

Jacques gave the roulant a shove; it drifted slowly across the floor, spinning slightly.

"I'm no traitor!"

Again, Grandpère could think of a dozen incidents that he could have named. A life many thousand years in length did not lend itself to purity of spirit, after all. But perhaps it was true that Jacques had betrayed them less than most.

"And yet you want me to tell you where the rest of the elixir is hidden," Grandpère said reasonably, even as his stomach lurched.

"I do!"

They could be back and forth at this all night. Jacques was just the sort to think that he hadn't lost, as long as he was still arguing: as if logic were a means of persuasion, rather than justification.

The roulant slowed and came to a gentle stop against the base of one of the displays.

Grandpère could see the entry doors without turning his head. Pierre had vanished. "I am bored, Jacques. You may leave now."

"I ought to kill you, old man."

Grandpère lifted his wrinkled old cheeks in a quick smile. "Yes, so you ought. But you won't. You'll rage and shout and shake your fist and argue the same point over and over. *If* you are a traitor, *then* you will continue in this manner, until you are able to pry some sort of admission out of me. But if you are *not* a traitor, then you will go, and moreover, you will go with a nod toward me for my wisdom at moving the elixir, and keeping it out of Armand's hands."

"But—"

"Are you a traitor? Or are you only asking to indulge your damnable sense that you are the only one who could possibly understand the situation we are in, and be capable of resolving it? Is that your opinion? When you have been unable to repair the ship for all these long years?"

The expression on Jacques's face turned crafty. It was as though the man did not realize that his expressions were the open mirror of his face—and they always had been.

Jacques waved a hand. "All right, you old fuck. You have me backed into a corner. Either I do what you want, or I'm a traitor, is it?"

"More or less."

Jacques gave him what he must have thought was an elegant bow, putting one hand against his chest. "Then let me prove to you, sir, that I am no traitor. You have your nod. I only hope you can protect the elixir, even though you apparently have no idea how devious Armand can be. I *do* believe that I am the only person who can protect it. But...as you say. I am no traitor."

It had never ceased to amaze Grandpère, that those who lived for thousands of years, had learned nothing new about the world, and reacted to in the same useless ways: Jacques was fooling nobody. He was backing off because he couldn't think of a way to convince Grandpère to give up the secret. That didn't mean he would stop trying, however.

It was not a new thought: *The Greek gods have nothing up on the likes of us.* Backstabbing, plots, using the same damned stupid tactics over and over again.

Grandpère nodded his head ponderously toward Jacques. "I thank you for the proof of it."

Mollified, Jacques bowed again, turned, and left the room, calling over his shoulder, "At least tell me something to make my trip worth the bother."

"Oh?"

Jacques stopped next to a case holding an antique vase decorated with a great ape, the like of which had never been seen on Thomàon and never would be, drawn in profile atop the skeleton of a building, throwing a barrel.

"*You* didn't suborn the Gold Stars from me and give them to Armand, did you?"

Grandpère barked with laughter. "No. But keep thinking like that, and Armand won't be able to twist them next time."

Jacques turned, grinned like the boy that Grandpère could only barely remember, and marched out of the room, letting himself out the doors. Pierre was still nowhere to be seen; a young woman with blonde hair let herself through the doors, saying, "Grandpère? Do you wish to go to bed now?"

She was one of his nurses; he recognized her. "No, thank you. I find that sleep has no hold over me tonight, Lucie. I shall stay up and watch the fires. Is there any word on whether they will be put out soon?"

Lucie was one of those small, unbeautiful, slight women upon whose backs an impossible amount of work is always carried. As Grandpère well knew, pound for pound, she was as strong as an ox.

Her shoulders pulled in. "I have heard that many of the firefighters have joined the revolution, and they are sabotaging the mechaniques so that the fires burn longer."

Grandpère nodded. "It's one of those times, then."

"Sir?"

"I have lived long enough, Lucie, to have seen it all. Sometimes the uprisings fall back down again; this looks like one of the other times. If you know anyone with the revolutionaries, tell them to hide. Do you know what the next step is?"

She shook her head, her eyes wide.

"The Gold Stars that seem to have joined the revolutionaries will turn on them, arrest them, and drag them to the Warden's prisons, if they don't just murder them on the spot. That was the Général who just left, child. He said he did not know what had made the Gold Stars turn their coats, but, as I have said, I have seen it all before. The streets will be full of bodies by morning, Lucie. Mark my words."

Her hand had flown to her mouth. "My brother…"

Grandpère held out his hand. "Leave me your badge. I will take it with me so that it seems as though you were here all night. Find your brother and bring him here, if you can. If you cannot, leave him and return. By dawn."

She ran across the hall, ducking around the exhibits, and handed him the tag that she wore pinned to her nurse's uniform. He dropped it in the spent cup of cocoa, where it clinked. "Go!"

She fled.

Grandpère found himself alone. He turned back toward the windows. The topiaries at the center of the Jardin were alight now. They all smoldered. The Archaeologist's burned.

Grandpère shook his head. He hoped that it was no portent; Marks Lemure was his favorite among those who had come with them to Thomàon, his favorite among the Twelve. Grandpère had not approved of what Lemure's wife had done, but he had been horrified at her fate—and disapproved of the way even her memory had been shunned.

Was that smoke he smelled, or was he imagining it? The Louvre had its own filtration systems, for the sake of the antiques that were preserved there. Temperature, particulate matter, and humidity were carefully controlled—even with a constant flow of visitors.

The entry doors opened again.

Who now? He looked over his shoulder and smiled, then gripped the arms of his chair roulant. It rose in the air, and he pressed upon the arms to move the chair toward his new visitor: the Scarabée Madame Opale.

Her beautiful shell shimmered as it caught the low lights of the exhibits around her. She trundled toward him, moving even more slowly than usual, to ensure that she did not disturb any of the exhibits.

"Grandpère," she said. "You are alone?"

Her low, nearly mechanical voice sounded disapproving.

Grandpère found himself blushing a little in shame, for having sent them all away. "It seems so," he admitted.

"I will wait with you."

"Ah!" he said. "I am glad of that. It promised to be a difficult wait. The Jardins are on fire, you know."

"I was sad to see it, as I passed this way," rumbled she.

They reached each other in the center of the room. Grandpère released the arms of his roulant, and it sank to the floor. She extended one of her upper legs, and he touched it gently. She ran a feeler through his hair; he was surrounded by a pleasant, calming scent—if he had been upon another world, he would have said it was fabric softener. He remembered the smell very clearly.

"Ah, Madame Opale. How wrong I was about you."

She rumbled with pleasure. "How glad I am to hear you say that."

"Will you—I find that there is something I regret not having done, and I am worried that I will find myself without the opportunity to do it myself. I could ask Pierre, but it is not quite the same. It is something I wish to have done personally, you see. As an individual. And not as Grandpère."

The feeler continued stroking his head. "I think I know what it is you wish you had done."

"I am sure you do. Madame Opale, if this body passes, will you tell her something from me?"

"Oui, monsieur."

"Tell her that I have been watching her progress, and that I have changed my mind. In truth, I changed it long ago, and now no longer disapprove of her. I might be the only one of us, other than her father, who feels that way. But now I am glad of it."

"It is no different than what you have done," rumbled the Scarabée, still stroking his hair, like a mother might.

"I agree exactly, Madame. That is why I at first disapproved. How it could be that such a thing could occur? It seemed monstrous at first. How could another of us be created? And how—how could she remain human? After all we have sacrificed, it seemed an insult. But how different is it from what we have done, really? We did it unknowingly, but we did it."

He leaned his head against her carapace.

"There, there," said she, in a voice the purred through his skull and into his ragged-feeling chest. "Is that the message?"

"Yes. No, wait." He thought for a moment. His eyes were starting to close; she was soothing him to sleep. "Tell her—when it comes time—tell her that I am glad of what she plans to do. I am an old man; I have not seen her since she was small." He held out his hands, remembering the size of the infant that Lemure had brought to show him, her perfect limbs and all. "She will not care what I have to say to her. But I remember a long time ago, when I made a brutal choice. I killed a man, to stop him from taking space away from me—from claiming it as his own, do you know that?"

He felt her shell tip in acknowledgment.

"I had him killed, cruelly killed. To keep him from becoming a worse man than I would."

"I know it, Grandpère."

Abruptly he was lost in a memory of Etoile, Lemure's wife, who had died shortly after giving birth to her daughter—the first of a new species. She had not died of giving birth; Carlton had killed her, draining her blood and leaving her an empty husk. What a clusterfuck *that* had been.

Etoile had been a red-haired beauty, tiny, a bright flower beside the dark and sombre Lemure. She had started out her life in one of the prisons, born to a woman who never made it back to the Silver City to celebrate the Season—at least, that was what Lemure had claimed. The girl was a shattered wreck when Lemure had first brought her to see Grandpère, shivering and staring at her feet. But, over the years, she had warmed, strengthened, become taller, more passionate: she had stood up not only for herself, but for the natives of Thomàon. She had once spat upon Grandpère, in the heat of an argument: then she had turned scarlet and spent *weeks* apologizing.

"I *miss* her, damn it."

Madame Opale did not answer. What could she say? The Scarabées had known and loved her, as well as anyone. And it was she who had triggered his memory of Etoile.

Grandpère sat upright, pulling himself away from her. "Thank you, Madame Opale. I am sure that I will sleep well—when I do sleep. But did you need something? What brought you here to me? Besides the desire to see to my comfort."

Madame Opale did not answer at first. "I wished to tell you, that we cannot regret what we have done, and what we will do. Your people are coming, despite all your hoping and praying that you had left them to destroy the Vieux Monde as they would. While there was a hope of your having contained the contagion, we were satisfied. But now that *that* hope is gone, we feel dissatisfaction, and must make our transformations."

He held out his hand, and she crossed it with one of her limbs. "If you are asking for my approval, you have it. Do you control Jacques, then? Is the ship operational?"

"We have exchanged favors."

During an earlier time, Grandpère and Jacques had exchanged favors. And the *Téméraire* had gone unrepaired. It was ruined beyond all repair, Jacques had said—at Grandpère's secret request—and they had believed him.

But now the ship was repaired.

The bastards from Earth had sent a drone packet ahead of them, with a pre-recorded message:

Colony World Thomàon. If you are receiving this, you are no longer alone.

Perhaps it was meant to be a message of hope. But to Grandpère, it had brought only horror: for twenty years he had lived under its shadow, not knowing when they would arrive.

But according to the Scarabées, it would be soon. A humble species that had never left its planet, and they knew the stars well enough to predict when humanity would reach them, across unimaginable distances.

"I am glad of it," said Grandpère. "I am tired...we are all tired. We are like children who wish only to sleep, but fight against it with all our strength."

"Some of you, perhaps," said Madame Opale.

"Was I a good man?"

She rumbled with laughter. "No, Grandpère, you were *never* a good man. But," she added, having spoken to him about it many times in the past, "a better man than you could have been."

He patted her leg, then pulled his hand back. "I thank you for taking the message, Madame. I will sleep all the better for it. But now, you must let an old man watch the destruction of everything he ever loved, in solitude."

"*Everything?*"

He laughed. "No, not everything. Be well, Madame Opale. And tell the girl what I said, even if it will do her no good. She should at least know that *one* person supported her."

"I shall."

There was a noise at the door, and Madame Opale dropped onto her legs, abandoning the awkward upright stance that the Scarabées used, when they were around humans, and moving as gracefully as any beetle, to the window and up it, then across the ceiling, disappearing into the shadows. Her shell went dull and dark, unreflective of the light.

Even in plain sight, she was well hidden.

Grandpère turned back to the window, hoping to conceal the expression upon his face until he could control it—then, as he saw how far the fires had spread through the Jardin, decided that he would not control it at all.

He wept openly, then.

The trees were on fire, the hothouse glass shattered. The long avenue lined with the aspen trees, one of the few plants to survive the trip from Earth, had burned to a crisp. Their leaves would quake no more. The topiaries and their arches had disappeared in a cloud of smoke.

Why burn it? Why burn any of it?

As a boy, in this lifetime at least, he had lived in a farming community along the coast south of the Silver City, and had learned how to sail boats there. It was like flying, he had thought, more like flying than operating an actual airship. He hadn't known, then, that it was a thought he had had many times.

And even when he had known, he had not regretted it for a second. He had not felt himself to have been wronged, to be the clone of a great man, to have lived the same life over and over again, to have made the same choices, without even knowing his own past history. He had felt embraced by the identity of Pierre, and then Grandpère, when he had taken over the position.

His name had been Louis Olivier, when he had sailed boats. Pete Johnson had been him, Pierre Delunay, Grandpère. One of the Twelve, and yet still his own self.

He was glad to have lived, after all.

He wondered who it would be: the Assassin? Armand?

It *should* be Paul Hong, the man he had most wronged. After all of this, the one thing he regretted was not righting at least a little of the wrongs that had been done to the man.

He watched the burning of the Jardin. He would see the rioters now, dark ants crawling over the avenues, carrying flambeaux and stolen gardening tools. And yet he was calm—Madame Opale's gift had not left him, although the old smell of fabric softener had dissipated.

There was nothing to do now, but wait.

Chapter 10

Beneath the Halls of Versailles

THE TWELVE HAD ALWAYS been reborn, or regenerated, or passed down in successorship, in a hidden chamber underneath one of the palaces of Versailles, that is, under the château that belonged to Grand-père.

During most of the year, it was a place that hummed with the calm and satisfied dance of those who knew their place and purpose in life—in other words, bureaucrats—and found that it agreed with them: a place of regular reports, calculations, and spreadsheets. A house of of small, quotidian problems, and even smaller solutions.

During the Season, it was abandoned. But death waited for no one, not even the Warden. The resurrection chambers were available, but unattended; one of them called up the Warden's preferred body and readied it to receive his consciousness, and the gift of life.

The memories of the Twelve were saved nightly. A certain type of clock that was common on Thomàon had been built to disguise the fact that it had a wireless receiver built into it. The bodies of the Twelve each had the transmitters embedded in their skulls.

This meant that a few memories inevitably went unrecorded, and had to be pieced together from the recordings of the day, from cameras and microphones scattered everywhere on Thomàon.

True privacy was not a luxury afforded to those effectively immortal.

Lemure found himself waking from one of the resurrection baths, feeling weak and ill—a typical case of resurrection sickness. He pressed his lips together and forced himself to lie at the bottom of the bath as the rest of the liquid drained out.

He wasn't a patient man, but the sheer number of resurrections he had endured had taught him that he would lose his balance if he tried to climb out of the bath before it was empty.

While he waited, he rolled onto his side and began laboriously coughing up the leftover preservative in his lungs. The liquid was a nauseating mixture of bitter, sour, and sweet, and was the consistency of a syrup. When one lung was more or less clear, he rolled onto his other side and repeated the miserable task, spitting into the drain.

When he was finally able to sit upright and climb out of the bath without falling, he got out and started his post-resurrection exercise routine. He had developed the routine in order to test the fitness of whatever body he found himself in.

He stretched upward, then bent forward to place his head against his shins. He stepped one foot back, then the other; he held his positions for a count of twenty breaths without his arms feeling the strain; he lay upon the floor, arching his back. Then he drew himself back onto heels, and reversed the moves until he was upright again.

Onward his routine continued, with tests of flexibility, stability, and balance. Reflexes, strength, and endurance, he would test later. One knee was a little loose on the forward lunge; he made a mental note to tighten the brace on that side, when he put it on.

Then he took a shower, scalding hot, and put on a robe, a waffled cotton one that wouldn't cling damply to his skin.

He walked out of the tiled, humid, high-school-locker-room-style resurrection chamber, passed through an airlock, and into the memory center. He booted up one of the ordinateurs to orient himself.

He checked it and found that he had lost a day; it was now the second day of the Season.

Although his personal reports didn't mention his death, he was pretty sure of how it had occurred: a brutal murder at the hands of Armand, during his latest damned revolution. The last sight Lemure had had of himself was of his previous body butchering a number of Gold Stars—or at least, men wearing their uniform.

He sighed. Saveur-Chausse was going to be pissed about losing his men.

A hundred resurrections ago, Lemure would have tried to discover the purpose of his death, and why Armand had done it: what part of Armand's plans had been forwarded. Lately, he discovered that he didn't give a shit.

Anyone who tried to figure out what Armand was up to was already caught in his trap, and doing exactly what he wanted them to do.

In addition, Lemure genuinely no longer gave a shit.

It used to seem vital that Armand be held in check, before his psychotic impulses could cause damage that couldn't be undone.

Thousands of years later, it was too late to prevent the damage. Soon, nothing Armand did would matter.

At all.

Lemure skimmed the news feeds to see what else had happened the day before. The feed was full of news about the revolution. Arrests of several prominent citizens had been mentioned, but none of the Twelve.

Lemure muttered, "The fucker didn't even bother to have me listed as deceased."

Corentin and Delphine were missing; Ammaline was not listed among the arrested or the dead; Madame LaFerme had not been reported dead or missing, either. There were rumors that some of the Gold Stars had turned traitor, throwing in their lot with Armand. The feeds *did* show Lemure on his murderous rampage down the opéra hallway.

He winced. Armand wasn't the only psychopath on Thomàon. He hoped that Ammaline wouldn't see what he had done—but he knew that she might.

The screen flashed.

BREAKING NEWS...PHILANTHROPIST GRANDPÈRE DELUNAY HAS BEEN FOUND MURDERED THIS MORNING IN A BRUTAL HOMICIDE...

Lemure flinched back from the screen, pushing himself away from it. The wheeled office chair rolled across the floor. Incredulous, he read the words scrolling across the screen:

ONE OF THE SCARABÉES STANDS ACCUSED...A WARRANT HAS BEEN ISSUED FOR THE ARREST OF SCARABÉE MADAME OPALE...THE MURDER OCCURRED DURING THE TRADITIONAL RIOTS OF THE FIRST NIGHT OF THE SEASON, WHILE THE ENTIRE CITY WAS REELING FROM THE THE UPRISING WHICH BEGAN DURING THE FEAST OF FOOLS...

Lemure found himself shaking his head. He stood up and began to pace back and forth across the memory center. The room was kept so cold and dry that the new skin on the bottoms of his feet tugged as he crossed and recrossed the tile floor.

Everyone knew there was something odd about Grandpère. He was always an old man and never died. The gossip sheets said that he *had* died, thousands of years ago, and his job was continued by a series of actors.

It was insane that anyone accepted Grandpère's apparent immortality—even if they explained it away—but accept it they did.

How would they take his *death*, though?

Grandpère was the force that held Thomàon together. Lemure never would have guessed it of the old man—the unethical software mogul he had met on Earth.

Lemure tossed himself back into his chair, rolled back to the keyboard, and searched the news feeds for any records of the death of Pierre Delunay, the name of Grandpère's heir-slash-clone.

Pierre was still alive. In fact, he was going to give a press conference on the front steps of the Louvre, at ten. Lemure wondered what Armand would do to disrupt it. Maybe nothing; maybe it was all part of his plan.

At least one thing was for certain: Grandpère had not been killed by Madame Opale.

Madame Opale was no killer, of that he was certain. In the end, the crime would be traced back to Armand. But not before Madame Opale had been brought in, imprisoned—perhaps killed.

Lemure spun around in the chair, chanting the word *fuck* out loud. Repeatedly.

Grandpère was like a father to them all. He stayed out of their conflicts and dramas, a neutral negotiator.

He had advised calm, patience, and tact from the very beginning, when they had discovered that the *Téméraire* had been irreparably damaged during the landing. When they had found themselves trapped on an alien planet without hope of ever getting home again, he had kept them sane. As much as anyone could.

That Armand had killed the old man was bad. Worse than usual.

Lemure pushed himself back to his feet and resumed pacing. His feet were dry enough now that they did not stick. He was getting sucked into the trap of wondering what Armand was up to—and he couldn't help it.

Armand must have gone to the Louvre to demand something of Grandpère. That he take sides.

And murdered him when Grandpère had refused.

But...why?

Armand never truly lost control. Every action was calculated. Armand had no native emotions; every subtle shade of nuance that crossed his face or tightened his voice was an act. A lie. The man was a psychopath. The only real, human emotion he was capable of was boredom.

Which meant that killing Grandpère and leaving his body to be found was a calculated act.

Why?

If Corentin and Delphine hadn't disappeared, they would have been the ones to handle the death and how it was played. They would have covered it up, no doubt. Delphine was the queen of maintaining a status quo.

So Armand must want Grandpère to be "dead." He wanted to take the old man off the playing field, at least until Corentin and Delphine took back power, and could "miraculously" show that it hadn't been Grandpère killed at all, but a body-double: some sort of soap-opera bullshit off *Days of Our Lives* or *The Young and the Restless*.

It didn't matter. It *couldn't* matter.

Within a few days, Armand himself would finally be dead, along with anyone else who had sided with him. His warren of incestual clone bodies would be a pile of corpses left to rot in his sealed-off château.

The elixir would be gone. The prisons would be destroyed—*thank God*—and Thomàon would no longer be ruled by the Twelve.

Either Lemure would be killed, or he would have the remainder of his life left to live. And then he would die.

Forever.

His personality, memories, and records would be erased from every database on Thomàon.

And so would the rest of the Twelve's.

It wasn't Lemure's plan, but he approved of it. They would use up the elixir...and *let humanity be done with them.* The Twelve would finally, mercifully end.

No more resurrections. No more of the foul taste of resurrection fluid in his mouth. No more testing to see what Paul's machines had fucked up this time.

No more trying to fit in with his old job under a new role.

No more starting over.

And over.

And over.

The plan was Grandpère's, but Lemure supported it. If he had been sure that Ammaline was safe, he would have been upset that he had been reborn at all.

He wanted rest. He wanted sleep.

But that could wait.

Lemure scrolled through more of the news feeds, but found nothing more of significance. The rioters had caused more damage than usual. They now controlled the Castle of the Silver Spire. The dome's tiles had been slow in handling the smoke from the previous night, but seemed to be running smoothly now. Many of the dead had been mutilated. Many were still missing. Armand would be making an announcement later in the day, with the support of the interim government of the People.

They were to have a Democracy this time, it seemed.

What horseshit. Anyone who had anything to do with Armand soon found themselves under a dictatorship.

Lemure tried to crack his knuckles and the bones in his spine, but they wouldn't crack: the body was too young. He sighed and returned to his files. While the information on his new identity had been implanted in his new body's memories, it was difficult to actually remember things he hadn't consciously recalled yet. The moving-in process for new bodies wasn't perfect.

His new name: Thomas Robida. His role was as one of the guards who had just returned from Shakes Prison; a man who had been newly hired to work for Warden Marks Lemure.

Lemure tried to remember who would take over the prison system after his death. His chief assistant, Paquet, had been killed yesterday—only yesterday!—at the North Pole. Who did that leave in charge?

No matter. The "Lemure" body had not yet been declared dead.

So...why not take over the life he'd just left behind?

The security systems weren't based on biological scans or samples; there had always been too much of a risk that the members of the Twelve would find themselves locked out of something important if one of the systems wasn't properly updated. Instead, there were elaborate encryption systems, passwords, and hardware tokens.

He could pick up a new hardware token and...use it.

Lemure got up from the chair and returned through the airlock to the resurrection room. The ventilators had cleared most of the humidity and sour smell out of the room, but the mirror was still fogged.

He used a sleeve of his robe to wipe it clean.

Did he look enough like his old self to be able to appear in public? What did he sound like?

The mirror reflected back the face of a younger man, in his twenties, instead of in his forties. The bone structure was similar, but the face was a little too full through the cheeks. Too young. The eyes were the same, the type of blue-green that shifted with mood. He had a cleft chin. Not nearly enough wrinkles.

He lifted an eyebrow, arched and sardonic, which made him smile, half-frowning. It made him look slightly demonic.

A familiar expression.

Give him a couple of years in the body, and he'd be able to pull off a credible impersonation of himself. But not yet.

He cleared his throat. Feeling like an idiot, he said aloud, "My name is Warden Marks Lemure. I am responsible for the recent deaths of approximately two to three dozen men of the Gold Star force. I would like to turn myself in."

Again, the voice sounded too young. Close, but no cigar.

He didn't have a couple of years to pass, to work as a second-in-command to the replacement warden; he didn't have a couple of years for his face to settle into the role. He could tell every ordinateur on Thomàon that this body now belonged to Marks Lemure, and the ordinateurs would believe it to be so—Saveur-Chasse had made sure of it in the programming—but human eyes and ears couldn't be as easily programmed.

Damn it.

He was going to have to explain things to Ammaline after all. If both of them survived long enough for him to finally do so.

Rage was rising up in him, the dangerous kind that he'd always struggled to control. He was a cool man—until he was a violent one. Lemure breathed deeply, concentrating on releasing the rage as if his breath were on fire. Heat would do him no good. Only coolness.

The airlock door opened, and Lemure had to restrain himself from picking up a nearby towel and using it to strangle the intruder.

It wouldn't have worked anyway; turned sideways, one of the Scarabées entered, waddling her enormous bulk through the narrow door. All but her hindmost legs had been pulled under her carapace, and her head and neck hung below the top of her shell.

"Yes?" he demanded. He didn't recognize her.

"Welcome back to life, Warden Marks Lemure," she rumbled. Two of her antennae protruded from her head, beady eyes glittering, and waved at him.

He frowned at her.

"I have come to announce news."

He took a step backward as she proceeded. She wasn't threatening him; she wasn't anywhere near him. And yet her presence seemed to fill the room.

"What?"

"Your daughter lives this morning."

The gravelly voice that wasn't quite a voice seemed to be speaking with pride in a job well done.

Still feeling tense at her presence, he asked, "Where is she?"

"She was to be found with Madame LaFerme, within the *Téméraire*. They danced in celebration."

Lemure's eyebrows pinched at the center of his brow. "Why would they go into the ship?"

"They were pursued but not captured." She rubbed her antennae together. "But after a time, they were joined by another."

"Another?"

The antennae fell. "The adversary came to the ship."

Lemure's skin turned to ice. He strode toward the Scarabée and clasped the edges of its shell. "The adversary? Armand? The Puppet Master?"

"None other." One of the antennae stroked the side of his face, as if trying to soothe a child.

"What happened?"

"The adversary returned to the ship to retrieve something he had left there. What occurred next is a mystery to all, for it was within a part of the ship that was unmonitored. But..."

He wanted to shake the damned giant alien bug. "But what?"

"But the two women emerged from the ship a few moments ago, carrying a case of the elixir."

Lemure whispered, "The elixir?"

The elixir should have been nowhere near the ship. It *should* have been hidden so deep within the Louvre that it couldn't have been found in a thousand years, not unless every priceless treasure within its sealed case were shattered all at once.

Just what the fuck had been going on last night after he'd died?

"They moved outside the range of our cameras, deeper under the city. We think they will approach the gondoliers soon, and sing with them."

Lemure rolled his head on his neck. "And Armand?"

The Scarabée's antennae writhed with pleasure, coiling and uncoiling from loose spirals. "It is my pleasure to be the one to tell you that his onboard chip has sent out a distress signal, as the body it inhabits reaches the threshold of death. We received the signal, then blocked it to all but ourselves. He will expire, in a few moments only."

The terror and rage that had been racing through Lemure's body transformed itself into something completely different, a kind of ecstasy that thrilled his spirit, as surely as any religeuse kneeling before a humble, carved statue of her Lord.

Lemure released the Scarabée's shell, his hands raising themselves upward. He was not a religious man, but he found himself with his face upturned, weeping freely.

Armand was coming back to the resurrection center.

He would be resurrected—because one of the final three cases of the elixir had been requisitioned for the medical center, and brought here by Scarabées, in case of emergency.

Lemure couldn't kill Armand permanently with one single, fortunate blow. He couldn't even stop the resurrection process or delete Armand's memories. Saveur-Chasse might be able to hack his own systems, but Lemure couldn't. Too bad; he would have liked to drop a virus into Armand's data and see him warp and mutate until he turned into a pile of goo whose last words were literally static.

But he could hold Armand here, incommunicado.

By killing him. And killing him again.

Armand hadn't been monitored on board the *Téméraire*. Which meant that his memories of that day couldn't have been recorded, either.

So Armand wouldn't know he had lost the elixir, or to whom. Or what had happened for most of the rest of that day.

The memory center was also not monitored. Nothing here would be recorded, either.

Which meant that each time Armand returned to life, coughing out the horrific fluids of his own rebirth, he wouldn't have a fucking *clue* about what was going to hit him.

It was a gift from the gods, whatever true gods ruled over such a damnable planet.

And Lemure intended to make the most of it.

"Tell me, good Scarabée," he said. "Would you have a knife?"

Chapter 11

A Father's Daughter

As Armand took the last few breaths that his body could endure, he felt the same thing he always felt at the end of one of his lives: terror that this time, there wouldn't be another life waiting for him, when this one stopped. That there would be nothing.

Death made the entire universe feel like it was coming to a stop; from his perspective, it did.

Once again, he had tried to hang on as long as he could. He'd known that it would be wiser to just let the thread of this lifetime go. But he could not.

He literally could not let himself die, no matter how much kinder it would have been on himself. He could not stop fighting for breath, even as he lay trapped inside his own body, even knowing the exact moment when his last breath had passed and he hadn't had the strength for another one.

Even worse had been the fact that he hadn't planned for what had happened to cause it. He literally had not seen it coming.

He, master of Fate, had been destroyed by—pure bad luck.

Temporarily, at least.

It had happened like this: he had come into the *Téméraire* to secure his own private supply of the elixir, one of the last three cases of the stuff that Lemure had brought back from Shakes Prison. The three cases had been separated and hidden; before he, Armand, had killed Grandpère, he had been able to get the location of two of them out of the man.

One of the two cases had been moved out of his reach via the underground tunnels to Versailles, and placed within the resurrection chamber hidden there.

The second of the cases had been placed in a location that Grandpère had thought was secure from Armand—but was not.

As for the location of the final case, well, it was too bad. Armand's knife-hand had slipped a moment too soon, and there happened to linger a drop of neurotoxin upon the blade. The old man's heart had simply given out.

Not only had he slit Grandpère's throat, he'd cut his own thumb—a matter which had not affected his own heart much at all, leaving him only briefly dizzy and distracted.

But it was an ill wind that blew no one any good.

As Armand had cursed the chance slip that had almost cost him his own life, he had chanced to look upward, and seen the glint of Madame Opale's unmistakable shell in the shadows of the rococo ceiling.

He'd stopped to call for the help of his minions, to try to catch her. A few of the Gold Stars had come as well, then—with no prompting from Armand whatsoever—spread the word over the police band transmitters across the city that she had been the one who had slaughtered Grandpère. They had even added the grisly, if fabricated, details of her shell, dripping blood.

By morning—was it morning yet? not quite—everyone would be on the lookout for her.

Following the directions he had been given, wending his way under the Opéra du Mendicant, down toward the reservoirs under the city—but not quite reaching them—he found himself at a seemingly blank wall, dull metal, a dead end at one of the catwalks running through the limestone caverns under the city.

His skin prickled with excitement. He would know that dull, featureless metal anywhere.

Fortunately, he still had his second-factor authenticator on him, and his biometric information was updated on a regular basis across the network—a network which secretly included this particular node, according to his source.

Armand had no memory of his old ship password—and he was *not* about to ask the system administrator to reset it.

He put a hand on the blank wall for a few seconds, then popped the red crystal out of the eyehole of his mask and held it against the wall, biting his lip, holding his breath.

The lock made a happy clicking noise, and then the door had revealed and unsealed itself, and Armand was able to open the heavy door easily.

He'd ducked through, bracing one hand over his head to keep him from banging it on top of the hatchway. As one foot stepped through, one of the bells on his red velvet costume jingled. He froze.

But no one seemed to have heard him. He stepped into the airlock and made sure the outer hatch closed and locked behind him.

Meanwhile, he mused that if his Gold Stars could catch Madame Opale, he would have to adjust his plans significantly. But it would be worth it.

Madame Opale, he had recently learned, wasn't just a freak of nature with a pretty shell. She was the mother-bug of them all, la mère des Scarabées, a sort of reservoir of all the past and future souls of that race. More than once, Paul Hong had tried to explain Scarabée psychology to him, from the confines of his cage. But Paul Hong was not called the Madman for nothing, and Armand had never really bothered to listen.

But Jacques Saveur-Chasse had. And when Jacques had finally cottoned on to what Grandpère was up to—letting the Twelve die off for good, without a fight—he had given Armand the information, in exchange for entry into Armand's plans.

Madame Opale was no mere servant, but the queen of the beetle-like Scarabées, the giant trundling alien bug creatures that had ruled the planet before humanity had come and disrupted their system, before the Grillons had turned violent.

And she could be used to control the other Scarabées—some of whom were inside Versailles, and presumably privy to Grandpère's secrets.

Covered in blood-splattered, particolored, red velvet jester's clothing and carrying a wand topped with a puppet face made to look like Richard Nixon, Armand had stood inside the airlock of the *Téméraire*, feeling as though he could hug himself. *Overjoyed.* With the door sealed, he could afford a jester's caper or two, and he did so, bells jingling, until he was panting for breath. He put a hand on the wall and took stock of his discovery. The ancient walls had held up well, even if they had made the stale air sour and plasticky.

How long had it been since he had been on their ship?

They'd all thought the ship was ruined, completely non-functional. They'd built the Silver City up around it, destroying plans and erasing the memories of the workers who'd known about it. Most of the workers had ended up in Shakes Prison for one reason or another and had died a premature death in the mines below the ocean floor.

It must have been at least three or four thousand years, Armand realized. It hasn't seemed to matter at the time; the damn thing had crashed. The *Téméraire* would never take them off the planet.

At least, that's what they'd all assumed.

But Jacques had brought more than one revelation: *the ship was fully functional.* Grandpère had fouled up the post-accident reports. After the crash, Jacques hadn't been able to get at the truth because Grandpère was the godfather of software programmers. He knew hacks into the system nobody else knew—because he'd helped design the original damned software.

Armand chuckled to himself at Grandpère's little joke, opened the inside door of the airlock, and stepped into the ship proper. The case of elixir was supposed to be in the server room. Just a short trip down a few corridors, and the elixir would be his.

It was vital that he get his hands on it.

Not only had Jacques revealed that the ship worked, but that its communication systems were still working. And that they had received a message:

Colony World Thomàon. If you are receiving this, you are no longer alone.

Earth was coming. And Armand intended to be ready to receive them.

There would be no "twelve" by the time the ship from Earth arrived. There would be only "one," that was, Armand himself. Or possibly two, if Jacques could stop being such a little pissant by the time the Earth ship arrived. The message had been sent via drone; the Earthlings were hard at work building a larger ship, and intended to send it as soon as possible. They were unsure how long it would take for them to reach their colony—but reach it, they would.

Rather than revealing the information to the rest of the Twelve, Grandpère had destroyed the drone.

Grandpère also had plans for the arrival of the ship from Earth: he intended to destroy the last of the elixir along with Paul Hong's other inventions and adaptations of alien technology. The resurrection rooms—the technology that allowed them to generate new human bodies—the mutations that kept them strong and healthy long past the length of an ordinary human life—the memory transmission, storage, and retrieval techniques—

Grandpère intended to destroy all of it, along with all of Paul's notes. And, of course, Paul himself.

Grandpère was insane. Worse even than Paul Hong. A megalomaniac.

If good old Pete Johnson couldn't control the universe, no one could.

Armand could have almost admired the reach of his planning—if it hadn't been for the fact that it meant that Armand Govender wouldn't be able to control the universe himself.

He almost whistled on his way to the server room. The hatchway opened smoothly.

On the other side of the door were banks of servers, air still chilled and dry, fans still buzzing like discreet bees.

He took a moment to admire the setup. How the fuck had the systems not crashed by now?

The case of elixir was just as Grandpère had described it, hidden in the last place anyone would look: nestled in one of the server racks. At first glance, the case looked just like any other server unit—except that the faceplate was blank. In addition, the case wasn't bolted in, it wasn't quite the same size as the others, and it wasn't connected to any cords or cables.

It was still an excellent disguise. If Armand hadn't known what he was looking for, he wouldn't have seen it. He slid it free and lifted it by the handle, which had been turned toward the inside of the server rack. The case wasn't heavy. What was inside weighed little, mostly padding to keep the vials of elixir safe.

He gave it a little shake but heard nothing moving around inside. Was the case, in fact, empty? He made a face and sat cross-legged on the floor of the server room, then passed his red crystal over the front of the case. The latch clicked and the top of the case rose a fraction of an inch, but he couldn't pry it open with his fingernails—he chewed them—so he dug the edge of his not-quite-clean knife under it and pried it open.

He needn't have worried about one last lie from Grandpère. Six vials lay inside their cradles of eggshell foam. The reason they hadn't sloshed was that they were completely full, airless on the inside. They radiated light dimly—the same way an old-fashioned radium clock dial would.

Armand let out a breath, then swallowed. He'd started drooling.

He closed the case and made sure it had sealed, then climbed to his feet. Grandpère had intended to hand the case off to someone else—but to whom? And when?

Time to go. He would hide the case under the opéra house in a place that only he knew, and carry out the rest of his plans to destroy the rest of the Twelve. He had set himself an optimistic goal of destroying them all by the end of the Season.

He put his hand at the top of the server-room hatchway, put one leg through to the other side, and—

The outward-swinging door slammed into him as he began to duck through.

The door knocked him back—except for his leg. Which was pinned.

He shouted in surprise, dropping the case on the floor—his stomach lurched—and fell ass backward onto the panels of the floor, leg wrenching as the door opened briefly, then slammed into his leg again. Harder.

This time, he felt the bones in his leg crunch.

Who the fuck was on the other side of the door? Who the *fuck* had made it onto the ship before him? Had Jacques betrayed him?

No. Whoever it was hadn't been expecting him. If they had, he'd have had a pistole to the face, not a door slammed into his leg. It was whoever Grandpère had sent to retrieve the case.

He pushed the case as far to the side as he could. Jesus! If they killed him—!

If they killed him and he were resurrected, he would forget about the case. He hadn't slept since he'd killed Grandpère. That day's memories hadn't been uploaded yet.

He had to live. He had to live long enough for his memories to be uploaded.

The door shoved harder against his leg, accompanied by panicked whispers. That meant at least two people stood on the other side of the door. The fact that they were trying to crush his leg with the hatchway meant they couldn't seal it, and furthermore that they hadn't brought weapons, or they would have attacked.

Armand stretched his arms toward the edge of the hatchway, caught it, and pulled himself upright, bracing himself on his back leg.

The pain from his trapped leg was finally starting to overcome the adrenaline coursing through his veins. He could feel the grinding sensation of the bone ends rubbing against each other as he moved upright.

All it would take was a knife to an artery and he was done for, memories of this day erased as if they had never existed.

At least the resurrection chamber at Versailles had been restocked.

Armand grasped the edges of the hatch, leaned his weight back as far as he could, then drew up his good leg and twisted to the side to give him every advantage of leverage possible. The pain was incredible.

Taking a deep breath, he roared, "I don't know who's on the other side of the damned door, but you better fucking open it and let me out. Don't you know who I am?"

The door twitched as the pressure eased up on it. Just a fraction.

He kicked.

The door did not fly open, but shoved itself wider by a span of a few inches.

He shifted his leg toward the door hinges, which had the effect of propping the door open even further as those on the other side of the door rushed to try to close it again.

Within a split second, he had his shoulder in the gap.

A young female voice shrieked, "He's coming out!"

Lower, a second voice added, with some disgust: "*Armand.*"

It was Océan outside the door! Océan who was Grandpère's secret ally!

He almost giggled. Who was with her?

Was it...*the protégée*? The Warden's daughter?

His skin pimpled in anticipation. He shoved his shoulder deeper into the crack. Océan had identified him by his costume, of course. Now that he thought of it, he could smell her perfume wafting around the edges of the hatchway.

"Hello, darling," he said, pushing harder.

She and the girl pushed back together, but Océan was weaker than he was—and the girl was only human.

Océan hissed a curse as he pushed his shoulder further into the crack.

"Open the door, my love. Let's not fight. You know that I only treated you the way I did in order to get a leg up on Grandpère. It was all part of the coup."

Something hard struck Armand's foot, crushing the toes. He clenched his teeth.

"Harder!" Océan urged.

It came down upon his foot again. The urge to try to withdraw his foot from the door was almost overwhelming.

He nearly sobbed as he cried, "Océan, my love! Why are you doing this? Don't you know what Grandpère has planned for us? Don't you understand that he's going to kill us all?"

Océan did not answer him, but said, "That's not heavy enough. Try something else."

"What? Everything is bolted down."

The other voice was young and filled with panic.

"He has betrayed us," Armand continued, tears of repressed pain pricking at his eyes and coming through in his voice. "Océan, this ship is fully functional, and it has been, the entire time we have been trapped here. The comms, too."

He pushed at the door again.

On the other side, Océan grunted, and he felt her feet slip.

"Worse, he concealed the fact that we have received a message. From Earth. After all these years."

The girl gasped, but the information only seemed to spur Océan to press him harder. If only he had been able to get proper leverage against the door! But with one leg trapped, his ability to brace himself was limited.

Armand winced at the pain in his shoulder. "The message came via drone. And do you know what the bastard did with it? He destroyed it."

The girl whispered, "Did you know?"

Océan growled, "*Try something else.* We can talk after we get this fucking door shut."

"But Madame!"

Cracks were starting to show between the two women. He could even hear Océan breathing heavily now. Excellent!

Armand raised his voice slightly, letting it grow ominous. "But Grandpère was not working alone. Lemure was working with him, too."

"*Papa*," whispered the girl.

He lowered his voice again, and let more of the pain come through. "They were planning to kill us all, Océan. I had to do it."

"To do what?" the girl begged.

"To kill him."

From the other side of the door: silence. Then the sound of Océan cursing under her breath, the repetition of the word *shit* in English, over and over again.

Then a thump.

Had the girl fainted? If so, Océan was all on her own. The weight upon the door seemed to have lessened—but was it only his imagination?

He wriggled further into the crack of the door and found that he had widened it far enough that his broken leg dangled freely. He dropped his other leg into the crack alongside it, and began using his hips to wedge himself closer and closer to freedom.

His arm fully free now, he reached suddenly around the door and grabbed a fistful of silk and flesh.

A breast.

Océan yelped and the door swung free.

He shoved the door until it swung all the way open, revealing the corridor, panels covering equipment and wiring, handholds jutting out here and there, padding everywhere. There were worse places to try to fight with a broken leg; at least here, he could hold himself up.

Ocean was backed against the far wall, her hair undone and missing the skirt of a pretty court gown. The Lemure girl lay on the floor in a blue dress, apparently unconscious.

Armand had to give her a second glance; for a moment he almost thought she looked like—but no. *That* fucker had been utterly destroyed, down to his last memory file. For hundreds of years now. And his stupid "prophecies" had all been bullshit, anyway.

Grabbing the nearest handhold on the wall, Armand had pulled himself away from the door. The thought of the case of elixir was an almost physical pull upon him, but he resisted the urge to look back over his shoulder to make sure it was still there. He couldn't have seen it if he *did* look, lying in the shadows as it was. He could only have given himself away.

The knife sheath pressed against his thigh. If only he had been able to dance! He could have been sure of sending Océan back to the resurrection chamber, and, even better, sent Lemure's progeny to oblivion.

"I cannot tell you how happy I am to see you," he said. "You must know what madness this is, Océan. In private, Grandpère calls us monsters and swears that all of us must be destroyed, for the good of humanity as a whole. But who has been the worst among us? Who has taken the most advantage of the planet?" Before she could answer him, he added, "Who has been responsible for the most murders, Océan? Among both the natives and among us? The Warden's butchery only follows his command. Jacques's pogroms after we landed? Those were Grandpère's idea, too. He is only going to destroy us because *he is afraid of getting caught.*"

Océan bent over slowly, keeping her eyes on him, and picked up a handhold that had been removed from one of the walls, a piece of solid black plastic molded into a U-shape. It wasn't much of a weapon. Two feet long, if that.

"*Fuck you*, Armand. You could be telling the truth for all I care. But *fuck you.*"

"Are you still angry about the performance?" He put on a charming smile. "Don't be. It was all an act."

Without smiling, she began to laugh, high-pitched, keening. The sound of madness. She lifted the handhold and raised it. "You worm."

Then she hesitated no further, but swung the handhold at his head.

He caught it but couldn't hold it, and she jerked it away from him.

He didn't have any balance or leverage. He had to keep one hand on his own handhold, or he would have fallen. His broken leg was a roaring furnace of pain, yet somehow also numb below the knee.

"Océan—"

She edged around him to his left, toward the hand that was clinging to the handhold, and swung again.

Unable to dodge, he twisted and earned another bruise on his shoulder.

But as he did, he reached down with his right to the slit in his pantalons and pulled out the knife, trying to hide it from her.

Then he slashed.

She danced backward before he could cut her.

He didn't bother to again. "Don't make me do this," he begged her. "I don't want to hurt you. I want you on my side, Océan."

She was afraid. He could almost taste the sweat crawling along her forehead, the sides of her neck. She was shaking.

She backed slowly away from him, moving down the corridor, holding the bar in front of her for defense. "I'm going to call for Lemure," she screamed at him. "I'm going to call for him and he's going to *slaughter* you the way he's wanted to do for millennia!"

Armand barked with laughter. "Lemure is dead. Didn't you hear me?"

"You're a liar!"

"Oh, he won't be dead for long, no doubt. But I took a few moments after the Gold Stars rose up in their righteous anger to get rid of him. Bricked him up in a wall, à la the cask of Amontillado, as a matter of fact. One of Paul's neurotoxins had left him unable to move...or breathe. He's long dead by now."

He brandished the knife. "Maybe there's even a drop of two of poison left on the blade, mingled with his blood. Give it up, Océan. You don't have anyone left to help you. But why would you even resist? It's only common sense that I'm talking here. You want to live, don't you?"

A pair of slim, smooth hands appeared in front of his vision, then clawed into his eyes. Blunt fingernails dug into them and he screamed, he *finally* screamed, not from the pain but from the sense of violation.

His eyes.

Océan wrenched the knife from his hand. He didn't care. He put his hands in front of his face, but the hands which had gouged his eyes had drawn away. He could still see, he told himself. It was only the blood covering his eyes that blinded him—

The knife found his solar plexus and ripped downward, sawing into the tough muscles of his diaphragm on its way out. It was a good knife; it didn't catch, as he finally lost his balance and fell.

When he finally stopped screaming, he heard the two women discussing what to do about him—and wondering why he had come onto the ship in the first place.

Did they not know about the elixir, then?

Had they not been sent by Grandpère?

Océan went over his clothing and took his red gem, apparently giving it to the girl as a trophy, saying, "Well *done*, Ammaline. You're your father's daughter, all right," Océan said. "But are you your mother's?"

The girl sighed. "I have no idea what you're talking about."

"Never mind. Let us clean your hands, darling."

Before they left him to die, Océan leaned down to his ear and whispered, "I don't care if Grandpère has betrayed us all. I just wanted to spite you once before I die, you son of a bitch."

Chapter 12

In the Madman's Prison

THE EARLY MORNING HOURS of the second day of the Season found the Silver City in chaos. The stars flickered on and off in fits and starts as the panels of the protective dome redistributed power and processing resources. Below them, parts of the city burned, were extinguished, and burned again.

The forces that should have been most concerned with restoring order in the city, were most involved in overturning it. The Gold Stars arrested rioters, politicians, business owners, performers—a list of citizens that seemed even among themselves without order or reason, but who carried upon their persons the symbol of an eye, peering from within a mask.

For what reason were these souls arrested? The reason that was given was that of public disturbance, and while that was often true enough, as *most* of the citizens within the Silver City were engaged in some sort of disturbance that night, it was not true in every case. Doors were broken down, innocents shot and killed, and the "guilty" dragged away, none the wiser about the nature of their crimes and coughing at the smoke that increasingly filled the atmosphere within the dome.

An onlooker, recording the events of those nights for the sake of History itself, might have questioned: did not the Gold Stars belong to the Général? And did not those marked as part of Les Yeux belong to the Roi du Rats, the Puppet Master himself?

Were they not allies?

The confusion seemed of a piece with the rest of the night that the panels of the dome were in ill repair, one more cursèd thing to go wrong.

But the failure of the panels protecting the Silver City from the madness of the Season was not caused by the fires—or by attacks upon the city's security systems by pirates informatiques—or by Fate.

It was an attack from without, an attack which soon would bear unspeakable consequences; it had been planned for longer than even the most cynical among them could have anticipated; and it could be said that everything else that happened that night, and through the nights that followed, were but distractions to prevent Thomàon's main forces of defense from being brought to bear.

The city, more or less unsupervised, attempted to defend itself as best it could. It had a sort of intelligence, not aware or conscious, but one that was able to adapt to circumstances in a limited fashion. A few human monitors remained to attempt to assist and direct that intelligence—thus the dome did not fail utterly during the long hours of that first night.

The Silver City had seen, and recorded, and studied, more uprisings than any but the Twelve had ever known. It knew—in its primitive way—of the loves, hates, betrayals, manipulations, and graces of every human that lay within its demesne. And yet even it was shocked, if such a distributed, sub-conscious intelligence could have been said to feel such an emotion, at what occurred that night, both within and without the bounds of its protection.

Within the protection of the dome, the denizens of the city were apparently more interested with their intrigues and conflicts and advantages than they were in their own survival.

The city began to set plans to announce what it identified as the larger emergency, the attacks upon the dome from *without*.

But the human monitors that watched the unfolding tragedy put a stop to the announcement.

The city believed that the mass of humanity that lived within its bounds of protection was *rational*, and could be entrusted with the knowledge that their survival depended on uniting in the face of external dangers.

But the humans who monitored their beloved city, even though they had lived only short, pitiable mortal lives, knew down to their bones that men, caught in the grip of emotion, were quick to abandon their precious rationality, and become the other things that men have always become, when they cease to be human.

The Grillons had attacked the Great Dome each Season, attempting to murder the alien species that controlled their planet, back to time immemorial. And each Season they had failed, and as the storms had passed, had returned to their territories, their nests, and their laying and raising of their young, as passive and servile as ever.

Without hope.

And yet.

Among the flickering stars of the Great Dome overhead, one of the panels went dark, and did not flicker to life again.

WHILE MADAME LAFERME AND Ammaline fought with the Puppet Master within the ancient star-ship, and while Warden Lemure slowly awakened from his latest resurrection—but before he had fully wok-en—and while Madame Opale fled along secret ways to a hiding place among her people, the Madman waited.

His cell was buried deep under the Castle of the Silver Spire, so deep that none but a few knew of it. The Scarabées knew, of course; it is difficult to conceal a subterranean chamber from those who burrow through soil and rock to build their homes. The Twelve also knew its location for much the same reason—although their burrowing was of a more metaphorical nature.

The Madman's prison cell would not have been out of place at Shakes Prison, and, indeed, during past uprisings, he had often been removed to that remote location for additional protection. His cell, however, did not resemble the cells of those other prisoners, who were housed together in large rooms, all the better to amuse and destroy each other, through sex and violence.

No, the Madman (who had once been known as the Scientist) had been isolated from all other living souls but the Twelve, and the Scarabées who were entrusted with his care—for the Twelve could not be trusted to such care.

His cell was large, so large that on those days in which he was able to recognize his situation, he did not mind it. He considered himself the master of infinite space, for tho' he was bounded, he suffered no bad dreams. His bed was a simple mattress upon a gray plastic slab; his meals were freeze-dried and tested for poisons after he selected one or the other. His cell—his quarters, really—had a living area, with facil-ities for eating, excrement, cleaning, resting, and exercise; it also had a room packed with ordinateurs, testing equipment, material storage (refrigerated and unrefrigerated), centrifuges, and other equipment.

He also had his own resurrection room, although he did not require it for himself, and it did not use any of the precious supplies of elixir that the Warden so assiduously mined from under the ocean floor.

He had mechaniques for company; he had waldoes to manipulate materials on microscopic levels; he had access to all the information of the world; and more, he had access to the Scarabées, as companions, mentors, and research subjects—but then the Scarabées did not constitute the limit of his research subjects.

Indeed they did not.

Every surface was easily cleaned and sterilized and tested; the air and water were filtered and tested; the information he received via the planet-wide ordinateur network was likewise combed through, to determine whether it might do him harm, or allow him to harm others.

The predominant scent that filled the Madman's life was that of ammonia, followed by blood; his food tasted dry and lifeless, no matter how much it was hydrated; his movements were so constrained by habit that he wondered if he should fracture his bones, if ever he were condemned to freedom upon the surface—if he were required to climb a staircase, or sit in a chair two centimeters lower than the ones he frequented, within his cell.

But why should he want to leave? He had everything he wanted, except for the love of his life, the physicist and his companion aboard the Téméraire, Simone Poulin—and he was in the process of recovering her. In fact, he had nearly reassembled all her memories from files that had been recovered by the Scarabées; the final data validation should be completed later that morning, in fact.

Then it would only require the presence of a good biological matrix in order to house and integrate Simone's consciousness—and the Scarabées had promised him that, too.

If Simone returned to him—if only she returned!

The immortality that he, Paul Hong, had been able to kludge together after the *Téméraire* had crashed on the planet had been a thin, frail sort of thing, adapted by a naïve young man whose intelligence had been limited to the paltry confines of his own skull.

What he was building for Simone was better, in every way; for Simone herself, for humanity as a whole, and for the universe.

The rest of the surviving Twelve had called Paul mad. But it was humanity itself that was mad; no one, not even Paul himself, was immune from the monstrous call that pulled all of them, that made them, no matter their individual minds or personalities, collectively a sort of horde of locusts, which made itself all the more deadly for its ability to limit its consumption, at least somewhat—and to turn upon their own species, when the winters wore thin.

Caught in his thoughts, Paul had not noticed that he had a visitor, and did not, until one of his chairs rolled across the floor and positioned itself beside him. Even then, he would have disregarded the sound, but for the fact that his own seat was spun around, so that he was turned toward his visitor.

She was familiar, and it only took him a scant second to put a name to her face: warm, friendly, pleasant hazelnut hair twinkling with a few gray hairs, her face lined more by laughter and happiness than by age.

"Hey, Sarah. What's up?"

She smiled, bringing the pattern of her wrinkles into a more pleasant prominence. "It's Delphine this time, Paul. Please remember."

"Delphine. That name means 'prophetess from Delphi.' The Delphine oracle. The French came up with some weird names sometimes, you know?"

They both paused, both recalling that Simone had once been called "the Prophetess," as a member of the Twelve.

"I...did not know that," Delphine admitted. "But that's not what I came to talk to you about."

"Oh?" He stared over her shoulder, at one of the grilled vents. "About Armand? He's doing the uprising thing again. I know how much you hate that."

He tried to keep track of what was going on above, but whenever Armand was involved—and that was most of the time—things got sticky and complicated.

"It's about the elixir. Have you found a way to manufacture it?"

Paul bit his lip. He *had* found a way to manufacture it, as a matter of fact; years ago he had had to develop a way of mass-producing it, not for itself, but that so he could use it as a way to bootstrap his understanding of the things he was being taught by the Scarabées. But he knew that she could not have found *that* out.

She sighed. "You didn't forget, did you?"

He shook his head. He *had* forgotten. But it didn't matter; he had long since improved upon the formula, and the Scarabées had tested it for him upon both human subjects and upon their own young: it had taken some time, but now they were at the point of unqualified success!

"Well?" she repeated, with emphasis: "*Have* you found a way to manu-facture the elixir?"

He had worked out a long time ago what he was supposed to say at this moment—for he had known it would come, in some form or anoth-er—but he had forgotten what he had intended to say.

Paul Hong had *always* found lying difficult.

He shrugged. "I think so. It probably needs to be tested on a few more subjects, though. I guess you can have some, if it's an emergency."

The lines on Sarah's—*Delphine's*—face eased, and he realized that her smile wasn't entirely genuine. "No, Paul, at least, not quite yet."

"I, uh, can pack some up for you? In one of those cases that Mark brought?"

Delphine corrected him gently. "His name is Marks now."

Paul made a face. "Like the famous socialist guy? I'm sorry, Delphine. I can never keep up with names. I know who you *are*, but keeping track of the labels when they keep changing is too hard."

She had leaned back in her chair, tucking her legs up on the seat beside her. She was wearing a pretty but torn silk top over the black stretch pants that she liked to wear under her braces. Everyone else liked to hide their changed limbs, even in private, but Sarah had always liked the aesthetics of seeing the metal rods and gears.

"You could call us by our titles," she mused.

She was staring at his computer monitor behind him, eyes unfocused. And her voice sounded like she was not really paying attention. She must have been worried about the elixir, really worried, and was now overwhelmed by relief.

He said, "Calling your friends by their titles is kind of weird."

She waved a hand idly. "At least the names wouldn't change."

"You don't call people by their titles, do you?"

She made a face. "Only when I'm pissed off at them."

Paul rolled his head on his neck, stretching it. "There you go. Calling people by their titles is weird. Unless you're pissed at them."

She gave him a half-grin, much more natural-looking. "You could write yourself a note and stick it on your monitor."

He rolled his eyes. "It would just rot after a couple of hundred years."

She put her hands over her head and kicked one foot on the floor, sending the chair rolling and spinning at the same time. "Oh, Paul. Do you know how good it feels to hear you say that you've synthesized the elixir? It feels like Heaven. Like everything is going to be all right again."

Paul didn't share her emotion. He understood that most of the Twelve didn't feel about Simone the way he did, but it was still hard to hear Sarah act so off-handed about his loss.

Nothing would be right until he had Simone back.

But Sarah was still talking: "Corentin and I will take a decade or so off while Armand fucks everything up again, and then he'll step down and we'll pretend to punish him again. Grandpère will putz along through his incarnations, LaFerme will sing, and we'll all keep ourselves amused." She paused. "Except Lemure. What's he going to do, without the prisons to keep him busy?"

Once again, Paul had to bite his tongue. *He* was in a prison, well, more or less.

"He'll find something, I'm sure," said Paul. "Unless...you want me to *do* something?"

Sarah went still, very still, her face turning into a mask.

"No," she said. "The last time we did that, it didn't work out, remember? Carlton."

Paul felt the tension of the name run across his shoulders. Carlton, who had gone by the title of the "White Gentleman." Mothers still used his name to invoke horror. They still brought out his old mask and costume sometimes, when there was a public killing to be done, and Jordan wouldn't or couldn't do it.

Carlton hadn't been the first of the Twelve who had been killed; that was Simone. But he was the only one they had agreed upon.

Skin crawling, Paul said, "I remember Carlton. We should have killed him a long time ago. Before..."

Before Carlton had killed Simone.

Now Sarah remembered. She scooted her chair back toward him and put a hand on her arm. "I'm so sorry, Paul. You've tried everything to bring her back. But it wasn't meant to be."

He bit his lip again, to remind himself not to let any emotion show on his face. Instead, he let his memories linger on the sight of Simone's body, butchered and bleeding.

Tears welled up in his eyes. "If only she were here. Imagine...what we could have accomplished."

Sarah took her hand away. "You've synthesized the elixir, Paul. That's achievement enough." She stood up.

"Are you sure you don't need a case?" Paul asked. "For safekeeping? To brag about? To use on some test subjects? I could always use more data points."

She stood over him and looked down for a moment. "I'm not leaving yet. If you don't mind, I'm going to use your shower and snag a change of clothes. Armand has been...particularly an asshole this time."

Paul waved a hand toward the facilities. "Mi casa es tu casa."

She got up and pushed the chair back to its original location, next to a second terminal. She'd always been very orderly and neat. "Thanks." She headed toward the facilities. "Oh, and Paul?"

"Yes?"

"If Armand or Jacques show up, don't let them in. Marks dug out the last of the natural elixir, and they're trying to find out where the cases are hidden. They might come here to find it."

Paul frowned, looking down at his knees. "Wouldn't it be better to let them in? To prove that I have nothing to hide?"

Suddenly, her hand was on his shoulder. He looked up, startled.

"But you *do* have something to hide," she said. "Remember? You're not supposed to tell anyone about being able to synthesize the elixir without Grandpère's permission."

He let his face light up with realization. "Oh! Yes, of course. And you're here, too—they don't need to know *that*. That would just be full-on drama."

She chuckled. "Yes. Full-on drama. Nobody wants that."

"What should I tell them?"

"Tell them…" She scratched the side of her face. "Tell them that you're in the middle of testing a subject and things are messy. Then waggle your eyebrows at them. They'll think you're trying to hide having sex with someone."

A fistful of grief clutched at Paul's heart and he blinked at her.

She patted his shoulder. "It's a lie, Paul. Just a lie. You want them to know you're lying, but you don't want them to figure out *what* you're lying about."

She turned and went to take her shower.

Paul relaxed as she moved out of view.

He knew the rest of the Twelve didn't really think he was capable of lying.

But he knew all about it.

Chapter 13

The Whistling Gondoliers

THE SILVER CITY HAD been built on a high plain, an area hundreds of miles long and a dozen miles wide at its thickest, where the ancient glaciers had built up a long ridge of moraine. The area was rich in limestone, which, as far as the citizens of the Silver City were concerned, meant two things.

First, that the easily manipulated limestone was available for making as many buildings as they wished—and turning the city that surrounded the final landing-place of the starship *Téméraire* into a pretty sort of fantasy architecture, a sort of combination of Cinderella's castle and French Seventeenth- and Eighteenth-century Rococo and Baroque architectures, with an impregnable dome of semi-self-aware panels surrounding it. They had designed and built it only a few hundred years after their landing.

Once the surviving crew and principal passengers had realized that they, and the other humans they had brought with them in cryogenic storage, would never leave the planet Thomàon, they had felt a combination of despair and freedom.

At the first, despair had reigned—but then Paul had discovered certain properties of the jelly used by one of the self-aware alien races upon the planet, the Scarabées, and had enhanced it with an admixture of genetic material that gave them all a surprising health and longevity—and then, with further modifications that allowed the surrounding technology to record their memories nightly, practical immortality.

Then were they gripped more by glorious freedom than despair, and designed a city beyond all cities—a limited city, a central city, a city that would bind the entire human race to them. *No* other place was to be made to be safe from the Grillons during the Season.

The Grillons could destroy limestone and even marble with ease. Even the sumptuous palaces of the Twelve, scattered across the planet, provided little shelter, come the Season.

The second significant feature of the limestone was that the water table had worn, over the countless eons, an enormous aquifer that ran underneath not only the moraine area of the city, but an immense area below that part of the continent, providing both an impregnable water source for the city during the Season, and a hiding place in the caverns below it.

The sudden, appallingly violent storms of the first few Seasons had terrified the new colonists, freshly wakened from a cryogenic slumber, and left their numbers literally decimated.

At first, the storms had been the only danger during the Season; the Grillons had not yet developed a taste for hunting humankind during such times.

Then, after only a few decades, as the human population began to replenish itself, the attacks by the Grillons began—only a few deaths at first, seemingly accidental, but then increasing in frequency and violence until to be outside the Silver City during the Season was to guarantee that one would be hunted down, tortured, and killed—and one's remains used as a trophy, preserved in the beautiful, delicate structures that the Grillons built to raise their young.

It was as if the sub-sentient race were using the dead bodies—preserved in a sort of extruded amber-like substance—to teach their young what to hunt for.

Fortunately, the Grillons didn't go underground, not unless they were following prey. Their nests were built above ground, and unless they were raising their young, they lived outdoors, on the surface, hunting the wildlife and even each other, if the population density grew great enough to prevent other meals.

Jacques sometimes compared humanity—not counting himself, of course, for he was above all that—to the race of Grillons: both were hordes of mindless, senseless eating and breeding machines with a taste for violence. The tale of both races was familiar, all too familiar.

Humanity had one advantage over the Grillons, that was all: intelligence.

Groups of humanity were occasionally able to reason out that they must focus their efforts on attacking external threats, instead of each other.

Briefly, anyway.

In the small hours of the night, Jacques had wondered if the human race had destroyed their home planet yet. They would; it was inevitable. When he had heard that humanity was traveling toward Thomàon, he smiled: no matter that the messages from the home world were a brief message of rescue for their lost colonists, he had no doubts as to whom wished to be rescued, and why.

In order to control this new, blind, all-consuming horde upon their arrival, certain changes needed to be made, and needed to be made immediately.

Those changes depended on whether or not Paul Hong had come up with a synthetic substitute for the elixir.

If he had: all could yet be saved from the encroaching Earth-born humans.

If not?

They would all be enslaved or destroyed.

Jacques whistled to himself as he descended through the tunnels and secret passages underneath the Silver City. He was almost positive that Paul had come up with a solution to the elixir question. Paul had never been stumped for this long before on any project that Jacques could remember. Therefore, he was hiding something.

Not lying, exactly—Paul couldn't lie—but concealing the truth. Misdirecting them.

It was time to force Paul to cough up the synthetic elixir. Likely, he was only trying to "perfect" some unnecessary feature of the improved elixir, and was reluctant to release the formula to the mechanique manufacturies under the city before he had perfected it.

After all, Paul *had* tried to do the same thing with the genetic modifications he had introduced into the natural elixir, the modifications that had given them all remarkable powers of healing, disease resistance, strength, endurance, and intellect, as well as helping extend their lives.

That was, he'd tried to hide the elixir from them, so he could "perfect" it.

The backward joints and extraordinary ability to jump were weird side effects, unintended. Paul had apologized profusely over the years for his "mistake." He'd had to introduce not only Scarabée but also Grillon genetics into the elixir in order to get the matrix of abilities that they'd asked of him. He'd thought he'd suppressed the modifications beyond what had been requested, but...

The only one who had actually been upset by the mods had been the Diva, LaFerme. The Assassin, Manon, had been fucking delighted. The rest of them had shrugged and said the changes were worth it in exchange for immortality.

Paul had wanted to perfect the formula to remove the unintended consequences, but Delphine talked him out of it: the people he was experimenting on were dying horribly, she argued, and the existing mods were a great eighty-percent solution. It was time for him to move on to the next research task, which was at the time—if Jacques remembered correctly—backing up their memories via ordinateur network.

Again, with the ordinateur network, Paul had tried to push for a better solution, one that didn't require REM sleep in order to record the day's memories, fearing that valuable memories might be lost if one were killed before one could sleep.

And once again, Delphine had been sent in to talk him out of wasting his time on refining a solution that already worked, when they needed him to move on to the next thing...and the next.

The synthetic elixir project had been going on forever. But enough was enough: Paul needed to wind up the project and get the elixir manufactured before the Earth-based humans arrived and it was too late to turn the Gold Stars into an elite cadre of warriors, able to resist—suppress—and even destroy the newcomers from Earth, as necessary to protect Thomàon.

And, because Corentin and Delphine had allied themselves with Grand-père and therefore were completely and utterly unreliable, that meant Jacques was the only guy left who could, or would, kick Paul in the ass and make him release the formula.

Armand would just kill Paul and take what he wanted. Not a good plan.

Don't kill the goose that lays the golden eggs.

Jacques took one of the tunnels from the Castle of the Silver Spire underneath the city and down into the caverns, descending past the first layers of stairs and walkways, the ones that looked like they belonged in an ancient sci-fi movie. His boots echoed on the metal, clang-clang, clang-clang, as he jogged along them.

Paul's prison was, no surprise, more than a little difficult to get to. The high moraine that the Silver City was built on meant that there was more than a little descending to do before Paul reached the water table.

The air in the caverns was damp and cold, smelling like mildew, that was, if mildew were made of minerals.

Jacques wore a red gem on a brooch on his shoulder. It looked like some kind of medal, but contained his second-factor authenticator as well as some other useful gadgetry. Currently, its GPS function meant that it flashed red whenever he was meant to turn from his current path: once for left, twice for right, three times to warn him to stop. It stored a map of the caves under the city, including the best paths down to the reservoir. He had it set to take him on an indirect route—never the same one twice—to take him to Paul.

In the dull red flashes of light, he caught glimpses of the caverns around him: dangling drips of stone, fissures in the high cavern roofs, the sudden enclosure of a tunnel cut through the rock, long-dead lights that hadn't been activated in thousands of years, darker streaks staining the pale stone as water dripped in from the surface, bringing iron and other minerals with it down into the dark.

Clang-clang, clang-clang.

He descended stairways, ducked under tunnel mouths, tramped along stone floors—splashed through them sometimes. The stone sculptures created by time were sometimes familiar, reminding him of caves he'd explored as a kid, and other times seemed alien, with the white calcium deposits reminding him of underground roots or the frost that hung off tree branches when he was a kid, before the temperatures rose. Pools of water surrounded by layers of built-up mineral deposits looked like some kind of funky paisley pattern. There were even areas where two layers of stone drips had formed, with blood-red platforms of iron-colored deposits balanced on thinner pillars, and long white strings of calcium deposits from above—a landmark he always remembered. One of the white calcium drips there used to look like a sort of Venus statue, the prehistoric Earth kind with big boobs and hips.

It wasn't there anymore; Armand had broken off one of the stalactites nearby and smashed it off its pillar, laughing hysterically and pointing at the smashed goddess below. The pieces had later disappeared—but Jacques still remembered the spot, pausing there as he reached it.

He had a brief moment of second-guessing—what the fuck was he doing, allying himself with Armand?—reminded himself that he was going to double-cross the fucker at the earliest opportunity, and jogged onward.

The tunnels grew narrower as he descended; they had had to be cut through the stone that ran alongside the edge of the reservoir, to provide stability. Otherwise, one good earthquake could have peeled the stairway off the wall of the enormous cavern, and they would have been screwed.

Finally, he reached the stairs, an enormous double-helix of steel stairs that ran down the last thousand meters or so, down to the edge of the reservoir.

A pole ran down the center of the stairs. Jacques tugged on a pair of gloves—one of them low-friction and the other a grip glove—from an inner pocket, then grabbed the cold, enameled metal with the left-hand, frictionless glove, and slid downward like he was on a fireman's pole, down a hundred meters to a small circular platform.

He scooted around the platform until he found the missing panel, lowered himself through with his right-hand grip glove, then grasped the pole again underneath the panel.

He dropped another hundred feet downward into the dark.

Below him was a dull blue glow accompanied by the usual faint humming echo. The gondoliers still navigated the cavern and sang their songs, even as the Season raged above, and humanity planned to consume itself—one way or another.

Jacques's brooch flashed three times as he slid, and he caught a glimpse of a Scarabée on the stairs as he fell. In the red light, it was impossible to tell the color of the shell. Had it been copper-colored or pearlescent?

Too soon, the round shape was gone.

He landed on the next platform, his boots echoing on the metal. He paused, listening for footsteps, and heard the thin, multi-pedal sound of a Scarabée delicately descending. If it was Madame Opale and she was headed toward Paul's prison, all the better—as long as he had time to talk to Paul first.

And if it was one of the Scarabées that reported to Grandpère?

He didn't want to have to kill one of the Scarabées. He had before; it had been repugnant in a way that killing another human being wasn't. He wasn't sure why.

But if he had to, he would.

He jumped again, and again, the faint blue light becoming brighter and the humming a little louder—but neither was ever more than faint.

Finally, when he landed, he landed on stone with a thump. The indiscriminate hum of the upper tunnel resolved itself into songs, songs that ranged from a deep, moaning bass to the highest of piping whistles, sounding almost like a church pipe organ—if churches had a hundred pipe organs playing at once, that was.

Jacques's brooch flashed three times. In front of him was the staircase proper. In the dull glow, he managed to work his way around it without tripping, then ducked under the low, irregular arch that led from the stairwell to the main reservoir without hitting his head.

It had taken him thousands of years to master *that* trick. He still flinched every time he passed under it.

The reservoir opened up in front of him, an enormous cavern that held only a millionth of the water of the full aquifer. It was down here that Paul had first found the elixir, and it was here that his prison had been built.

The gondoliers lazed on the surface of the water, throwing off their dull blue glow—a chemical effect like that of the fireflies, but not as flashy. They looked like tapeworms, and had rows of airholes along their sides that gasped and sang to each other. A few of them swam toward him, hoping that he would offer them a treat—meat, fish, seaweed, anything organic.

Jacques checked his pockets, found a package with some of the candy that was always thrown at parades during the Season, unwrapped a piece, and chucked it as far out onto the water as he could. The gondoliers whistled and puttered toward the candy, nudging it with their flat, ribbony coils, playing with it—singing songs of praise, no doubt, as the sweet candy melted into the water.

Underneath the gondoliers, the glow of their light revealed bulges and lumps in the water that looked more like the bulges of color in a lava lamp.

If only humanity were more like the gondoliers than the Grillons: stupid, non-violent, comfortable living in a limited, stoic environment, non-competitive.

Jacques looked around the cavern. A half-built, half-carved path led along the walls above the water, a ledge wide enough to drive a golf cart. The start of the path was half-hidden, or at least had been, until the turning of the years had worn a trail in the limestone.

The cart was gone.

That meant someone was visiting Paul. Likely Delphine.

But was she alone, or was Corentin with her?

Chapter 14

A Man of Noble Calling

Some are born great, some achieve greatness, and some have greatness thrust upon 'em—or thrust into their hands, anyway.

The roof of the basement under the apartment building was low, and Corentin had to duck a little to keep the support beams from bashing him in the head. He whistled. It was fine to make noise now; everyone else in the basement was dead, and the actual residents of the apartment house were more likely to sing his praises than report him to the Gold Stars.

He tossed his knife and caught it. It was coated with neurotoxin and would have sent him back to the resurrection chamber if he'd missed.

He didn't miss. He never missed.

The thing was, Corentin was nuts. He knew it, and privately had admitted it to himself a long time ago. Both he and his twin brother were nuts—as nutty as a fallout shelter full of squirrels.

They had their roles, Corentin as King, and Marks Lemure as Warden. And while they had grown up as identical twins, by the time they had boarded the *Téméraire*, their appearances had diverged, as had their tempers—Marks dying his hair brown to match his darker and more brooding moods, Corentin bleaching his hair to match his more cheerful and (some said) reckless ones.

And growing out his mustache, which had always been lighter and more golden.

Most of the crew hadn't even known Corentin and Marks were related, to begin with. Corentin had been a geneticist—if he could be called that, now. He was the one who was supposed to study alien species, but found himself bored with it, especially after Paul had moved in on his specialty. Marks, on the other hand, had gone in for geology and archaeology; he'd stuck with his chosen field, more or less, using the Warden job as cover for what he was really up to.

Delphine had known they were twins; she was one of those women it was impossible to lie to. And she had eventually wormed the truth out of him—or he had wanted to confess. He couldn't remember now which it was.

Didn't matter.

At the basement door, he stopped, wiped his boots on a fiber mat at the bottom of the steps, and checked his overalls. They were white and cast off stains. It was some damn gunk that Paul had made, coating the fabric. It made the cloth shed dirt, dust, oils, grits, and other materials like water off a duck's back.

Even blood.

Convenient.

Even after all the work Corentin had been doing that day, his overalls still looked pretty clean; he brushed a handful of red dust off the surface. That Paul! He was always up to something new and cool.

Corentin, well, he'd decided to take his specialization in a different direction, once it was clear that he was always going to be number two in genetics.

Still whistling, he climbed the stairs, jumping up them two at a time.

He'd tried one thing and another during the little "breaks" that Armand always gave him and Delphine from ruling the planet. He'd tried becoming a painter, a poet, and a philosopher (but he had no patience for writing his ideas down, which felt like little more than moving commas around); he'd spent a few decades womanizing, man-izing, and personne-izing, but had found his lovers boring; he had been a playwright for a short period when outrageous gore-fests were the style (*far* less boring than poetry or philosophy); when the style had passed, he had gone vagabonding over the planet to try to learn more about the Grillons and why they erupted into violence every Season. As far as he could tell, it was because they got bored—and who could blame them?

But then Carlton, the White Gentleman, had overstepped his bounds by killing Etoile.

She wasn't one of the Twelve; she was born and bred of unmodified colonist stock. Nevertheless her death had shattered Marks, who had gone so far as to *marry* her. When they had found out that Armand was behind the ugly killing—Carlton had drained her of blood, too, just to be an ass—then the fault lines had been drawn.

Armand on one side, Marks on the other.

Others might see the situation as being more complex, but it really wasn't.

Grandpère had his schemes. Jacques tried to play both sides. Paul Hong was insane, and resented the fact that Grandpère had put limits on his research. The others sided with Grandpère most of the time, but like any good family, switched sides and slept around as it pleased them.

But the real conflict, the engine of hate, came down to Marks and Armand. If they hadn't hated each other, Armand wouldn't have had Etoile killed.

And Corentin would never have known his true destiny.

Because the first time that the others needed someone killed after Carlton had been annihilated, something really blatant and indiscreet, which was not really Manon's style, whom did they turn to?

Why, Grandpère had practically shoved Carlton's old blood-draining knives into Corentin's hands, begging him to kill for the good of the Twelve, saying:

"No one would suspect *you*."

After his first kill as the White Gentleman, Corentin had felt happiness for the first time in his life. Oh, he'd *thought* he'd felt that emotion before, but now he knew that what he'd felt before was a dusty, dull, boring echo of what he'd felt after that first kill.

He'd found his true calling, and it had warmed the cockles of his heart.

When he had confessed it to Delphine, she had punched his arm and said, "Big surprise, psycho. Just don't get caught."

"What fun would that be?"

Her eyes had gone soft and distant, thinking—speculating. "You should see if Marks will switch off with you. You're twins, you know. He might go for it. A little makeup, and you could pass for each other."

He'd grinned at her. "Would you fuck Marks if he looked like me?"

She rolled her eyes. "No, but I'd fuck you if you looked like Marks. *God.* I know he's your brother, but he's such a downer."

The plan had meant giving up one of his knives to his brother, as well as whipping him into a frenzy about Etoile. Marks was always having to be talked into things, but Corentin was used to it. Fortunately halving the number of blood-drinking knives didn't reduce Corentin's pleasure in his kills, and it *was* nice to have backup, to be able to show up in public at the same time that Marks was making a kill—and vice versa.

Marks didn't enjoy himself as much as Corentin did, but he was (Corentin had to admit) the *slightly* better killer. Marks didn't let himself get distracted.

In short, the White Gentleman gag had been going splendidly and had taught Corentin many valuable skills, which he had only just employed in the basement, both to lure the Gold Stars into it, and to kill each one of them individually (except for the one who had shot his companion, dammit) and walk out with not a drop of blood on him.

Fun times.

Corentin emerged onto the main floor of the building. He felt eyes on him, on his white coveralls and his white mask—no crown, just the shiny sharp teeth: what passed for the full regalia of the White Gentleman, who usually went in disguise, at least when he wasn't killing.

He felt the watchers' fear, and it was delicious.

When he reached the top of the stairs, he found that one of the doors leading out onto the main-floor entrance was open, looking into an apartment kitchen. No one was inside the kitchen, but at the far end was a sliding panel door next to a large wall calendar decorated with a picture of Madame LaFerme. He could see the dim silhouette of someone standing beyond the crack. The entrance hall smelled—aside from the smell of blood and entrails that he'd brought up with him—like fried onions. He heard them hissing in a pan.

Still staring into the kitchen, he announced, "Someone ought to call the authorities. There seems to have been an accident downstairs…a *severe* accident. I'd hate for someone to slip and fall in all that blood."

His voice came out of the mask distorted, his words not only taking on a different tone, but no longer synchronized with the words as they came out of his lips. It was a good way to disguise his voice, but it always made him feel like he was being subtitled.

The silhouette gasped and stepped away from the crack in the door.

Corentin walked toward the double glass doors of the building, half off their hinges. The glass was shattered and muddy footprints had been tracked all over the place. Tsk, tsk. The Gold Stars had made a real mess as they had come into the building—they ought to be written up for it.

He shook his head sadly, knowing that they wouldn't be. There was just no justice in the world.

He stopped in front of the doors, turned, and gave his audience a bow—nobody important, but the *style* was what made this sort of thing so much fun—then swept through the doors and out onto the street.

A patrol of Gold Stars was crossing the street down the block.

He whistled through his mask—which was programmed to amplify the sound into a piercing shriek. He had their attention in a second.

The words "the White Gentleman!" echoed down the street.

Wishing he had a cape to flourish, Corentin waved, backed away from the façade of the building, crouched, and jumped—to the sound of running feet echoing down the street.

He flew upward. He wasn't the best jumper of the Twelve, not by a long shot. That was Manon, no debate. But he did all right. And of course even the cheapest tenement in the Silver City had been built to certain requirements, with easy-to-find handholds all the way up.

The Gold Stars couldn't follow and wouldn't be able to keep up, but they ran inside the building, nevertheless. Corentin watched them for a moment, thinking they looked like the Keystone Cops.

Something caught his eye and he froze for a moment: one of the officers had a red eye on the side of his neck, just above his collar.

No, not just an eye—a mask with a red eye.

Wasn't that the symbol for Armand's troop, Les Yeux? He couldn't remember. He'd have to ask Delphine. He tried to remember whether any of the ones he'd killed had had the eye on their necks. He couldn't remember; sometimes when he had more than five or six people to kill at once, it all tended to fade into a blur.

He ran for the edge of the roof and leapt. So far, things had been going according to plan: disrupt, mislead, sew chaos so that Armand couldn't just take the city quietly overnight. Don't let him have the last word, as it were, when it came to violence.

Then check in with Grandpère in the morning.

It was morning—at least, most of the dome tiles were lit up, although a few seemed to have gone dull and dark—and Corentin had ensured that, if nothing else, the transfer of power (illegitimate as it was) would not be peaceful.

He led his pursuers around by the nose for another fifteen minutes, dropped a few patio chairs on the Gold Stars, stared through a few windows at a couple of little kids, tapping at the glass until they woke up, shouted "boo!" and hissed at them to keep from laughing, smashed a couple of mechaniques—that sort of thing.

Then he took off his "disguise" and changed into a stolen set of work trousers and a pink satin festival blouse with lace at the cuffs. He smeared dirt on his face to give himself a black eye, picked up a fallen mask off the street—it was busted all to shit, a boot print on the cheap white plastic—tied it on top of his head, then started slogging toward the Louvre. He left the overall and vampire mask behind for the peons to find and scare themselves with.

He stopped for a minute at an all-night breakfast café to check the news and get a cup of shitty fake-coffee. The glorious uprising was glorious but (as per the news station, now no doubt controlled by Armand's thugs) not going quite as smoothly as it could, and citizens were advised to shelter in place where possible. Also, Grandpère was dead; long live Grandpère!

So Armand hadn't had Grandpère's heir killed and was supporting the story that "Grandpère" was just a series of wise old philanthropists who just wanted the best for Thomàon, and that a new guy had been appointed by the Twelve.

Odd. Unexpected. Nonsensical. But okay.

If Corentin had been Armand, he would have had the heir killed and the previous Grandpère denounced as some kind of traitor.

But that's the problem about guys with plans. Sometimes they got so in love with a plan that they couldn't update it on the fly.

Grandpère's death wouldn't change much.

There was a resurrection chamber under the Castle of the Silver Spire and one under the Louvre. With his heir already conscious, all that needed to be done were to upload the last of Grandpère's memories. It was a quick process, so the new guy should be up to date by now already. Good to go.

Corentin stumbled as he walked, staggering slightly, stopping to lean against buildings, breathing deeply and bending over as if he were ready to puke. He was stopped by a couple of Gold Stars and searched, but not well enough to find his knife. Which was good for them; they lived.

After a few blocks of dragging his ass down the white cement, breathing hard and wobbling on his feet, he was getting bored. And bored was not something Corentin could cope with.

Fortunately, he felt the hairs raise on the back of his neck, as if he were being followed or—even better—being watched.

His spirits rising with his interest, he began making plans for how to spot, catch, and kill his follower.

Unfortunately, at the end of the next block, he discovered that it was only Manon following him from over the rooftops, sailing overhead as Corentin crossed the street. He didn't even have the satisfaction of knowing he'd spotted them when they didn't want to be spotted; they'd waved as they flew above him.

A little later, there were two drunks, a handsome man in a pink satin shirt and a leggy personne in a torn, sequinned bodysuit stumbling along the street, arguing about how many drinks they'd had last night and whether the number was more or fewer than the year before.

The Louvre was just reopening to the public. The two drunks stumbled inside and the maze of exhibits soon swallowed them up.

The rioters didn't seem to have made their way into the museum the night before. A small army of mechaniques was rolling along the floor, but they were not cleaning or making repairs, only following the guests around to make sure they didn't start any problems.

Arm in arm, Corentin and Manon walked into one of the toilet stalls, each of which were separated from the next by floor-to-ceiling dividers and doors. The curious reason behind this was that there was a network of secret tunnels that ran outside of human view, in the interstices between walls, below floors, above ceilings—supposedly for the mechaniques—and their openings were often concealed within the stalls.

This secret network was not entirely secret; during the Season, citizens who were not native to the Silver City often became obsessed with looking for entrances. Sometimes they found a passage and smashed their way inside—but the locals to the city, who were perhaps a quarter of the population, knew that one could make little progress through the passages without a thumbprint and a second-factor authenticator to open doors for them.

Corentin's authenticator used to be in a medal he wore on his shoulder; now it was in the hilt of his knife, blood red even when it was not coated with blood.

Manon kept theirs on a cord around their neck and kept it tucked away, even when they were killing, which Corentin had never understood.

Corentin had never really understood Manon, not in any of their incarnations. Whatever thought processes went on behind the mostly silent façade were a mystery to him. It was as though the wide variety of bodies that Manon chose for their hosts had rubbed off on their mind, wearing off the unpolished surfaces. If ever there were a god with the personality of a pebble, it was Manon.

After a comedic bit of "after you—no, after you" between the two of them, Corentin took out his knife and held it against the flush sensor on the toilet.

The wall panels opened, splitting half and half around the toilet along a line of tiles. They both turned sideways and slid through.

The tunnel behind the toilet was narrow but clean and cool, with filtered air. They slid sideways through the tunnel until it joined up with a wider service corridor. Grandpère being fond of employing the Scarabées, it was necessary to build the service corridors through the Louvre a bit wider than they otherwise would have been, to permit the oddly shaped species to move through them. They did not see any of those creatures, however, and only encountered a few mechaniques hauling garbage and cleaning supplies.

After moving through the corridors for the length of several city blocks along their wing of the museum, silently they turned off the main passage and climbed a heavy ladder upward several stories.

They stepped out into a closet for mechaniques, checked a spy camera to make sure no one was watching, then stepped onto the upper floor.

They were inside Grandpère's private rooms in the penthouse; or, rather, Grandpère's private collection of objets d'art. His tastes were depressingly unoriginal: bronze reproductions of Rodin statues, a copy of the Mona Lisa, reproductions of several Earth painters who liked to layer on oil paint with a trowel.

The only piece of art up here that Corentin actually liked was Rodin's Gates of Hell, full of twisted figures trying to escape the door upon which they were sculptured. It was funny: why would anyone try to escape a bronze door, if you were bronze? He imagined one of the three sculpted figures at the top of the door—which couldn't open—jumping off the door and smashing onto the tile floor underneath it, then trying to drag itself away from its fate. Pointless.

Better to just grin and bear it. Why not put the same amount of effort into having a good time with all the other bronze sculptures trapped on the door with you?

Being trapped on Thomàon, as far as Corentin was concerned, was the world's biggest game of Fuck, Marry, Kill.

Suddenly, Manon stopped beside one of the other Rodin reproductions, the one with the group of people standing in rags, looking starved and despairing or starved and blank in the face, their hands dangling in defeat and ropes around their necks as they walked.

They touched the sculpted hand of one of the figures, the one with no facial expression whatsoever, then put their head against its shoulder. Corentin shrugged and walked toward the center of the room, where a wheelchair sat overlooking the big window over the garden. The new heir stood with his hand on the back of the wheelchair, which was empty.

"Hey, Gramps," Corentin said as they crossed the floor. Neither he nor Manon were in the habit of making noise as they walked, not even with boots on tile.

The heir turned and glanced at them, then turned back to the window. The man's face was a cipher, a blank. Grandpère's new faces always were, the first few days after he'd changed over.

Manon went to stand beside him, not touching him—but Corentin was reminded of how they'd stopped next to the Rodin. The two of them looked out over the garden together, either considering the wreckage or remembering the way it used to look. Rioters and fires had done a number on the place, toppling trees, slashing greenery, smashing greenhouses, even turning over the rocks on the ground.

The ring of statues dedicated to the Twelve had been toppled, with only Armand left standing.

Corentin snorted. Oh, yeah. Armand had a *special* touch.

"The insurrection has officially been disrupted and delayed," Corentin said. "Now what?"

Grandpère shook his head like a dog trying to shake a fly off its nose. "I'm trying to work it out, kid. I died without getting a backup yesterday. Give me a minute."

Having said that, he went back to staring out the window.

Corentin shrugged and started wandering around the room. There weren't any surprises; he'd been inside the rooms a million times and Grandpères never changed anything. But it was better than standing next to the window to soak up the sad and sorrowful vibe.

The thing was, he could have trashed everything in the room, and within a month or two, it all would have been fixed or reproduced. Copied. Nothing in the Louvre was an original. Everything set out in front of the public was a copy, a clone—easily replaced.

Just like the Twelve.

Corentin found himself next to the group of figures that Manon had touched. He considered the figures, trying to understand what Manon or anybody else could see in them that held any appeal whatsoever, then took out his knife and carved "Kick me" on the back of one of the figures. It might be interesting to see if it had been repaired or replaced the next time he came through.

Always thinking ahead, that was him.

Grandpère finally cleared his throat and Corentin walked back over to the pair—the trio, if you included the empty wheelchair.

The old man, who was not quite as old as he had been the day before, said:

"Lemure is at Versailles, having been butchered by Armand somewhere underneath the opéra yesterday during the uprising. It was off the network, wherever it was."

He pressed his lips together and lowered his head, his shoulders shuddering.

Corentin always had issues trying to read other people's emotions from their expressions and body language. The nuances escaped him.

Grandpère looked up. He was still pressing his lips together. "Armand's death was recorded within the *Téméraire*, early this morning. Before he had slept. He was also routed to Versailles for resurrection, that being the only one of our locations that has any of the elixir left."

Corentin chewed on the inside of his cheek. If Marks hadn't left the resurrection center before Armand had arrived, he was probably having himself a hell of a time torturing the fucker to death. But that would use up more of the elixir, and reduce everyone else's margin of safety significantly. Three doses gone. How many did that leave remaining?

"Any word from Delphine?" he asked. She had been supposed to go down to Paul Hong's prison and get definite word from him on whether he had developed a synthetic elixir or not.

Grandpère nodded. "She said he confirmed that the elixir had been developed. She didn't say she had it in hand yet; she was going to take a shower and change clothes first."

Corentin rolled his eyes. The woman hated to *stink*, worse than she hated death.

He asked, "And? What next? Have you noticed that some of the panels have failed? What's going on out there?"

Grandpère's facial expression changed, from repressed emotion number *one* to repressed emotion number *two*, whatever that was. "Lemure will ensure that Armand is restrained for at least a day, hopefully longer. As you know, the chambers cannot be set to refuse a valid resurrection request, so Lemure has set up an improvised solution."

He released the back of the wheelchair in front of him. "I am, unfortunately, not at a position to be treated with the same deference and trust as—as I had been yesterday. Legally, I occupy the same position as ever, but my recent death has changed matters somewhat. On the one hand, we have an opportunity here to retake the city from the troops that Armand controls; on the other hand, I suspect that I may not have the leverage that I need in order to do so.

"This leaves us in the following position: If possible, we will run out the clock, as it were, on Armand's resurrections. He will use up the last of the elixir in the Versailles facility, and then be routed to another facility, if any still contain any samples of the elixir. Then we can do with him what we did with Carlton—we can force entry into the systems and delete his data. I hope we can convince Paul not to restore Armand's memories from a backup. We then should be able to handle the other emergencies in good time, and return to a more regular existence."

Manon swallowed audibly, then cracked their neck. Carlton, the White Gentleman, had been a particular enemy of theirs—a bully. For someone whose genius was at killing without leaving a trace, Manon could be particularly easy to push around.

"Okay," Corentin said. "But if that's not possible? What if Paul decides to activate the synthetic elixir ahead of schedule, or if the other cases get found and plugged in to one of the systems?"

Grandpère gave a little wave of his hand. "Planning for that circumstance is of less importance. If Armand manages to put his piece back upon the board, then we will have to drop everything else and respond to his plans as best we can."

"We should kill Paul, at least for a couple of days," Corentin said. "I'll bet my bottom dollar that every one of Armand's plans goes straight through Paul and getting him to cough up that synthetic elixir."

Grandpère's expression resolved into something comprehensible: an ironic smile. "In this situation, Paul is the king of the chessboard. Removing him means the game is over—even I cannot get into the systems he has designed."

Corentin lifted his eyebrows. If Paul were a better programmer than old Pete Johnson, software mogul of Earth, it was news to him. "Yeah?"

Grandpère faced the window, the dull morning glow from inside the dome reflecting onto his pale white wrinkled skin. In a less authoritative voice, one that almost sounded impressed, he said, "He has been playing with a new type of encryption. I have no idea how he thought of it. I haven't figured it out yet. It's fascinating."

Corentin rolled his eyes again. This new body of Grandpère's had even more of a tendency than usual not to get to the point. "So we don't kill Paul until we get his encryption figured out, got it. And you say that we're waiting to find out whether we need to deal with Armand before we start making plans, which I'm going to take as meaning that you've worked out half a dozen plans and are waiting to see what happens before you confuse our poor little brains with too much information."

Grandpère gave him a dorky little bow. "As you say."

Corentin looked up at the ceiling, saw a shadow lingering overhead, wondered if there was a camera up there. Of course there was; the whole conversation was being recorded.

"So I'm going to ask my original question again," he said. "What next? What do you want me to do?"

Grandpère put his hand on the back of the wheelchair again. "I want you to bring your brother back to the city. He's digging in his heels, says we won't need him here, and that he doesn't want to leave Armand's corpse unprotected."

Corentin shrugged. "Sounds rational to me. Why not just leave him there?"

Grandpère extended an arm, hardly twisted by age at all, toward the window. "You asked earlier whether I had noticed that some of the panels were not working, yes?"

"Yeah. That, plus the way that the smoke built up at the top of the dome last night. That's not good. What's going on? Some kind of virus thing that Armand set up via Jacques? Or just bad luck?"

"Bad luck," Grandpère said. "Or fate, I do not know. It's the Grillons. They're breaking through."

Corentin felt his skin prickle and tighten. He blinked and found that he'd taken a step backward from the wheelchair:

"The Grillons can't break through."

Grandpère coughed dryly into his elbow. "I'm afraid that our plans have changed, Corentin. We need to gather ourselves together. I am abandoning Versailles. In fact, I am taking down its defenses, so that the Grillons will have another target to focus on for now. Here, in the Silver City, we will begin pulling our people under the city to the old safe rooms."

Corentin's head spun. On top of everything with Armand's latest scheme, there were the Grillons to contend with. What else could go wrong?

Worse, he imagined himself trapped in one of those innumerable survival shelters, with filtered air, filtered water, canned food, and barely room to lie down in—in shifts. Christ, he'd rather die than have to spend the rest of the Season in one of them.

"Are they even operational? Stocked? Is there air?"

Grandpère raised a hand. "You needn't worry about all that. I have kept them in order, well enough for a situation such as this, at any rate. Old habits die hard with me, you know that." He paused. "I have also kept the *Téméraire* in good order, for you and Delphine and a few of the others to retreat to, if needs must."

Corentin felt his shoulders relax away from his ears. Being stuck in the *Téméraire* wouldn't be pleasant, but there was more room and he wouldn't be stuffed in like a sausage. Plus it was familiar.

He took a breath, got a grip on himself, and said, "So you want me to make a mad dash to Versailles, drag Marks out before the Grillons overwhelm the place, and leave Armand there to whatever torture Marks set up for him—or, better yet, whatever the Grillons can come up with. Is that about right?"

Grandpère lifted an eyebrow. "Almost. There is one additional detail that I have not yet mentioned. I want you to draw the insurrectionists with you to Versailles. I have already been releasing information to the public that should have the effect of enraging that part of the public that sympathizes with Armand. And, one hopes, they will try to chase you down and kill you, or at least capture you. You will 'accidentally' reveal the path from the back of the Jardin here—"

He gestured toward the far colonnade to the right, past the toppled statues of the Twelve, and which butted up against the Great Dome.

"—And lead them out into the open, where the Grillons can do your dirty work," Corentin finished for him. "An unfortunate accident."

Grandpère leaned his head to one side, then the other, then rolled his shoulders, cracking the bones. He had a tendency toward arthritis. "Just so. And if you happen to leave some evidence of the White Gentleman having led our lambs astray, so much the better."

Corentin thought about it. If he wasn't careful, it might tie him, King Corentin, to his other persona, the White Gentleman.

Which might curtail his fun down the road; he wasn't about to spoil his big reveal on a simple battle with Armand. That wouldn't be nearly epic enough.

But he had a plan in mind that might work.

He nodded. "I think I got it. Stir up trouble as Corentin, lead the leaders of the uprising after me toward Versailles, grab Marks, and have him start slaughtering people in order to get to me. Make it look like Armand is turning against the Gold Stars, maybe."

Manon was cleaning under their fingers with a small, ordinary penknife, not really paying attention.

It reminded Corentin about a not-so-minor point, however.

"Only one problem," he said. "I don't have the other White Gentleman's knife. Marks had to have it on him when Armand cut him down, and as far as I know, nobody's found Marks's old body yet."

Corentin had spoken to Grandpère, but it was Manon who reached into their ragged, sequinned festival clothing and pulled out a sheathed knife, tossing it in Corentin's direction.

He caught it and pulled the blade half out. It looked like the twin of his own, all right, but it was too new. No blood ground into the join between blade and hilt. The hilt was set with a red gem to match Corentin's knife, but it didn't hold a second-factor authenticator the way Corentin's did. Marks kept his in a locket with Etoile's picture covering it.

One of the twin brothers was a romantic, and it wasn't Corentin.

"What's this?"

Manon cleared their throat. "Copy from Paul. In case the White Gentleman needed to kill while both you and Marks were in public. Pointless now. Have it."

"Where's the real one?"

"Left it for Marks. In case he came back."

"*Where*?"

"Under the opéra, down in some of the old walled-off tunnels. Armand bricked him up in a wall. Spotted some bricks that looked darker and checked it out. Left the body there with the knife."

Corentin snorted. "For the love of God, Montresor! That sounds like Armand's style, all right. Okay, Gramps, I have my job. I'll check back in when I can, but you'll know we made it back if you start seeing more bodies with one-eyed-mask tattoos piling up on the streets."

Grandpère said, "Understood," in a dry tone that Corentin took to be humor. Manon said nothing. Corentin saluted and left through the same janitor's closet he came in.

Chapter 15

Simplicity Itself

AFTER THE ATTACK ON the royal box at the Opéra du Mendicant, Yvonne la Gorge had gone into hiding. Her method of concealing herself was simplicity itself: she had climbed across the front of the royal box to the one next to it, then crouched in the darkness with a small group of courtiers until the Gold Stars had been led away from the area by Marks Lemure's dramatic, bloody exit.

She had asked the courtiers not to lie if anyone asked about her, but not to volunteer information either. She had given them directions to the safest way out of the opéra, via a set of back stairs the actors used to pop up behind the audience during some of the more modern plays.

One of the women courtiers had hugged her—some people were just huggers—and then Yvonne had excused herself, climbing across to another balcony to hide, then another.

She wasn't worried about being seen. People tended not to look upward unless their gazes were directed there, and the spotlight that Armand had trained on the Royal Box had long since been switched off. The upper sections of the theater lay in shadow, punctuated only by the red glow of exit signs.

She made her way into one of the toilet stalls, then used her second-factor authenticator to open the secret panel behind it.

The others used red gems to "conceal" their authenticators. Yvonne had an object decorated with a red gem herself—a pocket-watch that she always carried with her. But the gem was just a piece of red glass. *Her* authenticator was hooked on her chatelaine, that was, a type of old-fashioned keychain, as a perfectly functional, and perfectly clear, magnifying glass.

Using her magnifying glass to peer at security panels and open them, she followed the secret mechanique corridors toward the back of the opéra. The corridors were perfectly clean and dustless, and she left no footprints. She climbed down an aluminum ladder in her soft-soled shoes, then stepped out backstage. She grabbed a crate full of sound equipment, hefted it, and walked out of a backstage door, nodding at a couple of Armand's peons as she passed. They didn't question her. Once out onto the street, she depositing the equipment in the back of an unguarded, self-driving delivery truck. She located the control panel near the truck's cargo door, and hit the release button. Then she watched the door close and the truck pull away. She headed one direction while the truck headed in the other.

The back of the opéra house smelled like weed and booze and sex. Most of the time the Silver City was spotlessly clean, tidied by machines. But during even an ordinary Season, it was impossible for the mechaniques to keep up.

As soon as she turned the corner, she gave her dress a couple of artful snips with the shears that she carried on her chatelaine. They were gold-colored and shaped like a stork and they could cut or stab through virtually anything, having been modified by Paul to conceal thin blades of the same stuff on the White Gentleman's knives.

Snip, snip!

She smeared dirt on her clothes and face, then forced herself to cry a few crocodile tears so she'd look properly smeared. She shook out her hair and rubbed some leaves in it—voilà; she was now merely another celebrant.

She slouched, changed her stride, and kept the tears coming as she walked down the alley toward a small, tree-covered park tucked between two white apartment buildings and across from a café with its windows shuttered with metal panels.

It was a nice park most of the year. The trees were big native ones, sort of a cross between ferns and elm trees, native flora that the Scarabées called *Kathra* or *Gazhra*. They shed little succulent slivers of leaflike greens that dried flat and disintegrated into powder. Their trunks were rubbery and a little rough, and if you pushed hard against one, it would sway and bounce. Get one to swaying, though, and the other Kathra around it would sway, too, swinging their branches around and dropping their silvery succulent leaves. She wasn't sure why they did it, but it was fascinating.

Sitting underneath them on one of the smooth, slightly curved limestone benches always made her feel watched, too, in a good way. Watched over.

She sat on one of the benches and dragged out her phone to check the news. Above her on the Great Dome, one of the tiles flared brightly, then went out. She considered the dull metal surface, saw a haze in the air, and took a sniff: smoke.

Even if the entire city were on fire, she shouldn't be able to *see* smoke. She should only be able to smell it if she were practically on top of it. The tiles should have cleaned the air of particles as soon as they rose upward.

An ominous omen.

The news agencies had fully gone over to Armand's side, and were calling for all citizens to report any sightings of Corentin, Delphine, or the Warden.

As for herself, Armand's new "reporters" had said simply that "famed historian, Yvonne la Gorge, who was visiting the Royal Box at the time that the People retook their own government, has disappeared and is wanted for questioning."

She hoped that meant the people who had helped shelter her weren't being slowly tortured to death, but she wasn't going to count on it. Armand's peons tended to go more than a little over the top.

Other than that: the Gold Stars had been "cleansed" and were now working in support of the insurrection; all political prisoners were being released and their records removed; some of the many sins of the previous régime were being exposed, mainly the treatment of prisoners at Shakes Prison.

Armand always did have a hard-on for anything that inconvenienced Marks Lemure.

A little more doom-scrolling, and then she turned off the phone and smashed it underfoot, kicking it under a pile of succulent tree slivers. She had other gadgets on her, but they didn't connect to the ordinateur network and would be a little more secure, a little harder to trace.

The only way of tracing her would be as she used her authenticator and it recorded her passage. And only Grandpère had the authority to review those records.

She stretched her back until the bones in her spine popped all the way up her neck, wished she had thought to bring something to snack on, and circled behind the café, where she let herself in through a narrow door leading upward to apartments—and then downward via another panel that she unlocked with her magnifying glass.

She had known that the insurrection was coming, and she knew it was going to get worse, not only because she knew her history both here and on Earth, but because Armand only had one playbook, and he followed it to a T.

Every. Single. Time.

With Armand, tactics changed; strategies, never.

Step one:

Build support among those who thought of themselves as being denied their "natural" rights, particularly the right to oppress everyone who had had the bad luck to be "below" them.

Step two:

Infiltrate the cops and other agencies of authority with fifth columnists.

Step three:

Fundraising.

Raising money was about more than increasing Armand's working funds, it was about knitting tighter the bounds of loyalty and culpability. Charitable givers often found themselves pressured to give up more than their spare cash, but secrets and loyalty as well. Armand *loved* to build support by exploiting wealthy pedophiles, sniffing out predators and feeding them fresh meat. He also liked controlling those who had received profitable public contracts.

Armand was wealthy enough not to need the funds; this step was mostly a blackmail research & development phase.

Step four:

Cough up a wad of conspiracy theories to capture people's attention and disconnect them from outside influence.

Armand never developed his "causes" first. *First* he researched his audiences and found a sweet spot of overlap between them, whoever they all felt most guilty about bullying. Internal inconsistencies in these theories were a feature, not a bug. The only real requirement was that the conspiracies would "explain" why it was perfectly rational to dehumanize the hated group.

Step five:

Set up an alternate method of communication, one that further isolated the members of Armand's new followers from everyone else around them.

This was usually a separate communication channel combined with some kind of recognition symbol, often a tattoo, that was, a more-or-less permanent marking that couldn't be easily gotten rid of, and which could be used as part of a blackmail campaign to keep control of anyone who wanted out.

Step six:

Begin propaganda operations.

Find the most acceptable members of Armand's current worshipers and send them out to get ordinary people to agree to one minor, seemingly in-consequential point, being sure to send further agents out for recruitment if they received any promising nibbles.

These operations had a second purpose: to reframe anyone who resisted Armand's peons into being seen as irrational. Armand particularly enjoyed telling those who didn't get sucked into his plans that they were "living in a bubble" and "needed to be more open-minded" and "less divisive."

Step seven:

Start raising trouble against the rule of law (that was, Corentin and Delphine in their current royal incarnations).

This step consisted of two different wings.

First, Armand's crew began using the previously set-up conspiracies to justify violent, irrational actions by true zealots. These were tests of current system capabilities—the actors were clearly nutcases, solitary, and disorganized, and were disavowed until it the system had been so degraded that it was safe not to do so. The poor idiots were canaries in the coal mine, testing public opinion and response.

The second wing consisted of using high-ranking officials targeted and recruited during the fundraising step—the pedophiles and their ilk—to overturn laws, saying that they were unjust toward the group who was doing most of the oppressing.

Step eight:

Unleash the shock troops and terrorists, and aim them toward vulnerable members of the current society.

Step nine:

Take practical control over public communications and openly harass anyone who disagreed with the current set of conspiracy theories.

Step ten:

Find the most public possible method of overturning the current government by capturing or killing Corentin and Delphine. Sometimes he had them murdered outright; other times, he kept them in prison and had them publicly executed.

He never just let them go. If they escaped, he would just escalate the levels of violence perpetrated by his followers, send out public messaging that the only way to "reunite" society was by cooperating with his thugs, and repeat as necessary.

Whenever the phrase "we all just need to get along" began to crop up in the media, Yvonne penciled in her schedule for the next uprising—and planned accordingly.

Armand was like a natural geyser. His eruptions only *seemed* sudden; they were actually quite predictable.

She had tried to explain this to Delphine once when she was drunk. Delphine had patted her hand patronizingly and said that it was a nice theory, but Armand wasn't actually predictable. He was *crazy*, and insanity didn't run on a schedule.

Yvonne hadn't tried again. Paul had listened, and Grandpère had listened, and poor Simone had listened, and confronted Armand about it.

And now Simone was dead. Permanently dead.

Yvonne made her way down into the darkness underneath the apartment building, following her way down along the walkways and stairs toward the reservoir, remembering poor Simone, who had thought herself so worldly and sophisticated, but who was actually an idealist at heart, the kind of person who believed confronting a homicidal psychopath in private was a good idea, because if it was done in public, they would just be stubborn about changing their mind.

None had been so blind as the Seer; but then, Simone and Armand had been friends as kids. She had thought she "knew" him in a way that no one else could. That he had loved her, as a friend. On some level, at least.

But what she had known was just the mask of a "poor, wounded soul" that Armand wore over his true face—if he had a true face, that was.

It had been Simone who had been the wounded soul. Armand had only to reflect it back to her, and she believed that he was as essentially good as she was, despite her talents and instincts telling her ever the contrary.

But then, they had all been blind in one way or another, over the years.

Through the tunnels and caverns under the city the Historian made her way, her thoughts turning as her feet did: ever downward.

When she reached the nearest stairs-slash-fireman's-pole down to the reservoir, she pulled out a cube of chalk to dust her hands. Once, a long time ago, she had tried to slide down the pole with sweaty hands and had given herself blisters that had hurt worse than anything she could remember. The next day she had started carrying chalk with her, in a small silver box on her chatelaine.

Every time she put on the chalk, she felt like a famous gymnast, a Nadia Comăneci or a Simone Biles.

She clapped her hands twice, then raised her hands over her head in a vee, jutting out her chest as she turned one direction, then the other. She laughed at herself, then grabbed the pole with her hands and between her soft-soled feet, and slid downward.

Grandpère had given her a mission, to monitor the news networks and report back on anything she found significant. She ignored the mission; it was a time-waster, designed to keep her out of his hair while he was up to something else. He had "people" for that sort of thing. She had warned him months ago when the reporters had started to be replaced by their Armand-sponsored counterparts; any additional monitoring was his own lookout.

This time, there was more at stake than one of Armand's petty revolutions; she didn't have time to run around and pretend to be Grandpère's lackey, as usual.

No, what she intended to do was something different.

She landed on a platform, circled around to the missing panel in the plate, and climbed down to the next section of pole.

A shred of her skirt got caught in the panel and she had to tear it loose. She made a mental note to tear off her skirts before she went this way next time, or at least change into pants.

She slid downward again, down and down until she had reached the water table of the reservoir. The stairwell led out onto a shallow steel platform overlooking a small, low section of the reservoir cavern.

A light flickered to life as she passed out of the stairwell. An ancient steel box was bolted onto the platform, a calcium-encrusted power and data cable leading back toward the stairwell. The box cast a shadow past the platform rail and out onto the softly glowing water, where it disappeared.

This location was only a minor checkpoint set up for water purity testing. There was a bigger station that opened onto a larger, more open section of the reservoir nearby, but it was the one near Paul's prison trailer, and it was likely being watched at the moment—or would be soon.

Yvonne walked to the edge of the platform at the top of a ladder that led down into the water, and sat down, taking off her shoes, then swinging her legs and banging her heels against the ladder rungs. The gondoliers were elsewhere at the moment, or the air would have been filled with the soft hum of their singing, as sophisticated as Bach's Art of the Fugue but as improvisational as an extraterrestrial Charlie Parker.

She kept up at it, however, and soon they began swimming toward her. The water brightened even as the motion-detecting light by the testing station flickered out.

She took a handful of wrapped parade candy out of her pocket, and loosened one of the wrappers. One of the gondoliers surfaced under her feet, its flat, wormy surface bulging out of the water until it brushed against her. The openings along its sides rippled, flashing brighter as they stretched wide.

She dug her toes into the rippled skin and scratched gently with them. The gondolier pressed harder against her feet, making a sighing half-whistle of satisfaction.

She tossed a sweet into the water in front of it. It nudged the sweet with a coil of its flesh, sending the candy drifting further out into the reservoir, where other gondoliers jostled it, passing it around so the sweetness would spread through the water.

The gondolier flattened itself into the water like a cat stretching in the sun, then rose back up to her feet again, whistling an upward note that sounded like a question: *Want a ride?*

She pocketed the rest of the candy and slid down onto the gondolier's back, keeping a grip on the ladder rail until she had lowered herself onto her knees.

The gondolier began swimming through the water, an undulation that somehow managed to keep Yvonne steady on its back. Brushing her hand against its side, she steered it toward a dark spot on the far edge of the cavern, and then inside the tunnel there.

The inside of the tunnel was dark, but the gondolier did not hesitate to go inside. In one place, the roof of the tunnel was very low, and she lay flat on the gondolier's back; in another, she had to cling to its ribbony flesh as the tunnel plunged into the water, sharp stones overhead sealing off the air. But it was only a short journey, and in a moment they had surfaced again, the gondolier waiting to make sure she was all right—waiting until she had taken a loud breath and patted its side.

It left her, finally, at the edge of a gravelly underground shore that lay in darkness—except for the glow of the gondolier's flesh—until Yvonne clapped twice, and the lights turned themselves on.

What they revealed was a small fabricated trailer that looked more like a walk-in refrigerator than the refuge it was. It had been built to control temperature and keep out the damp. It was an old storage area that they had built long ago, then forgotten—one that she had found a few dozen years ago while researching an ancient text, in other words, one of Delphine's old journals. It was where they had left their reserves of Earth seeds, fertilized ova, and digital copies of their records. Since then, she had worked with Paul and the Scarabées to make it into something more: a vault that contained the genetic wisdom of Thomàon, as complete as she, the Historian, could make it.

She *had* mentioned it to the others, but they had been distracted about something or other, and had never gotten around to investigating her discovery. They wouldn't have cared regardless, sneering at her for being such a "history nerd."

After a while, she decided not to remind them.

She let herself in with her magnifying glass, then sniffed the air: it was as scentless as the air on a mountaintop, and as dry. She woke up the ordinateur and checked the life-support status on the rows and rows of drawers filled with seeds, slides, Petri dishes, thumb drives, and more. It all looked good. A few of the Scarabées had visited while she was gone, and had withdrawn a copy of the code for coffee and cocoa plants. They didn't need to take any of the actual genetic material with them; Manon had found a way to translate RNA from data into chemical elements the Scarabées could understand. Now they just needed the data.

It was the Scarabées who had taught the Grillons to hate humanity, during the Season. Humanity had attacked too many Grillons during their mating and nesting season, and their numbers had started to decline; the Scarabées had made adjustments until the Grillon numbers held steady.

When humanity had discovered the gondoliers and attacked them, disgusted by their strangeness, the Scarabées had modified the gondoliers until their songs lowered themselves into the range of human hearing.

Then, suddenly, the gondoliers were seen as magical fairylike creatures, instead of giant, monstrous flatworms. Yvonne had persuaded Corentin and Delphine to seal off the stairs, saying that nobody needed to have access to the reservoir anyway: it was an easy corridor for elixir pirates and smugglers.

Also, Paul refused to change prison quarters without a fight, and the last thing anyone needed was to have *him* be found.

The Scarabées had even modified themselves, making themselves smaller and rounder, more feminine in appearance, so the humans around them would see them as harmless and cute.

Yvonne served as their ambassador, answering questions, giving context, pointing out that humans weren't *all* bad. But the patience of the Scarabées was wearing thin. They wanted their planet back, or at least to be able to control human genetics directly, instead of using Paul as an intermediary.

The Scarabées had received the signal from Earth, just as Grandpère had, and knew that time was running out.

Yvonne sat down to transfer her latest data to the systems in the hut, and to wait.

After a few hours, the door of the hut opened, and a Scarabée bumbled inside, her outer shell opalescent and shimmering, but also dotted with blood on shell, legs, and antennae. It was Madame Opale.

Yvonne rose to her feet, her heart in her throat. "Are you all right?" Then she remembered that Scarabée blood was not red—only fully human blood was.

Madame Opale rumbled in her deep voice, "It is the blood of men. Armand came and killed Grandpère."

"Both of them?"

Madame Opale's head-antennae curled up, then relaxed: a shrug. "No. The elder had sent the younger one away. He had anticipated trouble. And yet I do not think he anticipated Armand's intensity of violence. In the end, he told Armand where to find two of the cases of elixir."

Yvonne lifted her eyebrows, but said nothing, opening the door of a small closet and removing some alcohol wipes from inside a sealed packet.

Wiping down Madame Opale's smooth shell, Yvonne said, "I am worried, Madame."

Madame Opale pressed against her hand, lifting her feet for Yvonne to clean between the pads. "Why do you worry?"

"The situation seems delicate, as if enormous weights are turning on small pivots. I never feel easy in circumstances such as these. I feel as if I carry some terrible knowledge of the doom to come, and while knowing that no one would believe me, if I spoke of it."

"You need not worry," Madame Opale assured her, her shell buzzing. "You do carry that knowledge, and no one would believe you. You may be secure in that knowledge, and have no fear as to its veracity."

Yvonne tried to repress a smile. "That's not exactly reassuring."

"Truth is always reassuring."

Yvonne sighed. "I wish it were. I wish I were that rational, that pure. But instead I am all too human, and I have doubts. I *wish* that I could say something and change the outcome of this conflict. I feel that my words will come to nothing, and it will be only actions that matter. But which actions?"

Madame Opale did not answer. Yvonne finished cleaning her shell and tucked the wipe in her pocket for disposal elsewhere; she left nothing behind, when she visited the hut.

The two of them went about their tasks, Yvonne checking over the genetic material and data, Madame Opale downloading information and withdrawing a few ova.

Part of Yvonne champed at the bit, to be busying herself with insignificant tasks, in the midst of such significant events. But what could she do? She had laid what preparations and alliances as she could, as she had known how to do. Simone would have known what to do, she thought miserably, but then, that was part of the reason that Armand had had her destroyed.

And so she tidied systems, backed up files, checked drawers, cleaned. Simplicity itself—but who else was there to do it?

And her entrance would help cover Madame Opale's presence in the records, if it came to that.

While they worked, they discussed one of the Scarabées' latest projects, that of increasing the sentience of several species of hawk-moth to sentience. As it was, the Scarabées had raised the level of sentience enough to make the curious creatures into excellent spies, able to pass down their information to the Scarabées via genetic encoding in scent markers, and, for more complex information, sterile eggs.

"But sentience?" Yvonne asked. "There are already three sentient species—excuse me, four, if you count humanity—on the planet. Do there really need to be more?"

"That is your human side talking," Madame Opale chided her, tapping her wrist with a leg. "As Grandpère would say, 'The more the merrier.'"

Yvonne clucked her tongue, corrected a typo in one of her batch commands, and hit *Enter*. "That's true. It seems so strange to think so, though. My first reaction is to think, 'That will only cause more competition.'" She chuckled under her breath. "As much as I love the hawk-moths, I worry what they will think of me, when they learn that I have treated them like pets."

Madame Opale touched her wrist again. "They will think of you with fondness, because you have treated them kindly. Anger at being treated like a lesser creature, that comes with the need to prove one's species, or even an individual creature, as superior to all others. No: what they will remember, passed down over the generations, is your love."

The Royal Historian—who was also a member of the Twelve known as the Hawkmistress—found herself relaxing a little, for the first time since the Season had begun, and she had been forced to leave her beloved pets—friends—companions behind, at Paul Hong's old retreat, Castle Frankenstein.

She found herself, thousands of years after she had thought she'd lost the last of her innocence, with the start of tears in her eyes.

Yvonne brushed her eyes with the backs of her fingers. "I hope they do. I hope they're not angry."

"If they are, you can apologize," said Madame Opale. "That is the way of it, the old to the young. We are always having to admit that even with all our love, we were unable to find our way to the miracles we needed, and were forced, instead of giving the world the miracles it needed, to fall back upon on the best we could do."

Madame Opale's timbre did not change as she spoke; it held only the deep, mountainous rumble of the voice of any Scarabée, a "voice" that was not her own, but an artificial one, made only to communicate with the human species. A rumble created by two concealed appendages deep within their shells.

Nevertheless, Yvonne seemed to hear tenderness in her words, a tenderness not meant for herself or for the human species in general—but for a specific individual, far more beloved than called for by the Scarabées' usual affectionate nature.

And who could blame her?

Yvonne closed her eyes, and sent up a prayer to her hawk-moths huddling against the Season's storms, to the Kathra trees swaying together in little parks throughout the city, to the gondoliers, whistling and singing down in the dark.

Let it all work out. Please let it all work out.

Her throat tightened. She had little to pray to, but then one didn't, when one was, of oneself, a godlike creature, set above one's fellows.

She rolled her chair beside Madame Opale for a moment, bumping her hip against the Scarabée's smooth, clean shell, then rolled back to her monitor and went back to work.

After a time, Madame Opale concluded her endeavors, bid her adieus, and left—but Yvonne remained, intent upon recording the events that had occurred since last she had brought the downloads here, and the thoughts of those who had participated in and been affected by them.

What she feared most, was that everything they had learned would be destroyed, and come to nothing—it was every historian's fear, that history should be doomed to repeat itself.

Chapter 16

Would You Kindly?

JACQUES STUDIED THE PAUL Hong's gray, metallic prison: a glorified prefab trailer house, little more than a set of cargo shipping containers welded together at the edge of an underground lake, connected to the world above by cables. Its main security system was its isolation. It was hard to get to, and it was hard to get away from. Paul had never really mastered the art of super-jumping, and the stairs back up to the surface were a real pain in the ass.

The electric cart normally parked by the entrance of the cave was missin g.—That was the last thing he noticed, before the motion-detection lights surrounding him went out.

What did it matter that the cart had been moved?

It didn't, really. Except that it was the first detail that didn't match up with Armand's predictions, and it felt like the kind of detail in a sci-fi horror movie that the audience would notice, but the characters wouldn't, as a portent of doom.

Who had moved the cart? Was it Paul? He could literally walk out of his "prison" any time he wanted to; he just never *did*.

It had to be Delphine checking up on him.

It had to be Delphine, Jacques decided, and she had to be alone.

Corentin would be out running Grandpère's errands like the good little boy he was. Yvonne wouldn't involve herself, Manon would be needed elsewhere, and Marks was probably tied up at Versailles after getting killed by Armand—Jacques had changed the routing on the resurrection chambers himself so that Marks would be outside the Great Dome when he woke up, a chess piece at least temporarily removed from the board.

Jacques nerved himself. Delphine he could handle.

As long as Corentin wasn't involved.

Because Corentin had become unnerving ever since they'd gotten rid of Carlton.

The White Gentleman had outlived his purpose. Even Armand, who had made use of Carlton to kill off Etoile, had agreed to get rid of him once they'd forced their way into Carlton's fortress at the South Pole, hidden in the ice, and seen what he had done there.

The guy had made a frozen Hell full of interbred chimeras, genetic monsters twisted out of both human and inhuman flesh, dead now, preserved by the cold as collections of twisted obscenities. It was like walking into a room where all the wings and legs had been pulled off the mutated flies.

Carlton had claimed he was just trying to recreate and improve the "slave races" that had been eliminated, by accident or otherwise, since the crash on Thomàon. And that they were all treating every other sentient creature on the planet as their slaves regardless, so why tiptoe around it? And that none of the others had had any right to debate what he did within his base, anyway.

All of which was nonsense.

But then he'd said that he was planning on breeding millions of those twisted things. Billions. He'd laughed at them and dared them to try to stop him.

So they had.

Corentin wasn't as bad as Carlton, of course.

It was just that once Corentin had stepped into the shoes of the White Gentleman, he'd changed.

Jacques shook his head. It didn't matter. Corentin was elsewhere; it would only be Delphine who was here. He and Corentin had never gotten along. That was all it was. He was safe.

He lifted a foot and leaned forward.

An old Earth cliché said that the journey of a thousand miles began with a single step. Why not the journey of a few thousand feet along a dirt road beside an underground reservoir?

The motion-sensor lights flashed back on again. Jacques's heart skipped a beat.

Anyone who cared to look could now see him on the security monitors housed within Paul's prison. A weird fucking inside-out prison, Jacques acknowledged to himself, if the security cameras were on the inside looking out.

Then Jacques's foot landed on the ground—onward with his single step—and he was carried forward. Further resistance to the ongoing act of walking seemed unnecessary at that point; he strode swiftly off the platform overlooking the water, then onto the gravel road. His boots crunched on the flat pebbles, which shifted fluidly underfoot. He stepped onto one of the ruts created by the golf cart's tires: more stable. The gravel was graded so large that it couldn't even hold his footprints. It hardly seemed as though anyone had passed this way at all.

Behind him, the entrance to the reservoir was a low arch in the cavern wall, cement shoring up the natural rock in disconnected patches. The cement platform was stained with mineral deposits but in good repair. The metal box with the power couplings, meters, and other monitoring equipment stood at one corner of the platform behind a red-enameled railing, which opened onto a ladder that extended a dozen feet downward to the surface of the water. The last visible stretch of the ladder was crusted with deposits; the water level in the reservoir was low, but not by much.

The gondoliers had gone dim, drifting away from the platform when it was clear that he wasn't handing out more candy.

Water lapped against stone and reinforcing cement.

The motion-sensor lights, installed over the mouth of the stair entrance, shone brightly after him as he walked along the cart trail, casting his long shadow forward.

He was missing something.

He seemed unable to stop and think about it; his feet seemed cursed to carry him toward Paul's prison, inexorably, step by step. The backs of his hands prickled.

He lengthened his stride.

He'd fucked up. Somehow, he'd fucked up.

It had to be Armand stabbing him in the back.

Jacques's breath came faster, and his fast walk turned into a jog. It made no sense; if anything, he should be listening to his instincts, turning around and running away—jumping back up the stairwell from handhold to handhold.

The lights behind him cut out, went dark.

They hadn't been on that long. They should have stayed on longer.

There *was* something wrong. He wasn't just being paranoid.

He ran faster, legs pumping, boots slipping a little on the loose pebbles, pebbles rattling as they went flying. The gravel road sloped upward and narrowed at the same time, the cavern wall arching inward to his right. Larger, rougher rocks lay on the road where they had bounced down from the wall. Dark patches appeared on the road where water had trickled down new crevices and moistened the rocks.

Any second, he could slip and fall, and—

He glanced over his shoulder. There was nobody behind him. He couldn't see anybody behind him.

His eyes snapped forward. The road lurched upward even more steeply, then curved sharply to follow a curve of the cavern wall. His footsteps were the loudest sound in the cavern. The dim light of one or two distant gondoliers was all there was to see by, but to Jacques's evolved eyes, it was enough.

He reached the golf cart parked in the shadow of the prison, and slowed to a jog. The motion-sensor lights above the prison came on. He looked over his shoulder again as he walked a few steps, then stopped.

He wasn't winded, but he still leaned forward and put his hands on his knees as if he were.

Behind him at the entrance to the cavern, the motion sensor lights hadn't come back on, and the dim light of the gondoliers had dimmed even further. If there *had* been someone behind him, neither of those things would have happened. The lights would have come on and the gondoliers would have swum back to try to beg a treat off whoever had arrived.

Then he remembered the Scarabée on the stairs, the one he had passed while jumping downward, and laughed. *Shit*, he had scared himself over nothing, over a half-remembered expectation that she would appear behind him.

But it would probably take the slow-moving giant beetle another half an hour to reach the bottom of the stairs!

He straightened up and turned back toward the door of Paul's prison. He leaned the authenticator on his shoulder toward the door, then pressed his left thumb on the recognition panel. The panel glowed, then flashed as it recognized him. The red gem on his brooch flashed in reply.

Handshakes completed, the door unlocked itself audibly. He opened it, calling, "Helloooo, Lucy, I'm hoooome!"

The door was heavy. He kept a grip on the handle as he let himself inside, then swung it behind him with a clunk. The air smelled slightly of air freshener, some kind of weak, old-lady floral perfume. The air smelled of dust and grime, several hundred years' of skin flakes and hair oils and other built-up essence of Paul—since the last time they'd replaced his prefab prison. He never aired the place out, and there was no breeze to speak of in the cavern, even if he had.

A voice called back, "Hey, Jack. How are ya?"

Casually, Jacques called, "Any visitors?"

Not answering the question, Paul called back, "No, no experiments today."

Jacques swallowed with a dry mouth. "The golf cart's been moved. Who's here with you, Paul?"

"Oh, no one. I moved it earlier. I went out for a walk earlier, but it was too tiring and I rode the cart back."

When was the last time Paul had "gone out for a walk"? He was lying. Someone *was* here. And if it were Delphine, he would have just said so.

Probably.

Jacques scuffed his feet on the square of industrial carpet at the entry, then stepped up two shallow steps into the receiving area, a small, windowless room full of monitors showing various parts of Paul's prison, as well as the area surrounding it.

Jacques checked the screens for movement.

Nothing within the cavern. Even the gondoliers were gone now.

Paul's part of the prison was guarded by a heavy door that was meant to lock him inside; it stood propped open; no alarms were going off.

Jacques paused to look over the screens monitoring the inside of the trailer. Paul was sitting in front of his favorite monitor, typing away on the keyboard.

"Hey, Paul?" he called.

The figure on the screen looked over his shoulder, responding to Jacques in real time. "Yeah?"

"Your inside door's unlocked. Is something the matter?"

Paul's head, covered with shoulder-length, thin black hair, bobbed several times. "Weird smell earlier. Had to run some fans. I thought leaving the door open might help, but it didn't. That's when I went out for the walk, while the smell in the trailer cleared. I must have forgotten to close it. Sorry."

"What was it?"

"What was what?" Paul called back, scratching his head.

"The weird smell."

"Preservative. I broke a specimen container from...four hundred years ago? There was something nasty growing in there. Don't worry. The smell's all gone now."

On the screen, he bent back over his keyboard again, typing furiously.

Jacques couldn't think of anything else to ask Paul that would test whether or not he was telling the truth. He *could* be telling the truth.

Jailbreaking his prison to get rid of an unpleasant smell, then forgetting to lock himself back up again, was just the sort of thing that Paul *would* do, in a case like this.

But that he had just "happened" to step outside for the first time in a hundred years, and it had "happened" to fall on the day after the latest of Armand's uprisings, and it just "happened" to be the first uprising after Grandpère had tried to conceal the message from Earth…

It was more of a coincidence than Jacques could trust. He hadn't survived this long by *not* being paranoid, after all.

Jacques took in a deep breath, ignored the dust particles floating in the air, held the breath until his lungs ached, then took his first step toward the door to the rest of the prison cell. It had been propped open with a rubber doorstop.

He put the toe of his boot on it and leaned on the door. The stop slid free. He bent over and picked it up, shoving it into a pocket, next to the crinkling parade candy.

Then it was time to stop hesitating, to stop freaking himself out. He stepped into the corridor, pulling against the heavy door behind him. It resisted being swung shut quickly but eventually did come to a close. It latched. The lock panel next to the door was supposed to switch from red to green with the door was locked, but it had been disabled and the lights were both dark.

It was narrow and a little too short for Jacques to feel comfortable standing up straight. He rubbed his fingernails across the pads of his thumbs as he walked, self-consciously pulling his elbows in. The doors on either side of him were marked things like *Specimens 889-44703* and *Animate Projects in Progress*. A paper note had been taped to the latter door, the tape peeling and a brown bloodstain on the paper: *Check monitors for escapees before opening door.*

Although Jacques's footsteps were muffled by the industrial carpet underfoot, the floor still creaked loudly. It was the prefab corporate version of a nightingale floor. The vents hummed as they circulated the dusty air. The filters needed to be replaced, the carpets cleaned, stains removed from the walls, metal plates covered in textured office-cubicle cloth.

And there *was* a sour smell in the air, one worse than caked-up layers of over a hundred years of human nerd body odor. It might have been preservative. It did smell kind of like formaldehyde.

Regardless, the filters definitely needed to be replaced.

"Hey, Jack?" Paul called.

"Yeah?"

"Would you kindly grab the meal out of the cooker as you go past? I figured I might as well use your manual labor as long as you're here. Save myself the effort."

Jacques rolled his eyes. "Sure, whatever."

On Jacques's right, the door of the kitchenette clicked open. Jacques hesitated, his heart racing at the sudden movement.

Jesus Christ, he mocked himself, *get a grip. He just unlocked the door to the break room for you.*

The truth was, Paul creeped him out, had always creeped him out. And, honestly, Simon had, too.

Jacques stepped into the kitchenette, which had a row of cupboards, a microwave, and a sink. The cupboards, which had their doors removed, were stacked with empty experimental equipment. Paul ate straight out of the container. All his food was kept in the fridge, stocked by Scarabées who carried the materials down the endless stairs, clattering across the pebbled road, entering using a private code, then shuffling sideways down the narrow corridor. Next to the fridge, half-tucked in a corner, was a dingy gray robot, mostly a pole with arms.

The microwave was alight and humming, a dark shape was moving inside. The timer counted down, ten seconds left, then five, then *ding!* it was done.

Jacques hit the button and the door popped open. The plastic covering the tray had a hole poked in it.

He reached in and grabbed the plastic tray, then dropped it with a yelp. "Shit! Hot!"

From the other room, Paul called, "Sorry! Uh, there should be some napkins or something in the drawer under the microwave."

Jacques opened the drawer, grimacing at the tacky grime on the underside of the handle. Inside were a pair of ancient potholders made of some kind of silvery fabric. They were charred and stained, at least a hundred years old.

He picked up the tray with the potholders and caught a faceful of steam that smelled like sweet and sour sauce. A world away from Earth, and Paul was still eating sweet and sour stir fry out of plastic trays. Disgusting.

Jacques backed away from the microwave and turned toward the door carrying the hot tray. It was at least bigger than the tiny meals that they used to buy in grocery stores on Earth. He should probably stir it, but he wasn't going to. Let Paul deal with the frozen middle and the burning hot outside. He probably wouldn't even notice.

Jacques stepped into the corridor, then into Paul's main living area. Paul was still at his monitor, typing furiously on his keyboard. The bathroom door was closed and had a metal broom handle jammed under the door handle to wedge the sliding door shut.

Not pausing, Paul said, "Hey, thanks. Would you set it over here?"

"What's up with the bathroom? Did another one of your experiments get out?" Jacques carried the tray over to Paul's desk and waited as Paul grabbed an armload of Petri dishes, long-handled probes and scalpels, pipettes, tongs, styluses, and other junk out of the way.

Paul mumbled something under his breath, ducking his head. His armload of junk slipped out of his arms and clattered on the floor, and he bent down to pick it up.

Jacques grinned as he set the tray down. "What was that? You created a hentai love slave and now it won't—"

Paul grabbed Jacques's jacket and pulled himself upright, knocking his chair so it rolled backward on the floor. His breath smelled bad and his eyes were squished shut.

"Sorry," he said.

Jacques heard the bathroom door rattling behind him, Delphine's voice calling, "Paul? Paul? Who's out there? Is it Jacques?"

"Sorry for what?"

Paul moved quickly.

It didn't hurt at first. Just felt like pressure against his coat, then having an itch scratched.

Then it was like a balloon popped and Paul's face was splattered with red.

The fucker had *stabbed* him, with something that was slicing through his ribcage like butter. Some kind of vibro-knife.

The room echoed with a banging noise, and Delphine's screaming.

Paul's eyes opened. They were two bright white spots in a face covered with blood.

"Sorry," he repeated.

Jacques thought: *Who queened the fucking pawn?*

But he couldn't say that. Not out loud.

Delphine screamed, "Paul! What the fuck are you doing?"

Jacques's legs lost pressure and he slumped backward. Paul was still hanging onto him; he tossed a delicate surgeon's vibro-scalpel down onto the desk, scattering red droplets across the food tray and the side of the monitor, then lowered Jacques down gently, making sure his head didn't thump on the floor as he bled out.

Stronger than he looks, Jacques thought. Silently again.

"Paul! Paul!"

The world grayed out.

Chapter 17

Into the Depths

AMMALINE HAD CLEANED HER hands as carefully as she could after gouging her fingernails into the Puppet Master's eyes, but there hadn't been soap or water, only ancient, rotted alcohol wipes. She chewed off her fingernails and spat them out over the walkways as she and Madame LaFerme ran through the darkness.

It didn't help; it only made her fingers taste more of blood than ever.

Their feet pattered on the metal grating; their breath echoed as they ran through the tunnels.

Madame LaFerme carried with her a small black case she had found in the server room; after they had been sure the Puppet Master, her former lover, was dead, she had climbed over the body and into the server room to see what he'd gone in there to retrieve.

"It's gotta be good," she spat bitterly. "Armand never makes a personal effort if it's something he can trust one of his peons with."

While Madame LaFerme had searched the server room, Ammaline had been unable to move, had been barely able to do anything other than pant shallowly for breath. The stink of Armand's death didn't help. She breathed through her mouth and felt herself getting more and more distant as she leaned against the wall of the ship.

A pair of latches clicked from within the server room.

"*Holy shitballs,*" said Madame LaFerme. That remarkable statement was followed by a string of other curses, each more incredible than the last.

A voice from deep within her own mind seemed to tell Ammaline: *Get your shit together! Are you a consummate artist? Or are you just a fucking fake? If you want to be a diva, be a fucking diva and put your big girl panties on. I know you can hear me! Jesus Christ, kid—at least fucking breathe!*

The voice seemed both outside herself, and to come from a place deeper within her than her own innate thoughts. But it was essentially, if rudely, correct: soon Madame LaFerme would emerge from the server room with whatever she had found, and it would be time to take action, even if it was only to follow Madame's orders.

And, if Ammaline was not to soon pass out from lack of air, she *must* breathe.

She breathed slowly, deeply, down into her diaphragm, exhaling while humming tunelessly through her nose, then began to run through her vocal warmups.

The ship echoed shallowly with the sounds: *me may mah mo muuu...*

Madame LaFerme had emerged from the server room with her eyes wide and nearly bulging, holding the case. "I'll explain later, Ammaline. Right now, we need to move."

Breaking off from her exercises, Ammaline said, "Where are we going?"

"Down past the gondoliers."

And so Madame had gathered a few things and shoved them into a bag, and the two of them had left the *Téméraire* as precipitously as they had come. Madame left behind her, in addition to the still-warm body of her former lover, the full skirt and bustle she had torn from her clothing, as well as her wig.

Madame's twisted limbs were revealed, then—but there was no time to study them, or to consider what they *meant*; for they must run, and run, and run.

They fled this way and that along the echoing catwalks, claustrophobic tunnels, and damp-smelling balconies crossing beside trickling caverns that whispered from half-caught sounds, perhaps from the surface, perhaps from below.

No matter how far they ran, they seemed always to have further to run, until finally Ammaline, who had already been forced to use her vocalist's control over her breath to keep herself from collapsing, finally must beg for rest:

"Madame! I—I cannot!"

She came to a stop, clasping the railing of the platform upon which she stood. They had reached the top of a spiraling staircase that ran along the inside of a narrow chimney of rock, leading down into darkness. A pole ran down the center of the staircase, with a small collar of metal at one place upon it, with a panel missing on it.

Madame was halfway down the first flight of the metal staircase when she came to a stop, her odd-looking knees bending backward as she descended, as if she were a faun from one of the ancient paintings in an obscure room of the castle. One hand lay lightly on the railing, and the other grasped the case in an iron grip.

"Ammaline?"

"I—I—" Ammaline felt disconnected from the world about her. She was about to faint. Suddenly she was kneeling upon the metal grating of the platform, unsure of how she had come to lower herself.

Madame appeared at her side. "Oh, Ammaline. You are exhausted, of course. You are—you are—you are exhausted!" She put the case between her ankles and stroked the top of Ammaline's head. "I will carry you—"

She froze, then lifted her chin, her nostrils flaring as though she had scented something. "We have been followed."

In a heartbeat, the case was shoved into Ammaline's arms, and then she was herself within Madame's arms, thin and elegant, yet seemingly made of hardened steel—or some other inarguable material. Madame strode toward the top of the stairs, turned toward the pole—sighed—and then began to jog down them.

Her footsteps echoed in a way that made Ammaline's stomach lurch. She clutched the handle of the precious case—what could possibly be inside?—and tried not to become too dizzy as Madame increased her speed, nearly leaping down the stairs.

Overhead, a soft noise followed them through the darkness.

Madame hissed through her teeth, more of the same awful curses as before, and tried to go faster, but caught a hip on one of the turns, and was forced to slow again.

She turned her face upward and shouted, "Show yourself! Who are you?"

There was another soft sound, and then—

A light appeared above them, descending quickly, as if falling from the sky.

Landing on one of the small collars of metal surrounding the pole, a few feet above them, was a figure dressed in dark gray, their disguise even covering their face. A button light shone from their shoulder, diffuse light spreading across the chimney of rock and the metal stairs.

The figure's legs had that same backward-facing bend to them—a trait that Ammaline had previously noted in her father, who wore braces on his legs and called it a birth defect which his daughter fortunately did not share.

The knowledge that *all* of the Twelve had these legs came to her in a flash: Madame had them, and her father—and, too, Manon had had them.

Manon had become one of the Twelve, which had involved some terrible change that had required them to disappear—seemingly for forever.

Whatever had changed, it was marked by, or accompanied by, the odd changes to the limbs of those who had been changed by it.

And (with a further flash of insight) Ammaline realized that whatever made the Twelve the Twelve, *must* be found within the case she clutched.

Yes, said the voice that had spoken to her before. *Yes and no. It's complicated.*

Ammaline clutched the case tighter.

Madame snorted at the figure in gray. "Well? If you're going to kill me, get it over with. I know when I'm backed into a corner."

The figure let one hand go from the pole and used it to reach under their chin, lifting the featureless gray panel of fabric from their face and revealing—Manon.

"I'm not here to kill you. I'm watching your back."

"Did Grandpère send you?"

They shook their head. "I was tracking the Puppet Master. But you beat me to him. He's dead?"

"He's dead. The two of us took care of him. At the ship. Which is—"

"I know where the ship is," Manon said. "The real question is—"

Madame and Manon both tilted their heads in thought, as if the same thing had occurred to both of them at once.

Madame said, "He would get resurrected at the Castle of the Silver Spire. That would be closer, unless Paul has his chamber turned on?"

Manon said, "I doubt Armand would let himself be resurrected any-where near Paul's experimental facilities. And the castle's chambers are out of elixir. So Versailles, if anywhere. What about *her*?"

They both looked at Ammaline, Madame frowning as she did so.

Madame said, "I am going to try to take her to the gondoliers, and see whether they will carry us to the archives. I doubt that Paul's is safe at the moment. I'm sure someone is already there, trying to bully him."

"What are you trying to achieve?" Manon asked.

"Can I trust you?"

Manon shrugged, turning out one hand at the elbow. "It depends. I know that you don't like politics and that you want to stay out of them. If you trust me with something, I may use it to further my goals."

"What are your goals?"

Manon grinned, showing teeth. "I am not prepared to discuss them with someone who wants to stay out of politics."

Madame inhaled, exhaled slowly, then put Ammaline down onto her feet. "I cannot believe that you have become so cold, Manon. I remember when you were just a little gamin."

"You remember a charming, sweet little child who was desperate for any advantage. Now, you see a member of the Twelve, one who has purposes of their own which have nothing to do with you."

"Nevertheless," said Madame, "There is one thing I can trust you with."

Manon's thin, arched eyebrow rose.

Madame held her hand out for the case, which Ammaline gave her. Madame lifted the strap of her bag over her shoulder, made a face—the case was too large to shove inside the small bag—then threaded the strap of the bag through the handle of the case and looped it over her shoulder.

Taking a step away from Ammaline, then putting her foot onto the railing, Madame said, "Take Ammaline to safety. I will get the case to the archives, one way or another, and leave it for Yvonne to look after—I'm sure she had places to spirit it away that the rest of us have never seen. Or I will give it to the Scarabées, or sink it into the reservoir."

"Oh?" Manon asked, their eyes passing over Ammaline's face in a way that made her shiver. "I thought you were uninterested in politics."

"My politics," Madame announced, "are now and forever whatever inconveniences Armand and makes him grind his teeth. But also I am fond of this girl. Do you know that she clawed his eyes out for me? I..." she lowered her head, and Ammaline could see sudden bright tears in her eyes. "I was wrong to say what I did about her. She's a good kid. Keep her safe. Hurt Armand, help Ammaline get on her feet—away from this madness, if possible. Those are my politics."

Then, without another moment's hesitation, Madame LaFerme threw herself over the railing and down into the darkness.

Ammaline gasped and rushed to the railing, looked over the side with her mouth agape, but fearing to call after her, lest it alert any other pursuers to her location.

Manon leapt off the collar of the pole and landed behind Ammaline, then leaned at the railing with her.

Distantly, a thump echoed up the chimney at them.

"She is well," Manon said. "She's jumping down the landings built onto the pole. It's faster for us." They pointed upward toward a section of staircase opposite them on the chimney, where a handhold was bolted onto a landing platform. "We can jump back up, too, but it's more work."

Ammaline turned toward her friend—the friend who had knocked her out the last time she had seen her. "You're the Assassin?" she said. "Why you? Why did they pick you? Why did they take you? Where did you go? What happened to you?"

Her throat tightened and her eyes filled with tears.

Manon made a small noise, and their shoulders dropped. Their eyes were filled with pity, sorrow—worry. "Oh, Ammaline. There is so much, isn't there, that you don't know. I'm so sorry. We will talk soon. But for now, we must go. Madame is right to try to hide the elixir—don't ask me what it is, not now—but you must go elsewhere. May I carry you? I would like to go quickly, and you—are not able to use the fastest route."

Ammaline nodded.

Then she was swept up, carried like a child once again in the arms of one she had known both as a playmate, and now as a sort of god.

Those arms smelled of soap and cinnamon and Manon, and something else. They walked down the stairs with Manon holding her tight, soon beginning to jog, and finally to bound and leap.

Chapter 18

The Scent of Someone Else Upon Her Skin

MANON DESCENDED WITH AMMALINE in their arms, trying not to jostle or frighten her.

Ammaline's long, curly black hair bounced into Manon's face as they leapt from platform to platform on the way down the helixed stairs. Last night at the opera, Ammaline's hair had lain loose underneath a piece of silver netting, its only restraint its own weight. This morning, after the night's adventures, it had matted a little, and smelled of sweat. Her clothing, a beautiful blue gown that was completely different than the robes of Thomàon's so-called nobility, was horrifically stained and reeked of blood and other foul material.

Manon could feel the questions radiating from Ammaline's body like heat. But her breath came slowly and steadily, under disciplined control.

Underneath all that, she smelled of powders and soaps—and of someone else.

At first, as Manon jumped down the interminable stairs, they thought it must be the traces of Madame LaFerme's perfumes lingering upon her skin. Yet the scent was *not* Madame LaFerme's, not completely, but still not unfamiliar. Had Armand been wearing cologne, when LaFerme and Ammaline had killed him?

The mystery remained unsolved by the time Manon reached the bottom of the stairwell, where it was interrupted by the necessity of lowering Ammaline to her feet, then taking a bow towards the figure awaiting them at the bottom of the stairs: Madame Opale.

The pearlescent Scarabée stood on her hind legs, awaiting them with one of her sets of middle arms extending toward them, and the other set trying to position them with more dignity. Her antennae shivered with excitement.

In her low, grinding voice, she said, "Greetings, Manon. Greetings, my child."

Manon said, "Did Madame LaFerme tell you her news?"

"She has." Madame Opale's antenna shrugged, as if to show that she was not agitated about the case of elixir being found, but by something else.

If it came to that, Manon was not particularly concerned about the elixir either. Paul had long since developed a synthetic replacement for the elixir and modified it to the specifications of the Scarabées; the golden draught of immortality was no longer a scarce substance, one that needed to be controlled—although Grandpère and the others would, for the most part, wish to control it.

No, what upset Madame Opale was likely the same thing that upset Manon: what was to be done with Ammaline?

Manon walked with Ammaline toward Madame Opale and offered their wrist to the Scarabée, who scratched it delicately with one footpad, laying down a thin line of scent, which was both personal to the Scarabée and the collective identification of her nest. It would serve as a password, of sorts—at least, until the next time that Manon bathed with soap and water.

Awkwardly, Ammaline also held out her wrist.

Madame Opale leaned forward, balancing delicately on her hind legs, and lay her mouthparts against Ammaline's cheek, her antennae reaching forward to familiarly stroke and pinch the girl's skin.

Ammaline yelped, then giggled, turning her head away from the Scarabée and exclaiming, laughingly, "I am too old for you to pinch my cheeks!"

Madame Opale said, "Do you remember me yet, my child? Do you know me, then?"

Ammaline froze, swallowed, blinked eyelashes suddenly dotted with tears. "No—no. I'm sorry? Did you know me from when I was younger?"

"I helped to raise you," said the Scarabée. "Before your father was forced to banish me from Shakes Island. I was sent away after your mother died."

What Madame Opale said, Manon knew, was the truth—but not the truth entire, presented pure and without taint.

The Scarabées did not lie; sometimes Manon supposed they had taken up the habit of telling the truth so that they could be less easily caught in their continuous deceptions.

Ammaline, with that open heart which always belied her intelligence, but which was so entirely charming, threw her arms around Madame Opale's shell, laying her head upon her smooth, perfectly ovoid shoulder. "I knew you seemed familiar!" She squeezed the Scarabée. "But no, I still cannot quite exactly remember."

Madame Opale's antennae brushed through the girl's hair affectionately. "Your memories will return to you, I am sure. Even in difficult times such as these, there is always hope that what has been taken from us will be returned."

Ammaline pulled back, still leaving her hands resting lightly upon Madame Opale's forelegs. "I hope so. I feel...I must admit, I have felt as though everyone were keeping secrets from me, secrets that I should have already known."

Madame Opale rumbled from deep within her shell, wordlessly, then said, "But we are lingering here, when we should be elsewhere—my child, will you come with us?"

Ammaline raised her eyebrows. "Come with you? Where? To where Madame LaFerme took the black case?"

Manon cleared their throat. She hated to be caught like this, pinned between the Scarabées' agenda and the love of an old friend.

Madame Opale said, "No. Madame LaFerme will meet someone who will take the case to a safer place. The three of us have another task to complete."

Manon's throat had throat closed up, refusing to emit any other sound than a harsh sigh.

Ammaline reached out to them. "Are you all right?"

Manon forced themself to swallow. They could not lead this innocent girl onward, not like this, not unknowing. "I am afraid. Ammaline..."

Their vision swam with tears, which they dashed away with the back of one hand. In doing so, they caught sight of the blue glow shimmering on the other side of the entrance to the reservoir, which brightened until it turned Ammaline into a shadow and erased her face—even to Manon's dark-adjusted eye.

Gently, with Manon looking the other direction, Madame Opale said, "You are being called, my child, to take up a task that is not yours, and which may hurt you greatly, and which will surely change you into someone you do not know or understand. But that call is a cry for justice, in benefit of one who was greatly wronged."

"I don't understand," said the girl.

Manon gestured toward their body, with its modified joints and alien motion. "I have been changed, and become one of the Twelve. The Scarabées would like you to become one of the Twelve, too."

Ammaline clapped both hands to her face to muffle a shriek. Her face was instantly coated with tears. When she breathed again, she said, "*What* have you done to Madame LaFerme!"

Manon drew their head back, looking at Madame Opale for assistance, not understanding what Ammaline meant by her words. "Why, nothing? As far as I know?"

Madame Opale said, "My child, I see that you do not understand, as well you do not, for it is very difficult to explain. The Twelve are not elected from the People, as stated in the legend, but bred. Manon was not chosen at random, but bred from long before her birth to become the Assassin's incarnation. Nothing has happened to the Great Diva. You could never take the Diva's place, for you are not of her plasm. It is another of the Twelve that you carry within you, La Voisine."

"La Voisine? The Seer?" Ammaline frowned. "But isn't she…but I'm not a seer or a fortune-teller. I'm a singer."

Remembering Simone—whom Manon had often considered forward, crass, and unpleasant, if not unlikable or unlovable—Manon said, "Simone was a singer, too. It was her hobby, just like it was the Diva's. A performer."

Ammaline went still again, her silhouette as motionless as a statue.

Abruptly she turned toward the mouth of the stairwell; the light outside had brightened even further, and was almost as bright as daylight. The humming of the gondoliers had risen into song.

"What's out there? I hear singing."

Ammaline pressed past Madame Opale as if hypnotized, the silver threads of her gown sparkling as they caught the light of the gondoliers in the cavern. Manon followed. The water of the cavern was a mass of gondoliers, their long, ribbonlike, segmented forms packed tightly together in the water, so that they seemed a carpet or a cloth, so eager were they to greet Ammaline.

She walked to the edge of the platform and leaned over the rail.

"Oh! There you are!"

She reached an arm over the railing. A loop of one of the gondoliers' coils rose up to reach her, and she scratched into the flesh as the gondolier purred with pleasure, then began whistling to her, an intricate song with harmonies layered upon harmonies.

Ammaline laughed. "I don't understand! You're whistling too fast! Please slow down!" She whistled a trio of notes that sounded like the chirp of a bird, perfectly clearly.

The gondolier's song paused, then repeated itself as a simple melody, without harmony.

The cavern, filled with more gondoliers than Manon could ever remember seeing during the course of a very long life, had gone silent with anticipation.

Ammaline whistled a trill, tilted her head, and thought. Slowly—as if she were speaking in a foreign tongue for the first time after years of ignoring her practice—she whistled a short series of notes, stopped, then whistled them again, with more confidence.

The cavern erupted with swooping, tuneless whistles—cheers. The gondoliers bumped up against the platform, crowding each other and swamping the cement with water as they crashed into each other, glowing brightly.

Ammaline turned away from the railing, pressing both hands to her face. Her face was coated with fresh tears. "I know them! Oh, Manon! I know them!"

Manon held out their arms, and Ammaline went into them, sobbing with what might have been confusion and relief.

Madame Opale said, "And they know you, my child. They have never forgotten you."

"Never!" Ammaline sobbed, muffled. "Tell them I am overwhelmed with joy. Tell them I am so sorry I forgot them. I didn't mean to."

Madame Opale purred from within her shell. "Tell them yourself. They will be taking us where we are going, deeper within the caverns."

"Where are we going?"

"To a place that belongs to the Scarabées alone. It is where we raise our young. There, we will explain to you what we are asking of you, and give you time to decide whether it is what you would like, or not."

Ammaline drew away from Manon, her face shimmering with reflected blue light. "I will like it."

She returned to the railing, leaning over it once again.

Manon shook their head. Ammaline could not know what she was agreeing to—she must be told the painful details before they, Manon, would allow it to happen, as desperately as it needed to be done. She could not allow this girl, this wonderful girl, to thoughtlessly destroy herself, in the name of rediscovery.

To be *one* person, whole and complete—then to be tricked into becoming *another*!

To be Manon was one thing. To be the Assassin was to have so many contradictory voices inside one's head that they hardly knew which ones to listen to, at any given moment—or, in fact, who listened. The awful sense of déjà vu, the constant sense of being doubled, or tripled, had always haunted them, left them feeling accompanied every moment, cutting them off from any real sense of integrity or solitude.

They could not allow it to happen again. Not to Ammaline.

Without a word, Ammaline edged along the railing, then turned and climbed down the ladder off the platform, stepping onto one of the backs of the gondoliers. She swayed for a moment, then steadied, hiked up her skirt, and knelt down on the gondolier's back, reaching down to stroke its white, slippery skin.

She whistled to it, and it whistled back.

Madame Opale climbed down next, ignoring the ladder and climbing over the rail, then dropping lightly onto the back of a gondolier who had risen to meet her.

The gondoliers began to move away from the platform, taking Ammaline and Madame Opale to Madame's nest, where the transformation would surely occur—if Manon did not go with them and try to stop it.

Manon felt their throat tighten as they climbed down the ladder and stepped onto the back of one of the gondoliers. They had no tenderness for the creatures, no trust.

And yet the gondoliers treated Manon as gently as they treated the others, and made their undulating way from the caverns bordering the human city, to places far more strange and foreign.

Chapter 19

Whistling While He Worked

IT WAS THE DAWNING of a grand and glorious day beneath the halls of Versailles which saw the moment Marks Lemure finally gained control over the fate of his long-standing tormentor and opponent, the man who had ordered the death of his wife.

But it was only many hours later that *that* dawning, so glorious in its inception, could come to fruition.

The unfamiliar Scarabée who had arrived to inform Lemure of Armand's timely arrival in the resurrection chamber had, as soon as she had made her announcement, dropped to the floor and scurried away in an almost indecent haste, leaving him alone with his thoughts—his simmering, violent, impatient thoughts.

He could not blame the Scarabée for leaving so quickly. Scarabée chemical receptor organs, that is, the organs which in humans led to taste and scent, were quite sensitive.

A rancid, peppery emotional stew filled the room, the scent of a pressure cooker about to overboil.

But there was nothing else he could do to speed up the process.

Armand's new body had been brought up from the depths of the storage system underneath the chamber, but it still needed to be "decanted," or taken out of its cryogenic stasis and prepared to receive the mind and memories of a man who had lived for thousands of years. If nothing else, it would take some time for the body to come to temperature.

The Warden paced. He intended to wait just long enough for Armand to finish the process of resurrection so he could kill him again.

Armand would not remember killing Lemure, would not remember what had killed him.

Even setting that aside, there was no point in questioning the man. Truth, falsehood: those words meant nothing to Armand.

The question—the delightful, undeniably joyous question—was this: just how should he, Lemure, do the deed?

What sort of butchery would most satisfy him?

What sort of revenge would most quench the rage that had overwhelmed him since his wife's death?

What sort of assassination would be most likely to heal his very soul?

If Lemure had known how to dance, he would have danced—for a time, at least.

He was not the sort of man who had ever much expressed his joy, and when he had, it had been in the presence of his wife, with such profound gestures of affection as men such as he bestow, after a lifetime—after many lifetimes—of repressions: awkwardly, tenderly, with a sense of miraculous delight, and ensnaring all love and loyalty of those to whom they are given.

But that was another lifetime, and besides, his wife was dead.

And so dancing would have been impossible. He was, however, good at waiting. And he was good at keeping himself busy.

While he paced, he occasionally stopped at the ordinateur terminal to look again at this record, or that one, records both of the recent past that showed the manner of Lemure's death, then of Grandpère's.

The records showed that he himself had disappeared off the public map of the Opéra du Mendicant and had gone down into the hidden corridors that ran through the theater. His body had not been located, as of yet, and was likely buried under a floor or bricked up behind some wall out of reach of the mechaniques cycling through as they cleaned and repaired even the most hidden areas.

If the cleaning machines had found a body, they would have reported it, even if they were off the official map.

Grandpère's death had been recorded in full, for it had occurred within the Louvre, and within his own private quarters at that. The cameras in Grandpère's private rooms were inaccessible to anyone but Grandpère himself, but he had—or, rather, his heir had—sent Lemure a copy of the murder for his files.

Armand himself had also died under mysterious circumstances, having once again disappeared from the cameras and records and tracking devices that lay nearly everywhere within the Silver City.

And yet that was not the greater part of the mystery:

The Scarabée, before fleeing, had told him that Armand had gone to their lost and ruined ship, the *Téméraire*, and been attacked by Madame LaFerme and—wonder of all wonders!—his own daughter.

His own daughter: yes, his own, even though she was not flesh of his own flesh, nor truly blood of his wife's blood either.

When Simon Poulin had announced that he was finished with being male, and *she*, Simone, was now a woman, some of the others had laughed at her. Lemure had felt only a sense of rightness, as of a puzzle piece having been jammed into the wrong spot, then moved slightly to where it truly fit.

Lemure had not been—not on Earth—the sort of man who accepted such changes easily; in fact he had felt unable to conceive of them at all. He had not been able to sympathize, in similar situations—before leaving Earth.

But here, on Thomàon, he had grasped the essence of the matter immediately upon being informed of it. Paul Hong had just given them all the doses of the elixir that had changed them from men to monsters—or to gods, as men like Armand would have it—and the profundity of that change, that dizzying, sickening sensation of having been cut off from a common humanity, had forced Lemure to realize how little it meant to wish to change something so simple as one's gender.

One would still have been human, after all.

Better to feel fitted to one's flesh, than to lose one's internal integrity.

The thought would not have crossed Lemure's mind afterwards, except that Carlton had murdered Simone, and claimed it because of the "monstrousness" of her change in gender.

Of the change in *species*, Carlton had said nothing.

Lemure had seethed with the injustice of it—to have come so far, and to have finally found one's place in life—all the more so when it became known that it was Armand who had manipulated the killing. But he had soon forgotten it, in the daily necessity of sending prisoners down into the deadly cavern depths here and there about the planet to bring up the elixir, then refining it.

He had taught himself to ignore many things, over the course of the history of mankind on Thomàon. To forget justice, to cease to know that it existed as a matter of convenience, was a daily matter for him, for all of the Twelve.

But, one day, his wife had come to him, announcing that they would have a child—the child he had thought Paul had prevented them all from having—and that the child was a reconstruction of Simone Poulin, introduced into Etoile's womb by the Scarabées.

He had been shocked: he had thought his love for his wife would die with her at the end of her natural life. And although this child would not carry either of their gene plasms, it would be nurtured daily upon their love, and upon the body of his wife.

That much, he had grasped immediately. His wildly scattered emotions assembled themselves as a flight of starlings became a single swirling mass: love.

He was not, in essence, a good man; he knew that. The best he could say of himself was that he was not as soulless as his brother, nor as vain as his brother's wife; not as blind as Océan, nor as monstrous as Armand; not as mad as Paul, nor as spineless and weak as Jacques.

The truth was that Lemure was a good man, but it was by choice only, and not by temperament.

And so it had taken him until now, now that he was here, pacing in the sterile, dull room outside the resurrection chamber, to realize that the man he was waiting to kill had not only killed his wife, but had also, in a sense, killed his daughter—had her killed before her own birth.

Once again, he was crushed by emotions. He loved his daughter; therefore, he hated Armand, even more than before. He could not have imagined such a thing, but such it was: an irrational ecstasy of hate.

Why had Armand not been destroyed, erased as Carlton had been destroyed and erased, and as Simone had been destroyed and erased? They were no longer on Earth, where the considerations of the man's heritage and wealth might have carried some weight—Armand was the son of he who was once the richest man on Earth, after all—but on Thomàon.

What, then, was the cause of Armand's not being eradicated—they were, after all, ten to one, at that point. Even Carlton, Lemure knew, would have voted to have Armand killed, if it had been possible to countenance such a vote.

And why had Thomàon become what it had become? Why these cycles of monarchy, rebellion, collapse, and renewal of the monarchy? Why the fucking French influence?

Only one of them was originally from France: and that was Armand.

They called him the Puppet Master—or he had named himself such, Lemure could no longer remember—but *why*? Why did they all dance to his strings? How had he begun pulling them?

Lemure could not remember.

He did not feel weak; he did not think that he was easily controlled; he did not believe that he had ever said to himself, "Come, now, if I don't do what Armand wishes, it will go all the worse for me." He had never consciously yielded to the man.

Rather, he had fought; he had fought Armand's influence every step of the way; he had treated the man with contempt; he had undermined Armand's every whim and desire, as he was able. So had many of the others, at least at the beginning.

How had it come to this?

He did not know. He realized that, if any of them knew, it would be Yvonne, that odd little creature, painfully shy, playing with her hawk-moths and her histories at Castle Frankenstein.

He tried to remember if she had ever made a comment directly upon Armand, rather than his actions. He seemed almost to remember that she had, but could not remember what she had said, other than that it was something about Armand being predictable—which was laughable.

Armand could not be predicted. His actions were unfathomable.

Lemure shook his head, trying to bring himself back to the present moment. It was useless to think of such things. Every time Armand did something so monstrous that Lemure found himself actually shocked by Armand's influence and actions, he had this same conversation with himself: they all *ought* to have done something about him. They *ought* to have done something different.

But what?

There would be no answer, and the latest offense would blow over, leaving all of them devastated—but Armand unscathed.

And then they would somehow to find a way to accept an even more egregious offense the next time.

No, there was no stopping the Puppet Master; they were all dancing to his strings.

The thought made a flash of inspiration come to Lemure abruptly. He stopped pacing, walked over to the terminal, and shook the computer mouse awake. The software reported that Armand's resurrection was progressing perfectly, but that several hours remained before he would be available for Lemure's nefarious plans.

Well *and* good. That meant he had time to make his plans even more nefarious.

Lemure began whistling. He was an excellent whistler; he caught himself whistling the merry tune of "Il n'y a pas de cordes sur moi." It wasn't a French song, but it had been so long since he had heard the original English version that he couldn't remember what it was called in that ancient tongue.

He wandered over to a storage closet and looked through the boxes until he found a plastic crate filled with a jumble of coils: spare extension cords, data cables, and other cabling and wiring. He carried it into the resurrection room. He also found there a metal mop handle that was quite strong, strong enough not to bend or break when he knelt on the propped-up handle. He lay it next to the box of cords, along with several not-too-ancient rolls of duct tape.

Then he led one of the larger mechaniques from the kitchenette area, which was mostly unused, and made sure it was working well enough for his purposes—it was. He jammed the mop handle through the open spaces in several overhead support beams above the resurrection pool and taped it down, then began attaching the various cords to it.

The last piece of material he required was a restraint harness; fortunately, the resurrection room was already well-supplied with spare restraint harnesses, for they were used on each of the bodies that were resurrected, to keep them from floating loosely around in their tanks and damage themselves by getting jammed into a corner. In fact, for a time, Armand himself would already be so restrained, until the servos inside the capsule removed the harness as part of the process of waking him up.

Lemure went to work on the mechanique, training it to trigger the emergency release of the resurrection pool cover, then clip the cords to Armand's restraint harness before the servos could remove it, then hoist him up above the resurrection pool, anchoring the cords by means of one of the handgrips on the lip of the pool.

He tested this first part of the mechanique's programming several times, then began programming the mechanique to perform the rest of the required actions: disemboweling Armand, pulling out his intestines, and wrapping them around his neck.

Soon enough, he had the movements working smoothly, or as smoothly as they could, without first being tested on a live subject.

Lemure would have to stay and oversee the first few times—the first few dozen times, if necessary—to ensure the process worked perfectly. After that, he would depart, secure in the knowledge that the Puppet Master would be strung up and disemboweled over and over again, until the cords broke or the mop handle bent.

Armand would be trapped in place, unable to make plans, manipulate anyone, or even to remember what had happened to him the day before. An eternity of waking up and being murdered. When Lemure got the chance, he fully intended to return to the resurrection room with something better than a mop handle and electrical cords to bind him with. Steel cables and a titanium rod, perhaps.

Then he remembered that the elixir—these last few doses—were so scarce, and so difficult to find and extract, that they would be the last immortality that any of them knew.

He was wasting them, to ensure that Armand would die in agony repeatedly, never understanding *why*.

What he was doing would destroy both Armand, and the rule of the Twelve upon Thomàon: wasting their immortality on something painful, pointless, repetitive, cruel, and stupid.

It was a miniature reflection of their history entire.

Lemure smiled, and whistled while he worked.

Chapter 20

A Prayer

THE JOURNEY THAT AMMALINE, Manon, and Madame Opale took upon the backs of the gondoliers was not one of any great discomfort. The gondoliers were slow and gentle, and carried their passengers no faster than at a swift running pace. Their dim blue glow came to seem quite bright to Ammaline's eyes, as she sat upon the back of her gondolier, her legs crossed so that her knees stuck out on either side of the creature's skin, but perfectly balanced so that there was no worry of her falling.

Manon seemed sullen and Madame Opale nervous, a soft scratching sound emanating from her chest that Ammaline associated with biting one's nails, or gnashing one's teeth.

Once or twice along their journey, they had been required to submerge themselves under the water, clinging to the backs of the gondoliers as they dipped below the surface. Ammaline grasped her gondolier with her knees and elbows, laying her head flat against the gondolier's skin, as cool as a mannequin's or a fish's, so that the pressure of the water would not get under her torso, and make it all the more difficult for her to cling.

When they rose to the surface, Manon spluttered and shook their head indignantly, dashing water from their eyes as if they were wiping away tears, then rose off their stomach and knelt upon the gondolier's back, retching and gasping.

Manon, Ammaline remembered, had grown up in poverty on the streets, and did not trust the water, having never lived on an island, or had a father to insist they learn to swim.

How had Manon grown up in such poverty, if they were an incarnation of one of the gods?

It was a mystery. Ammaline had no idea how the process worked, how the gods were reborn into different bodies, then reawakened to themselves—even though she was about to join their ranks, as the youngest and most naïve of goddesses indeed.

Moreover, she was afraid to ask.

The gondolier under her seemed to sense her troubled thoughts, and whistled softly to her, a simple tune that she seemed to have remembered having taught to it—or to its distant ancestor—once upon a time. But then Thomàon was a small world, after all.

She began to sing along with the gondolier, at first only to herself, then raising her voice so that Madame Opale and Manon could hear also. Madame Opera could not sing, but only buzz along with her; yet Manon joined their voice with hers in harmony, for the two of them had sung the little tune often enough, as children. The gondoliers joined them, their song weaving and echoing through the caverns as they slid across the surface of the reservoir.

Finally the song ended with a "Il n'y a pas de cordes sur moi!"

Manon was smiling a familiar, yet half-forgotten half-smile that indicated that they were pleased enough to set aside, at least for the moment, the difficult circumstances under which they all found themselves, and to feel a little happiness.

To Ammaline, it was the finest smile in all the universe.

Gently, Ammaline asked, "Manon? Are you all right? Are you worried about me?"

"Yes!" they burst out. "I have been biting my lips to keep from shouting at you this entire time, not to simply take Madame Opale's words as a matter of unquestioning faith!"

Then they ducked their head, still kneeling on the gondolier's back, and with a great deal of awkward, self-conscious movement, turned around until they were sitting straight-legged upon the gondolier's back, arms crossed across their front, looking stern and unflappable once more.

Ammaline pressed her lips together, trying not to smile. It would have been all too easy to slip back into the merciless teasing of her friend that they had both been used to, as children—but she would rather reassure them, if such a thing were possible.

She made a face. The fact was, she hardly knew what to say to reassure herself!

The gondoliers swam onward as the two of them seemed to ignore each other, but in reality thought of nothing else.

Finally, Ammaline said, "I think you and I have different ideas of faith."

A dry sniff. "Oh?"

"It is true that I am behaving the way I am out of faith rather than reason. Reason says that those of the Twelve I know, or have met, have not found their transformations easy or pleasant. Then, when they have achieved whatever apotheosis—" She stumbled slightly over the word, "—they can achieve, they then use their transformation as a driver of power and prestige, and those things do not make them happy, either. Reason says that if I wish comfort and happiness, that I should turn away from the choice that Madame Opale would so transparently have me make, and remain among the merely mortal."

Madame Opale buzzed, a sound without tone or meaning but which nevertheless sounded sympathetic.

"Exactly!" Manon exclaimed. "It was pure torture. I hated every second of it, and you will, too."

"My dearest friend, I don't doubt you," answered Ammaline.

She was rewarded with a vulnerable, startled look.

Ammaline continued, "And yet, reason is not the only argument possible. There is also an appeal to justice, which is entirely unreasonable; and to compassion, even less reasonable still."

Manon snorted but made no other response.

Ammaline smiled to herself, while outwardly frowning, trying to match Manon's stern demeanor. "And who is to say that I would ever be happy in remaining mortal? For, as we have all seen this night, this world of ours is plagued by chaos and strife, and I might remain in my current state, and be killed in a heartbeat, before I am able to achieve what I wish to leave behind me, as a legacy."

Manon snorted. "People will not remember your singing. Trust me. They only ever remember the Great Diva."

Ammaline still found the mention of the destruction of her previous dreams—to inherit Madame LaFerme's beauty, grace, elegance, and—above all—her talent, most painful indeed. But she ignored the desperate stab she felt at her breast, for it was her purpose to soothe her friend, rather than to indulge in maudlin reminisce of long hoped-for times which were now never to be.

Taking a deep breath, she concluded: "Finally, there is my instinct, that having learned that there is a part to myself that is missing, and which might be recovered, I may be able to reclaim myself as a person, to become whole."

Manon snorted again. "Why, do you feel broken? Have you been walking around, saying to yourself, 'My self as I know it, is insufficient?'"

Ammaline felt another poignant stab to her heart, a moment of agony and longing, for had she not felt entirely inadequate, upon leaving Shakes Prison for what she now felt to be the final time?

Had everyone not said, that Ammaline would be a wonderful singer, if only she were to have her heart broken a time or two?

Those feelings seemed childish, now, in the face of the chaos she had seen the night previous.

Ammaline thus prevented herself from biting her lips, and instead said the following: "No. When a part of oneself is missing, and it is that very part which would be wise enough to know that one limped when one might fly, then one does not feel insufficient. The ability to *feel* insufficient is itself missing." She sat back on her knees and pressed a hand to her chest, feeling her heart beating rapidly beneath it. "But when that part of oneself begins to waken, then one knows. I *recognize* myself. I am coming to remember myself. There is a voice inside me which has begun speaking to me."

Manon screwed up their face, as if trying to hold back tears by sheer force of cynicism. "And this mysterious inner voice? What does it say?"

Ammaline stuck her tongue out at her friend. "Mostly it says, 'Don't be such a fucking baby! Get on with it! The show must go on!'"

Manon burst out with a harsh bark of laughter, then clapped a hand over their mouth, their eyes softening into concern above their fingers. They lowered their hand. "Oh, Ammaline. When you speak like that, you sound just like her—like Simone. She would have...she would have loved to *be* you. Perhaps she would have even felt at peace, for once."

Ammaline smiled slightly, trying to hide her confusion.

Where did the voice inside her come from, if she had not yet been transformed into one of the Twelve? For she had never heard the voice before. And that Manon said that Simone had never felt at peace worried her: it did not sound very pleasant, or even goddess-like.

But Manon was still speaking: "You know what I'm really worried about? I only just came to realize it, when you made me laugh."

"What is that?"

"That you won't love me, when you're the Seer. Simone loved Paul Hong, not me. I always liked Simone. But she didn't love *me*."

Ammaline reached a hand toward her friend, and the gondolier upon whose back she rode swam closer, close enough for them to touch. Manon took her hand as they had once often done. The skin was smooth and cool, the fingers long and elegant, but moving oddly. With a start, Ammaline realized the joints in Manon's hands had been transformed, too. She rubbed the pad of her thumb over Manon's skin, feeling the musculature and bones beneath, different than the ones she had known.

"What will happen to me?" she asked her friend. "Tell me the truth, Manon. What was done to you, to make you so changed?"

Manon choked and tried to pull their hand away, but Ammaline gripped it tight, knowing that if Manon pulled any harder, they would pull her off the gondolier and into the water—and *that* they would not allow themselves to do.

Manon's arms went limp, and their head dropped forward on their chest. They mumbled something, but Ammaline did not hear it.

Madame Opale's shell buzzed, a descending glissando of grimness, yet also of sympathy.

Once again, Manon dashed their hand against their face. They lifted their head and stared directly into Ammaline's eyes. Their face looked hollow, the cheeks sunken, with dark circles suddenly appearing beneath their eyes.

Their hand tightened on Ammaline's. "First, they implanted a transmitter in my head. Then they forced me to sleep. While I was unconscious, they recorded my memories, my personality, the arrangement of the nerves and neurons in my brain, the wavelengths of my mind, the chemical imbalances of my brain. Every flaw, every disturbance, every doubt, every nightmare was recorded for all time."

Ammaline dared not blink, but she did nod.

Manon dug their fingernails into the back of Ammaline's hand. "Some of the Twelve simply have themselves copied onto a blank body, a soulless body that has never lived. But I—the part of me that was the first Manon, that is—rejected such a thing. I felt that I would become frozen in place, stuck reliving the same life over and over again. I would be unable to change."

They paused, their gaze turning inward. "And I have always felt this way. Even though the transformation is so horrible. I always give myself a choice beforehand. And then afterwards, I ask myself if I want all this to end, to be deleted. And I never do it. I'm such a fool...such a coward. I should have let myself die a long time ago. I have no freedom. I am just as trapped as the others. Every time."

Ammaline pressed her lips together and kept her hand within Manon's, although she felt like giving them a slap and shouting at them not to say such a thing.

Manon did not notice, but shook their head, then raised their eyes to Ammaline's again. "So when I take on a new body, it is always a personne, an innocent who only happens to share my genetics, who has lived a life away from the Twelve, who has gathered their own experiences. They are always poor, have always faced hunger and injustice and want. And then I offer them a chance to become more than they ever dreamed of. All they have to do is to be able to kill upon command."

Manon's face became even more drawn, even more hollow. "But that choice is never truly a free one. In every lifetime, I am a desperate personne, often one who has had to kill already in order to preserve their own safety. I tell them that they will be free, if only they do this one thing for the Twelve. This one thing, which the Twelve already do so well! Especially—" Their voice became strained. "They *all* know how to kill."

Ammaline suspected that Manon was thinking of her father, the Warden. But had not Ammaline herself had blood on her own hands recently? She did not know what to think, but she did know that her ideas of guilt, and of innocence, must necessarily undergo some review.

With a long, slow inhale of breath, Manon licked their lips. "Then, when I have agreed to be transformed again, as I always do, I am injected with the golden elixir, which is itself a monstrous thing. Your father mines it from veins deep under the ground, refines it, murders everyone how knows of its existence or erases their memories—the prisoners—then sends it to Corentin and Delphine to be distributed to the resurrection pools, where the Twelve are reunited, minds with bodies. Do you know what that elixir is?"

Ammaline shook her head.

Manon glanced at Madame Opale, then back down toward the water. "It is the memories of the Scarabées, their genetic material, their history, their souls, recorded and hidden away for safekeeping. The immortality of the Twelve comes from destroying the past of the Scarabées themselves. It is nothing but injustice. And I drink of that cup every time I am reborn!"

Their shoulders shook, out of grief or shame.

Ammaline's fingers had become numb from the tightness with which Manon clutched them, but she did not remove them from her friend's grasp. The gondoliers swam forward through the dark caverns, bringing their own light with them. Madame Opale buzzed a little, while her antennae shifted this way, then that.

Manon wept silently to themselves for a time, then dried their tears and asked in a low voice, "What do you think of that? What do you think of me now?"

"I think you are my friend," said Ammaline.

"Why?" Manon cast Ammaline's hand away from them, in order to throw their own hands up into the air.

"I do not know," Ammaline admitted. "It seems as though we must always have been."

"Your heart is too good," Manon told her, accusingly. "You ought to reject me, to reject all of us. You should cast us out of your thoughts, your feelings. You should go with the Scarabées to some forgotten cavern, and live out your life in peace, away from the evil and idiocy that we have brought with us to this planet!"

Her heart in her throat, Ammaline looked upward, to the ceiling of the caverns above them. They were currently in a large, open area, whose ceiling was so distant that the light of the gondoliers could not reach it. Her heart felt heavy, and seemed to pull her eyelids with it, trying to lure her into sleep—into avoiding the rest of the conversation, into avoiding painful truths.

She breathed deeply and slowly, trying to clear her thoughts.

Manon was ranting, trying either to drive her away, or to make her declare how they were of course forgiven for all the crimes they had committed, in the name of the Twelve.

But it seemed as though no words would be good enough, or true enough, to soothe Manon's damaged soul for them.

It would be foolish to continue arguing.

There was nothing that Ammaline could do, or say, that would make her friend accept that life was not meant for shining goodness and purity, and neither for the blackest despair.

Her father sometimes fell into such moods; it was useless to speak to him then, or to otherwise attempt to make him see reason. This was likely no different; Manon was determined to make them both miserable, to drain the charm and wonder of the moment, and that was that.

Ammaline decided to ignore her friend and their pleas that she should reject what Madame Opale both offered and requested. Manon's upset was about their *own* past, not about what was, or was not, wise for Ammaline to do.

Instead, Ammaline would attempt to discover what *she* thought and felt.

She breathed deeply and slowly, and felt the struggling of her heart, the twitchiness of her nerves, the uncertainty of her scuttling thoughts—stirred by Manon's need to have them *both* be upset—dissipate like the illusions they were.

Who am I? she asked. *If I am, and have always been, one of the Twelve, who am I? What does that make me? Have I, too, sinned against the Scarabées by, time and again, choosing to have myself resurrected at their expense? How long have I been alive?*

Would it be better if I died?

In the depths of her heart, she knew that she was unlikely to ever receive straightforward answers to these questions. But it felt as though she knew an answer, nonetheless:

If I am, and have always been, one of the Twelve, then I am, and have always been, myself—no matter in what body I have found myself, or what changes have occurred to me; regardless of that which is perfect and that which is imperfect about me, all of this has happened before, under slightly different circumstances.

And, if I do not hold myself true to what I believe in, if I am weak, it will happen again.

Ammaline's throat tightened. She felt the truth of that statement, a truth that reached back into a past that she could not remember, but was coming to feel underneath her, like a pile of stones upon which she stood.

The voice with which she *now* spoke to herself was not a new one; unlike the other, it used no words or figures of speech that she would not have used herself.

And yet it was *not* the same voice with which she normally spoke to herself. It felt like a prayer, a connection between her present identity, and her past lives, come now back to haunt her and advise her.

Below her, her gondolier whistled the old, familiar song again, but this time very softly, and with complex embellishments that enriched the simple melody as well as concealing it from anyone without an intimate knowledge of how music was written.

The simple tune, transformed, spoke of freedom; it was a declaration of independence; but it also spoke of having forsaken one's connections in order to obtain that freedom.

Was that what she wanted? To declare herself independent of the influence of the Twelve, of Manon in particular, as well as of the Scarabées?

In her heart, she knew that the Scarabées had first claim upon her, a claim that took precedent even over that of her father. Every human creature who lived upon Thomàon ought to submit themselves to that claim: this was not a human planet, and humankind had no right to it, and never had.

But she, *she* was one of the few members of the human race who might do what all ought, and submit herself to the will of justice.

Would it be enough? To offer herself to the will of the Scarabées? Would it make up for what had been done to them, what had been so casually, so selfishly taken and used, and destroyed?

It would not be enough. Yet that did not mean it was not worth doing.

She did not want to live the life of Simone Poulin. She did not want to repeat Simone's cycle of existence, whatever that might have been. She did not wish to be trapped within fate; nor did she wish to struggle against it, only to be caught in its webs all the tighter.

Instead, she would simply give her trust, bow her head, and submit.

That was the secret to change: again, it seemed as if the knowledge came from within her, not as a strange voice, but as a knowledge that she had always had, and would always have.

If one wished to escape one's fate, one must submit to change, change that seemed unjust—irrational—unkind—unfair!

Ammaline smiled to herself, knowing that Manon would rail and argue against the knowledge that she carried; that they would be unable to stop themselves from doing so. Manon wished to fight injustice. But injustice could not be *fought*, it could not be killed, it could not be erased or prevented.

It could not even be amended.

Injustice was a current that flowed through all of them, all of humankind. They were not Scarabées, who shared among them a calm sense of patience and purpose, a patience that—Ammaline suddenly realized—had waited eight thousand years, since the landing of the Twelve and their starship, to come to this moment, watching as their memories were consumed by selfish creatures who wished, like spoiled children, to avoid going to bed at night, and having to sleep.

For to the Scarabées, whose memories could be stored as a golden elixir, *must* live forever, in their own way, a way that the Twelve wished to steal for their own.

Poor Paul!

That strange voice which belonged to her, yet did not, had returned.

Who is Paul? she asked that inner voice.

Paul Hong. My—our—lover. A genius. The Twelve use him to create their mad inventions.

Ammaline nodded. Manon had named this Paul Hong a little while ago as Simone's lover across their reincarnations, but she had forgotten.

She asked the inner voice, *Will you forgive me if I do not love him? If I love Manon instead?*

Ammaline felt herself sigh, felt the other voice within her sigh. *I don't want to love Manon. Manon is so...full of drama. Constant fucking drama. They're like a smoke machine of drama.*

Ammaline snorted, but kept silent, even in her thoughts.

The voice considered the matter, and Ammaline saw memories of her own childhood flash before her eyes, as an older soul looked through them.

She saw herself and Manon playing as children. She saw them reuniting joyfully after a long time away from each other, Season after Season. She saw Manon ranting about a neighborhood bully; she saw herself defeating the bully, not by fighting with them, but by finding points of alliance and methods of manipulation and bribery.

She laughed at herself as she remembered the year the bully—there was always a bully, under the shadow of the Silver Spire in the Silver City—was swayed by a particular type of ice cream, which she, Ammaline, had persuaded several of the local sellers to stop carrying, mainly by sabotaging a few cleaning mechaniques and blaming the vandalism on the bully.

Or the year she had caught one of the Hawkmistress's spy-moths in order to keep it from seeing Manon as they broke into a bully's hiding-place to leave a handkerchief filled with greenish boogers on her bed.

Or the year she had to get Manon off the prison-ship before she was taken to Shakes Prison—the fool personne had sneaked onboard, thinking that they and Ammaline could spend an entire year together. In the end, Ammaline had had to trick someone else into taking Manon's place, a prisoner who would otherwise had to have gone, and who had thought themselves freed.

They had died in the underwater mines a few weeks later.

Ammaline knew herself not to be good, the kind of pure goodness that Manon tried to assign to her, but she had never thought of herself as delightful or interesting. The only thing she had valued about herself was her voice.

But apparently the voice within her—the Simone that had been—found her entirely worthwhile. Ammaline's soul was filled with the sound of wicked chortling and sympathetic groans.

I like you, the voice concluded. *I could have turned out worse. Fuck it. Love who you want. Manon and Paul and whoever are just going to have to work their shit out for themselves. We're good.*

Ammaline reached tentatively toward the voice. *I like you, too. Will you come back? I want you here with me.*

She felt Simone smile within her. *Aren't you afraid that I'll keep you trapped in the same cycle of life? The same stupid way of being me, over and over again? I'm not that great, you know. I can be a real bitch, no lie.*

Ammaline smiled. *I think we might need that quality of yours very soon.*

She felt the other side of herself smile back. *Just you wait.*

Why wait? You are welcome now, here, whoever you are.

Then she felt Simone's presence come closer to her, closer...until it was pressed up against Ammaline's cheek, until Simone was breathing into Ammaline's face a perfume of musk, flower blossoms, and smoke.

Ammaline exhaled. She felt Manon's eyes turned toward her, the prickle on her skin of being watched.

Then she inhaled, taking in Simone's scent like it was a prayer.

Chapter 21

The Seven Valkyries

Within the Silver City, it was mid-morning on the second day of the Season, after a rather long and harrowing night. It had seemed to more than one soul that the hours had passed with unnatural length, and that each of the clocks had come unstuck from the bounds of the natural rise and fall of the sun around which Thomàon revolved.

That may or may not have been the case; had those distracted souls been able to see outside the dome, they would only have seen the cruel storms of the Season wreaking havoc across the planet.

From polar ice cap to polar ice cap; from ocean to ocean; from mountain range to mountain range; from one wooded forest of odd yet familiar Kathra trees to the next: all were punished by the brutality of the storms.

The Season had formed Thomàon into what it was, a Paradise whose cost was the destruction of all that had been built throughout the previous year. To be above ground during the Season was to be destroyed. All were punished by the storms. Thousands of tornadoes stripped the earth of its greenery and woodlands. Thousands of hurricanes lashed the coasts, as if a multitude of angry sea gods pointed their tridents toward the uncertain lines of the land and said, "These are the enemy of water, these are what prevents us from true dominance, across all the planet. They must be destroyed."

Thomàon had no true moon, although it had several small satellites which the crew of the *Téméraire* had deployed upon finding themselves so close to a habitable world, upon being awakened from their cryogenic sleep.

Instead of a moon, Thomàon possessed for itself a captured comet, enormous, large in gravity, in an orbit which brought it past the planet year after year, and which served to destroy it—and to cause it to renew itself.

The cycles of life upon Thomàon revolved around the comet, as the comet revolved around the planet.

The Season destroyed all; the rest of the year, incredibly, rebuilt it.

The life which survived the harsh Season, survived it either because it was able to find shelter during such times, or it was too tough—and too quick to reproduce—to need to. The Scarabées evolved to retreat underground, while the gondoliers remained there for ever; the Grillons evolved to leap through the storms, turning hurricanes into wings.

But there was yet another way that life survived, a vegetative sort of survival, that life which was able to leave reserves of itself deep in the soil of the planet, and regrow itself from the roots which remained. The Kathra trees followed this manner.

As for structures, the only ones which regularly survived the Season were those built by the Grillons of a tough, yet rubbery excretion. These beautiful, alien, castle-like structures shifted and swayed, seeming to dig themselves in all the more securely, the more they were lashed and pulled by the storms.

When the storms were over, the eggs of the Grillons would hatch, and consume the material from which the castles were built, a sort of dense, vitamin-rich protein, that served as both egg-food and cement.

It was ironic, that the only structures which regularly survived the Season, were those built to be destroyed shortly afterward.

But, regarding the structures of the Grillons, there was a second cycle of life which occurred.

As the structures worked themselves deeper and deeper into the earth, they finally reached the depths habituated by the Scarabées. There, the Scarabées would dig into the nesting-castles of the Grillons, and fertilize those eggs which were not too close to the surface, while claiming some of the curiously durable proteins of the castle for their own.

In this way did the Scarabées and the Grillons communicate with each other: the Grillons raised the doubly-fertilized eggs as if they were solely their own—yet the offspring carried traits, instincts, and memories the Scarabées had implanted in them.

For that was the great talent of the Scarabées: they were able to absorb, modify, and adjust other creatures' genetics.

The Grillons raised their cuckoo children, never dreaming (if they had been able to dream) that they were being taught to hate humanity, to drive humankind away from the surface during the Season, to limit their numbers, and to destroy their homes and structures so that humanity, too, must learn yearly to start all over again.

In short, it was the Scarabées who had driven the Grillons mad; their bastard children, carrying no more intelligence than the natural Grillons, knew only that they must kill, and kill, and kill, even that which they could not eat.

Additionally, the Scarabées claimed some of the durable protein matrix built by the Grillons for their castles, in order to store their own and the

Grillons' memories, safe beneath the surface—the same material which became the golden elixir.

No Scarabée ever truly died, but was reborn through its fellows, intermingled and intermixed, a consciousness that was both individual and collective, intelligent enough to span a planet—if somewhat too slow in its communications to be considered a single entity, or telepathic.

The Scarabées, those master engineers of all things protein and protean, communicated chemically, that is, by scent.

For one of the Scarabées to smell another was to have communicated both practically and spiritually.

For one of the humans to smell a Scarabée was to be controlled—and changed. The pleasant smells wafting about the city reprogrammed human hormones by the hour.

What the Scarabées wished to know was: how little could humanity be changed, without letting them become a plague upon the universe?

And so the humans upon Thomàon were carefully programmed to find themselves trapped there, to be led by the Twelve, gods who were themselves experiments altered by a mixture of Scarabée and Grillon genetics encoded into their bodies and minds, a combination which both gave them lives of a suitable length for meaningful study, and which allowed the Scarabées to modify their subjects in an ongoing manner—every time they switched consciousness from body to body, their codes could be subtly changed.

This was the Scarabées' fundamental question: could humans change? And still be human?

And still be allowed to exist in the universe?

Or should they be destroyed, erased from the genetic record?

The Scarabées hoped, and prayed, that humanity could be saved. They were a gentle folk, but a wise one.

The gondoliers stayed out of such politics; they had come from another planet entirely, and were monitoring the situation.

The intelligent species of the local cluster agreed: the humans were charming as individuals, but, as a species, they were intolerable, and ought to have been long since destroyed. They consumed; they destroyed all but the barest minimum necessary for the survival of a few monarchs, who then invariably enslaved the others, destroying them in a thousand different ways. They destroyed their environments; they destroyed each other.

The problem with humanity, it was jointly decided, was that it had no sense of continuing existence; it was maddened by the fear of death.

Would humanity grow past this primeval terror if they were given something close to immortality? If their fears were removed, would they learn to care for each other?

Or would they continue to dominate and destroy?

It was both unlucky for Thomàon that humanity had been inflicted upon it, and lucky for the universe as a whole that it had. What other world had any hope of containing them? The Scarabées maintained their environment, kept the human population under control, and carried out their experiments with affectionate, yet brutal, efficiency.

But it was time for eight thousand years' of experiments to come to an end: more humans were coming, and it was time—as the humans might say—to sink or to swim.

Outside the Great Dome, the storms raged and the skies were dark and tumultuous, so much so that it would have been difficult for anyone to ascertain where the sky ended, and the surface began. Wind spouts hurled stone and earth; trees smashed through trees; cliffs rose, bulged, and spilled over as great walls of water erupted from suddenly overflowing underground streams.

Throughout the storm leapt the Grillons.

They were between thirty and fifty feet tall, this alien race, with long, thin, aerodynamic shells that exploded with power as they leapt. They were all legs; what need had they of wings? Their jaws and claws were powerful, enough so to tear through concrete and steel.

The storms grasped them, flung them, shook them, twisted them into knots but were unable—most of the time—to tear them apart.

The Grillons destroyed everything before them that the storms had not, with a deliberate appetite for the destruction of all things human. Even the dwellings of the Twelve did not go untouched, although generally it was the interiors of the buildings which were destroyed, rather than the structures themselves, which were well-built indeed.

Still, it was not as if the creations of the Twelve could be considered *safe*. Their interiors were ruined, flooded, and gutted.

The Great Dome itself was smooth and a little flexible; it was defended both via surface electricity, and by armies of mechaniques which scuttled about its surface, repairing the damage caused by the storms to the outer surface, detaching those Grillons who were able to find purchase, and using their own bodies to create patches as needed. What seemed impregnable was, in truth, merely efficient in repairing itself.

The inhabitants inside the Great Dome would have been shocked to discover that the outside of their sanctuary was a battlefield, one that seemed every year to come closer and closer to being penetrated by the twin foes of weather and Grillon attack; but such was the nature of humanity to believe that it was invincible for ever, simply because it had not recently been vanquished.

WITHIN THE GREAT DOME, the inner surfaces of the tiles had been repaired from the damages they had suffered the previous night, and once again shewed the pleasant blue skies of the day before. They filtered the air; they regulated the temperature; they shone with a bright blue light that made everyone within the Great Dome feel as though they were being bathed with the sort of sunlight that makes one crave a languorous nap. The air was scented with flowers, a calming perfume that had been pre-programmed to offset the revels of the previous night—even though those revels had not proceeded entirely as planned.

And yet it could be said that the Silver City had been damaged by the storms within, as well as the storms without.

No buildings had been burnt to the ground, but a few windows that had been smashed were, in the bright light of an artificial mid-morning, not yet repaired. The shops had re-opened, but the plants of the Jardin were not yet replanted. Grandpère had been replaced, but the fact of his replacement had not yet been forgotten. The entertainment and news networks had all returned to their regular programming for the most part, yet still interrupted themselves, from time to time, to remind all citizens that certain persons were still being sought by the New Republic, including the former King and Queen, the Warden, and certain others.

There was a hush in the bright, warm sunlight flooding the interior of the dome; a hush that could not be heard, yet was felt, for it was so unexpected.

The citizens of the Silver City asked themselves, "But where is word from our new ruler?"

But the Puppet Master, being trapped at Versailles by an ingenious machine of the Warden's making, was entirely silent.

The people of Thomàon were used—by both history and personal experience—to accepting the unacceptable; they were used to the sort of actions that, had they been perpetrated by a lover rather than a government, would be called *abusive*; they were used to being told that day was night, and night day, that four was five and also quite the reverse, that any lack of justice or mercy were *their* doing, or the doing of whosoever their political opposites might be.

What the people of the Silver City were *not* used to, was not being told what to do.

While they awaited word from the Puppet Master, they began to feel the weight of the dome above them, and to look toward the cheerful blue tiles, so heaven-like, above them with a sense of crushing dread.

Where was the Puppet Master? If all was well, why did he not announce, at great length, the superiority of his views? If all was well, why did he not denounce, at even greater length, the flaws in his former opponents? Why did he not crow in victory?

And if all was not well, why was not there a deafening hue and cry, that it should be made so?

There began to spread rumors:

Armand had been killed.

Armand had done something so unforgivable that he had had to go into hiding.

Armand had murdered Corentin and Delphine, or they had murdered *him*.

Armand had murdered the Warden, had murdered the Général Jacques Saveur-Chasse, had murdered the Royal Historian, Yvonne la Gorge, had murdered, in fact, each person who had disappeared during the night of the revolution—of which there had been many, more than usually disap-peared during the Season.

Armand *was* the hated Warden.

Armand had murdered Madame LaFerme—everyone could see that he was abusing her on stage during the Feast of Fools! He was a violent man.

Armand had raped men, women, personnes—he had robbed construc-tion workers, refused to pay overtime to his domestic help, and had spat in another patron's food at a fine restaurant one night, just to spoil it!

Armand was a monster—no, he was a saint! He was one of the Twelve. He was *not* truly one of the Twelve, but had assassinated the true Puppet Master and taken his place. He was Grandpère's secret son. He was a cyborg, part man and part mechanique. He was from another planet. His mind had been eaten away by the Grillons, and they now controlled him, in a plot to bring down the Great Dome.

The Puppet Master's entourage and loyal following did not spread these rumors; some of the more savvy of them attempted to find the source of them, and found nothing: neither confirmation nor denial.

Damningly, the harder they searched for Armand, the less of Armand there was to find.

His records prior to a dozen years ago were thin, artificial-seeming. It was discovered that those who had schooled him did not remember him; the businesses that had made use of him in the earlier parts of his career had failed, their owners sentenced to Shakes Prison for unnamed crimes and never returned; his parents themselves had never existed, or had changed their names.

The Puppet Master's worshipers turned their faces aside from the damning evidence, saying only that he was clever about concealing his past.

But they worried at the rumors, trying to swallow them whole with their denials, and discovering for the first time that it was harder to suppress a rumor, than it was to start one: those who had excelled in disinformation in the service of the Puppet Master found that their skills had little to do with preventing, or stemming, disinformation's consequence.

Their only solution was to add further to the layers and layers of untruths upon which the citizens' fragile sense of stability was built:

Corentin and Delphine were brother and sister, and had ruled the kingdom incestuously.

The Warden was the *true* monster here, and he had personally slaughtered every man, woman, and personne who had died in Shakes Prison with his own bare hands, often bathing in the prisoners' blood as he laughed, and laughed, and laughed.

His daughter Ammaline was a mutant, a cross-breed between human and Scarabée genetics that would soon "hatch," her human body splitting open to reveal a nest of larvae; alternately, she was known to be a clone of her mother, and the Warden had been making love to her since she was a babe. Her voice was a modified recording of Madame LaFerme's; it was not her own, but *synchronisation labiale.*

Grandpère—the new one—had been a poor man, a body double who had killed the wealthy businessman he was supposed to protect. Grandpère secretly controlled all the finances on the planet. Grandpère had plans to wipe out all human life upon the planet as soon as the Season was over; the only survivors would be those who had joined him at Versailles, at his own personal invitation.

Deeper and deeper the rumors collected, as does detritus in the wind-shadows of a storm.

As the bright blue morning burned brighter and became midday, then early afternoon, none of the Twelve were left untouched by rumor; even Armand's ally Jacques was assumed to have betrayed him, and was denounced as the traitor he must be, having fled to la Tour de Défense—for was it not true, that the Général was also that member of the Twelve known as the Player?

And as the blazing afternoon began to dim and redden, the members of Armand's entourage began to turn upon each other, each one blaming the others for not having been loyal enough to have protected their leader from the doom which he must have encountered.

Outside the Great Dome, it was not late afternoon; the external hour had turned past midnight, on that long and significant day. The clocks themselves seemed to be biting their nails, seeming to understand that if the sun should set without Armand, then the sun would set on his new empire as well. The true time did not matter, however; during the Season, no one could see outdoors, and the clocks adjusted themselves, either to give more time to the daylight, or more time to the night, depending on which was considered to be the more amusing for the People and the events that were scheduled, day by day.

Inside the Great Dome, the long afternoon stretched on and on, but still the Puppet Master did not return. Eyes rolled with impatience, the sober became drunken, and the fearful began to laugh, too loudly and too long. Each began to see their fellows' faces as somewhat twisted, foreign, strange, and alien.

When the sun finally set among a thin lace of simulated clouds and the evenings' festivities finally began, the People felt at once a sense of relief—for time had been allowed to progress once again, and would surely proceed forward as a prodigious rate to make up for its previous delay—but also a sense of doom, a fruit that had ripened from their previous sense of weight and dread.

It was a sweet fruit, in fact over-sweet, and had turned from nourishment to rancid alcohol, during its long stay in that impossible day's overbright sun.

That night, the second "night" of the Season, was to be celebrated not with parades, not with another Feast of Fools, but with a full performance at the Opéra du Mendicant of the newest opera of one of the best playwrights on Thomàon, an opera that showcased Madame LaFerme's talents, an opera whose plot had come to him in a dream: the tale of seven warrior women, so-called angels, who had descended to defend a prison camp whose prisoners had been abandoned to the storms by the authorities, when one of the last transports had broken down. They had been left behind to be murdered by the Grillons, and only these seven angels, sent by the Great Diva herself, could defend the camp.

But the angels were at odds with each other: their leader was cynical, another of them was naïve, another was too old to fight properly, and the main character—named Val Kyria and to be played by Madame LaFerme herself—was a braggart and a fool.

It was to be an immense spectacle, one whose preparations had begun long before the previous Season—as all such performances must, even though they must be performed from year to year.

And although Madame LaFerme was missing, the opera itself would go on: for of course Madame had several understudies, women with the same dark hair and same flashing eyes who could sing the part in her absence, although without quite the same voice or spirit.

The People, looking suspiciously at one another as they proceeded along the streets, began to make their way to the Opéra du Mendicant. Along their way, they saw that most of the damage of the previous night had been repaired throughout the long day, damage which had still been obvious in the morning's light. "Ah!" they said to themselves. "The mechaniques have been hard at work, have they not?" and they felt themselves to be relieved of their fears. The mechanisms of society still turned, after all; surely all would be explained soon.

Their festival-clothing was this night more subdued than it had been upon the previous evening, and their eyes more wary, and less unguarded in their madness and inebriation. The seductions were quieter, the crimes less overt. No one pushed over the statues that stood within the entrance to the opéra this night; no one tore the clothing from the attendants; a few people took the food without paying, but they were the sort who would have done so regardless, the way that some people, in the presence of a sickness, will expose themselves to it, as if to dare Fate itself to condemn them, or to seduce Death—for such was what they risked, if they were arrested and sent to Shakes Prison.

Life on Thomàon was often short, brutal, and extremely pleasant: caught between torture and luxury, a life without true change for eight thousand years, without war, without true poverty, without serious disease, without isolation and lack of purpose—even criminals had a purpose, on Thomàon, to destroy the weak, and to play the villain, so that the true villains could prove their bona fides in their pursuit.

The citizens of Thomàon had become a people of about a million souls who did not look toward the depths of spirit or philosophy for answers, but only to the stage, and the news. They lived their lives, enacting their dramas, their comedies and tragedies, as if they had meaning, surely enough; they did not notice that they themselves were never elected to one of the Twelve, and never anyone that they knew. They worshiped their gods, saying that the great benefit of the Twelve was that "anyone could become one," but knowing, in their heart of hearts, that nothing could be further from the truth.

In short, there was no hope; there was such an absence of hope that they were unable to sense how hopeless their souls must truly be. Life was frozen in place, as it had always been, other than passing fashions, such as the political movements that revolved as surely as a clock, each revolution only serving to hold the People more securely in place.

They entered the opéra with interest and excitement, curiosity and anticipation. The interior of the theatre had been rearranged from the previous evening. Where before the theatre had only open flooring, on that night there were countless rows of folding seats upholstered in red velvet.

Overhead the crystal chandeliers had been cleaned and reordered. The brass railings along the edges of the boxes had been cleaned of fingerprints and scratches; the hallways, of dirty footprints and blood. The door of the royal box had been repaired, as had its walls. The air had been circulated, and now smelled perfectly fresh; the toilets had been cleaned and repaired and restocked; the ladies in their enormous court dresses would find no inconveniences. The lights shone brightly above the stage; and even backstage and in the secret rooms and corridors under the stage, all was in order.—The body of the Warden had finally been found by the mechaniques, and both Grandpère and the Warden alerted, but both men had declined to have the body removed, and so it was sealed up in the wall where it had been found.

The audience was shown to their seats as befitted their rank. The entirety of Thomàon could not fit itself into the confines of the Opéra du Mendicant; there was a significant portion of the populace that was not interested in music or culture, or even crowds; but still it was a structure that could hold nearly a hundred thousand souls at a pinch. The floor was immense, but it was the balconies that held the majority of the attendees. Each of the seats was stocked with its own viewer, a pair of opera glasses that was held toward the stage to receive a live projection that was unimpeded by the swaying feathers, broad shoulders, or towering headdresses of some of the attendees. On the floor and upon the upper levels of the balconies, food and drink were served by small armies of mechaniques, or human attendants, for the more opulent boxes. Intermissions, as throughout all of history, were chaotic, but controlled by holding the patrons in separate areas off the opera floor, so that those in Section A could not cross the hall and find their way to Section Z. The way it was done was not obvious; only a truly determined soul would discover that each section of the outer court—its toilets, its bars, its booths, its meeting-areas—were each separated from the other, during the performances. Parallel labyrinths created the illusion of space and freedom, but in reality the crowds were treated like cattle to be pinned down at the end of a narrow passage, to be branded. And although the Silver City was small, there were small trains that circled the city, to help disperse the crowds after the performances; otherwise, the streets would have been choked with the merry, the drunken, and those who had eaten so many sweets that their fingers had become sticky—sticky with the possessions of other people's pockets.

But with the performance yet to begin, the streets were empty, abandoned, all but for a few romantic souls who wished to look up at the starry underside of the Great Dome, and wonder what it would be like, to travel among those stars.

Inside, noise baffles had lowered between the groups of the audience, to keep the enormous cacophony of a hundred thousand souls (or slightly fewer, there having been so many abductions and arrests the previous evening) from deafening those within.

This night, the dress was somewhat less outrageous; clothes remained upon their owners, and were of a more modest, if not less expensive, sort. The wealthier one was, the more room available to sit; the more room available to sit, the larger and more impressive the court dress worn. Broad skirts, cascades of ruffles, wigs that were not so much styled as engineered were seen in concert with the most desirable seats; more modest gowns that fell straight to the floor—as Ammaline's had, the night before—were more evident in the less privileged boxes and upon the floor, with tight breeches and long suit-coats being sported among those who preferred not to wear skirts. The attire was more formal, signaling that the People were prepared to pay attention and behave as humans ought that night, rather than as locusts: such had always been the mood of the second night of the Season.

It was as much of an illusion as the rebellions of the first.

The crowds entered, were sorted into their sections, and were seated. The emptiness of the Opéra du Mendicant became its fullness. The audience was even larger than the previous night's. Friends gossiped; personnes of business discussed what they would do first, upon leaving the Silver City and traveling to their stations; workers sighed at each other, saying how difficult it would be, to assist the mechaniques in repairing the damage this year; artists spied their rivals' works in the corridors and gnashed their teeth; families gossiped about children or grandchildren who were taking some small part or other, either on the stage or behind it, this night, either with pride or with annoyance, that their bloodline should participate in such foolishness, when instead they could be harvesting crops, or working as prison guards, or monitoring mechaniques, or teaching, or—

The lights began to dim, voices quieted; those who were still up and about returned to their seats. The opera glasses were attuned to retinal scans of those who were meant to be using them, and only the pair at one's assigned seat would operate as designed, once the performance began. (Of the blind, there were none—not on Thomàon, nor the deaf, either; all such gross physical differences had been long since bred away, or repaired before birth, using Paul Hong's many strange techniques.)

The lights having darkened and the audience becoming at least a *little* more quiet, the sound-baffles rose, and the spotlights aimed themselves at the curtain.

The audience raised their glasses with such a clatter, that no other sound could be heard for a moment. One and all turned their eyes toward the stage, where the immense red velvet curtains were beginning to rise, their gold fringe a movable horizon that revealed the opening tableau vivant of the opera:

A bloody battlefield stretched across the stage, with backdrops and scrims used as trompe-l'œil to create a sense that the battle had stretched on forever into the past, throughout all history, and would stretch forward throughout the future, too. Smoke rolled across the set, dark clouds of it, and spilled onto the proscenium like a living thing, oozing and creeping about as if hungry for more. Red lights lit the scene from underneath and behind the tableaux, revealing here a man without a head and there a personne without any legs, a woman whose insides had gone outside for a bit of sun and a stroll. The lives—and deaths—of children were not ignored, and were pitiable to see, with the little forms being posed manikins, and therefore all the more disturbingly silent, and still.

Lights from above brightened, lighting the scene with seven pools of blue light.

Dangling from harnesses, seven angels descended, dressed in shining silver armor, with brilliant white wings outspread and arms stretched forth to the dead below. Seven voices rose in harmony, a harmony of such divine and painful sweetness that it raked the soul raw, and was more discordant to one's nerves, than outright discordance itself.

Clever eyes noticed that the angels cast no shadows, and called them hologrammes, each whispering cleverly to their neighbors.

Then the angels' wings—the voices of the angels still shimmering through that dreadful, sublime harmony—began to beat, and to stir the hair, the clothing, the dreadful wounds of the dead and dying below, and those who had just been annoyed to hear how clever the observation that the angels lacked shadows had been, had the pleasure of whispering in return to their neighbors that they could not be hologrammes, could they, if their wings stirred the air so exactly in time with the beat of those several wings?

Disregarding the whispers from the audience, the angels themselves landed upon the stage, each in their own circle of blue light. Their wings folded, and each of the angels—still singing; would they never stop singing that dreadful tune?—gave themselves a little shake, and the wings, so powerful but a moment before, became silk overdresses, which draped themselves over the bright and shining armor.

Before the clever ones among the crowd could explain how it was done, the angels gave themselves another shake, and their armor disappeared.

The seven were angels no longer, but women. They began to search among the dying and the dead, dragging several of them away from the center of the stage, to leave a clear area in the center of the lights.

The celestial blue lights were no longer the lights of the divine, but turned white. From above descended a ship, and it could be seen that the women's mouths were no longer open, but the dreadful harmony continued—then modified, and became the sound of a ship's landing, and not the singing of the women at all, women who were not—when had it happened?—wearing diaphanous white overdresses at all, but severe olive-green uniforms, with red and white crosses as armbands.

The ship having landed, the dreadful harmony faded, and then became silent. The sound of weapons fire echoed in the distance, sounding almost as if it were a heavy rain pattering against the opéra's roof.

The dying began to stir among the dead, and moaned for help, for water, for assistance.

One of the women called, "Got another live one over here."

Another replied, "The Grillons really did a number on them, didn't they?"

"Why did they drag them all outside? That's the question," interjected a third.

A fourth shrugged. "Who knows why the Grillons do anything?"

A fifth and sixth were silent, having occupied themselves with loading bodies onto floating medical platforms and pushing them toward the ship, where they bumbled like animals waiting for their supper. The door of the ship opened, and the bobbing platforms pushed their way inside.

The seventh of the women, the tallest, wore a white scarf tied around her raven-black hair. As she stood in front of the ship, she said, "I'll tell you what I think. The wreck of that transport ship over there—" She gestured toward the end of the stage, where a heap of rubble concealed whatever she might have been pointing at— "tells me that there was a wreck. And the lack of anyone wearing a uniform—" She gestured toward the dead and the dying— "Tells me that *some* have already been rescued, but others were not."

She inhaled to begin a song, planting her feet firmly upon the stage. The orchestra, down in the pit before the proscenium, lifted their instruments and raised their bows.

The weapons fire in the distance began to get closer, and louder, and the other six women, attending to the dying, looked up, startled at its approach. The leader, Val Kyria, seemed unshaken by the increase in the noise, and sang:

What injustice is this? I cannot understand what has happened here! My soul cries out—

The weapons fire increased in volume suddenly, ending in a powerful *crack!* that seemed to rend the stage itself, with chunks of plaster and plastic falling from overhead, landing heavily upon the stage.

Some of the women, and some of the dying, and even some of the dead, screamed, as if in surprise.

The actress playing Val Kyria did not notice; she only continued singing:

—at the monstrosity of those who selfishly abandoned—

One of the other warrior women crashed into Val Kyria, knocking her to the side, as a very large piece of ceiling plaster fell atop of the ship, crashed through part of it, and bounced onto the stage where she had been standing but a moment before.

The actress playing Val Kyria was knocked away to safety, but the one who had saved her was not, and was caught by a chunk of the plaster, which knocked her to the stage with such force that her wig had come askew, revealing a wig-cap covering the woman's own natural hair, now splattered with blood and embedded with a white chunk of plaster.

The woman lay unmoving on the stage. Behind her, in the wrecked ship, it was revealed that a trapdoor had been opened in the belly of the ship, so that the actors playing the dead could be removed from the stage, without interrupting the flow of the plot, and thus had escaped the doom that had attended the dead warrior woman.

The audience did not know what to make of the scene; they had been so often entertained with such surprises, that they were unsure how much of it was real, and, more importantly, when they should begin their applause.

A few hesitant claps echoed through the opéra.

Then a scream came from the stage, a scream such as only a trained soprano might emit: all eyes, and several spotlights, swung toward the actress portraying Val Kyria upon the stage.

She was at the very edge of it, half-behind a pile of rubble, and pointing upward, not toward the ceiling of the stage, but to the chandeliers, now only dimly lit, hanging above the floor.

Once the length of her scream had ceased, she added after it a question, not as loud, but nevertheless, due to the technology projecting her voice across the immense Opéra du Mendicant, quite audible.

"What the fuck is up in the chandeliers?"

A hundred thousand opera glasses turned themselves upward, and saw what crawled, and readied itself among the dimly glowing lights. A sigh passed through the audience, as the realization spread through them, and the shadows upon the ceiling of the opéra spread, and all felt blackness descend upon them, a doom more apparent, and less escapable, than the one that had first marked the actress playing Val Kyria, but which had been then moved to another source.

The Grillons.

The lights went out.

Chapter 22

The Stench of Fear

THE CAVERNS OF THE aquifer were moist and echoing with the sound of dripping water. A scent of purity filled the air, freshness—a waiting sort of scent. It was not the scent of the surface, which was livelier, full of growth and death and transformation. *That* was a different sort of freshness. This was the simple freshness of the cool underground outside the nest, a place of solitude and disconnection from the sisterhood of Scarabées. Sometimes one needed to be alone with one's scents, to undertake the work of discovering one's own true mind, when one's thoughts seemed full of reassurances and satisfaction, but one's scent was acrid and fearful.

Madame Opale shuddered.

This was one such time. She felt ashamed of her own stench.

Next to her, the sweet young human Ammaline had fallen back into the arms of the glowering Manon. They glided through the water on the back of the ribbony aliens the humans called Gondoliers, which glowed, and whistled, and sang as they swam, taking them ever forward.

Madame Opale wished to growl, "Take us back! Undo what I have done!"

But it was too late. The process of Ammaline allowing herself to be integrated with her other identity had begun, even without the use of human technology that the others required: she had opened herself fully to transformation.

At least the Gondoliers seemed satisfied with the events as they transpired. They had often carried Madame Opale where she wished to go, but never had they sung while doing so.

The humans thought the Gondoliers to be native to Thomàon. But that was not the case. The Gondoliers had come from the depths of space, unthinkably far, and had lain under the surface of the world for untold generations, standing aside from the affairs of the planet.

They had only awoken when the humans arrived—at first the sisterhood of Scarabées had thought that the humans had brought the Gondoliers with them, as some pest they had inadvertently brought on their ship. They had brought all sorts of infestations with them, uncaring.

But the sisterhood soon had found evidence that the Gondoliers had been there for an eon, a billion years—the remains of their bodies had marked ancient stones, freshly mined.

How had they come to Thomàon? Their genetics were nothing like the Scarabées had ever smelled or tasted; their proteins were truly foreign. Even the humans were closer in nature to Thomàon than the Gondoliers.

Madame Opale was convinced that the Gondoliers had come to watch Thomàon, that the arrival of humanity was itself an experiment that the Gondoliers wished to observe.—And yet the arrival of the Gondoliers had been long before the development of humanity.

And yet.

As the sisterhood of Scarabées had debated what to do with humanity, to destroy them, to be destroyed by them, to embrace them, to *become* them, Madame Opale had felt, down in the most foul and unseemly of her scent glands, that the fate of Thomàon hung upon how the challenges of humanity were addressed.

That they were being judged.

To destroy humanity outright would have meant that any challenge Thomàon faced would likely be addressed in the same manner. Internal factions within the sisterhood? Why, better to destroy those who had caused such conflict! The Grillons encroaching upon their nests and eating their own shared young? Better to destroy them, than to accept them as co-generators of their intertwined species.

To co-opt humanity and make it serve the sisterhood's purpose—as they had done with the Grillons—was a constant temptation among their kind. But the Grillons had become warped, turning ever further toward violence, shedding their native intelligence, turning further and further toward the regression of their species. Had binding the Grillons to the Scarabées genetic cycle made them unable to adapt?

What responsibility did the Scarabées carry for the Grillons? And what responsibility did they carry for themselves?

Madame Opale had wished to find another way—to bring humanity into the sisterhood itself. But her identification of the females with the sisterhood of Scarabées and the males with the Grillons had twisted her perceptions.

She knew—it was a matter of faith for her—that it was *her* scent that had caused the humans to destroy Simone, the Seer.

Simone had been born with male genetic markers, and had, during her purely human immaturity on her home world, been raised mainly excluded from her essential femininity. Madame Opale, of a species that relied on scent to establish information, had made the assumption that Simone was lying about her gender. She had treated Simone as a male of her species—and had treated all the human males as if they were Grillons, waiting for their season of madness to attack!

The other Scarabées, looking to her for leadership, had assumed the same.

They had rejected Simone's overtures to discuss her hopes and fears about humanity with the sisterhood, even rebuked her cruelly for trying. Eventually, after thousands of reincarnations influenced by the Scarabées' genetic influence, the other humans turned on Simone as well and had had her killed by the White Gentleman, no longer able to tolerate her presence among them.

Were the Scarabées so different than the humans?

Was it so difficult to believe that the Gondoliers had come to influence—or test—or observe how the Scarabées handled the conflict?

It shamed Madame Opale, as well as terrified her.

Madame Opale had come to carry poisonous guilt inside her, a scent that had built until her own nest had driven her away, to be alone and to find her own thoughts.

Madame Opale rubbed her inner legs together, worrying them against each other, feeling every nick and scratch on them like a polishing stone. But no matter how much she rubbed them together, they did not wear each other smooth. The movement only stirred up the ugly scents from her glands, forcing her to smell herself—her doubts, her guilt.

It was so strong, even the humans must smell it.

On the back of the Gondolier and still gently cradled within Manon's arms, Ammaline breathed shallowly, her skin pale blue in the glow of the Gondoliers. Her eyes darted beneath their lids, her breath came in pants, then seemed to stop. Then began again, a slow, inward sigh, that, upon exhalation, became a hum.

The memories that she carried of Simone were beginning to integrate.

The sisterhood had agreed, finally, that Simone had been wronged. That Madame Opale was to attempt to bring her back. The humans thought her memories and awareness had been destroyed, but of course nothing was ever lost, as long as the sisterhood of Scarabées remained.

Humanity wished to know the secret of immortality: the sisterhood had mastered it.

The sisterhood did not agree that Simone could help them resolve the human question, but were willing to listen—now, when more humans were soon to arrive, and it might have been altogether too late.

They had recalled Simone within themselves, from within their own memories and protein files, and re-encoded her memories into the Warden's child.

Madame Opale put her worrying legs against her thorax. Scarabées did not pray; they did not create gods as humanity did. They carried their ancestors within them, and that was enough.

But Madame Opale had learned to pray, to listen to a small, silent, foreign voice within her, one that she carried with honor.

It had been Ammaline's mother, that human soul untainted by Scarabée genetics, who had offered them all a chance at peace, and allowed Simone's memories to be brought back within the realm of humanity. Upon her unjust death, her awareness had been brought into the sisterhood, and honored as one of the ancestors, with Madame Opale as her special vessel, carrying her consciousness, hidden yet immortal.

Madame Opale held her worrying legs still and prayed.

To Ammaline's mother, Etoile.

Chapter 23

Death Rises

Within the Opéra du Mendicant, all was darkness, and cries of terror and pain, as the Grillons descended upon the crowd.

The roof of the opéra lay before the Silver Spire. The roof of the opéra was a silvered, arched dome that was hung inside with a chandelier. It was covered with glass, but cleverly silvered over, so that the dome could be made translucent, or opaque, depending upon the effects that were wished to be produced. That night, it had been darkened, so that *The Seven Valkyries* might begin in velveted blackness; it had been planned that the building's dome would be made clear at the triumph of the play, and a panoply of lighting effects be played upon the inside of the dome that protected the city.

Alas, plans had much been changed.

During that night, the dome was not so beautiful as it once had been; it had been punctured and violated in a hundred different places, where the Grillons had cut silently through the glass, and set it aside, and pressed themselves inward along the inner surfaces of the roof, clinging with their pads and claws to the joints between the panes of glass, to the supports for the chandelier, to the scaffolding that ran here and there among the stage lights.

The shapes of the Grillons, numberless and alien, gushed into the dome, all with only the barest whisper of sound, a fluid motion made of enormous but sticklike figures.

They had entered—it seemed impossible, how many of them had entered—but finally they were all inside, and the artificial moon glowing from the inner surface of the dome shone down on the silvered glass and the bare, gravel-covered flat areas outside the curves of the dome. The rest of the roof was only interrupted by a pair of access doors on opposite sides of the roof past the dome itself, for maintenance and for lovers to escape to, to stare out at the Silver City.

One figure remained: a man, or rather what had once been a man.

His figure was elongated and distorted. If the Twelve, those demi-gods that had been given gifts of Grillon genetic material thousands of years ago, were tall and slender, this man—if such he could be called—was a giant, over ten feet tall, dressed in wispy rags that danced with the slightest breeze.

He sat on his haunches, peering into the darkness below, watching what could not be seen, only heard, with the greatest of relish.

His face was a grimace of joy, the face of every human monster at the moment of the revelation of their true nature: wide, dark blue lips, stretched unnaturally far; bulging eyes that were pure white, enclouded with strange blindness; teeth that were far too many, and far too sharp; a nose that had been bitten down to the bone; and blue veins running below the skin, in animate mockery of the signifiers of death. Against them lay the fact of his tongue, bright and red and sensuous, running against his dark lips.

His limbs, where they emerged from his raiment, were pale white, except for the claws of his fingers, and the talons of his feet. Stiff black hair emerged from his head, a steel-stiff crown. The white rags that hung around his body were fastened at the waist with a black belt, covered with loops and tools and pouches, and set in the center with a red gem: a gem that gave him entry to many locations, and access to many tools.

He rose from his crouch and paced around the silvery dome, listening to the screams below with relish. From time to time he would press a hand to the edge of a broken pane of glass, as if in doubt whether to slip inside and join the chaos below—but he did not.

If he had been human enough to remember himself, he would have called himself the White Gentleman; but he was no longer that human—or was it that he had never been that human?

The rest of the Twelve were monsters, it was true, monsters of one form or another. Any list of sins would have found them out: Grandpère might be despair; the Diva vanity; the Warden the soul of wrath itself. The Général was greedy; the King held impatience in his heart; and the Queen—although she seldom showed it—was constantly afraid. The Assassin was a deceiver; the Scientist, with his stolen science, the soul of sloth; the Seer Simone was wracked with envy, envy, envy! The Puppet Master boasted; his evil acts were carried out, that he might lord his superiority above all others, that was, hubris. And the Historian, that is, the teller of this humble tale, had much to her regret indulged for long years, years beyond all human feeling, the deadly sin of passivity and indecision—the foolish notion of being above the world's tragedies.

And then there was the White Gentleman, the embodiment of lust.

The White Gentleman considered himself perfected, when he considered himself at all. He told himself that he wished to destroy all of humanity, in just revenge upon those who had wronged him, but he deceived himself: he would have come to this pass, whether humanity had ever wronged him or otherwise. The reason for his bloodlust was his bloodlust itself, self-referential, whole, and complete.

The Scarabées had no notion of human personality; it did not drive their species or their world the way it had driven life on Earth. The powers that they had given the Twelve had fed the worst aspects of the Twelve; it had disconnected them from their fellows; it had raised them above them and turned them against them. The Scarabées had no notion that such a thing could exist: that humanity, when fed upon the nectar of the gods, when granted immortality, would cut itself off from itself, and allow their inner predators to conquer, warp, and destroy them.

The Scarabées had no way of saying that *power corrupts*, or that *absolute power corrupts absolutely*; they had no need of it—although they themselves were neither saints nor blessed innocents.

They did not know that their gifts would corrupt the Twelve. They did not know that humanity is best when it is beset, when it is challenged, when it must struggle for survival. *Then* it can aspire to kindness and generosity.

And how could they know, with their collective sense of each other and the universe, that among the various characters of humanity, there would be One who had been bred, across countless generations of humanity, repeating itself as surely as a musical theme, to predate upon the enemies of the group, or, if they were not available, the weakest of the group, to become the living nightmare that is used to scare children—how could the Scarabées know, that among the monsters there is always one who is worse than a monster?

Humanity itself refused to know it; how could the Scarabées have guessed?

They knew that the others had murdered the one called Carlton after the death of Simone, and that the survivors had felt a great relief afterwards. They did not understand why the remainder of the Twelve had forced themselves to forget their compatriots—either of them. They did not understand why Lemure, or Corentin, would take on the rôle of White Gentleman from time to time, as if to keep his memory alive.

It was not they, however, who brought back the White Gentleman. That was the Grillons, who could not understand why they had brought him back either, but found themselves attracted to the man, who had heretofore walked among them without fear or pity, but only understanding. They resurrected him—they were more intelligent than even the Scarabées knew—and rebuilt him in their image, and reinstalled him at the south pole, in Dorakyura Fortress, and called him their God.

The White Gentleman paced around the edges of the dome of the Opéra du Mendicant, and waited for the Grillons to finish their work with the thoroughness for which they were renowned.

They had asked but one thing of their God: that he remain outside the dome of the opéra, while they performed these first ablutions. It was their only acknowledgment of that gentleman's past: they feared that they would murder their own God, in the throes of their initial bloodlust.

All things considered, it was a reasonable precaution—but it did not suit him.

He paced; he ran his claws against the surface of the dome; he crouched once again, attempting to peer inside.

The night was stifling and warm, airless and dark. The stars had gone out on the underside of the Great Dome; no lightshows lit its surface; no clouds roiled, brooding and dark. The weather systems had been deactivated—or, rather, there was no one left to keep them running, after the Grillons had gone into the secret spaces that controlled the Great Dome and the rest of the equipment maintaining the city. Such things had been easy, with the White Gentleman and his red gem at their side.

The rest of the city held its breath, understanding that something was afoot, and gladdened by the fact that they had not gone to the opéra; they were safe from whatever trouble stirred up by the Puppet Master and his rebels; they need only wait until the morning and—they told themselves—all would surely be well.

Only furtive shadows stirred on the streets in the darkness, when they stirred at all. Small fires smoldered; fountains lay still; the lights of the city, such few as there were, showed the smog hanging in the air and cast it in a greenish light; what sounds there were, were soon hushed.

What was happening?

Those within the buildings who could still contact each other, asked that question of each other, but received no answer. Rumors spread: *there is screaming, coming from the Opéra du Mendicant...I see movement outside the apartment...I see movement near the Louvre...within the Jardin Botanique...on the rooftops...across the street...upon the stair...*

It as an old fear, coming from the depths of humanity, or at least that part of humanity which had been selected to travel to Thomàon: that they would go to strange new worlds, conquer what they found, crown themselves as kings, and then make some critical, tragic, unavoidable mistake in not having conquered and dominated thoroughly enough: that they would have let some small element of resistance escape, and have it turn its revenge—surely not deserved!—upon its rightful masters.

Upon Earth, against the rest of humanity against which the colonists of Thomàon had turned their backs, such resistance was small, or subtle, or limited by ethics, or otherwise undermined itself with infighting, as each group fractured itself upon the other. It was more often that those who would resist were the ones inflicted with annihilation, than the colonists.

Upon Thomàon, the resistance was, however, not human. And the Grillons had had enough of subservience. They could not touch the Scarabées, who controlled their reproduction.

But they could, and would, unleash their anger against humanity.

Among the dying cacophony below, there was enough silence that the White Gentleman could hear sounds behind him: human footsteps upon the gravel of the roof. He twisted to look over his shoulder and found that a small group of survivors had escaped their murderers, and gained the roof.—or they had been driven there, by the Grillons, for the White Gentleman's amusement.

Even those in the grip of bloodlust could be thoughtful, it seemed.

The White Gentleman rose from where he crouched, unfolding his limbs. His white flesh seemed to glow, even in what little light there was inside the dome. He was utterly silent, but the fluttering of his rags caught the eyes of the four survivors, bloody and limping, as they emerged from the stair.

One of them pointed and cried sharply, but silenced themselves immediately, having learnt the cost of making a sound, no matter how hushed. The others did not point or cry out, but only froze in place, and looked, and shuddered.

Not one of them moved to defend the others, or to attack. They had no weapons; they had not found or made any. Those who would have done so, had already sacrificed themselves. The ones who had escaped were in the habit of making themselves small and immobile, so that their braver fellows could grapple and delay and die.

Throughout the course of humanity, it had mattered little that the brave had died and died and died in that cause or the other; humanity carried its Twelve in its flesh, and they emerged once again, even from the mildest and most sheeplike among them.

Such sheep lay before the White Gentleman.

He smiled—he had carved his face so that he could hardly have stopped—and walked slowly toward the survivors.

They huddled against each other, seeking comfort, showing their weakness as if it were a playing card: *we will yield, if you only let us live.*

Among humanity, it was often an irresistible card, as conquerors took their brides and slaves from among the weakest of a race.

But the White Gentleman, even when he had been human, had not been one to live and let live.

One or another of the survivors, not the one who had pointed, whispered the truth: "It is him, the White Gentleman. We will die here."

They pushed away from the others, who stared at them in horror and surprise. Surely it was better to huddle upon the roof, and show only weakness, and beg for mercy.

The one who had pushed away from them turned and ran, not back toward the questionable safety of the stairs, but in another direction: their party clothes torn and soaked with blood and fluttering behind them as they fled the fate of the others.

They flung themselves from the edge of the roof and into nothingness, praying for a quick death.

The White Gentleman let that one go; it amused him to see such wisdom.

The rest, he kept. Such friends, at such a moment, were only to be treasured.—We will leave him to his particular pleasures without further description, and turn our attention back to the rest of the Twelve, and their pursuits as Thomàon fell to darkness.

Chapter 24

The Lodestone of Thomàon

WHILE AMMALINE, MADAME OPALE, and Manon traveled via underground caverns upon the backs of the Gondoliers, to some location that the human passengers hardly knew, as Ammaline's body shuddered and shook, and frothed at the mouth; and while the Grillons completed their slaughter of those within the Opéra du Mendicant and began overspilling into the surrounding streets, and the buildings where the survivors huddled; and while the White Gentleman looked up and said, "I apologize, but I really must be going" and lavished upon his lovers an end; the rest of the Twelve had not yet realized that their doom was upon them.

In the Silver City, Corentin had paused in his plan to draw the Gold Stars and others who belonged to the Puppet Master's retinue to Versailles, to note the darkening of the Great Dome, and to lick his lips and turn toward the Castle of the Silver Spire, as if he were a compass needle pointing toward true north.

Grandpère, after his death and the transference of his memories, had earlier that day—or was it night?—returned to his place in the Louvre, watching redouts collected by the sensors of the Silver Spire and understanding that the situation was worse than he had known, or had even thought to dread: it had not occurred to him that the Grillons might rebel, not now, not while the ships from Earth were coming.

Below the city, in the caverns at the edge of the reservoir, Queen Delphine screamed—she seemed to scream forever—as Paul emerged from the kitchen of his prefab trailer, covered in Jacques's blood, and looking apologetic. He endured as long as he could. "Sorry to interrupt," he said eventually. "But you can either stop screaming or I can cut your throat."—She did; she had lived long under the eye of powerful men, and had subsumed herself to their personalities, their hopes and dreams, leaving nothing for herself, a nothingness which she called *stability*, not recognizing it for the corruption of the soul that it was. That was, she was used to silencing herself, but not for that useless nerd *Paul*.

Paul crossed the trailer, making a face, and eventually pulled a towel from a closet and soaked it with rubbing alcohol from his laboratory supplies, cleaning his hands and arms as best he could.

From a corner, the Queen said with a shuddering voice, "Your face, Paul. Wipe your face."

He did what he was told, then sat down, still covered in blood, at his terminal, where he typed a few characters, lifted his right hand in the air with one finger extended, hesitating.

"What are you doing, Paul?" asked the shivering queen.

Lowering his finger slowly, he gently pressed the *Return* key, then rose from his seat at the terminal. "Just sending a message to Yvonne."

He glanced over his shoulder; Sarah's face was greenish, washed out of all color. She was going to be sick. He made plans for how to move her unconscious body. Jack's, of course, could be left behind. He was no longer present within it; Jack himself had moved on.

Paul walked toward the door to the corridor. Had Jacques brought the golf cart with him? The golf cart would do nicely to carry Sarah, and then he, Paul, would not have to walk.

Sarah tried to shrink further back into her corner. "Did Yvonne tell you to do this?"

"No," said Paul. "She didn't know what I was doing. She does now, though."

"What you were doing?" she asked. "Paul, *what* have you done?"

It was too much, and Sarah's mind too small, and too terrified to understand what he *had* done; he did not answer her. He was himself abruptly gripped with the knowledge that his own mind, however much it had been improved by the Scarabées, was sorely lacking. It felt as though the world outside his trailer were haunted, had always been haunted, not by a ghost but by some idea that he was too stupid or too foolish or too ignorant to comprehend.

"We are going *out*," he said, hesitating at the door of the room. "To meet Yvonne. Are you coming? Do I need to knock you out and load you into the cart?"

It was not a threat; he only meant to offer her the brief surcease of unconsciousness. He knew how terrified she was.

Sarah stared at him, her eyes bulging in her face, her cheeks hollowed out, dark circles under her eyes. "Don't leave me."

He nodded, then beckoned toward the door. "Come, then."

She preceded him out of the room, and the two of them climbed into the cart and drove back toward the stairs leading upward, to the Silver City.

Meanwhile, the man who had been killed by Paul Hong, that is, Général Jacques Saveur-Chasse, was in the process of being resurrected: but not in the nearest resurrection center, which would have been more or less directly above him in the Silver City, but in Versailles—Paul had not wanted the man to be able to return *too* quickly, but had qualms about leaving him no way to return to the supposed safety of the city.

Jacques had always been a light sleeper, never quite trusting himself to the arms of Sleep, not out of fear of death—who of the Twelve feared Death, on Thomàon?—but simply because he felt Sleep to be a thief of his time, removing hourly that which was most precious to him.

He came to himself while the supporting gel still surrounded him in the resurrection tank. It was an uncanny, but not unfamiliar experience, and he found himself unable to move. His brain was active, and his nervous system gave him notice of the pressure of the fluid upon his limbs, but also the awareness of the fluid still found within his lungs, so that he felt as though he were drowning: a sensation impossible to endure, and yet he must.

As soon as control of his limbs had been returned to him, he would tear free of the connections holding him fast within the tank, but until then, he was forced to think: to turn his awareness inward.

Jacques Saveur-Chasse thought constantly, and thought *of* himself nearly as often: his discomforts, his insecurities, his wounded pride, his sense of being an outsider from the others. But seldom did his attention turn upon itself, so that he must think of who he was, and what he had done, rather than what had happened to him.

Why had Paul killed him? It had *hurt*.—How had he, the Player, the Général, been so deceived by the man? Aside from being merely offensive, what *reason* had the Madman for removing the Player from the board? And why had Paul let Jacques retain the memory of that death?

Trapped inside the nutshell of his own skull, Jacques was forced to answer his own question, or rather to be unable to find an answer to it, and thus turn his inexorably active mind upon the question itself.

Was he, Jacques Saveur-Chasse, the Player? Or the Played?

Was he a general, or was he a tool, being used against his own will, as a piece in games that not only was he not in control of, but had not even known existed?

He was quickly forced to realize that the answers to *those* questions were obvious: He had thought he was playing a game to control Thomàon, himself against Grandpère, with the Puppet Master as his own Black Queen, sowing discord at the Player's discretion.

But he was not.

The unquestioned assumption upon which he had built his existence on Thomàon was itself false. It was not a matter of who was in charge—the Player or the Puppet Master—but that the two of them were very nearly peas in a pod, manipulators who were themselves always having been manipulated.

Jacques took a moment—without external reference, he had no notion of how long such a moment stretched—to acknowledge that he had been a fool.

The awareness was brutal, and he wished for death; if he had been at liberty of self-eradication at that moment, he might have done so, even as he knew that he would be resurrected once again, and have to kill himself again, and again.

But his limbs were not at their own liberty, and the gel that supported his weight also performed the exchange of oxygen and carbon dioxide within his bloodstream via his lungs, and in short he was trapped within his own mind without surcease.

His mind was a dragon, and vicious when stirred.

The moment passed, and he shook aside the wish for oblivion. Curiosity drove him. *If* he himself had been manipulated, *then* who had done so?

His old enemy, Grandpère? No: Grandpère had been too long fought against, like a familiar chess player. Too often had Jacques tested him past his limits, and seen where Grandpère had been forced to yield, to concede defeat. If Grandpère had secrets, they were secrets about the arrival of the ships from Earth, and his fears that humanity would conquer the universe.

Could instead it be Armand who had undermined the game, as Jacques had so often wondered? No: for the same reasons as Grandpère. They had too often struggled against each other.

Jacques ran through the others, letting his instincts guide him through his questions—knowing his own mind as the imperfect tool it was, he also knew that it was, at the moment, the only one he had—among possibilities. Corentin was a tool, Delphine his helpmeet; Yvonne thought herself objective and did not wish to play; Marks belonged to Grandpère, body and soul—there was some secret about his wife, Jacques knew, but it was likely only that he was attempting to find a way to resurrect someone who could not be resurrected; Océan threw herself this way and that, depending upon who offered her the most pleasures or least pain; Manon also threw in their lot with Grandpère; and Simone and the White Gentleman were dead.

The thought of Marks attempting to resurrect his wife occurred to Jacques again: what if Marks was not the only one trying to resurrect a lover?

Paul had never recovered from the death of Simone. Grief had lingered within him like a cancer.

Was that it? Had Paul found some way to bring Simone back after the White Gentleman had so foully murdered her and all her existing clones, and the Puppet Master deleted her memories and genetics?

Was that sufficient explanation for Paul's behavior? That he had found a way to bring back Simone?

But, wait: Jacques felt gooseflesh creep across his skin like the wind ruffling up waves on a placid lake. His temperature rose with the fever of his brain—the gel surrounding him chilled slightly, in order to compensate.

Why had the Puppet Master deleted Simone's memories and genetic code from the systems?

The other members of the Twelve likely did not know that the Puppet Master had done it: they had thought that the White Gentleman had been the single, sole force behind Simone's death.

That was not how things worked, among the Twelve. No one of them could work alone, independently of the others. They were all bound together by the resurrection chambers, and, moreover, by the Great Lie that they had told the rest of humanity: that the Twelve were chosen from among the people, that the people ruled Thomàon.

Jacques's mind turned upon his own thoughts again: *was* that the extent of the Great Lie that the Twelve had told the rest of humanity, so that they would remain their playthings? Power corrupted, Jacques knew; whether absolute power corrupted absolutely was a minor point up for debate, but it tended generally to be true.

But was part of that corruption ignorance?

Who ruled Thomàon?

Why had the Puppet Master helped the White Gentleman destroy Simone?

Jacques had considered the matter at the time: the Puppet Master had helped the White Gentleman to destroy the Seer because Armand had always hated Simone—they had been friends on Earth, which meant that Armand sensed in her the constant risk of her exposing some part of his past—and he had later denounced the White Gentleman to shift the blame off his own ass. Getting rid of the White Gentleman was merely the cherry on top, removing another threat to his own power from the board.

Jacques had thought he had understood the situation. But it was becoming clear that he had not.

Who ruled Thomàon?

Truly, who?—The resurrection pool began its next cycle. Jacques shuddered from head to foot as his muscles responded to the impulses of his nerves. The gel surrounding him began to cool, and become oppressive. He swept his arms about, pulling them free with a hundred different stinging sensations, then heaved himself above the level of the gel. More carefully this time, he pulled free the intubation that circulated the gel inside his lungs, soft, rigid material that branched several times, an incredible mass of complex tubing that always repulsed and shocked him to see it, it was so large.

Then he coughed into the pool, forcing the rest of the gel out of his lungs as best he could. Had he been a better sleeper, he would have slept until the tubes had pumped most of the gel out of his body for him.

But he could never sleep so long.

As he shrugged out of his restraints and lifted himself out of the pool, he saw a mechanique waiting next to the other pool. He climbed out of the pool and vomited back into it further amounts of gel. Later, he would have to shit the rest out in the other direction.

The room felt cold, even though it was kept warm. He shivered. His feet slapped upon the clean white tiles underfoot, feeling the subtle, sharkskin texture that kept the newly resurrected from slipping on their gel-coated feet.

A white robe waited for him. He slipped it on; it was softer than he liked. It was fuzzy, not waffled cotton. But whatever. He had more important things to think about. He headed for the door, which opened as he approached, spilling colder air toward him. He shivered. A long, hot shower would not be a waste of time, he decided.—Then he glanced back at the other pool. Who else had been sent back to the start of the level that day?

Arms spread wide, long hair floating in the subtle currents of the gel, the body of Armand lay in the second pool. Jacques checked the flat gray readout panel built into the side of the pool: Armand was nearing the end of his process.

In fact, as he glanced, the monitoring system beeped, the gray digital countdown switched from "ANI" to "W-R," that was, from "animation" to "withdrawal and resurrection."

The mechanique came to life and began to lift Armand from the gel using a contraption rigged in the ceiling, which Jacques had not noticed at first. The clone had a loop of intubation wrapped around its torso, which the mechanique fastened to a hook leading to a pulley overhead. Armand's clone rose from the gel, the wires attached to his torso and limbs ripping away, and the intubation coming out of his lungs with a rough jerk and streaks of blood.

Jacques frowned. What had happened, that Armand's body needed to be attended by a mechanique? Was the clone damaged? Had yet another aspect of the world gone awry?

Who was actually in charge of this shitshow?

Armand shuddered, came awake, and opened his mouth, bloody gel rolling down his chin. His eyes looked blank, horrified. Out of the mechanique emerged a waldo equipped with a surgeon's razor. Something with the clone must have gone *really* wrong. But why had the resurrection pool not caught it?

Armand's clone began to struggle, so vehemently that the mechanique was pulled forward, moving something behind the pool.

Jacques took in the shape down in the shadows without conscious comprehension.

He reached forward, took the scalpel away from the mechanique, and used it to cut the intubation material on Armand's chest. The clone fell clumsily back into the pool and continued thrashing and struggling. The mechanique went into standby mode to await further instruction, having been interrupted in its tasks by one of the Twelve.

Behind the pool lay a disembodied foot, surrounded by a dried pink stain that peeled and curled—dried gel. That was all.—That was all that had been left behind.

If someone wished to trap one of the Twelve in one place, setting up a trap of resurrection, murder, and further resurrection would accomplish it, as long as there was no one to set them free.

Who would do something like that?

Any one of them, given enough pressure to do so.

The question came to him again, and this time he was not distracted from answering it:

Who rules Thomàon?

No one.

No one theory could comprehend the situation; only a mess of conflicting interests could explain it. And that meant that—literally—no one was in control of the situation.

That meant Simone *might* be able to return. And if Simone might be able to return, then so might Marks's wife Etoile, and if Etoile might rise, then Carlton also, looking for revenge against them all.

Further, if no one truly ruled Thomàon, then the unthinkable might happen: the Grillons *might* be able to rise up against them all.

It was illogical. Impossible.

Yet: that did not mean it was not true.

Jacques set to work with helping Armand out of the pool.

As for the Hawkmistress, she had completed transferring, validating, and setting in order the records that she had brought with her to the little hut, in order to preserve them against loss.

That being done, she soothed herself by checking the seeds of the vault, reviewing both the files on the computer systems and the physical samples stored on slides, freeze dried and carefully preserved in sealed containers. The seed vault was a small trailer, smaller than Paul's, and made to feel smaller still by the endless deep gray plastic cabinets that lined the wall s.—The process was entirely unnecessary; the seeds and their genes were carefully recorded all across the mechaniques of Thomàon. It would take nearly the destruction of the planet to eradicate them all.

Nevertheless, it comforted her. She had just received a message from Paul, saying that Delphine had been sent to watch him, and that Jacques had come as well, to murder him.—But not to worry, that he would carry out his part of the plan as agreed.

Paul's part of the plan was to extract the information he had collected, the devices he had engineered, the insights he had made, and to give it to her, so she might preserve it. Until he had done so, she was to wait at the archives, and try not to chew her fingernails to the quick.

Yvonne put on scrubs, gloves, and a mask and scanned the files while she waited for the air to cycle and clear, so that her presence didn't pose a genetic risk of contamination. Paul had set up the system, and she tended to trust it. When she got a notification that it was safe to proceed, she did so.

The cabinet doors opened onto rows and rows of slim drawers. The handles of the drawers were of smooth, cool plastic that stuck slightly to her blue nitrile gloves. The drawers themselves slid out smoothly on their rails, revealing columns of glass slides inside clear, sealed boxes. Each slide was sealed, each box was sealed, and the vault itself was sealed.

The boxes contained the genetic material of every human who had lived on Thomàon—although not their memories or personalities—and several samples from every type of species upon the planet. There was even a single sample of Gondolier material.

With this information, the entire human race on Thomàon could be replicated.

The Historian looked through the drawers, peering at random samples of the material within, taking heart at the thought of all the wealth before her. Then she resealed the cabinets and updated the files that she had stored on her magnifying glass. The matter of updating the files was simple; she had only to lay her glass atop a wireless pad and wait until the mechanique informed her that the data had been synchronized. Later, she would need to validate the data against her system at Castle Frankenstein, to ensure it had transferred correctly.

She picked up the glass and kissed the frame.—There is nothing that a historian loves so much as primary sources, but the digitized encoding would have to do.

Paul's signal finally arrived: the data had been archived, and needed but to be transferred to her keeping, and brought back to the hut to be stored with the rest of the data. He could not come to her; Delphine was still with him. She would have to get it herself.

Yvonne looked around the vault to ensure that she was leaving nothing behind.—She was sure to return soon, but it was a particular habit with her, to leave the place as if she were never to return, so that it would always be in readiness.

The mechanique had already gone back to sleep; the cabinets were closed and sealed; the desks and ledges clean; the floor unbroken by footprints, smudges, or dust.

She let herself out of the vault door. The lights flashed on as she emerged, showing her the stark, barren ledge of the reservoir, the reflections of the light on the waves of the reservoir, the line of sandy grit that had been cast upon the subterranean shore.

A glowing ribbon was coming toward her, across the water; it had a dark figure upon its back.

Yvonne tensed, wondering if she were about to be killed: wondering if the seeds were about to be attacked and destroyed.

But the figure was not Armand, was not Jacques, was not—a figure from her nightmares—Carlton, his waxy, cruel face half-translucent in the Gondolier's light. The Gondoliers had refused to carry Carlton, when he lived. Yvonne gave thanks to whatever gods there might be in the universe, that he had been finally killed.

It was Madame LaFerme who rode the Gondolier's back.

This surprised Yvonne; Madame LaFerme did not like to ride the Gondoliers; she said that it only reminded her of navigating the *Téméraire*, and saddened her that she could no longer fly the stars, and must prance around the stage and sing, which she had not done since university.

"Yvonne," said Madame LaFerme, holding up a black case, "I have something that I want you to keep for me."

The case was familiar enough: it was one of the cases that Marks Lemure used to transport the golden elixir, the honey-like substance that the Scarabées used to store their memories, which the Twelve had been consuming in monstrous quantities, erasing the history of the Scarabées as they did so, a fact that filled Yvonne with shame.

Why, oh why, had she ever agreed to such a thing?—But if she had not, there would still be the Eleven, and everything which had occurred would have gone unrecorded, and, eventually, unremembered.

"The last case of elixir, more or less," Yvonne said. "Where did you get it?"

"Armand had hidden it on the *Téméraire*. I took it off his corpse when Ammaline and I killed him."

Yvonne backed into the side of the hut, startled more by *who* had helped kill Armand than that Océan had killed her lover. "Ammaline? Is she—?"

"She's all right."

Underneath their words was the question of whether Ammaline had gone mad, or gone into shock, or worse—the experiment that was her flesh had gone wrong somehow, and she had changed, uncontrolled, into the monster that her mother and father had made of her.

She's all right. That meant that Ammaline had not been transformed, only that she had fought, and killed, as so many must do, to survive on Thomàon.

"And you want to keep the elixir here?" Yvonne asked. "At the archive?"

"It needs to be somewhere that can't be found. Off the network. Temperature controlled. Just in case."

Yvonne licked her lips; what followed was a touchy subject indeed, among the shifting alliances of the Twelve: "Does Grandpère know where this is? Or that you have it?"

The Gondolier bumped against the shore, and Madame LaFerme disembarked. She held out the case. "I don't know, and I didn't tell him."

After a moment's hesitation, Yvonne took the case from her, then placed it out of sight behind one of the stalagmites near the hut. "Thank you."

"I'm sorry." Madame LaFerme stretched, rolling her head on her shoulders, locking her fingers behind her, then lifting them over her head. "Aren't you going to put it inside now?"

Yvonne could not have explained the real reason she did not unlock the door of the hut, and begin the laborious—but not *that* laborious—process of storing the elixir safely.

Lying, she said, "No. I have to pick something up from Paul and store it. I might as well wait until I pick up Paul's materials and file them both at the same time."

Madame LaFerme nodded, as if Yvonne had not just been speaking so completely out of character. "Sure. Then you can just lock yourself away here until all of this blows over."

"If it all blows over," Yvonne corrected her.

The Gondolier that had brought Madame LaFerme surfaced from the water, whistling at the two of them.

The wrapped candy in Yvonne's pockets was still damp from her earlier submersion. She unwrapped it carefully, making sure the wrapper would not get away from her, and tossed her few remaining pieces to the Gondolier.

She was never sure how much they understood, but had long since decided to err on the side of *too smart to talk to the humans.*

The Gondolier rolled a loop of its flesh toward the two of them. Madame LaFerme stepped casually atop the creature, but Yvonne climbed aboard on hands and knees, letting her feet dangle into the water, the weight of her shoes dragging against her legs.

It whistled at her again.

She patted the Gondolier's side. "As much as I'd like to go to Castle Frankenstein and play with you, I need to go to Paul's trailer first. If you don't mind, please."

"They don't really understand," Madame LaFerme told her, not for the first time.

"And yet I always arrive where I ask to go," Yvonne answered her.

The Gondolier whistled to her and began undulating away from the shore.

Madame LaFerme yawned. Yvonne followed suit. She *was* tired. Exhausted, in fact. She lay against the cold, wet flesh of the Gondolier, sighed, and let herself doze. The Gondolier whistled to her soothingly; Madame LaFerme joined it in song; soon Yvonne had fallen deeper into a sound sleep.

The reader might rightly ask: Did she know what was happening above, as the Grillons entered the city? She knew that such events were possible; she was no Seer, but she was not talentless in the realm of prognostication. But the worst of what was about to occur, she did not know, and had not even suspected, for Paul, in his mercy, had not told her.

Book the Third

Les tempêtes de la saison

Chapter 1

Re-emergence

When Ammaline returned to herself, from the tempests of resurrecting the memories of Simone, little had changed—or everything had.

She looked about her. The Gondolier, its white flesh cool but soft underneath her, still swam toward whatever destination Madame Opale had chosen for them. The reservoir was still dark but for the dim greenish glow cast by the Gondoliers above them, lighting only dimly the cavern roof above.

She lay upon Manon's lap, their crossed legs under her head, and their arms resting upon her shoulders, or stroking her forehead. She smiled up at them; they had been looking elsewhere, but looked down at her as she tilted her head upward.

Manon's form was no longer as familiar as it once was, but now Ammaline understood the changes: their long, foxlike face no longer seemed unfamiliar to her; she had, after all, seen it over thousands of years. The history between herself and her friend had changed, become richer.

Ammaline lifted a hand, noting that it felt weak and shaky, as if she were exhausted. She placed her hand upon her chest, letting it rest lightly there.

Did she still love Manon? Had the introduction of Simone's memories and feelings so changed her that she no longer felt for her friend what she once had?

Her feelings *had* changed, but not lessened: Simone had never considered Manon as anything other than a being without a will of their own, in thrall to Grandpère, and therefore predictable. Not a person.—Such opinions must change, when an entire childhood is witnessed from within a lens of affection and love.

Ammaline lifted her hand and put it over Manon's, where it lay upon her shoulder. Their fingers intertwined, cool and smooth but for rough pads on Manon's narrow fingertips, a small change wrought by the Grillon genetics they carried. Ammaline felt her heart lift.

A scraping sound caught Ammaline's attention, and she turned her head in Madame Opale's direction. The Scarabée balanced precariously on the Gondolier's flesh, sitting upright. The rustle of Madame Opale's worrying-legs came from within her shell, which scintillated in the soft glow coming from the Gondolier beneath her.

With a raw throat, Ammaline asked, "Where are we?"

Manon grimaced comically, looking around again. "I am with you. Does it matter?"

Ammaline snorted.

Madame Opale's deep rumble answered her: "We are crossing the reservoir outside the Silver City. We are traveling toward my nest. The transformation can be finished there."

Ammaline felt the smile that played upon her lips fade. "No, Madame. The transformation is finished. The rest of what you might transform is unwanted."

The rustle from beneath Madame Opale's shell became a rasp.

"You do not wish it?"

"I do not," Ammaline answered firmly. "I have brought Simone into my consciousness, and we are in concurrence. What we have is enough."

"You will not be resurrected, if you die." Madame Opale's voice, even though it was no true voice at all, sounded strained.

"I will not be resurrected the way that the Twelve are resurrected," Ammaline reminded her.—For it was not just Simone's awareness that had come to life within her. "I am one of the Scarabée now. I feel the connection. As would you, dear heart, if you stopped worrying so much."

The rasping stopped. In unison, the Gondoliers slowed, then stopped, the water gently lapping against their sides, whistling softly.

Ammaline struggled to sit up, Manon helping her. In a voice that seemed to echo back from all around them, she pronounced, "We will not go to your nest, Madame Opale, and you know that we should not. We were not born for safety. We are no warrior, no general, no leader of humankind, but we were not born to be conquered by fear, either. We have come this far. We will continue with the destiny that we have, in our several selves, for ourselves chosen."

It felt strange to use the royal *we*, but it would have felt stranger, talking to Madame Opale, not to.

Madame Opale rattled her shell. Ammaline caught the sour sulfur smell of her fear as it dissipated. It had surrounded them all so long that Ammaline could no longer smell it, until it lessened. In its place, a perfume, not quite strange, not quite familiar.—*Her* perfume, Etoile's, her mother's.

Of the three of them, Etoile was the faintest, standing back from her daughter's consciousness as a mother should, offering support and kindness rather than dominance. But she smiled at Madame Opale, a corner of her mouth twitching, then retreated again.

Ammaline crossed her legs and straightened out her ruined, blood-splattered clothing as best she could. She wondered, briefly, how her mother could have loved her father, but only briefly: she herself loved him still, even knowing him for a monster.—She had forgiven him, and thus released herself from hatred as well.

The back of the Gondolier under them tilted slightly. It was turning, but slowly, so as not to disturb its human passengers.

Manon cleared their throat, then doodled a finger-drawing on the back of the Gondolier, leaving glowing lines on its flesh. "If you're done with the scary voice, can you tell me what's going on? In simple words that I can understand?"

Simone drifted forward, Ammaline as curious as any of the others to find out. She found that her sense of herself continued no matter who controlled her flesh, but that her mind could only think so much at one time, and she felt herself somewhat slowed.

"Don't mind me. *I'm* still trying to wake up from being dead for so long and put together everything Ammaline knows," Simone said, using Ammaline's voice. "What is happening is that it's all coming to head. Before I died, I talked to Yvonne about what was going on, and she gave me a lot of information I didn't know."

Manon dragged a finger along the Gondolier's flesh, leaving another glowing line behind. "So?"

Ammaline let her mind open and her eyes close, feeling Simone extending herself outside their body, reaching into Madame Opale's knowledge, into Manon's—into the Gondoliers.

Before we came to Thomàon, I joked that I had "women's intuition," said Simone, adding a flash of herself as a young man in a suit. But once I came here—after the first resurrection—my women's intuition became something different.

Ammaline let the knowledge flow into her, not trying to understand what she was learning, let alone how it worked. It *did* work; that was all.

It went beyond what the Scarabées could do, with their scents and their shared genetics.—Something new in the universe.

Aloud, Simone said, "The Grillons will have attacked by now. Carlton is back."

Manon swayed; Madame Opale reached out as if to steady them, but her arms were too short, and too slender, and shaking with such violence that they should have steadied no-one.

"Carlton? But he is dead," she said.

"So was I," Simone answered her.

"But that means..." Manon fell silent.

Madame Opale said, "It means that the Grillons have brought him back. The Scientist would not have done so. No human, no Scarabée could, or would, commit such a thing. The Grillons have brought him back."

From her shell emerged a rough scrape that whined high and tight, almost the saw of a shuddering violin.

Simone said, their shared heart aching, "It means that your entire race, as well as mine, is in danger. You planned to bring humanity to the crisis, I know; it was the only way you could save us from the rest of your race, when they wished to see us all killed. They think you are a monster, a freak." She paused. "They are breeding another queen to replace you."

The whining rasp softened. "I know. When they sent me out of the nest, I knew they would. If I do not justify myself, I will be cut off. I will die."

Simone and Madame Opale considered each other, the water moving between them more quickly now as the Gondoliers swam faster, still protecting their passengers from upset, but speeding now, stirring up wakes behind them.

Manon said, "And, Simone, the human ships are coming. I found out from Grandpère. They'll be here in twenty years, if not sooner."

Simone lowered her face. "They will arrive sooner. They are almost here, I think. Paul ran the numbers of the earliest time they could reach us, before I died. I think it will be soon."

Manon slapped the back of the Gondolier, leaving a glowing handprint behind. It whistled sharply at them, and they smoothed the handprint away, their demeanor softening.

"The Grillons will kill us all, won't they? First every human on Thomàon, and then the ones from Earth." They continued petting the Gondolier. "Maybe that's for the best, though. Maybe we all deserve to die. That's what you're saying, isn't it? But the rest of the Scarabées don't know about Ammaline yet. When they find out what she can do, they'll want her. A human who can do things with memory that they can't. They'll want her."

Ammaline felt a clutch of fear at her heart. She did not want to be wanted, not in that way! She loved the Scarabées, but she was not blind to them, and with Simone's understanding of events, she knew them even better than she had before; they would destroy Madame Opale as defective, without hesitation although not without misgivings; and they would enslave her in order to plumb her talents, although not without bewailing the unconscionable violation of doing so.

In short: she had better keep Simone's talents a secret.

"How did you not know what Simone could do, before?" Ammaline asked Madame Opale.

But it was Manon who answered: "Simone couldn't do *this* before. She was uncanny about what she predicted. But not like this. She couldn't read minds."

"I can't read—" Simone paused. She turned toward Manon, studying their presence behind her, her nostrils flaring. "I can't read minds. I can't. It's just the smell. The smell of…" Simone broke off, the strain of a frown between Ammaline's brows. "Six times seven? How many roads must a man walk down…? I don't remember."

Manon reached forward and touched Ammaline's lips with a cool, smooth finger. "We talked about that book. Back on Earth. Do you remember?"

"Over eight thousand years ago. It's…been a while."

"I was thinking of that book on purpose, to see if you'd pick up on it," Manon said. "You read my mind, Simone."

Goosebumps rose on Ammaline's flesh. She did not feel Manon's thoughts—whatever it was—but Simone, who shared the same brain that Ammaline did, had.—She and Simone might share a brain, then, but did not share a mind. They *were* two different people.

Manon took her finger away, leaning back a little.

Simone was too flustered to speak; Ammaline said, "Do not use me as a bargaining piece with the Scarabées. I do not want them to take possession of me."

Manon nodded.

When Madame Opale did not answer, Ammaline knew that she would betray her, if she deemed it necessary; to her, Ammaline was a bargaining piece, of less importance than the survival of her species.

Well, then, she would not trust Madame Opale implicitly, and she would have to make her own plans. Whether those included sacrificing herself for the greater good or not, she herself did not know.—She had never before had to make such plans. Her father had protected her, kept her away from the others. He had thereby protected her secrets and kept her safe from the others' cruel machinations, but he had also taken the gifts of freedom away from her. She did not intend to squander them.

Something in the caverns had changed; some shift in the humidity or the scent of the waters, or echoes—Ammaline did not know—had occurred, and Ammaline knew that they were very close now. It seemed to have taken them hours to ride away from the Silver City, but only moments to return.

Ammaline looked down at her hands, studying them. They were small and slight, still seeming childish rather than womanly in her own eyes.

Madame Opale's worry legs rasped softly under her shell. "What will you do now?"

"I don't know." The words emerged from her own mouth, but Ammaline did not know who said them. "But we will go back, and we will try to come to some sort of resolution."

Ahead of them, a distant light flared to life, revealing the shore ahead: a small, metallic building; a cart that rolled away from it, carrying two figures; a third figure that emerged from the shadows beside the cavern, holding a hand above its eyes, then pointing toward the approaching Gondoliers.

Chapter 2

The Worst Possible Moment

The underground tunnel, or tunnels, leading from Grandpère's palace of Versailles in the countryside back into the Silver City quickly informed the Warden, Marks Lemure, of much of what he needed to know about the events which had occurred in his absence.

He had left his grisly work in the basements of Versailles after watching his contraption slaughter Armand twice.—He had programmed it to believe that Armand was showing signs of enfeebleness which might lead to madness. Armand's clones tended toward catastrophic failure at the best of times; it was not difficult to trick the system.

He had shed the white robe, and taken copies of his standard belongings from the locker room adjoining the showers. One of the lockers blinked red at its lock plate. He had gone to it and pressed his thumb against the pad. The lock had clicked open, and he had pulled out his preferred dress, which he never otherwise wore: gray sweatpants, gray sweatshirt, white socks, white underwear and undershirt, and white trainers. His knife, his terrible knife, had been recreated for him, lying lovely and seductive in its soft black sheath. He shook his head. He had hoped against all hoping, that the machines would not bring him what had been lost. At least the other knife would be deactivated, wherever it was.

He exited the basement, following his usual route through the corridors toward the tunnel to the Silver City, the sorts of corridors that avoided all public spaces, avoiding all décor to celebrate the austerity of their function.

Passing several Scarabée workers, to whom he nodded, he was struck by the aura of the tunnels. They did not smell quite clean and fresh, as they usually did.—They were clean, but not fresh, he decided. They carried a metallic scent. They also hummed with a tense rasping sound, more felt than heard, as if a worried cellist were scraping a fingernail softly upon their strings. He dismissed it as the Scarabées worrying about the uprising in the Silver City, and moved on.

When he reached it, the tunnel was long, and dull, and gray, and two tracks ran along the bottom of it, where a small engine with cars would carry supplies and personnel back and forth. Lemure had been tempted to take it, to shorten the long walk back to the city. He had in fact stepped onto the engine, which had come to life as he entered, and unlocked it using the gem in his locket, opposite the image of Etoile.—It was a new locket, a new gem; the attendants had left it for him, when he had been resurrected. Which was good, because he had no idea where his body was, and therefore no idea about the location of his previous locket. They were not things in and of themselves, the gems; they were only tokens to validate access to a system, as easily replaced as his body itself. Nevertheless, he kissed the small gold locket as he tucked it back inside his clothing, as he did every time he remembered it.

He even went so far as to put his hand upon the lever that would have started the engine moving, when he paused; the road was long and dull, but it would force him to exercise his new body, and—well, he had no great desire to return to the Silver City; only a sense of duty in doing so.

A slight delay would be tolerable, he decided. So long as Armand's plans were disrupted, there were no pressing matters. The ship from Earth would not arrive in five minutes; the elixir would not run out; the uprising might eradicate some of the humans of the city, but they could be rebred quickly, and perhaps the following year's culling of "criminals" would not have to be so harsh.

He gave a little sigh, kissed the icon of his dead wife once again, then climbed down from the engine, performed a few perfunctory stretches, then started down the long tunnel at a jog.

The tunnel stretched out in front of him, the darkness turning light as the bulbs came to life in front of him. The air was not exactly stale, but it had gone flat. It was cool, slightly damp, and carried an earthy tinge to it, in the way of a cavern near a fresh water might. Other than the two rail tracks in the floor, it was flat, slightly textured, and easy to run upon. He did so, passing by a number of darkened side tunnels, and also several cracks in the walls outlined with orange and white streaks, where stormwater had leaked through over the long years. His footsteps echoed as his trainers struck upon the floor, and the walls carried the sound of his breaths back to him. His stomach growled; he would have to find some breakfast after he arrived in the Silver City, which might prove difficult, what with the uprising's disruption of services. He wondered how high the price on his head would have risen, and whether Armand's minions had yet begun to panic. He chuckled to himself. He was glad to have skipped the train, he realized; he would have arrived at the Silver City already by then, and not had time to clear his head before he had done so.

It did not smell of the Scarabées' upset, he realized. They had not come this way.

Instead, he began to smell a different scent hanging in the air. If the scent of the Scarabées' fear was nearly the smell of rusty iron, then this was the scent that hangs in the air after an electrical fire.

Marks Lemure was never a man to take things for granted; his skin prickled with a sense of awareness at the most calm and soothing of times, and he did not deny himself the awareness of what he had smelled.

Thus it was no surprise to him when the two Grillons crawled out of two side-tunnels. He reached under his gray sweatshirt and pulled out his knife.

The two Grillons were not in their best element: the underground was the realm of the Scarabées, and Lemure made quick of them both, sharpening his blade on their shells.

When it was done, he shook the ichor off his knife, then set it to vibrate until the blade was clean. The handle was still sticky; he was forced to wipe it against the leg of his sweatpants, between other the other stains that covered them.

The bodies of the Grillons settled upon the tunnel floor, making small sounds as the long legs and light bodies slid flat. He waited at the crossing, listening for the sound of other movement from the tunnels.

He was sure he could hear the whisper of movement; he was unsure of its direction. It seemed to be coming from every direction at once.

"Which way were they going?" he finally asked the tunnels, softly.

The lights went out. He had been standing stationary for so long that the lights had gone back into sleep mode. He stared into the darkness, watching for the light that would have indicated movement, saw nothing.

He waved an arm and the lights flickered back to life.

Then he sheathed his knife and resumed running along the tunnel, this time with earnest speed. He did not worry himself with wondering what had happened, how the Grillons had come to be within the tunnels. He simply assumed the worst, an assumption that had oft stood him in good stead.

The Grillons had rebelled, as he had feared; the golden elixir produced by the Scarabées had been very nearly used up—and would be used up even faster by the trap he had set for Armand; his daughter, the experiment that his beloved wife had pressed upon him, was in danger; and according to Grandpère, a ship full of humans from Earth was coming. The ship was meant to have arrived later, but—Lemure assumed—it would arrive soon, if it had not already, in order to time its arrival for the worst possible moment.

Shivering, Grandpère looked out over the devastation of the Jardin Botanique, holding a folded card of heavy cream paper, and saw the dark shapes creeping under the cover of the trees, which were not much cover at all. The trees had been burned, slashed, wrecked, ruined. The Puppet Master's peons had focused on the garden, knowing that Grandpère had an especial fondness for it.—Armand always targeted what others loved, when he went on these destructive rampages.

Smoke rose from the smoldering trees. The strange ferns of Thomàon did not smolder; they were too damp to burn, and snapped quickly and easily during storms, saving their intertwined, fungus-like rootstock against the time when the storm had passed. But the trees in the Jardin Botanique had come from Earth. They scattered their seeds, trusted that the ash the fell from their burning leaves and trunks would fertilize the land below it, and allowed the cycle of life to pass forward to their children.

The mistake had been in allowing the Scarabées to give them immortality. Only twelve of them had it—and look at the horrors they had done.

Unlike the rest of the Twelve, when he had died, he had not experienced a sudden resumption of consciousness. He had had an entire lifetime isolated from the truth, having immersed himself in the work of daily living on Thomàon. He had fathered children: he had married, and loved, and seen his wife die.—One of his children, Philipe, had been sent to the prisons for a year, after having beat a personne almost to death. He had returned alive; had the Warden protected him? Grandpère had, when he had first been apprenticed to his earlier self, refused to inquire.

Grandpère had, as a young man, railed against the injustices of the world, as young men will. As an old man, he struggled to accept his own part in those same injustices—as *old* men will. He had not created the injustices on Thomàon. He had not even been born!

But, as the previous Grandpère had shown his younger self the reasons they had all done what they had done, he, the new Grandpère, with heavy heart, had taken on the mantle of responsibility. *He* had benefited, it was true; but, all in all, the terrible realization was that *he* would have made the same choices as his predecessors. At his core, he was the same man, burdened by the same terrible senses of fear, of ambition, of loyalties too strong to be denied.

He *would* have made the same mistakes. And it was his sombre task to try to repair the errors of what he had done, all the while knowing that he would make the same mistakes again, and worse—but that the situation would have been even worse yet, had he not.

Without him, there was only Armand.

And so he looked out over the burning gardens, and wondered: which of the rest of his clones would he select to be his own apprentice—would he follow the same line of succession set by his predecessor? Or change it?

No: he would keep to the same order. There were dozens of Grandpère's clones scattered among the citizens of Thomàon. The next in line needed to be notified and brought in, or, if he were dead, the next afterwards. It was best simply to go in order, and to give the order that another clone be wakened, and fostered, when the madness died down again.—If it ever did.

There was one piece of information that had been kept from him by the former Grandpère. The man's final memories had been transferred to the new Grandpère's mind, but did not contain the information, for the simple reason that Grandpère had forgotten it.

Forgotten it!

With his immortal, ever-refreshed memory, Grandpère could not have forgotten any item of significance without concerted effort: he had *made* himself to forget.

It was the opposite of everything that Grandpère stood for, and in fact, in opposition to his nature. And yet he had chosen to forget.

The card shook in the new Grandpère's hand, which seemed older and more frail by the second, as if it were the knowledge that lay within the card itself that would put him in the wheelchair that had sustained the previous Grandpère through such a long life.

Would he read it? *Could* he?

He must.

Even if he was not the same man as his line of ancestors, and had therefore not committed their sins, the simple fact remained that he was responsible for their actions now: he had inherited, he had *chosen* to inherit this place, these duties, these sorrows.

He opened the card; it appeared to be blank.

Nevertheless, Grandpère found himself striding through the halls of the Louvre, breaking into a run. He had seen nothing written on the card—had felt only a sudden lurch in his heart—and knew only that he must get to the Silver Spire as soon as possible.

The card fluttered to the floor behind him, dropped in his sudden haste: upon it, were in clear script written the words which Grandpère had been unable to see:

THE EARTHMEN HAVE ARRIVED IN THE SYSTEM AND ARE EVEN NOW IN ORBIT.

Chapter 3

The Nest

Underneath the city at the edge of the reservoir came together several members of the Twelve: Paul Hong, the Madman, driving a golf-cart of ancient design; Queen Delphine, riding with him, still shaken with fearfulness, from what she had done and seen; upon the backs of the glowing Gondoliers, Manon the Assassin, and Ammaline the Seer, with the honorable Madame Opale accompanying them; and, creeping out from the shadows, Yvonne la Gorge, the Historian, and Madame LaFerme, the Diva, with her.

The caverns were dark, and damp, and echoing with the sound of water, and the gentle splashing of the waves against the platform extending above the waves. The metal staircase rang softly with the footsteps of Ammaline and Manon, then louder as the Scarabée climbed after them, her chitinous shell a clear bell against the dark.

It was a rushed meeting.

They met upon the platform near the top of the ladder, the six of them and Madame Opale. Half of them were humans who carried the secrets of a flawed immortality within their flesh. Paul was spattered with blood;

Delphine was dressed in a common woman's tattered Season frock, having wisely changed her clothing after the attack upon the Opéra du Mendicant; Manon was dressed in gray, having shed their nobleman's costume long since; Ammaline's starry blue frock had been stained with blood, but the blood had flaked away, and the dark cloth looked more or less clean, especially after her dunking; Madame LaFerme's gown was nothing but glittering tatters over a silvery undergarment and the braces she wore on her legs; Yvonne's dress was dirty, and she had a smudge of something black and oily on her face—a not particularly unusual state.

Ascending lastly from the ladder, Madame Opale turned sideways and slid awkwardly through the gap at the rail. Her worry-arms rasped against each other underneath her carapace. The others stared at each other, not knowing who was friend or foe.

Simone, who would have otherwise been the first to announce herself and greet her friends, found herself within the body of Ammaline the Seer, was too shy to introduce herself to the others—to Paul. What would he think of her? What would he think of the body she wore?

She felt the itch of Paul's attention on her. Seeing her.

Seeing...*Ammaline* instead of his lover, come back from the dead.

A child.

Simone looked at him and thought of everything they'd shared—everything that she had remembered—everything she had known about him since then. Her heart burned in her chest.

Paul looked at her, then at Manon, then at her again. Smiled fondly, like a father.

Then blinked and let his face go blank.

He had abandoned her! Her cheeks tingled, as did the backs of her hands. How *dare* he! How dare he let her go! After he had loved her, and loved her, and loved her across thousands of years! *How dare he take all that history between them—*

Paul swallowed, and turned his face away from her, and wiped his eye.

—and let it flutter away, falling off her like a veil falling from her eyes.

He loved her, and she loved Manon now. Of *course* he had let her go.

Simone was no longer Simone. She was part of Ammaline now, and to cling to him as though nothing had changed would have been exactly the sort of selfishness that had caused the Twelve to come to being, and to rend and slaughter for so many thousands of years.

He had released her from the cruel wheel of humanity striving for permanence.

The least she could do was accept his gift with grace.

She closed her eyes and breathed deeply, sinking away from the front of Ammaline's mind, wracked with grief but sealing that part of herself away so it would no longer torture Paul, and so he would not have to pretend not to notice.

Paul looked away, and began talking to Yvonne. History moved onward.

And Ammaline sighed, and held onto the memory of the moment, then continued looking at the others: a standoff between the gods, none of fully trusting anyone else—but no, she trusted Manon, and she trusted Paul, and she trusted Madame LaFerme.

Lines of possibilities were forming, connecting one future to another, opening doors.

It felt almost as though everything had already happened, and yet was laden with the possibility of surprise.

Delphine put her hands on her hips but her hollow eyes belied the confidence of her stance, as she leaned upon the golf cart and snarled at Madame LaFerme. "Where have you been? Has anyone heard word from the others? What's going on up there?"

"I've been out on the reservoir," Madame LaFerme said coldly, crossing her arms over her chest. "Paul's the one with server access. Why didn't you ask him?"

Paul had just handed Yvonne a small, cloth-wrapped package. He looked up, startled, then began pacing back and forth in front of the golf cart's headlamps, throwing his shadow toward the cave leading to the long ladder upward. "I...uh. What's going on? The Grillons are attacking the city. Killing people."

Ammaline gasped. The others did not seem surprised.—Startled, perhaps.

Paul cleared his throat. "It gets worse. They brought back Carlton. On their own. Without using the resurrection pools."

This time, it was Madame LaFerme who gasped. "No!"

Ammaline could not move, felt herself to be locked in place, completely numb. The hair had risen all over her body; she was chilled to the bone. The man who had murdered her! was now at large in the city above them, helping the Grillons to slaughter innocents. Simone felt like screaming in terror. Ammaline clung to her spirit, offering what comfort she could, through her own terror. She did not know who *else* Carlton was, until Simone moaned his name:

"The White Gentleman!"

That name, Ammaline recognized. The White Gentleman was a figure of children's nightmares; her father had often told her tales of the monster, laughing as she shrieked in fear, within the isolated confines of their rooms at Shakes Prison.

Everything I have ever known was a lie, she thought. Poor Simone, to have been killed by such a monster.

Yvonne la Gorge, who had gone to stand apart from the others on the far side of the platform, put a hand over her eyes. "And? And?"

Paul did not answer her, not at first, but lowered his head and slumped to the cement of the platform, his elbows balanced sticklike upon his bony knees.

Delphine walked to his side, and bent down to shake his shoulder. "Paul! What else aren't you telling us?"

He murmured something. Delphine stepped back from him, both hands over her mouth in horror.

"And? And?" Yvonne repeated. "And what else?"

Ammaline swallowed. She did not know—and yet she knew. "They are here. The Earthmen have finally come."

Yvonne lowered her hand, showing cheeks wet with tears. "You told me they would come, Simone. You have always said that they would come."

Ammaline spread her hands, unsure how Yvonne had known—as she seemed to do—that Simone was awakened within her.

Paul turned his head toward her, his eyes empty, almost as though he were walking in his sleep. "Yes. It is true. I have hidden it from you all. They are here. We are all too late."

"Can't we talk to them?" Ammaline asked. Simone's prediction included nothing that seemed to require responses of such horror. "Why is everyone so upset? Aren't they here to save us?"

They stared at her, unable to respond.

Manon knelt beside her, and took her hand in her own. "You are innocent of what we have done, Ammaline. Remember that, no matter what else you hear of us. You are innocent."

"But I don't understand!"

Inside her, Simone murmured, *Look what we have done to life on Thomàon, Ammaline. Don't you think that Paul could have gotten us back to Earth, if he had wanted to? We all agreed to trap ourselves here, so the rest of humanity wouldn't have access to the golden elixir, to genetic modification, to...everything. We couldn't resist taking the power ourselves. It was the price we demanded for keeping the rest of humanity from finding out how to become gods.*

And now they have come. And will learn Thomàon's secrets, and destroy the universe.

There followed scenes from Simone's memory, her imagination, her destiny as a Seer:

Being strapped into a seat on a starship, checking over her boards, clenching her toes inside her boots, wondering whether her understanding of the theories were right—knowing that the drives that would carry them across space were part of her own damn doing—smelling the stale cycle of air as the fresh air inside the ship had been exhausted as they waited on their launch platform off the coast of Florida.

Lying down in a cryo chamber after they were sure they were on course, understanding but not really believing what Paul had told her about them: that there was no "sleep" as such in them, only death, one they hoped they would be able to waken from, feeling the gel around her chill her, shivering, her heart racing, finally panicking, thrashing against the walls of the container, choking, swallowing the thick gel, feeling herself smother—then ceasing to care at all, as the cold took her down into the depths.

Waking—the horror of it—as they emerged from the ages of darkness and death—the torture as her body came alive again, the awful coughing that she had to do, to get the gel out of her lungs.

Looking over her board with satisfaction, knowing her understanding of the universe had been *right*.

Waking the rest of humanity from their "sleep." Exploring the planet. Setting up the first research stations. Working with Paul on a multitude of projects, sending communications with Earth—when they had first arrived, they were still able to communicate using technology that Ammaline could not understand, even with knowledge of the inside of Simone's mind—testing assumptions about gravity, about time, about space, when halfway across the galaxy from Earth.

Then: the first Season.

The planet went mad; the storms wrecked the settlements, and the humans took shelter in the Grillon's strange, giant's-anthill structures.

Ammaline walked with Simone through one of the structures during a storm, staring upward in wonder at the cavernous ceilings, the walls that thrummed with the energy of the storm outside, shaking and shivering, in places outright swaying—but not falling, not being ripped from the ground and smashed against each other.

The appearances of the Twelve in Simone's memories differed: the ethereal beauty of humanity on Thomàon was missing. They looked plain, with spotty skin of different colors, none of them very tall, nasal voices, limp hair, evidence of age. *Fat*. Humanity's root stock had not been very attractive.

Ammaline found herself walking beside Simone, in her memories.—Or more than Simone's memories, perhaps; the air smelled sour and musty, with a gagging sweetness. Ammaline reached out to touch the wall of the nest. It was warm and moist and spongy, with small openings that closed as her hand came close.

"But...the nest! It's alive!"

Ammaline startled herself with the sound of her own voice.

Simone responded in a low voice: "All of them are. Apparently, until the Scarabées modified them, they were conscious, too, the guiding essence of the race. But that was thousands of years before we arrived. The Grillons were their main predators and drove them underground. The Scarabées fought back by genetically modifying the nests and cueing the Grillons to instinctually believe that the Scarabées were their breeding partners."

Ammaline looked upward. The flesh of the nest swayed as the storm howled, bulges in the walls showing Grillon eggs and younglings underneath, rocked in their sleep by the storm.

She pointed upward. "But—couldn't they *see* that it wasn't true?"

"We can only see what we are bred to see." Simone took Ammaline's hand, the texture of her hand feeling awkward.

Ammaline turned toward her partner—her other self—and looked at her: a middle-aged face, stubble on her cheeks and lip and chin, Adam's apple underneath. Her mouse-colored hair was pulled back in a ponytail, and she was wearing a stained coverall with a patch on the chest that said *Earth Expeditionary Force* in the old tongue. Her eyes pled with Ammaline not to judge her.

Ammaline studied her, seeing a little of her own face in Simone's: the eyes, the proportions of forehead, chin, and brow, the tiny attached earlobes, the bowlike lips.

It was true. She carried Simone's genes inside her.

"I hate for you to see me like this," Simone said. "But I can't change my memories all that much, or I start feeling crazy."

Ammaline nodded, and took Simone's hand, rubbing her fingertips across Simone's palm. It had lines and folds, and soft patterns at the fingertips. The backs were hairy, the knuckles misshapen.

"What's wrong with your hands?" Ammaline asked.

Simone frowned. "Wrong with my hands? Nothing."

"They're so smooth. And crooked."

Simone looked down at her hands, turning them back and forth. "Oh. I thought you meant—no, this is what hands were like, before Paul and the Scarabées changed us. I was probably developing arthritis."

"What's that? and I thought only the Twelve had been changed."

Simone's gaze rose upward to the inside of the swaying towers. "Arthritis was an ancient ailment. It doesn't exist anymore. The things that used to kill or disable humans before their time, they're all gone now. We changed *all* of humanity. Not just the Twelve. We tired of having to take care of people who were ill. They all live longer lives and take less hurt from injuries, so they can work harder and longer. They also go a bit mad from time to time, if they can't act up. We are all changed. This is what it used to be like."

"Oh."

Ammaline looked around her, catching sight of another human walking past an arched entry into another one of the nest's chambers. It might have been Madame LaFerme; it might have been someone else completely. The woman's nose was crooked, and she was wearing thick-lensed goggles over her face. She, too, wore the same coverall uniform.

"Is that some kind of eye protection?" Ammaline asked, pointing.

"Glasses. For...bad vision."

"What's that?"

Simone shook her head. "It's not important now. Look, Ammaline, what is it that you're not seeing here?"

Ammaline saw another human walk past an opening. What should she expect to see, in a Grillon nest?

She nearly slapped her forehead: "Grillons."

"Look at the floor."

Ammaline looked down, saw streaks of dried ichor, a few pieces of chitinous shell on the floor of the nest, and, in one corner, a dark opening that led downward. It was stuffed with dismembered Grillon bodies, their dead black eyes dry and dull.

Simone said, "We slaughtered them and shoved the bodies underground. Soon we will seal the openings."

Another voice called through the tunnels, "Okay, folks. We got a problem over here."

Simone led Ammaline through the tunnels toward a large, open chamber whose upper reaches rose at least twenty feet overhead, the walls shuddering and swaying. Even the floor thrummed. Other primitive humans were coming into the room, all of them wearing the uniform. The walls were thickly covered with the blisters that held the young Grillons in stasis as they grew.

A blond man in the center of the room pointed upward. "Look. One of them is hatching."

It was King Corentin's voice! Ammaline gaped and stared at the man. How old he looked! He looked curiously starved, too, as if his flesh had melted away from him. The cords of his neck strained as he looked upward.

Ammaline followed the line of his arm upward and saw movement. One of the Grillons had cut through its blister and was struggling to crawl out. Around it, others also stirred.

A woman's voice shrieked, "They're going to kill us!"—It was Queen Delphine, her hair pulled back tightly in a bun, silver-gray. "What can we do? Paul?"

A short man with darker skin crossed his arms over his chest. "How about nothing?"

"But they're hatching!"

Paul rolled his eyes. "They're babies. They do that."

Queen Delphine ran to her husband's side, clinging to his too-slender arm. "They're not babies, they're monsters!"

A series of explosions echoed through the room, making Ammaline put her hands over her ears. Everyone turned toward the sound. A trio of men stood at one end of the room, holding antique weapons that shot explosive projectiles like a pistolet, but louder.

The projectiles burst through the walls above them, letting the storm come howling in.

Queen Delphine raised an arm to shield her eyes from the splattering flesh of the nest. "Look! It's getting away!"

Several of the Grillon younglings skittered out of their blisters, out into the storm, where they were torn away by the winds as soon as they left the safety of the nest.

"Stop shooting!" ordered one of the men, white-haired and -jowled, with watery eyes and dark glasses. He stood with a cane. "You'll destroy the nest. *After* you went through all the work to take it from those monsters. The younglings won't be any more difficult to kill than the older ones."

One of the men had not used his weapon. Ammaline recognized him immediately as her father—although he was a small man with dark skin—by the stern look on his face. He said, "If you're not done with your bloodthirst, at least use a fucking knife."

The three men who had fired were the Général, looking embarrassed but with the same styled sideburns upon his cheeks, and two men that Ammaline did not know.

Simone whispered to her: "The one in the middle is Armand, the Puppet Master. From your memories, you must not have seen him. Sometimes he goes through phases when he isn't around court much. The other one, the one on the right, is the White Gentleman."

Ammaline frowned, studying the man, whose eyes had fixed upon the young Grillons within their blisters, regardless of how the storm howled and threw debris in his face.

She had heard all sorts of nightmare tales about the White Gentleman, and she knew that he was the madman who had killed Simone. He had pale skin, with scars over his cheeks, a bald spot at the top of his head, peeking through his colorless hair, and deep-set pale blue eyes under a large brow. The skin under his eyes sagged, making his eyes look even bigger. His cheeks were hollow, covered with stubble, and his pale lips were downturned. He was a large man, muscular, but also had a belly that pressed against his uniform.

He didn't *look* like a monster, only pale and colorless, with the brightest color about him being the red skin that sagged under his eyes. In fact, he looked to be made of wax.

"That's him?" Ammaline asked.

Just as Simone was about to answer, Queen Delphine screamed again: "More of them are hatching! Kill them!"

It was true, more of the Grillons were hatching, but Ammaline didn't see why Queen Delphine was terrified of them: she had always struck Ammaline as being brave, and sophisticated, and, well, *queenly.*—But this had happened a long time ago.

The three men raised their weapons again, although the storm was still tearing away pieces of the nest that had been blown open by the explosions.

Ammaline's father grabbed Grandpère's walking-stick away from him, and began to tear open the blisters with the tip, then flinging the younglings out into the center of the room, oozing and wet from blister-fluid.

King Corentin dodged out of the way of one, then pinned it down with one boot and kicked the rest of its legs away. "There, Sarah. Happy now?"

Queen Delphine turned her head away. "That's only one of them. We have to kill them all. Before they kill us."

King Corentin rolled his eyes. "Fine. Whatever."

The men proceeded to slaughter the young Grillons, using knives, sticks, metal bars, and even their feet. Queen Delphine led them from room to room, finding Grillon after Grillon within the shuddering walls and ceiling of the nest.

Ammaline felt eyes upon her, and saw, time and again, that the White Gentleman stared at Simone whenever he thought he was not being watched, with his pale, cold eyes. Simone became nervous, tugging at Ammaline's hand, one moment leading her away from the chamber, the next shaking her head and leading her back.

"No. You have to see this. You have to know who we are."

Ammaline squeezed her cold, soft hand. "Why is he watching you?"

"I wouldn't kill the Grillons. Neither would Paul—no, I take that back. He did kill one who came for me when we first rushed in to try to find shelter. Carlton was never a fan of mine. He mocked me behind my back and pulled away whenever I had to come near him. Armand was nasty to me, too. Contemptuous, even though we'd gone to school together. I think I was a...measuring stick for Carlton. He kept testing other people to see what he could get away with. Would Delphine join him in mocking me? Would Marks? Could he convince enough people to cut me out of the herd?"

Simone pulled her hand away from Ammaline and put it on her chin, cupping her entire face thoughtfully as the others slaughtered the young Grillons. "There are things I hate about all of us. I see us all as monsters, as greedy bastards who sold our souls for the promise of immortality. We all had our buttons to be pushed.

"But Carlton? I don't know how to explain it. Armand's a fucking bastard, but at least he could be charming. He was human enough to put on a charming face, that is. But Carlton is different. He really is the boogeyman that lurks in the dark. I mean, we Twelve have more than our fair share of psychopaths, narcissists, and histrionics. But Carlton? A whole other level of wrong. The incarnation of genocide."

Ammaline didn't understand, but she squeezed Simone's hand harder. Paul came to Simone's other side and took her hand, too, and the three of them witness the slaughter. Ammaline had been brought up to fear the Grillons, but also to take as an article of faith that they could never come inside the Great Dome during the Season. It just couldn't happen.

Paul said, "They don't see intelligent life. They just see the monsters from fucking *Alien*."

Simone said, "You'll get through to them someday."

Paul lowered his head, muttering at his ichor-stained boots: "Is that your instinct? Or just a desire to soothe me?"

Simone let go of Ammaline's hand, and wrapped him in an embrace. "Paul. I'm so sorry."

"We can never leave this place," Paul mumbled into her shoulder. "*This* is what humanity is like."

Simone put her chin on top of his head. "Where are the others?"

"Jennifer has Yvonne and Jordan in a side chamber, one of the outer ones that doesn't have any younglings in it. Yvonne is in a fugue state and Jordan had to be tied up. Before they got slaughtered trying to attack the others after Carlton killed their 'pet.'"

Simone turned to look at Ammaline. "Your Manon was called Jordan then. Their whole history had revolved around the possibility of finding alien life and learning to communicate with it. Yvonne, too, had hoped to learn to speak with them and gather their history. They had befriended one of the Grillons, and were learning to speak to it. It rescued us when our shelter near the ship collapsed and blew away, and brought us here. When we startled the other Grillons, Carlton took especial care to rip its limbs off. He left it to die, then came back to burst its eyes with his fingers."

Ammaline felt gorge rising in her throat. She watched Carlton with the Grillon young, tearing them apart, slowly and intently, flinging off limbs, ripping off entire sections of their carapaces. When they stopped struggling, he tossed them aside and looked for more—more—more!

Paul had turned to watch Carlton too. "Why does he even exist? Tell me, Simone. I need to know. Is there some purpose to him? Or is he just some kind of mutant genetic line that has raped its way into long-term survival? A throwback? What?"

Without taking her eyes from the White Gentleman, Simone said, "Talk to someone who's a psychologist, not me. Talk to Yvonne. Or Manon. They know history...genetics."

Paul balled up his fists and turned to her. "I'm asking *you*, Simone. I'm asking the smartest person I know."

Out of the corner of her mouth, Simone told Ammaline, "Which was ridiculous of him to say, but sweet." Then she closed her eyes and let her shoulders sink. "I don't know, Paul. I don't know where Carlton's genes came from, and I don't know why is the way he is. I don't know if something in his brain is broken, or if he's the next evolution of humanity. All I know is that someday he's going to kill me and hang my head up like a trophy."

Paul stood there, unmoving. Slowly the slaughter finished, and the others pushed the bodies of the younglings down into the holes, while Queen Delphine searched from room to room for any other survivors.

Ammaline felt tired—as if she would never again see sunlight or hope. *This* was humanity, *this* was the secret behind the secret of the Twelve. Not the immortality, not the false identities, not even the way they had stolen her childhood playmate Manon from her, and twisted them into a sort of god.

The White Gentleman was the worst of them, but none of them had stopped the slaughter, not even her father, and it was Queen Delphine who had led the worst parts of it, demanding the murder of the helpless.

And they *all* had benefited.

Ammaline inhaled the scent of the nest, musky and sickly sweet—the sweetness was the smell of ichor—and vowed to herself that she would never forget the moment where she had come from.

The arrival of humanity was terrible indeed, if this was what humanity had brought with them.—If humanity had not changed, or better elements had not improved it. Eight thousand years had not changed humanity upon Thomàon for the better; it was unlikely that eight thousand years had improved humanity anywhere.

"Can we go? Have I seen enough?"

Simone reached a hand to touch Ammaline's face; it was wetted with tears.

"It is enough."

The memory dissolved around them, leaving Ammaline staring upward at the roof of the caverns above, shaded and dark, but only just visible in the pale glow of the lights, and the greenish radiance of the Gondoliers. A cold cloth lay across her forehead. Manon glanced down at her, eyes angry.

"Ammaline!" exclaimed Madame LaFerme, who knelt near her. "What happened?"

Roughly, Manon said, "Simone took her into her memories without thinking. And didn't make her sit down first. *You let her fall.*"

Simone tried to speak, but Ammaline silenced her, saying instead: "She showed me the slaughter at the Grillons' nest, during the first Season."

The others shifted uncomfortably, their clothing rustling, footsteps dragging against the cement.

A long pause followed. Then Manon said, "I don't expect you to forgive any of us. But you understand us now. And you understand why we have to destroy the humans from Earth. Every one of them. Before they find out how to become like us. Or worse."

Chapter 4

The Seed at the Center of the Storm

HUMANITY CAST SHADOWS UPON the storms of Thomàon in three colony ships so large that they had no little effect upon the tides. Their mass and gravitational pull were immense; their materials were so heavy, that they had to be harvested from countless asteroids.

The presence of the ships worsened the storms of the Season and maddened the Grillons. Like all creatures of electricity, iron, and water, they felt the compass pull of the ships from the Vieux Monde and responded with ever-greater madness.

The engineers had calculated the effects of the stars, the planets, and the oddly wandering moon had upon the planet, and understood the conjunctions of those things that powered the storm. Yet they underestimated the effect of their massive ships, which were like moons themselves, upon such chaos.

These were the first ships humanity had flown of such a size. They did not think to make such calculations.—Or if any of them did, their voices were disregarded, "in the face of the mission."

They monitored the signals coming from the planet, and found no active radio communication.

They concluded the civilization below, which seemed to consist only of scattered ruins and a remarkable dome that covered a single square mile but which also emitted no signals and released no heat, to be a failed one, long dead.

The storms of the Season continued on.

Humanity waited, long past their calculations, for the storms to end. They paced their halls, too cautious to land upon the surface, too impatient not to. They sent down drones to collect data.

The storms, worse than any hurricane or typhoon or tornado on Earth, smashed the drones.

They sent down a small landing ship, with a few brave souls whose curiosity and desire for advancement outweighed their desire for survival.

The storms tore the ship to pieces before it even landed.

They dropped bombs into the hearts of the storms.

The storms accepted the seeds that humanity planted, and let them grow and blossom, stronger than before.

Those upon the ships did not do the one thing that might have ended the storms: they did not retreat, they did not turn away.

They could not.

The secret of the three colony ships, the reason they had seemed to appear out of nowhere, was that Vieux Monde had long since been destroyed. An asteroid had torn through space toward the home planet. The humans had shattered the asteroid with missiles. Fragments of the asteroid had struck a mining settlement upon the Moon, which was testing experimental explosives.

The explosives went off—the moon began to fragment—fragments struck the Earth—the impact was terrible. Billions died.

But the particulate matter suspended in the air was worse than the impact itself.

Plants could get no sunlight, and died. Temperatures which had been too high from the way that humanity had poisoned the composition of the air itself, plummeted. A long winter followed, which reduced humanity to little more than animals. Life itself starved, and withered, and died.

The fragments of the moon turned the space surrounding the Earth into a minefield.

The three colony ships had been stationed far away from Earth and near the planet Mars, in order to take advantage of the many asteroids that lay just past its orbit. Upon those three ships, which were already near to completion, were genetic stores, and frozen fertilized embryos, and landing-ships, and everything the colonists would need to travel the darkness of space in cryogenic sleep, to reach the planet of Thomàon. The planet, which had been named after its discoverer's Scottish terrier, had long been remembered in song and story, as a place of hope, where humanity would one day be reunited, and find a paradise.

It did not seem a paradise then, as they looked down into the continuing storms.

They studied the surface of Thomàon, desperate for its richness, unheeding of the warning of its storms—just as those on the *Téméraire* had done.

Humanity saw the Grillons emerge from the storm and climb the Great Dome, their slender bodies buffeted by the storms, but resilient within it, and recoiled in horror.

Thomàon was populated by monsters, ones that would need to be exterminated, before humanity could feel itself safe.

They signaled the planet again; no one responded. Thus they felt the planet was theirs to claim, to do with as they willed.—Already, plans were drawn up to secure a landing away from the monster-infested dome. Several dozen landing ships filled with trained troops would begin clearing the surface of the planet of the horrific monsters which lived there, first establishing a landing site, then making their way to the dome to investigate it.

The landing party began to gather itself upon one of the colony ships, the *Octavius*, in preparation of the invasion. Crew and settlers were moved to the other ships, the *Lovibond* and the *Celeste*, to make more room and to keep the soldiers from distraction.

The soldiers prepared for war, the engineers prepared for landing, the scientists prepared reports showing that the air was breathable, and the life on the planet not inherently incompatible with their own. The generals swore there was no need to fear, no need at all, that the risks had been assessed and determined to be minimal, should the worst occur.—To sum up their findings, there was no downside to landing, none at all, once the storms had settled enough to allow the ships to land.

Families said *au revoir* to each other, rather than goodbye.

Then the unthinkable happened: pilots startled from their sleep, which had been filled with nightmares, and exclaimed to their superiors that something was wrong with the ships. Soon after, alarms began to sound. Their orbits had become unstable, and all three of them were sinking toward the surface of the planet.

How could this be? The scientists soon answered the question: the planet had wobbled. Their own ships had destabilized the planet's orbit, which was itself affected by the moonlike satellite which caused its Seasons.

The ships' combined mass was small, relative to that of the planet. But they were, at that moment, enough.

An age-old cry arose from the ships:

But we didn't mean to!

The universe, as always, shrugged and moved onward. Whether or not humanity had intended the consequences of its actions meant little; they had done what they had done, and the consequences had followed.

The *Lovibond* and the *Celeste* were able to escape their decaying orbits, but the *Octavius* was not so resilient. It had transferred much of its fuel to the landing-ships in preparation of the invasion. The fuel that drove the ships across the stars was collected by the ships themselves, but it would take time to refill the *Octavius*'s coffers.

Everyone who could flee the *Octavius* via lifeboat did so. But there were not enough landing-ships, and not enough time. Those who remained sent their farewells to their loved ones, saying not *au revoir* this time, but *goodbye.*

The *Lovibond* and the *Celeste* watched as the *Octavius* began its mad descent.

Chapter 5

Fate, or Coincidence

It was not so strange that Grandpère should encounter first Corentin, then Marks, as he traveled toward the Silver Spire in the heart of the Silver City, for he knew that the streets themselves were filled with danger, and therefore he had chosen to travel through the secret ways that led through, and below, the city, in parallel to the more open routes, slower to navigate, but more secret and secure.

Grandpère showed each of the doorways the red gem that lay in his cane, and ran as quickly as he could.—He had brought his children and grandchildren into the Louvre, in remote places where the treasures of Thomàon were hidden. Still, he trembled in fear for them; the Puppet Master's hoard might let them live if they found them, but the men from Earth? Never! Grandpère knew the sins of mankind deep within his bones, for they were his sins, battled within himself for thousands of years.

Through shadows, through tunnels, through passageways: the ways seemed to stretch on forever, yet the Silver City was not large; it was tightly built, with only a few parks or open places within it, and occupied but a single square mile. To be sure, to place an entire planet's spare populace within a single city during the Season was a challenge, but the populace had been trained to it, to breed slowly and to murder quickly, to feel the cheapness of life as a mark of pride, to tolerate injustice as they tolerated being packed so closely into such a confined space.

In short, there were not so many secret ways through the Silver City as to call Grandpère's encounter with Corentin a coincidence.

Grandpère had stepped out of one tunnel into a low basement. He listened for a moment, heard little, smelled death.

He lifted his hand, turning one of his rings about with this thumb, then caught a switch with his nail, so the gem on the ring lit, and showed him the contents of the room.

A cement room, ill-decorated, was filled with a chaos of heavy, ruined plastic separators, glittering party clothing, torn bedding, and human bodies, butchered and left where they had fallen, staring eyes not quite glittering in the light of the gem: killed, and not long ago.

Grandpère cursed and coughed as he stepped into the miasma, holding one sleeve before his face.

"Hello?" A voice called to him from the darkness. "Who's there?"

It was Corentin.

Grandpère called back, "It is I, Corentin. Stop killing, would you? We have more important things to do. We must go to the castle, quickly."

A noise overhead prevented him from continuing his words; a Grillon was positioning itself quietly but quickly overhead.

"Hold!" shouted Corentin, and from the darkness flew silver and red, the vibro-knife that Corentin carried burying itself within the Grillon's carapace like an arrow flying to its target.

The Grillon fell.

Grandpère felt the air move as the creature brushed against him, and stepped away.

The Grillon landed upon a pile of trash and human bodies, its legs still scrambling, trying to pull itself upright. Now the smell of sweet ichor lay atop the reek of human death.

Corentin bounded past Grandpère and kicked at the Grillon's legs until they were all of them knocked away; it was easy enough to do, once the trick of it was known, and Corentin had been one of the first to learn it.

"I didn't kill any of *these*," Corentin said, recovering his knife. And it seemed true; the fluids that had leaked upon him were the copper-green of ichor, not human blood—for the most part. "I was stirring up the Gold Stars for a while, but then the Grillons made it in and I switched targets."

Crossly, Grandpère began working his way through the tangles of trash and bodies. "I don't care what you do, as long as you do what I tell you when I need it."

Corentin snorted. "What, not going to thank me for saving your life? What's the hurry to get to the castle, anyway?"

Grandpère felt a sickening lurch within him. He told Corentin, feeling his lips move—and knowing from their shape what he had said—but did not hear his own voice.

Corentin said, "What?"

He stepped over a child's blood-soaked stuffed Scarabée. "They. Are. Here. In orbit. Above us. Only the storms are holding them at bay—*if* they are holding them at bay at all. They may attempt to land."

Corentin pushed a piece of plastic board out of the way, shoving it atop a bed. A small sound from under the bed made Corentin stop to fling both board and bed aside, uncovering a small personne that had been lying underneath them.

The personne was dressed in blood-soaked white, and had cuts upon their arms and feet, claw marks of the Grillons. Their eyes saw nothing, and they cowered on the floor, awaiting death.

Grandpère considered the personne for a moment, thought to himself that he had surely failed humanity, and walked on. Corentin glanced down at the knife in his hand for a brief moment, then followed Grandpère to the other side of the room, leaving the personne behind.

"Someday," Grandpère remarked, as he found the cement-faced secret panel at the other end of the basement room, "I'm going to have this stretch of the route built over. I had forgotten that it would be full of people, because of the Season."

Corentin shone the hilt of the knife toward a small hole near the panel, and the panel shifted inward silently, opening to one side. He ducked as he entered, then waited for Grandpère to pass and closed the door behind him.

"They have to live somewhere," he said pleasantly as he slipped past Grandpère and led the way down the narrow, low corridor, ducking his head as he went. "And you're getting ahead of yourself, aren't you? If you think that we'll survive—" Corentin's voice went blank for a moment. "—if they really *are* here already."

Irritably, for Grandpère did not like to be reminded that he had forbidden himself from knowing what he *must* know, he replied, "If Simone hadn't been killed, we would have known when they were coming."

"We all agreed."

Grandpère grumbled.

Corentin laughed. "I was worried that this time, you might have found an incarnation that could actually act differently than you always do. But you're the same old bastard, aren't you? The same old bastard as always."

This irritated Grandpère even further, for he did not like to know that, once again, even with the span of several generations, he had failed to change his own mind, to make any difference in his character whatsoever.

A second tunnel ran crosswise to the first. Corentin paused, held up a hand to keep Grandpère from proceeding, and extinguished his light. After a few breaths, he proceeded forward.

"So the humans are coming," Corentin said. "What's the plan? Are we going to pile into the ship and see if she can still fly? It's been thousands of years since anybody's been in there. "

Grandpère had to stretch his legs to keep up with Corentin, but they were both almost jogging. "Océan was there a few days ago and checked it over. She says it can fly—whether it can get out of the confines of the castle is another matter."

They came to a fallen area in the corridor, a place where the cement roof had split and fallen in.

"Huh." Corentin heaved the roof panel up. "How does it look?"

The corridor past the fallen area seemed clear, in the light of Grandpère's gem. "Well enough."

"Duck under."

Grandpère scuttled under the section of roof that Corentin was holding easily aloft, then waited. Corentin ducked under, balanced the section on his shoulder, turned then backed out from under the section, which rumbled back into place, almost to the floor.

"Wonder what happened up there," Corentin said. "There haven't been any earthquakes or anything."

Grandpère let Corentin lead again, and they resumed their swift walk down the corridor. "It doesn't matter. The main thing is that we are going to have to destroy everything we've built here, everything we didn't have when we arrived."

Corentin looked back at him, a skeptical, amused tilt to his eyebrow and lips. "Seriously? You think that's even possible? Going to scrape up all the flakes of skin from the atmosphere that might give us away? Or, what? Shatter the planet in half?"

Both courses of action had occurred to Grandpère, long ago. "No, no. Nothing like that. But we are going to have to destroy the records of how we did it, as well as Paul's equipment."

"And Paul," Corentin said casually. "He couldn't keep his mouth shut to save his life. Even Simone was better at keeping secrets than he was."

Grandpère did not answer; Corentin sighed. "So. Guess who gets to do it, am I right?"

"You or your brother."

—The *next* coincidence occurred, not at that moment, but not soon after. Out of the corridor they emerged from a doorway of reinforced steel more heavily built than the ones they had taken to enter at the other end, into a sort of underground station.

The station was plain, made of cement, and cramped, with only a narrow platform on one side, beside a set of tracks that led into the darkness, toward Versailles. There was another route that led from Versailles to the Louvre, but it would have taken too long to use it. The small train that led from one end to the other was missing, but they were not quite alone in the station: the sound of running footsteps came from the tunnel, a steady rhythm that could easily eat up the thirty or so miles from Versailles.

Corentin called down the corridor: "Marks, that you?"

A response echoed back: "On my way. Watch out, there are Grillons in the corridors outside town."

"They've taken the city," Corentin shouted.

No answer followed; in a few moments, Lemure emerged into the dim light of Grandpère's gem. He was wearing jogging pants and a sweatshirt and was splattered with sweet-scented greenish ichor.

He slowed to a walk, then put his hands on his knees and breathed deeply. "What's that you said? Do you have any water?"

Corentin walked to the mouth of the tracks to watch for movement. "Sorry, no. The Grillons have taken the city. They're all over the place."

Lemure panted, "The dome must have failed. Something's gone wrong. The fires just about smothered us all the other night. The ventilation systems aren't working."

"Well, it's a good thing we've got the people's genetics all recorded, because otherwise we'd be facing a lot of overbreeding in the next few thousand years, that's all I have to say." Corentin settled into a fighter's stance, holding his knife out. "Oh. And—"

Again, Grandpère's mind did not register the words that he knew must have been said. He gritted his teeth and unscrewed the top of his cane, pulling out the slim blade within: one he had rarely used, and never in this body. He had always disliked violence, but there was something about Thomàon that brought it out of all of them. He pulled the ring from his finger, and tossed it against the wall. Lemure's and Corentin's shadows spun as the light passed them.

Sounds came from within the tunnel, a sort of hissing, slithering sound; the sound of many small movements occurring all at once.

Lemure turned around to face the tunnel, drew his vibro-knife out of his pocket, and tiredly settled himself into a fighter's stance as well. He was chuckling.

"I knew it."

"You did not," Corentin said. "You're making that shit up."

"All I had to do was ask myself what else could possibly go wrong."

"You're such a fucking pessimist."

"Tell me I'm wrong."

The sound within the tunnel stopped, or rather softened, as the Grillons stayed in the shadows, considering whether they wished to attack the humans that stood before them.

Apparently, they did not: from the corridor sounded a long and irregular purr, the strange sound of the Grillons' speech, which Paul and Manon and Yvonne had learnt, but which none of those facing the Grillons at that secret underground station knew.

"Well?" Corentin shouted down the corridor. He glanced at his brother. "What the fuck, you know?"

Lemure did not answer.

The sounds within the tunnels began again, and they both tensed for attack. Grandpère glanced about, wondering whether they were about to be ambushed from behind—but there was nothing.

After a moment, the sounds lessened—the creatures were in retreat.

Grandpère took up his ring, and threw it into the tunnel, the light now illuminating that which lay within: only the swiftly retreating forms of a few Grillons, surely insufficient to have made the noises which they had heard but moments before.

"Scared them off," Corentin announced, but not with any faith in his voice.

"They got commands from somewhere," Lemure said.

"Where, though? They're clever fuckers but they can't use technology."

They both turned toward Grandpère. He pointed toward the ring, and Lemure jogged forward to retrieve it.

"I don't know," Grandpère admitted. "But it doesn't matter. We need to get to the ship."

On its opposite side, the station led to another heavy, reinforced door, which Corentin unlocked and they passed through. Here, the corridor was dimly lit by low red peanut bulbs, and showed signs of footprints, bloodstains, and paint. They were under the Opéra du Mendicant, the very corridors that the Puppet Master's peons had cleared of those still loyal to King Corentin and Queen Delphine.

It seemed ages ago—although Grandpère had only just heard of it, having stayed at the Louvre with his predecessor that night—but it had only been a few days.

They all began to jog, not as quickly as before, Corentin ahead of Grandpère and Lemure behind.

Corentin called back, "We have to destroy everything before the humans can get hold of it. You want Paul?"

Lemure jogged in silence, then answered, "You take him. I want to find my daughter. Get her on that ship."

"Océan apparently went over it and it's good to go—good enough to try to get off the planet, anyway. Could get hung up on something and go off all half-cocked, who knows?"

Lemure's footsteps stopped behind them, and Grandpère looked over at his shoulder. Lemure stood before a stone wall, one of the older parts of the opéra house. He studied the stonework.—Then suddenly he shoved his shoulder against the stones.

They tumbled inward. He pulled others toward him; the stonework was only loosely set. Behind the wall came a gagging stench. Lemure bent down and pulled something out of the hole: a sheathed knife, seeming twin to the ones he and Corentin both held.

Corentin burst out with laughter. "This is where Armand stashed your body? Like some sort of damn horror movie."

Lemure wiped the blade on his sweatpants, then stuck it into his waistband. The red gem in its hilt did not glow. "Let's go."

Corentin led the way again, slowing a little as he worked through the corridors and into the areas under the stage with the dressing rooms. The floor was sticky there with blood, some of it sudden and fresh.

A long, chitinous leg lay in a corner beside a set of stairs, leaking ichor.

"Grillons here, too," Corentin said. "Ready for trouble?"

Lemure stopped beside the leg, picked it up, then tossed it back down. "A couple of hours at most. Maybe they've moved on."

They both looked at Grandpère.

It was time to make decisions: a task that Grandpère had never loved, but always found himself shouldering.

His family, huddled in the basement of the Louvre, was doomed. Grandpère could not end humanity, without also dooming those of his blood.

Love, it was irrelevant. He steeled himself.

"Corentin—clear out Yvonne's archives, on the other side of the reservoir. Then do what you feel necessary with Paul."

Corentin made a face. "I don't want to be away from the action."

"Don't argue. The archives are almost as bad as Paul himself. It needs to be done.—Lemure, go to the control room and trigger the self-destructs for the Louvre, Versailles, Shakes Prison, anywhere else that might have any stores of the elixir left. Then you can find your daughter. Bring her to the ship."

Lemure nodded. "And you?"

Grandpère knew that he could not tell either of them the truth. "I will be destroying the dome, using the codes that only I possess."

The brothers nodded, and dashed up the stairs. A moment later, Corentin's voice called down, "All clear."

Grandpère climbed the stairs, putting one hand on the rail to steady himself. He was still holding the naked blade that had rested inside his cane, with the sheath tucked under his arm. His footsteps felt heavy, as though his own body were attempting to hold him back from what must be done.

"Go on ahead," he called. "I will do what must be done."

If he did not act, the destruction wreaked by humanity would seem only happenstance, to those who inflicted it; but when the labyrinth of time were drawn, the path would reveal destiny. The Great Coincidence of humanity was that everywhere it found itself, extinction followed.

The Twelve must fall, and take the Scarabées with them.

Otherwise, all of this would begin again—and sprawl across the universe.

He would go to the room that held the controls for all the networks and mechaniques across Thomàon. And then he would go to the place that had once held all his hopes and dreams:

To the *Téméraire*.

Chapter 6

The Téméraire

AFTER THE HALF OF the Twelve that had found itself together in the caverns under the Silver City had concluded their discussion—what little of it that followed Simone's vision from the nest—they began the long climb up the stairs toward the surface. They all agreed that the first thing to do was to reach the control center hidden in the upper rooms of the Opéra du Mendicant in order to locate the ship full of humans from Earth, and determine what might be done to stop them. Yvonne said that she wished to return to the archives, to take with her the latest data that Paul had collected, so that if tragedy occurred, at least the events of the previous days would be preserved. Madame Opale said that she, also, must go—but to her own nest, to try to persuade the rest of her kind to assist the Twelve against the humans from Earth.

Queen Delphine protested at their leaving, saying that she did not trust them, but was overruled. Whenever Ammaline looked at her, she heard the voice of the woman Delphine had once been, screaming to have the youngling Grillons killed. She pulled away from her whenever the queen approached. Delphine seemed not to notice.

They said farewell to Yvonne and Madame Opale. Ammaline shook Yvonne's hand, but embraced Madame Opale fiercely, joining her mother's love with her own.

"You carry our hopes with you," murmured Madame Opale. "As well as my love."

Ammaline wiped tears from her eyes as she turned away.

The rest of them entered the chimneylike cavern. Delphine, Paul, and Madame LaFerme began their ascent.

Manon carried Ammaline on their back; the rest leapt up from platform to platform, disappearing into the darkness.

Manon and Ammaline spoke little; Simone was silent, heavy with thought.

When they emerged into the tunnels, they found that the others had left them behind; not even a dim glow remained in the dark vault, where the enameled metal staircases rose up in levels, to the corridors under the opéra. The two—or three—of them proceeded, Ammaline now on her own feet, until they had reached the side of the *Téméraire*, and the sealed door that protected it, in the blank and silvery wall, slightly curved, at the end of the walkway.

Manon passed it without comment, but Ammaline stopped. "We must stop here, Manon. Let us in."

Stopping a few dozen feet away, Manon turned back to look at Ammaline. It was dark; the only light came from a small red gem that Ammaline had taken from her clothing.

It had once been stained with the Puppet Master's blood; the blood had all flaked free, and only the gem remained.

"Where did you get that?" Manon asked. "Who...?"

"The Puppet Master. When...when Madame LaFerme and I killed him. His body is still here, I think."

"I knew he was dead, but I thought Océan had killed him. Alone." Ammaline shook her head.

Manon returned to her, took the gem, and studied it. "I don't think it'll work. It's keyed to the Puppet Master, not to you. And the mechaniques would have deactivated it, when they resurrected Armand?" Their tone belied the words, rising to a question. "But it shouldn't be glowing. You're not Armand."

Ammaline took the gem back, then held it to the same place upon the ship that Madame LaFerme had done. It had been such a short time before! And yet she hardly remembered what Madame LaFerme had done, whether she had entered a code or made some gesture, had submitted to any tests of identity or otherwise. It seemed an age ago that she had come to the ship.

That she had awakened Simone within her, seemed the least of the changes she had made.

The ship's door sank into the silvery surface and slid to the side: within, the air was fresh, and did not smell of death and blood.

"Shit," declared Manon. "Holy shit. You should *not* be able to do that."

They ducked inside the door of the ship. Ammaline followed. The door at the other end of the short white corridor crowded with plastic panels opened, and once again the air was fresh.

Manon turned to the right, but Ammaline turned left, toward the server room.

"Where are you going?" Manon called after her, but followed.

Ammaline stopped in front of the door to the room, where not so long ago the Puppet Master's body had lain: the place in the corridor was clean, spotless, and fresh, as if nothing had happened.

Manon was tall enough that they had to crouch a little, to stand inside the corridor, and put one hand on the plastic panels to steady themselves. "What's wrong? Why are you stopping here?"

"Are there mechaniques on board the ship?" Ammaline asked. "Modern ones, that is?"

"No, why?"

"The body is gone. This is where we left him—we sealed up the ship."

Manon stared at the spot. "Why here?"

"He was coming out of the server room when we saw him. He had hidden a case there, which Madame LaFerme later recovered, and took to the archives for Yvonne to keep for her."

Manon's jaw dropped. Then they held out their hands a little over a foot apart. "Was it about this big? Sturdy but not heavy?"

Ammaline remembered the weight of the case, the size of it crushed into her stomach as Madame LaFerme carried her. "You saw the case—it was the one she had when you found us."

Manon exhaled, their chest deflating and their shoulders drawing in. "I wasn't paying attention, not really. That was the last case of elixir that your father brought from Shakes Prison. Grandpère had me bring it here and leave it, for safekeeping. A few days ago. Armand shouldn't have known it was here. I can't even begin to think what that means anymore. Who betrayed who. I can't keep track of anymore."

A red light flashed overhead, and an alarm beeped once, then went silent.

Manon barely blinked. "What now? Someone's at the door."

Ammaline's fists clenched. *Armand.* Her body burned with heat, prickled across the backs of hands. "Should we let them in?"

"We don't have much of a choice. They're already coming in."

Manon waved her away, directing her to move further down the corridor. Then they waited on the far side of the door, out of sight, their hands loose and relaxed beside them, still in the same half-slouch.

They waited for several long seconds. The person who had entered the ship was moving slowly. Something tapped on the floor, followed by a cough. A clicking sound. A beep.

Then a grunt. "Hello? Who is here? The door is open and the readout says someone just came in.—Manon, is that you?"

Manon stepped into view, unfolding a little, losing all appearance of dejection or weariness as the light from the entrance struck them, their confidence inside their streamlined gray suit like a costume that made them appear to be a stranger. "Hello, Grandpère."

"Manon. What are you doing here?"

Ammaline could not see Grandpère. His voice sounded different than the one she knew—and wasn't Grandpère confined to a wheelchair? She hadn't seen him that often, to be sure, but he had always seemed so ancient! This man was on his feet, sounding much younger. She could not imagine how such a thing could have happened—unless Grandpère had died and been replaced by a clone, that was.

Manon shrugged. "You know how it is."

Grandpère chuckled. "Here to check on the elixir? Is it safe?"

Manon was still crouched a little, to keep from hitting the ceiling, but they no longer leaned against the wall. Their hands were still easy at their sides, but in no way did they seem to be relaxed. Acid rose in Ammaline's throat. Somehow, she knew that the situation would call for violence.

Manon did not so much as glance away from the door. "No, Grandpère. I am not here to check on the elixir."

"Then what are you doing here? Get out of the way. Let me pass."

Without moving, Manon said, "Give me your cane."

A pause followed, which was so long that Ammaline began to look around the corridor, to see whether there was anything lying around that she could take and use for a weapon. There was nothing, not even the piece of plastic that Madame LaFerme had used earlier. It had all been cleaned up. Ammaline did not want to have to use her bare hands again. She could still feel what it had been like, to attack Armand's face and eyes.—But she would do it again, if she had to.

Manon reached out a hand, accepted a cane with a red gem at its top, then held it out for Ammaline to take.

Don't touch it, Simone cautioned. *Grandpère would never let go of it if it wasn't booby-trapped.*

Ammaline kept her hands close at her sides.

Manon glanced over her, and she shook her head. Manon tossed the cane down the short hallway, where it came to a halt at the curved far wall.

Grandpère sniffed. "There's someone with you, isn't there? Well? You have my cane. Let me in."

Manon stood aside.

An older man entered. He did not look like Grandpère, but it would have been difficult for anyone who had not been as ancient as Grandpère to look as Ammaline remembered him. This man was of medium height, only just barely an old man, straight-bodied, with steel gray hair and heavy eyebrows. Even his voice was unrecognizable. She could scarcely believe it to be the same man.

"Ammaline," the old man said. "Come here, child. Let me see you."

The voice *was* similar, and how he addressed her seemed much the same, but it was not exactly so, and not merely because it was a younger man saying it. Ammaline's skin crawled.

Don't, Simone whispered again.

Manon interrupted: "What are *you* doing here? The elixir is gone, by the way."

The man's eyes widened and his jaw set. "Where is it? What have you done?"

Ammaline breathed slowly, trying to stay calm. The cane seemed to have a living presence, like a predator lurking at her back, waiting to attack. She pressed against the wall, wondering if Manon could handle both the old man and his cane, if it came to that.

Manon spread their hands. "I didn't do anything with the elixir. Océan took it. I saw her, but I didn't realize she had it. I ran into her and Ammaline near the stairs down to Paul's trailer. I had just found *her* again, and I wasn't paying attention."

Grandpère cursed. "If only you had stopped her. What was she doing with it?"

"Only trying to keep it safe, I think. Armand had attacked her and Ammaline inside the ship, and she was afraid that he would come back when he had been resurrected."

Grandpère's eyebrows beetled downward and he hunched his shoulde rs.—Now he looked familiar, his old self. But there was still something off about him, an aura—almost a scent.

He growled, "Armand should not have known it was here."

Manon's hands fell, and they leaned back against the far wall of the corridor, but their eyes stayed fixed in place. "I've been trying to work out how he knew. Who would have known? Who would have told him? Jacques, maybe? Anyway he was here and attacked Océan. He put her through some shit during the first night of the Season. So there was no love lost there." They crossed their arms over their chest. "More than that, though. The ship has been cleaned up since the last I was here, too. Wakened. And Ammaline says they left Armand's body by the door of the server room, and there's no trace of it. Not even a smell. So how did the mechaniques get in here to take care of the body?"

Grandpère waved a hand carelessly. "That would have been Océan. She hated that the ship slept for so long. She would have wakened it just to feel its presence, and a few of the automatic programs could have started running and let the mechaniques in. She was always convinced that it was intelligent and that it missed her."

He snorted.

Still leaning casually against the wall, Manon repeated, "What are *you* doing here? Why have you come?"

Grandpère looked toward the cane that lay down the corridor, his squarish face looking like the most genial, least threatening thing in the world: yet terrifying.

"To get the elixir," he said. "Manon, you must get that case back for me. Go now. Ammaline and I will wait here in the ship for you."

Manon didn't budge. "It should be fine where it is, with Yvonne."

"I need it," Grandpère said.

"For what?"

Grandpère's face began to turn pink. "Is there any particular reason that you won't do what I tell you?"

Manon didn't answer. If anything, as the situation had grown more tense, they had relaxed against the wall, their eyes half lowered, as if they were going to sleep. "Everyone has a line in the sand, old man. And you have come up against mine."

Grandpère's fists balled up; his pink skin turned redder. Then he put up a hand: *stop*. A few deep breaths later, and his color had returned to normal. He opened his mouth, closed it, then said, "I don't know how much you know. The Grillons have attacked the Silver City. They have broken in and are killing everyone they can get their hands on. And the ships from Earth are in orbit above us, about to land. I was off. Twenty years off! And, as Lemure said, the worst possible moment."

Ammaline's heart leapt at the sound of her father's name. "My father? How is he?"

Disgustedly, Grandpère snarled, "Covered in ichor and bloodlust in his eyes. He and Corentin both. They've been out slaughtering Grillons all day and night, instead of getting anything useful done."

Manon scratched their chin. "And Armand? Is he back yet?"

"Armand? No." Grandpère's hand reached out to steady himself on his cane, the one that wasn't there, and he had to quickly bring his hand up to the wall. "He should be back by now, demonstrating the difference between bad and worse. Where *is* he?"

"And?" Manon asked. "What else?"

Grandpère glanced again at Ammaline, then shook his head. "Isn't that enough?"

Did he know about Simone? Ammaline wondered.

"Then I know something you don't," Manon said. "The Grillons brought Carlton back."

Grandpère exhaled so heavily that it was as though a ghost exited his body. "No."

"Armand was dead when the Grillons got in," Manon said. "Someone had to let them in. Someone with access. The Grillons have access to the same tech that we do, up at the North Pole. We just assumed they were too stupid to use it."

"The resurrection pool was deactivated and all the elixir removed. And none of us would help them turn it back on again."

"They can get at the elixir, though," Manon pointed out. "They have access to the entire planet, Season or no Season. And maybe it wasn't as hard to turn the damned thing on as we thought. Or Armand convinced himself that turning it on was the most outrageous betrayal he could ever commit. You know how he is."

"Not even Armand," Grandpère insisted.

"If you say so." Manon pushed off against the wall. "So the Grillons are here and the humans, too. What comes next, Grandpère? It's not a question of preparing for the humans to get here anymore, or trying to defuse the situation with the Grillons. What comes next? And don't tell me to bring you that case of elixir. As I said, there's a line in the sand now. I'm done taking orders."

Manon was not angry, or at least did not seem so. Only cool and distant, relaxed, and still slouching from the low ceiling.

Grandpère stared at them.

The truth unfolded in Ammaline's mind like a piece of gossamer fabric, translucent but dotted with stars.

She said, almost as though she were making a prophecy: "He's going to destroy the ship. He only wants the elixir because he wants to destroy it. All the resurrection chambers have been sabotaged. The second the ship from Earth touches ground, they'll go up. The files with your memories have all been deleted already. It's just a matter of cleaning up a few loose ends. Boobytrapping the Silver City. And killing the rest of the Twelve."

The events that would occur if Grandpère had his way played out in front of her as if she were watching the recording of an opera on stage. The humans' enormous ship descending from above, crashing to the ground, and causing an earthquake so large, that it threw an explosion of particles into the atmosphere, which the Season quickly spread all over the planet, bringing darkness, while the Silver City erupted in flames, as Grandpère's sabotage destroyed it from within.

She saw her father killing Queen Delphine, and King Corentin killing him in turn. She saw Armand and Jacques returning together in some sort of train, arriving at a place underground, as the tunnels collapsed around them. They fought their way to the surface, and were surrounded by Grillons, led by a man dressed in stained white rags, his body so horrifically twisted as to seem more than half-Grillon himself.

She saw Océan return to the ship, only to fall with a knife in her back: Corentin's. She saw Paul try to flee, and to fall under the same knife.

And then it was *her* turn, as King Corentin stalked her, calling her a monster, saying that she should never have been born, that of all the foul things that had been spawned on Thomàon, she was the worst. Manon lay at his feet, pale from loss of blood...and nothing she could do to prevent it...

But before all that, clear yet wavering in her inner vision, came another task she must complete.

She blinked, and her eyes cleared. She had not fallen this time, but still stood upon her feet, close to the wall of the ship. Grandpère watched her; Manon still watched Grandpère.

"You're afraid that the people from Earth will come, learn our secrets, and become just as bad as we are, or worse," Ammaline said.

He's not wrong, Simone told her.

"I'm not *afraid* of it; I'm *certain* of it," Grandpère said. "There is no question about it. That's what they'll do. That is what we are all made of. Even if *you* are innocent, that doesn't mean your genetic lines don't contain predators within it, waiting to be born. There will always be another vile monster waiting to slaughter the weak, wear their skins for coats, and bathe in their blood."

He's still not wrong, Simone added.

Ammaline bit her lip. She didn't want to have to say what she was about to say. "How would you know that it's not you who is the monster?"

Grandpère chuckled, sounding uncannily like his older self. "Oh, I know I'm a monster. I know what *I* would do. I am a bad man, standing between the innocent and those who are even worse than I am."

She knew the cause was hopeless, and yet she must make the attempt:

"How do you not know that what you do defends us? and does not make the situation worse? If you are a monster, if you are a bad man, how could you be sure that what you do is right?"

He smiled at her patronizingly, his voice cooing in a soothing singsong:

"You are innocent. You have not seen what men who are worse than me can do."

Simone said, *I have always wanted to ask him that. I had hoped that he would give me another answer. I searched the possibilities to see if there was anything I could say or do that would change his mind. I couldn't. So I didn't ask.*

Ammaline replied, *You have your answer for Paul. The White Gentleman exists, so that men like Grandpère can control the destiny of humankind.*

Manon glanced at Ammaline, then nodded. She had a moment of panic: what was that nod for? What had Manon just decided to do?

Grandpère took a deep breath, then exhaled, looking around the corridors. "I had thought that I was long past arguing with childre n.—It seems strange to see the ship in person. I have spent so many generations of myself without stepping inside it, half wondering if it was real. Now that I am here, it seems small and unimportant. Not worth the effort that has been put into it, over the eons."

He patted the panels of the wall. "We should never have gone to space. We should have stayed upon Earth and learned to be better, before we reached so far. Everything that humanity touches, is tainted."

Ammaline pinched her lips together. It was a fine time for him to say such things, now that he thought that what he had taken from Thomàon would soon be taken from him, by someone else!

A door that had been opened inside her began to close: if this was what it meant to be human, she would have no part of it.

Ammaline?

Her guts lurched, shivered—shifted.

Moving carefully, she walked to the curving terminus of the corridor and took up the cane with the red gem at its end, then walked back to Grandpère. Her fingers knew what it was that they should do; by the time she had reached Grandpère's side, she had pulled the cane's sword-blade from its sheath.

Grandpère blinked and drew back, coming against the doorway that led into the ship.

Her fingers moved again, and the blade began to vibrate and shimmer, as if it were cutting the air itself.

Ammaline was close enough to him that she could feel the warmth of his presence. That which had shifted inside her shifted once more: she wavered, and the blade touched Grandpère's shoulder.

The blade leapt through the cloth of his jacket and his shirt, which parted themselves and lay aside to reveal Grandpère's wrinkled white skin, but came to a rest on his flesh, shimmering with menace but unwilling to cut its master.—If she had wished, she could have stabbed him in the guts with it, forcing it within him, or chopped at his shoulder with it. The metal was sharp.

She pressed the blade a little, and a bead of blood appeared underneath it.

Ammaline? What are you doing? Simone sounded frightened. Ammaline herself was also frightened—but it was what she had seen, and she had chosen not to try to avoid it.

If she wished to change the path of time she had seen, she would have to give herself to it.

The shifting in her guts came up into her throat, a burning sensation that was not pain, not grief, not heartbreak, but a little of all of those things. She opened her mouth to release it, with Grandpère as her target.

What emerged was curious, strange—wonderful.

A song.

It had no words, no melody, no rhythm. It was a sound that felt as though it were a living thing in and of itself, the end point of everything that the species united in its creation had attempted to do. Humanity's love of data and measuring was in it; the Scarabées had brought to it a certain communality of spirit; the Grillons had contributed the workings of the paths of time that they had learnt, in surviving and even thriving during the chaos of the Seasons.—That was where Simone's ability to see the future had come from, from them. *They* were the ones who had been destined to travel the stars, if the Scarabées had not hobbled them.

Ammaline turned away from that other future, a path it was now too late to take, and allowed the song to move through her.

She formed words around it, words that had long been familiar, but she could have chosen any song, or none: *Les beaux rêves...*

The song curled through the air; Ammaline and Simone watched its course, seeing it as a physical thing that distorted the air, darkened it but made everything seen through its lens sharper, more clear.

The song surrounded Grandpère, covered him, considered him.

What would it do with him?

Judge him?

Embrace him?

Make him stronger, weaker?

Kill him?

Or could it do nothing? Was it all an illusion? Had she, in fact, gone mad, the voice of Simone a symptom of her separation from reality?

Even Ammaline did not know.—If Madame Opale had been there, they could have asked her, for she had been the one who had engineered the material which made up Ammaline, and which had laid her potential at her own feet.

Grandpère's eyes watched her, puzzled. He did not see what had emerged from her mouth; he only knew that she was singing, and holding a blade to his shoulder; that she had forced it to scratch him, and he was annoyed by the cut, which felt as though the blade had betrayed him.

He said, "Sword. Sting."

Whatever it was that he had meant the sword to do—poison her, perhaps—the sword did not do it. It was within the nimbus of the song, and she held it in place.

The song crept within the blade, worrying out its secrets, and tuning them to Ammaline's command. Then the song ended, echoing in the room but no longer physically present.

The blade sank deeper into Grandpère's flesh, and he howled in surprise, more than pain.

He attempted to grab the blade with his bare hand.

Ammaline stepped away from him before he could catch the blade, raising her other hand to waggle a finger at him. "Don't. It'll cut your fingers off. It's mine, now."

The sword still retained its sense of presence, but now the sense of it being a threat had gone. What remained was a sense of curiosity, that the blade knew it had gone against its own protocols and did not understand why—but it was open to discussion, for it had never spoken to one of the programmeurs before. The sense of awareness that it carried, radiated from the gem at its hilt.

"What have you done?"

The question came as blood ran down Grandpère's shoulder, and soaked the white cloth of his shirt and the dark blue of his jacket. His eyes were wide and fearful, the whites showing around the watery blue pupils.

"I have taken your sword," Ammaline said dryly. She was no sword-fighter—although it was a pastime taken by plenty of young people, all the better to demonstrate their prowess during the parties of the Season—but she had learned a little play-fighting for the theater.

She stepped backward into a fencing stance, holding one hand up and behind her, the sword upright but within easy reach of Grandpère's throat.

"How?"

"How would I know? I am an innocent, remember?"

For a moment, all remained balanced, with the paths of time spread out before her. Simone said nothing, too engrossed in the possibilities—not only of what might lay before them, but in how Ammaline had taken control of the sword; it felt to both of them as though it were connected to them in common, as if it were a new node on a mechanique network.

Then: the ship began to scream.

Chapter 7

An Effective Method of Unlocking Doors

CORENTIN, ON HIS WAY to destroy the archives and recover the black case filled with what might have been the last of the elixir, leapt down the long stairs to the reservoir. He eschewed the central pole, instead flinging himself from platform to platform. Around him echoed the sound of his striking the metal stairs, the long, booming sounds announcing him to anyone who might listen. He imagined dark figures attacking him out of the darkness, forcing him to dodge, and weave, and stab.

There was no one.

He knew where Yvonne's secret hideout was; the Puppet Master had told him ages ago, just to stir up some shit. Corentin had gone once to check it out. It was too lame to bother with, even less impressive than Paul's trailer down by the water. He'd decided to let Yvonne have her little hobby; it didn't hurt anyone and it kept her from spending so much time mooning around the castle.

By the time he alighted upon the cavern floor, he was nervy. He wasn't sure why.

Outside the chimney-cavern that held the stairs, the reservoir was dark, and damp, and depressing. Paul's golf cart was parked just outside the stairs. Not a single Gondolier was in sight. The lights had come on as he reached the floor, throwing garish shadows out on the immense underground lake.

Corentin made a face. He needed the Gondoliers if he was going to make it to the archives anytime soon. They always seemed to know when they were needed—but he didn't have any candy in his pocket. That was probably it. The Gondoliers came when there was sugar to be had, that was all.

Paul should have some candy at his hut somewhere.

Corentin jumped into the electric cart, backed it around, and bumbled off toward Paul's trailer. The trail ran along the water, the cart's headlamps lighting up the darkness. Behind him, the lights at the platform turned off.

The water remained dark. The cart whined and its tires crunched on the path.

Why couldn't the Gondoliers understand that he was in a hurry? Why couldn't they have remembered all the times that he'd brought them pieces of candy, and just come? Stupid beasts.

He pulled up at Paul's trailer and parked the cart, leaving the lights on. He walked to the door of the trailer and banged his fist on the door. The trailer was sturdy, but any of them could have torn the door off with their bare hands. No answer. He banged again. A red light flashed on the panel by the door.

Corentin snorted. Paul had locked the door.

The knife was hanging in its sheath at Corentin's side. He put a hand on it, then pushed the small, smooth metal loudspeaker button on the panel.

"Open the door, Paul. I know you're in there."

He let go of the button. Still no answer.

In order to go back to killing Grillons without Grandpère getting on his nerves, he had to take care of the archives. In order to take care of the archives, he had to get across the reservoir. In order to get across the reservoir, he had to ride a Gondolier. In order to ride a Gondolier, he had to get some candy. In order to get some candy—

"Fuck it." Corentin drew the knife, flicked it to life, and stabbed it through the door of the trailer.

The knife sank into the door, punching through it like it was a tin can. The noise sounded like a string being pulled tight, until it snapped free with a twang. The blade hummed as it rested inside the door.

When he didn't get any answer from the intercom speaker at the side of the door, Corentin dragged the knife downward with a sawing motion. The metal parted with a rancid smell from the insulation that was melting inside the door. It sounded almost musical as it cut. The vibro-blade got hot, transferring the heat to the metal but the metal heating up and radiating the heat back to Corentin's hand.

He slashed down to the bottom of the door, then cut across at chest height, and downward again.

"Paul, you have nobody but yourself to blame," he shouted.

He kept working, making it to the bottom again. Now he had a tongue of metal about a foot and a half wide, and five and a half feet tall.

He sheathed the knife again and pushed the tongue inward. It bent, the edges complaining loudly as they scraped against each other. He put a foot up and pushed the tongue of metal down further, until it touched the floor, then ducked through.

Inside the trailer it was dark. The inner door that led past the foyer area was shut. It was locked, too, with another light that flashed red when he tried to open the door.

Corentin stabbed the inner door, this time planning his attack a little more efficiently, cutting through the bolts that held the door in place rather than cutting a hole in the door. The bolts went quickly, if more loudly, as the knife split them apart. He yanked the door open.

On the other side of the door, a few peanut bulbs glowed near the floor.

"Paul!"

No answer. Corentin stalked down the corridor to the back room where Paul spent most of his time, still living life like a teenager in his mom's basement. The door to that room was locked as well. He hacked through the bolts and let himself inside.

This room was dark, too. Paul was gone.

Corentin tried to wake up his mechanique, but it was powered down and would be password locked as well. Stabbing the terminal would hardly unlock the system, even if he did get it powered up.

Where was Paul?

When did Paul *ever* leave his trailer?

Wasn't Delphine supposed to be watching him?

Where had *she* gone?

Corentin stared around the room. Besides the fact that Paul was missing—and so was his wife—the place felt off somehow. The air hung thick with the reek of the burnt metal and other materials of the door. It was silent.—That was it. It was too quiet. The loud noise of fans cycling air through Paul's massive servers had stopped.

There must be something wrong with the power at the trailer. It was running on backup.—Maybe Grandpère had already done whatever he was going to do with it, to sabotage it so the humans from Earth couldn't fuck around with it.

But why hadn't Delphine contacted him?—Because if the power was out at the trailer, then her messages wouldn't reach him. Not this far underground.

It didn't matter. He only needed a couple of pieces of candy.

He left Paul's room and stepped into the corridor, then stopped in front of Paul's kitchenette. The door was locked there, too. As if Paul were afraid that someone was going to steal his snacks. He'd always been like that. Paranoid about people taking his food.

Corentin cut through the bolts on the door, then kicked it open.

The stench of death gusted out at him.

Corentin put his sleeve in front of his face, the vibro-knife still switched on. The blade caught some of his hair and burned it. He thumbed it off, then messed around with it until he found the flash-light settings around the hilt.

The light shone red through the gem at the hilt. He aimed it around the kitchenette.

Against the far wall lay Jacques's corpse, gore everywhere, splattered around the room like Jacques had been attacked by a high-powered blender.

"The fuck," Corentin said.

A noise from the room caught his attention. In the far corner, trying to hide behind the open door of a microwave, was a big mechanique. It was covered with blood.

It wasn't too hard to work through what had happened. The mechanique had attacked Jacques and killed him, sending him back to the resurrection pool.

Whether that was a good thing or a bad thing was for Grandpère to decide.

Corentin stepped inside the room, trying not to slip in the blood, working his way over to the cupboards. Paul had to have a store of candy lying around somewhere in here. He ordered enough of it for his stores. The man practically lived on frozen meals, soda, and gummi worms.

The first cabinet was full of napkins and paper plates. The second was empty.

The third had a couple of cardboard boxes wrapped in plastic, the words *32 PIECES* written on the side. A strong possibility. Corentin took one of the boxes down, set it on the counter, and cut it open with his knife.

Inside were plastic bags full of gummy candy: miniature Scarabées. Kids' candy.

"About time." Corentin put the knife down to shove a handful of packages into a pocket and closed the cupboard door.

Something dark and heavy slammed into his face. Corentin saw stars and stumbled backward. Blood gushed into his face.

A whining sound followed.

"What the fuck, Paul?" Corentin felt around for his knife. His hand slapped the counter. Nothing. He swept his hand around, and felt only the box. Where the fuck was his knife? He was going to stab that fucking weirdo Paul to death.

Corentin didn't find his knife; his knife found him.

He shouted as the knife cut through his other hand, which waved in front of him. Fingers went rolling.

"Paul! Knock it off!"

The pitch of the knife rose higher. It felt like his eardrums were splitting. The knife sliced through his forearm, dragged against bone, and burned through it. The rest of his hand went dangling off his forearm with a crack of the last snapped bone shard.

That was it. He no longer cared what was going on. Every moment of frustration that he'd had to deal with over the last few days was going to get dumped on the stringbean freak.

Corentin swept his leg out to knock Paul's feet out from under him and encountered only hard plastic.

The mechanique.

It skidded a few inches, then rolled closer. The whine of the knife rose in pitch even further, cutting through the metal brace on his leg, then down through tendon and bone.

Corentin dropped onto the floor.

The mechanique rolled over his foot. Blood loss was starting to get to him, making him shiver and retch. Christ! He was being taken down by a fucking *robot*. Wielding his own vibro-blade.

He must have triggered the trailer's defense systems, running on emergency backup power.

Corentin tried to kick the mechanique off his leg but only wrecked it further. He swore, his voice fading and the gray building up around the edges of his vision. Fine—they weren't out of elixir yet. Or he didn't think so. And even if they were, there were still a few doses at the archive.

The mechanique wobbled, dropping the vibro-blade. It landed on top of Corentin. He suddenly remembered that there was supposed to be a safety mechanism on it that kept it from attacking its owner. Too bad he'd never figured out how to reset it. It sank into his flesh, tearing through muscles, bones, and organs as it dug down.

What would stop it, Corentin wondered, as it worked its way through him and onto the trailer floor. The rock floor of the cavern, maybe.

Then again, maybe not.

He passed out.

Chapter 8

A Predator's Amusements

Lemure ran through the Castle of the Silver Spire, slaughtering Grillons as he went. The corridors were stained with blood, the white and gilded plaster covered with it, the thick carpets, the parquet flooring, the intricate tiles, the rococo furnishings a sort of history of gore: the blue-green ichor of the Grillons was the freshest, but the red human blood showed different colors, indicating where the Grillons had recently slaughtered them, and where Armand's thugs had earlier culled those who might be allied King Corentin and Queen Delphine.

He passed into the Hall of Masks. The giant masks that represented the Twelve hung high above them, untouched by most of the blood and ichor, but still showing signs of disturbance. Several of the masks had been tilted. The King's mask had fallen and cracked into two or three large pieces in the center of the floor, and dozens of others scattered everywhere else.

Lemure looked away from it, as he jogged around the sides of the room, to the staircase leading upward to the more private areas of the castle near the Opéra du Mendicant.

Up the stairs and into the corridors full of ballrooms, meeting rooms, and small assignation rooms—fancy names for a convention center, to Lemure's way of seeing things.

He recalled the moment when he had given himself over to Grandpère's plans, to limit the expansion of humanity throughout the universe. It had been in another banquet hall, not far distant in space, but quite distant in time, and in origin: inside the Grillons' nest they had fled to, during their first Season.

Their shelters had been blown over, smashed to smithereens. The ship still lay on its side, half-plunged into the depths of the reservoir, and, they all thought, ruined and uninhabitable. The twelve of them had not yet made their foul bargain with the Scarabées. They had not yet learned what it meant not to die.

The rest of humanity had not yet been reawakened; they lay in their cryogenic death-sleep on the ship, or were merely fertilized ova, waiting to be placed in the wombs of the women they had brought. The cryo-sleep passengers were women, all of them; the only living men were those that had been frozen to help operate and maintain the ship.

Once they had landed, they had all gone for each other's throats. Only the threat of the Grillons—one contrived by Grandpère, for the most part—had kept them from murdering each other, for one reason or another.

The Season had struck, destroyed their shelters and most of their equipment, and the damned pet Grillon that Manon and Yvonne had tamed led them to its nest. The Grillons guarding the nest while the rest of their species were out celebrating the storm were old and weak, too weak to survive the buffets of the wind, too frail to survive being carried hundreds of miles in the storm, to begin their lives at new nests halfway around the continent.

The Grillons tried to push Corentin out of the nest. He had shot one. The rest had attacked.

Humanity was more than a match for the black-shelled aliens. Even without their most powerful weapons, it was nothing to slaughter them: knock off a few legs, and they'd bleed out quickly. They were the kind of species that overbred itself to ensure its overall survival. Humanity had chosen a path of toughness instead, with fewer kids but more resilient ones.

When all the adults were dead, Delphine had freaked the fuck out and had them kill all the kids. First, though, Corentin had once again done the stupid thing, and fired at the wall of the nest, blowing holes in it and letting in the storm. They'd had to scream to hear each other talk.

Lemure had showed them that it was more than possible to slaughter the Grillon young without using guns.

That had been the moment that he had given himself over to Grand-père's plans. He hadn't even heard them yet. But the first person to propose to him at that moment to keep humanity from spreading through the universe would have had his loyalty.

He had hated himself as he killed the Grillon young. He had murdered the innocent to keep his twin brother from killing them all with his own stupidity. And he hadn't really stopped murdering the innocent since then. They'd put him in charge of the prisons, which were nothing more than an engine to control population growth.

Grandpère had capped the human population of Thomàon at one million people. And every year after the Season was over and the damage cleaned up, Marks Lemure set his hand at culling the weak from the herd.

Then he had met Etoile, marked for death at the prison, and had taken her for his own.

His wife. His commoner wife.

She had had faith in him, a faith he knew he didn't deserve. *She* had tried to bring him back from despair.—He had always wondered whether she had given herself to him as a trick, in order to survive longer. He had taken her from a subterranean work crew that was digging a dangerous vein of Scarabée matrix. The others had all eventually died.

She had lived.

And had born his child.—He hadn't known he *could* bear a child. Paul had told him that the elixir had made him infertile at best, that any child he conceived would die in the womb or kill the mother—would be born a freak.

Ammaline shouldn't have been able to exist. She hadn't killed her mother, and she hadn't been a twisted mutant of a thing, her flesh half-Grillon and half-human, a predator of her own species. She was perfect and pure.

Paul had not lied—he never lied—but he had been wrong.

When the others had let Carlton murder Etoile, then refused to resurrect her—refused, that was, to make the Twelve into Thirteen, for that was what her resurrection would have entailed—Lemure had called them to get rid of Carlton and they had. He had called them to leave him to raise his daughter, so long as he ensured that she didn't become a monster. And they had. Manon had killed themselves in order to be raised with her, to keep an eye on her when they were children. Even as a child, they would have murdered Ammaline, if she had shown the slightest sign of making the horrible change that they all feared.

But Ammaline was perfect, and pure.—In truth she was Etoile's daughter in spirit, not his.

Grandpère had let her live, and thereby purchased Lemure's loyalty, to a depth that Lemure's reason would never have agreed to.

But now? Now that the humans from Earth had arrived?

Would Grandpère still allow Ammaline to live? Or was she, an innocent, marked for death, as a precaution against the Earthlings learning secrets which they would wield against the universe?

Lemure had passed through several of the corridors leading toward the control room, when he heard a sound behind him. It was a distant sound, but one which echoed.

He retraced his steps, unwilling to leave unknown danger at his back at such a moment.

At the top of the staircase leading from the Hall of Masks, he easily spotted the source of the sound. The shining black shells of Grillons crept along the top of the room. They were unmistakable, set against the pretty gilded patterns of the wallpaper. They were attempting to throw the masks off the walls and onto the floor. As Lemure entered the room, they managed to loosen the mask of the Général. It toppled from the wall and crashed upon the floor, landing atop the King's mask and shattering it further, while itself sustaining a long crack down its center, and falling in two.

Laughter rang through the room, a sound that was neither sane nor human.

For a moment, Lemure could not see who had made the sound; he looked about the hall and saw no human figure upon the floor. But the laughter continued, on and on, and Lemure followed the sound upward, and saw a pale figure which made him shudder.

It wore white rags, stained red here and there, dangling from its limbs, which were nearly as pale as the walls upon which it clung. It had been human, once, but was no longer.

Carlton.

The White Gentleman wore no shoes or gloves, but hooked its pads and claws directly into the texture of the wall. Its head was framed with straggled white hair, stretched to be twice its previous length, and whose mouth gaped open, revealing an odd, bulging mouth without teeth. He wore no shell upon his outer flesh, and bent oddly as he clung to the wall.

"That's it!" he cackled. "Keep working! We'll soon have them down!"

Lemure felt his skin creep at the sight.

Carlton, the White Gentleman, warped by the Grillons, and apparently now their leader, or their God. Lemure looked about the room, and considered turning his back and walking away, climbing up the stairs until he reached the control room, and following Grandpère's orders.

He thought about the man who had killed Etoile, his wife.

He thought about the slaughter of the Grillon young, in that first nest, so long ago.

And he thought about humanity, both that which had established itself upon Thomàon and that which was only just now arriving.

The Grillons were working at another of the masks—that of the Diva—when Lemure put his fingers in his mouth and whistled.

The sound startled the Grillons, whose shells rattled like pebbles on a beach, then went deadly silent as they each one turned their long heads in his direction.

Lemure shouted, "Hey there! Carlton! Is that you?"

The Carlton-monster had not moved. Its jaw hung open still, its eyes blank, and Lemure feared he would have a dozen of the Grillons leaping onto him in a moment. He drew the knife and started it singing.

Now he had the Carlton-monster's attention. It leapt down from the wall and onto the floor, then began gracefully picking its way through the shattered fragments of masks. The Grillons still clinging to the walls made soft purring noises at him, questioningly.

Carlton rose onto his hind legs, then waved a hand—or claw—toward the Grillons, purring back at them. They settled, and stayed where they were. Carlton stopped at the base of the stairs, an easy leap for either of them, to instantly be at the throat of the other.

Lemure switched off the knife and sheathed it. He breathed deeply, then exhaled.

"You're alive."

Carlton sneered at him, the corners of his lips wet with spit. His voice came out in nearly a toneless monotone. "So are you, bootlicker."

Lemure reminded himself that Carlton was a complete psycho, and had always been a complete psycho, and there was no need to react to anything he said as if it had actual meaning.

"I see the Grillons follow you. Are their attacks your orders?"

Carlton licked his lips with a dark-red tongue. "My encouragement. Do you have a problem with that?"

Lemure shrugged. "I just want to know if you're done killing yet."

"Why? Do you want to take revenge for the slaughter of your wife? I ate her, you know. When I was still more or less human. Her body was sweet, as sweet as fresh shrimp, back on Earth. Do you remember what that tasted like, Lemure? Or have you forgotten? I hadn't."

Lemure felt his heart racing, struggling inside him not to explode. His lips went numb with the strain of trying to control himself. He blinked, forced himself to breathe, and came back to the world. The back of his neck prickled.

The knife was out of its sheath again, and back in his hand, whining as it vibrated.

"Sure I remember, Carlton. But are you done killing, or are you busy?"

"Busy? Why, I'm a busy little bee. But if you want to have a duel to the death, I'm available."

Lemure shook his head. "I was just wondering if you wanted to sink your teeth into some new victims."

"Oh? Finally decided to betray Grandpère?"

Lemure shook his head again. "The humans from Earth have arrived. They will land soon."

Carlton considered this. His jaw fell and he began laughing again. "Bullshit."

The lights flashed in the Hall of Masks, just as if it were time to enter the opéra for a performance. A loudspeaker called, "Warning, the Great Dome is in danger of being breached. Please move to the nearest hallway or corridor without windows and crouch down. Warning, the Great Dome is in danger of being breached. Please move to the nearest hallway or corridor without windows and crouch down."

Lemure said, "There are several large ships. One of them is coming down outside the city. Any of the humans who survive the landing are going to be ripe for the picking. Armed, too, and probably dangerous, but that shouldn't bother you too much. They'll take one look at what you've become and piss themselves. They'll probably try to surrender."

Carlton kept laughing, but hooked one claw upward, toward the Grillons. He purred at them, still laughing.

A few of the Grillons raced away along the walls, leaving claw-marks in the wallpaper behind them.

"They'll be back soon," Carlton said. "Tell me, while we wait, how have you been doing, Lemure? How is your daughter? Still tasty? Or has your lord and master, Grandpère, gotten rid of her yet?"

Lemure didn't answer. Over eight thousand years of experience in surviving Carlton's needling. He'd learned not to respond unless it was truly necessary. Instead, he tossed his knife from hand to hand. It had been Carlton's knife, or the pattern of it had, before they'd killed him.

After Carlton had killed Etoile, and after they'd all agree that Carlton deserved not only to be killed but to have his memories erased and his genetic code destroyed—not that it had done any good—they'd had to plan how to kill him.

Grandpère hadn't come up with the plan. Neither had Jack. Armand had refused even to try.

Yvonne had come to them and sketched it out for them: Jack would hack into Grandpère's systems and leave himself a backdoor to exfiltrate information. The information would show a flaw in the security at Shakes Prison. Armand would set up a plan to take advantage of the flaw, to try to get a few extra doses of the golden elixir.

The flaw in the Shakes Prison security would also expose Ammaline to danger. She would be the bait for the trap. An infant.

Lemure had refused.

Carlton would only come if he had a chance to get at Ammaline, explained Yvonne. He was watching them all. Even if he knew that they were laying a trap for him, he would come. Even if none of them contacted Carlton, even if none of them asked for his assistance in any way, he would know.

And he would come.

He *would* come, Yvonne had told them. Either he would come at a time that they controlled and had prepared for him, or he would come at some other time, one they could not control.

Lemure had refused again: Grandpère had ordered him to do it. He had still refused.

Corentin had turned to him and said, "And if Grandpère authorizes it anyway? Without your permission? Do you want to know when it's coming, or do you want to be forced to respond at the last minute?"

Lemure had agreed. Still strangled with grief for his wife, knowing that not only was his daughter targeted for the same torture or worse, and believing that the others would use his daughter as part of their plan, whether or not he agreed—he agreed.

The plan had gone smoothly enough. Jack had hacked into Grandpère's system to get some files that he had his eye on; Grandpère had scrambled to stop the exfiltration but had been unable to completely prevent it; Armand got into Jack's systems in turn and reviewed the files, finding what had been hidden from them all, and found the flaw in the Shakes Prison security—it involved a long passage underwater, several complex mechaniques, and only a couple of flawed samples of the elixir, which had been discarded as not being worth processing—or were they?

Armand developed the mechaniques as well as a few modifications that would allow him to stay underwater for longer, then set up a diversion at the prison: a prisoners' riot.

None of this had been arranged with each other, after that first meeting. Lemure had found himself asking whether the first meeting had been a dream, or if the others had changed their minds and gone behind his back. Yvonne had given him a space of three days in which to be most prepared, a week after the first meeting. Madame Opale had come to Shakes Prison in that time, in order to care for Ammaline. Lemure hadn't told her of the plot, and yet she seemed to be aware of it, showing him a spray that she had smuggled with her into the prison, that would stun a certain man, if she sprayed it, but do nothing to the baby—or to him, Lemure.

"It is attuned," she had said.

It was like something that Simone would have come up with, if Simone had not already been killed.

Armand had crept into the prison through the underwater passage and gone to where the samples of faulty elixir had been disposed of. He had taken the elixir, then returned the way he had come. He had seen no sign of Carlton anywhere. The hair had not even risen on the back of his neck.

That night, after quelling a mysterious prison riot that had ended almost as soon as it had begun, Lemure had received a message from Yvonne, asking for some records regarding the elixir. What happened to samples that were deemed unusable, she had asked. She had found a report of a woman having been brought to a hospital in the Silver City with some pretty terrible injuries: mutations, that seemed almost similar to those suffered by the Twelve.

He had frozen in front of the terminal after he had read the message. Did it mean that Carlton was coming? Was it some sort of hint? It was the first sign that he had received that anything unusual had happened, or would happen.

He decided to try to behave naturally, that was, with extreme paranoia. He checked on his daughter, sleeping peacefully with Madame Opale watching over her, then locked their personal rooms as if for a siege. He brought a pistolet à aiguille with him, but went alone to check on the samples of elixir he had discarded, down in the storage areas under the prison, where bodies and other waste were discarded. A gruesome place.

The samples were gone!—Stolen by Armand, a contemptuous little scrawl on the safe where they were kept: *Thanks for the research materials, asshole,* with the little mark that Armand always signed shit with, that of arrows pointing in all directions, an old symbol for chaos.

Of Carlton, there was no sign.

Lemure ran back to his apartments, calling for security to assist him in searching for Armand or any other unauthorized personnel. He did not call for anyone to meet him at his apartments; he would not have trusted his own men not to have been subverted, and bring Carlton directly to the place he was wanted least. Carlton had persuasive ways, one that did not take Armand's subtlety to inflict.

When Lemure reached his apartments, the heavy outer door had been sliced open like a rind. He ducked inside, drawing the pistolet, and ran toward the room where his daughter was.

That door, too, had been sliced open.

Looking through it, he saw a broad back blocking the room, moving as if he were struggling with someone else, trying to keep them from the door.

"Carlton!" he roared, lifting the pistolet to shoot.—Then, hesitating, he pushed his way past the figure. It was his brother, his feet just off the floor, being strangled with a loop of wire around his neck.

Lemure ignored him. Corentin got a foot up on his shoulder.

The room was small, little more than a cement box with ventilation and drainage, a plastic bassinet and a platform for Madame Opale so she could rest comfortably while watching Ammaline. There had not been time to decorate with anything more appropriate.

Madame Opale lay on the platform, legs raised upward, her shell cracked and fluids oozing from it. Carlton stood beside the bassinet, his arms gathering Ammaline to his chest. His pair of knives were at his sides, still sheathed.

Lemure had attacked.

Behind him, Corentin had dropped to the floor, gasping and choking.

Carlton tucked Ammaline—wrapped in a light blanket—under one arm and drew a blade with the other. He had started to say something, but Lemure had ignored him, running straight at him, and buried the blade in his own guts, hugging Carlton to his chest.

A mist sprayed the side of his face, smelling of sickly sweet perfume.

Lemure coughed, feeling the vibro-blade eat deeper and deeper into him, knowing that he was about to die, praying that he had saved his daughter. If *she* died, the others would not bring her back to him.

Carlton struggled against him, but slumped. Ammaline began to whimper and kick, inside her blanket.

"Whoops, there." Corentin took Ammaline from Carlton's side, as Lemure bled out. He lay Ammaline in her bassinet, then took the knife out of Lemure's side and wrapped his dying fingers around the hilt and moved hand and hilt up to Carlton's neck.

Lemure pushed and the knife slid inward.

After that, it had been easy enough: Carlton was not resurrected; his clones were destroyed, his information deleted, both his memories and his genetics.

Lemure and Corentin had each taken one of his knives, and—when it was time to manage their herd of humanity a little more severely than usual, committed the same sort of brutality that Carlton would have, at least, as much of it as they could stomach.

Manon had had themselves killed in order to watch over Ammaline as she grew. *Someone* had to do the killing.

Lemure flipped the knife over and over in one hand. He was sure that Carlton could see it.

Carlton purred at the Grillons, who purred back. He shook his head. "Just a little longer, Lemure. Do you want to know why I am back? Who brought me?"

Lemure shrugged. "No."

"Then I will tell you. At the north pole, I have my fortress. Inside it are the experiments that I have conducted upon humans and Grillons. Monsters, you would call them. They are my children."

Lemure knew that Carlton didn't have children, only playthings. He kept flipping and tossing the knife. "Or we could just wait in silence."

Carlton tilted his elongated, distorted head upward to where the Grillons struggled with another one of the masks. It was stubbornly stuck.

"Without using the systems that Grandpère controls, over time, I was able to reproduce them. It was simple. Once I discovered that I did not need any of *you* to ensure my immortality—"

Several Grillons entered the room. Whether they were the same ones or others, Lemure did not care. They purred at Carlton, who laughed, once again extending his monstrous jaw.

When he had regained his composure, he looked back up at Lemure: "If you will excuse me."

Lemure nodded. Carlton sprang out of the room, heading through the archway that led to the lesser areas of the castle complex. Behind him, the rest of the Grillons fell to the ground, landing with a rattle, and scurried after Carlton.

When they had gone, Lemure took a deep breath and sheathed the knife. He turned back toward the corridor that would lead him to the control room and strode away.

Behind him, the mask that had been loosened fell to the ground with a crash.—Lemure did not return to see which one had fallen.

Chapter 9

A Procession of Scarabées

Within the halls of Versailles was a certain amount of violence, but not as much as there was within the Silver City.—Versailles had been evacuated of all but the Scarabées underground, Grandpère's trusted servants. The resurrection chamber and certain other areas of the palace were still intact, but the palace itself lay in ruins.

This was no surprising thing; every year it fared a similar fate. The storms which consumed every above-ground structure on Thomàon were so severe, that it was considered foolish to try to out-build them. And why anyone would attempt to do so, when the means of rebuilding them was so simple? One had only to send an army of mechaniques into the rubble, and they would rebuild most of the palace from whatever wreckage remained.—Some part of the buildings was lost every year, flung halfway across the continent or into the ocean by the winds, but the missing materials were easily dug up from the earth, or harvested from other structures which had left their inadvertent gifts of tile and struts nearby.

The buildings were so easily replaced, that they were hardly built to last longer than a year's time. Even in the Silver City, much of the city would be torn down and rebuilt in sections, throughout the year.

Versailles's golden plastic structure, with its high arched windows, columns, gardens, walkways, and courtyards, its meandering wings and its fountains, its chandeliers, its gilded ceilings, its frescoes and marble, its candelabra and its clocks, all had been torn asunder, and flung to the winds, leaving only the socket of a rotted tooth behind.

It crawled with Grillons, who clung to the surfaces and worked their way slowly from brick to brick, as the winds shifted and tried to snatch them away.—Sometimes, one or another of them would be smashed to bits, by the arrival of some piece of construction that happened to land upon them. Others would be knocked away, and flung into the storm.

Those who remained picked through the rubble, searching. For what they might search, was not immediately clear. They seemed not to find it, whatever it was.—Then a flare went up, fired by one of the Grillons, who had planted it into the ground.

The other Grillons turned in that direction, watched the storm snuff out the flare and scatter it to the eight winds, then began to make their slow way toward the signal.

Rain and hail battered them; winds shook their bodies as they crept, and screamed at them for attempting to defy it; rubble flung itself at them, or rolled underneath them, and a moment's unsteadiness meant death, or banishment to the maw of the storms.

The Grillon who had attracted the others with the flare, clung to a heavy stone banister next to the last few shreds of a red velvet curtain. A painting had been trapped under the banister, one that showed Grandpère's genial face in a gilded frame, but which had been ruined by the water.

Underneath the painting was a thin slit of light, where the marble flooring had cracked, and revealed a glimpse of a world that lay underneath the palace.

The Grillons began to drag the wreckage away from the crack: the banister, the curtain-rod, the painting, and other things as well, until the flooring was visible underneath.

Then they began to work at the flooring. They were creature of air and storm, and were too light to lift the heavy pieces of marble and cement underneath. But some of them carried cutting tools with them, vibro-blades strapped to their bodies along with power-sources, in slings of human invention.

They began to cut downward into the tile, into the cement, and then, the steel bars that reinforced the cement, and more cement, then a layer of steel mesh, and finally another layer of cement, which they did not have to cut into minuscule pieces, and carry out with their own quivering, struggling legs—this last layer simply fell inward, and crashed at the bottom of the room it had suddenly ceased to protect.

The Grillons entered, dropping to the floor and out of the worst part of the storm.

By the time the Grillons had made their way into the resurrection pools of Versailles, it was too late: Jacques and Armand had already left. They had climbed into the train cars underneath the palace and set the engines running, and had rolled along the tracks to the underground station at the center of the city.

They had been delayed by the thought that they ought to take whatever remained of the golden elixir of the resurrection pools of Versailles, only to discover that there was none left; nothing remained of what, eight thousand years ago, had seemed an illimitable supply.

If Jacques had not stopped the mechaniques from killing Armand yet again, he would not have been able to return at all—unless there were any doses of the elixir left to be had, at another pool. But neither of them thought it likely. There *were* such doses, but Grandpère had hoarded them, Grandpère and his peon Lemure.

If they experienced death, it would likely now be permanent.

It had been so long since either of them had faced such a possibility, that they did not speak to each other of plans, or intentions, or possibilities.

They knew that the humans were coming, and they knew that Grandpère wished to sabotage everything that they had built on Thomàon, so that humanity could not take it and use it to conquer the universe, the way that they had conquered Thomàon.

The end is near, was the thought which hung between them. What each of them wished to do, in the face of death and extermination.—They did not know that the Grillons had overtaken the city, or that Carlton had returned; they had both expired too early, and had left the palais too casually, to have learned *that*.

The end was near, and Grandpère would attempt to kill them all, in a misguided effort to "save" the universe.

What could they do?

Armand considered that Grandpère was unlikely to change his mind, no matter what inducements were used upon him.

Jacques considered the same, and concluded that he had better find the humans when they landed, and offer to lead them to the secrets that he had preserved in case of such an eventuality, at la Tour de Défense, his own fortress, not far from the Silver City.—Or at least, the secrets that he stored underground in the safe-rooms near his tower, for the tower itself had no doubt been obliterated by the storm. Further, he considered the best method of approach, as well as the time likely to remain in this current Season. He thought that it seemed to have been continuing longer than it ought, or shorter: it was hard to remember the date or the time, when the Great Dome had been sealed, and the days and nights stretched long past their natural hours. And if one had been killed, in the course of the Season, and had to be resurrected, it destroyed one's sense of time entirely. He resolved, when he had returned to the Silver City, that he would check the date and the time, and berated himself for not having done so earlier.

Armand considered that Jacques was likely to run straight to the humans and tell them *everything*, without consideration of what would be beneficial to reveal, and what would be beneficial to hold back. It was, after all, what Jacques did when he came running to Armand.

Jacques considered how much of what he knew he should reveal to the humans. If he doled out too small an amount, they would not expect much of him, and would not grant him any power, after they had finished establishing themselves, and sorting out which of them would rule and which obey. If he doled out too large an amount, he would have given them enough that they would not need any more, and he would be destroyed, as a threat to their power. The best of all strategies, he concluded, would be to hide until after the humans had faced their first Season, and had been nearly, or very nearly, destroyed by the Grillons. After that, they would be nothing more than desperate survivors, who would place great value on whatever Jacques should reveal to them. They would hail him as a savior.

With that pleasant thought, Jacques swayed as the train came to a stop at its underground station. He stood up. The door of the car opened, and Jacques ducked out the door, and onto the narrow platform, where he encountered the bodies of the Grillons, which Lemure and Corentin had so ably separated from Life.

"What the shit?" he asked.

Armand ducked out of the door after him, and also surveyed the wreckage, bringing a light at his wrist to bear on the brothers' handiwork.

Grillons, deep inside the Silver City. And underground—yet Grillons hated to go under the surface. They left it to the Scarabées to dig through the rock, and crawl in the dirt.

How had they come inside? A trail of ichor led across the cement platform, back toward the tunnels that the train had come from. Armand shone his light down the tunnel. They both half-expected to face a wall of Grillons staring back at them from the tunnel—but there was nothing.

They both listened to the self-echoing silence.

Jacques's eyes were dry. He blinked, held them close for a moment, then opened them again. "Did you do that?"

The two of them still stood in front of the tunnel. Neither moved; they barely breathed. Still there was nothing more than silence—the dripping of water—more silence still.

Armand felt smaller and more uncertain than he had while being repeatedly killed and resurrected at Versailles. The sweet smell of the ichor was almost making him gag. "What?"

"Did you let them in? Is this all part of your plan?"

"No."

His voice hoarse, Jacques said, "That's almost worse, isn't it? The devil you know and all that."

Armand's throat tightened. He felt himself rocking as he stood, his knees locked. It was ridiculous, the way that finding the bodies had surprised him. So what? What did it matter, if the Grillons had broken into the city? It wasn't like he couldn't turn the situation to his advantage: get rid of the Grillons when Corentin and Delphine couldn't, and come out of the situation looking like a hero. He'd have to do something if he wanted to regain the People's trust, after being gone for so long. But he'd have to do it quickly; and without being sure of what resources he would be able to muster on short notice. The Grillons wouldn't have made a distinction between his supporters and the others.

How long *had* they been gone? Armand checked the gem on the cuff at the back of his wrist. It lit up but didn't connect to the mechanique network, not down here in the secret underground station, naturally enough.

It didn't necessarily mean that the network was down, only that he couldn't access it. Angrily, he snapped at Jacques, in order to release his nerves, "Am I the devil you know? Or just the devil?"

Jacques sighed. "Not now, Armand."

A white heat spread through Armand's chest. In a second he had drawn the pistolet that had been in his resurrection locker and aimed it at Jacques's head. "This is more than just another annoyance now, isn't it? It's the end. That changes things between us."

Jacques's eyes stared over his shoulder. A cramped line of sweat rolled down Armand's back, the nerves prickling like pins, like eyes were upon him.—Armand often felt as though invisible eyes were upon him, calling him a fool.

But nothing leapt upon Armand's back; he was not attacked from behind.

Jacques said, in a placating tone, "Look. We both have the creeps here. Let's get up to the nearest mechanique network station and get a better idea of what's going on before we start turning on each other."

Armand lowered the pistolet, then holstered it. He felt disconnected from himself, as if he were being controlled by an outside force that made him do exactly what he would have done, if he had felt in control of himself.

Jacques straightened his military-style jacket. "I'm sorry I thought you were behind all this. I just couldn't think of how it could have happened. It almost seems like Carlton's style, you know? If he'd still been alive, he would have been the one to let the Grillons in. He just didn't give a fuck."

The hairs rose on the back of Armand's neck. *There was something behind him.* He couldn't hear anything, but he knew it was there.

Slowly he turned.

The train they had come in on was short, no more than a single passenger car and a few cars for materials and equipment. But the far end of it lay in the shadows of the tunnel leading to Versailles.

Armand stared into the darkness, wondering whether he saw movement, or his eyes were tricking him.

"Did you hear something?" he asked.

Jacques drew his pistolet and aimed it into the darkness. "No. But I feel it now, too."

From the darkness, a grinding, stonelike voice rasped, "We apologize for startling you. We had hoped to avoid startling you. We will enter the tunnel now."

Coming out from under the shadow and into the dim light of the station, with shadows that danced as Jacques and Armand moved the light that shone from their wrists, was a double-row of Scarabées, their shells various shades of dull metal.

They moved silently, making only the slightest of sounds, eighteen or twenty of them, and then no more.

One of them said, "We will pass into the city now." And the double-row of Scarabées marched past the two men, neither saying nor indicating anything further of their purpose or necessity.

They exited through another of the tunnels, one that led toward the Castle of the Silver Spire.

"Let us follow them," said Armand. His feet were already carrying him in that direction. "And see what it is they have come to do."

"Do you think they know about the Grillons?"

The Scarabées had shown no sign of battle, but their feet had left dotted trails of ichor as they passed.

"They know."

THE PASSAGE TO THE castle was not so easy as the tunnel that led from Versailles. Every year, when the Silver City was rebuilt after the Season, the layouts of the streets would change; the buildings would be moved, rebuilt, redesigned; the secret passages would change course, like an underground stream that had been damned and had to find cracks through which to flow.

The Twelve had never seemed to notice it. They had traveled the routes without considering how they knew where the doors were, or how to find and unlock them. The knowledge had come from the genetics of the Scarabées, who had tinkered with humanity for so long, that it was as though their genetics had become their toy, a game carried out over generations, the rules changing so subtly that the pieces never questioned their movements.

As the Général and the Puppet Master traversed the spaces underneath the Silver City, they noted that the route seemed strange and unexpected—different than the one they themselves were used to. They did not recognize the basements, and sewers, and storage areas through which they passed. The corridors were wider; the ceilings lower. They hit their heads on pipes in the dark.

The Scarabées passed solemnly and silently before them, their bodies trundling slowly through the dark. Their progress would have been lightless, had the two men not followed them; but they did not seem to notice their presence, or the weak and wavering light they cast. They walked two by two, or one by one, where the passage and doors were too narrow.

They entered through a heavy steel door marked with the sign of a white mask, with a crown at its head: the sign of the Castle of the Silver Spire.—They were at the castle, then, about to enter into its warren of underground rooms.

Jacques found himself increasingly nervous, with a grinding sense of dread that he carried in his vitals, as if he had been swallowing pebbles by the handful. Heaviness weighed his steps, and dizziness lifted his head, disconnecting it from his body, making him feel as though he had been elongated.

He took a deep breath. It seemed as though he smelled a scent that he had not smelled in a long time: vanilla, a smell that he had not smelled since Earth, as the plants themselves would not grow on Thomàon.

A song began to repeat itself in Jacques's head, a sad song about the consequences of virtue, "Heureux celui qui n'en a point." It was from an old play of the Vieux Monde, all the way back on Earth. It told about how wisdom had killed Solomon, courage had killed Caesar, and honesty had killed Socrates. It was one of those damned songs that Armand had whistled all the time, after they had killed all the Grillons as the nest that first year.—Jacques attempted to whistle it, but his lips were too dry to bring out the tune. He licked his lips, pursed them, and tried again: a tuneless sound emerged, frightened and small.

He swallowed, bit his lips as if to crush the blood out of them, and tried a third time. The tune came wavering out, strengthening as he continued it.

Armand gave him a glance as the two of them passed down the humble corridor, far from the heart of the castle. Then he, too, puckered his lips, and the two of them whistled together in harmony, a sort of dirge for the Scarabées' strange procession.

They turned a corner, and Armand began to recognize where they were in the castle. They were behind the Opéra du Mendicant, on one of the several routes that led toward the reservoir. It was not a route Jacques had used before, although he had been in that part of the basement for some reason or other, several years ago—or a hundred. He could not now remember.

They reached a hidden door that the Scarabées opened, paneling upon the wall that slid back to reveal a heavy steel door. The heavy steel sank into the cement around it, and pulled back to reveal a wide, low opening about a foot off the floor.

The Scarabées climbed over the lip of the door, then dropped out of sight, into the darkness.

The door began to close as the two men approached. They quickly ducked through—they were almost to the end of the song, which ended on a long musical passage. They both began whistling it together.

On the other side of the doorway were enameled metal grillwork platforms. They followed the Scarabées down them, their great beetlelike shells bobbing and dipping as they went down the stairs. Their feet made no sound whatsoever.

The two men finished the song; Armand began whistling "Mack le couteau," which was another song from that old Vieux Monde play. Jacques elbowed him and he stopped. They continued following the Scarabées as if enchanted.

They passed the curved wall of the *Téméraire* and glanced at each other.

"What are we doing here?" whispered Armand.

"Trying to find out..." Jacques started to say, then drifted into silence. The smell of vanilla returned to him. "Following a scent," he concluded.

"Fucking Scarabées," Armand whispered. "Why are they dragging us along with them? I have shit to do."

After that, they walked in silence, surrounded by clouds of pleasant scent, until they reached the long stairs down to the reservoir.

The Scarabées arranged themselves single file, and began to descend.

"Fuck that noise," Armand said, and flung himself down the central platform. His boots banged on the little circular platform on the pole, then banged again as he dropped.

Jacques followed him, moving slower and more cautiously. Soon he was out of the cloud of scent and able to think more clearly; still, he descended toward the cavern floor. Curiosity had got the better of him. What was so important, while the Grillons were murdering their way through most of the city above—apparently—that the Scarabées, their sister-wives, were marching away from it, at a stately pace? Were they fleeing the carnage? If so, they were not moving very quickly.

Armand had gone out onto the platform and activated the motion sensors. The lights over the reservoir were blindingly bright. Paul's golf cart was parked at the trailer. Jacques shuddered. He hoped the Scarabées would not force him to go to the trailer. The idea of facing the mechanique that had murdered him gave him the creeps.—He had come too close to a final death.

Grandpère *had* to have more of the elixir stashed away. It couldn't end like this.

Armand stood at the railing, looking over the edge. For a moment Jacques wondered whether he, too, were being beset by dark thoughts.

Then Armand said: "The Gondoliers are here. A fuckton of them."

Jacques walked to the edge and joined him. The paint on the rail had built up over the years and was tacky to the touch.

Below them was a thick mass of spongy white living ribbons, hardly glowing at all, and silent, bobbling gently on the water. It truly seemed as though they had come to meet the Scarabées.

Jacques looked over his shoulder, back toward the cavern. The Scarabée procession had not yet arrived.

Armand hawked up phlegm and spat onto the Gondoliers. "Fucking things."

Jacques turned his back to the water. "You know they probably like it."

Armand snorted and spat again.

They were both wearing their "starting" gear. Jacques was wearing a pair of gray sweatpants and a t-shirt with English writing on it: *I'm a GAMER not because I don't have a LIFE, but because I choose to have MANY*. At the time he'd picked it out and programmed it into his profile, he'd thought it was clever. As the years had gone by and he'd found himself living the same life over and over again, using the same strategies, never quite min-maxing his score, it had turned into a dark and private joke. Armand was wearing brown corduroy slacks, brown Italian leather shoes, and a gray t-shirt under a brown tweed blazer, all of it tailored to his taller height.

One of them looked like a joke. The other one looked like…a billionaire's kid slumming on another planet. Which he was.

Jacques said, "What are we doing here, Armand? Not down here, here. But…overall? What are we *doing* here, on Thomàon?"

Armand exhaled on a groan, slumping over the rail even further. "Christ. Don't get philosophical on me."

"Why not? Don't tell me you don't have a plan to take advantage of all this." Jacques waved a hand toward the cavern entrance. "I just want to know how you see the game overall."

Armand straightened back up. "Why the fuck would I tell you?"

Because, unless we can figure out what the fuck is going on, we're both going to die. Because the humans from Earth are almost here. Because I got caught flat-footed by all this and I'm having a panic attack and I want some reassurance that, no matter how bad it gets, at least some asshole has a plan to survive all this.

"No reason." Jacques's voice came out rough, vulnerable.

Armand's eyes sharpened on him, as if he had smelled Jacques's insecurity. "I see it as fucking Pete Johnson deciding to get one up on Joel Govender, my father if you've forgotten, dragging me along for the ride to make sure that dad's legacy on Earth got fucked. I didn't want to come. I see 'the game,' as you call it, as a stupidly drawn-out attempt to get back to fucking Earth and take my rightful place there."

Jacques blinked.

It didn't even make sense. If Armand wanted to get off Thomàon, why hadn't he just taken the ship?

The answer to that question came to Jacques like a switch had been flipped inside his head, his lungs, his guts. His heart rate sped so fast and hard that it felt like it was going to burst in his chest.

Armand didn't know how to run the ship.

Jacques could program the ship. Océan could pilot it. Together, Paul and Simone could find a solution to any other problem they encountered. But Armand? He was just a billionaire's kid, slumming it on another planet.

He'd spent the last eight thousand years trying to get the right people on "his" side. All that effort, and he couldn't be bothered to pick up a basic textbook on programming or physics.

Eight thousand years of pulling people by their strings, because that was all he knew how to do.

Armand was watching Jacques's face closely. He took several steps back away from the rail, drew his pistolet, and fired.

The needles sank into Jacques's chest and abdomen. He felt the pain blossom as the needles ejected their contents, but whatever Armand had loaded them with had not yet hit his system.

Jacques put his hand to his chest, then held it out to the light. He wasn't bleeding badly. His hand showed only a few dots of blood.

He didn't ask why Armand had shot him.

Instead he put his hands on the rail behind him, to steady himself in case his legs went numb or collapsed. "You know that if I die you're missing an engineer."

Armand lowered the gun, his face turning red. He held out his other hand, palm down. "You shouldn't have asked. You shouldn't have looked at me like that. You shouldn't have asked that question."

At the mouth of the cavern, the Scarabées had reached the stone floor. Before they emerged into the bright lights over the platform, they regrouped, forming up once more in their double rows.

Jacques licked his lips again, and began whistling the same old tune.

His skin prickled with gooseflesh.

Once again, Armand joined him, but this time, the Gondoliers whistled with them as well, as if they had long ago been taught the tune, or as if it had come to them from the Earth itself—they whistled not only the tune, but the rest of the song itself, accurate as far as Jacques remembered it. The sound almost seemed to shimmer in the air, becoming light as the Gondoliers turned themselves luminescent.

The double row of Scarabées began to move toward them again. This time they did not limit themselves to silent marching, but began to buzz and hum and click as they walked.

White pinpricks of light flashed in Jacques's vision. The ends of his fingers and toes, the end of his nose, all became cold. He smelled the same scent of vanilla, but it was subtle.

The Scarabées walked to the ladder leading down to the water. They did not descend, but stopped, one at a time, to cast something past the rails and into the water below.

Jacques felt himself start to slide down on the rail. It didn't hurt—it didn't hurt any more than it had a minute ago, and it hurt even less by the second. His whistling grew fainter.

Still, he struggled to turn around and face the water, to see what the Scarabées were throwing over the edge. He lowered himself down onto his hands and knees and crawled up against the railing, leaning his head over the edge.

The Scarabée nearest the opening in the rail threw a piece of something over the edge. It was not large. It turned as it fell. The platform cast a shadow on it from above, but the soft glow of the Gondoliers lit it from below.

It landed on top of one of the Gondoliers. Jacques's eyesight was failing. He squinted at the object that had fallen, trying to make out what it was. It shimmered in the light of the Gondoliers, but did not become more clear. It joined a few other objects on the back of one of the Gondoliers.

Another piece fell from the platform. This time, Jacques turned his head toward the next of the Scarabées as she came to the edge. There, in her jaws, was a piece of shell, shimmering like a piece of abalone.

Opalescent.

Jacques had had no special affection for Madame Opale, but no repugnance, either.

Armand, though, muttered from behind him, "There goes that old bitch. They're throwing pieces of her shell over the edge. Something must have happened to her."

Jacques felt the edges of his vision going gray. "What did you shoot me up with, Armand? Am I dying or just passing out?"

Armand grunted an *I don't know* at him.

Jacques felt tired, and old—he felt like one of those sci-fi immortals from movies back on Earth, the kind where you removed the spell or curse or whatever that was keeping them immortal, and they shriveled up and died, then turned into dust. There would be a moment where their jaws would come loose, and fall off the skull—then the whole skeleton would blow away in a Hollywood breeze.

His arms were shaking with the strain of keeping him up. He lay down on the platform and curled onto his side. He felt a little nauseated, but it could have been worse. He studied his hand, turning it back and forth, but it looked fine. Just a little pale.

The song he was whistling faded from his lips so that only a little hiss remained. Armand was nowhere to be seen now.

The Gondoliers continued their song.

The main thing was that he didn't feel afraid. If now was his moment, if this was how he died, he was okay with that. He wasn't afraid and he wasn't alone. The Gondoliers were there.

The Scarabées kept throwing things over the edge, until they had all taken a turn. Then they turned around and marched away. Jacques tried to wave at them as they left. His fingers barely twitched.

Inside his head, and with the barest movements of his lips, he formed the words:

See here Jacques the Général The master of all games Who never sacrificed a pawn That he did not take a King and more besides And as he planned his next daring move The poisoned needles plunged into his side The world, however, didn't wait But soon observed what followed on It's strategy that had brought him to that state...

From then on, Jacques smelled nothing more.

Chapter 10

The Substance of Memories

Yvonne la Gorge rode the back of the Gondolier toward the Archives, relieved to be away from the terror of the Silver City. She knew she should feel something more than pity for those who were trapped there. She knew she should see the people who were dying as just as important as she was.

She had seemed fine, even to herself, until after she had begun moving away from the platform and the others. Then she had been gripped by an awful, panicked feeling that had left her in such pain that she felt she must cry out, and terrified of what might happen—she had no idea what that might be—if she did.

Sweating and shaking and ill with dread, but as silent as a mouse, she could hardly cling to the back of the Gondolier as it carried her across the reservoir.

The Gondolier swam slowly and gently, whistling softly to her, a soothing song that somehow made her feel worse, rather than better.

Over and over, she asked herself, sometimes silent, at times aloud: "But what could *I* do?"

The caverns echoed around her, twisting her words: "What *could* I do?"

The water was cold, the back of the Gondolier little warmer, spongy and nubbled under her clutching fingers. Whenever the bitter salt of her tears pooled on its back, it had to duck down into the water to swirl the salt away.

When she had come to the cavern and looked out over the edge of the platform, she had seen a mass of Gondoliers waiting there. Surely they had not waited for her, alone and afraid. As the Gondolier moved slowly forward through the waves, and as she regained control of herself, she began to wonder more and more about what had brought them to wait there.

The soft tune whistled by the Gondolier stopped. The sounds of the water moving throughout the reservoir echoed, the drips of water, the wavelets against unseen rocks. Her eyes adjusted, and the distant cave roof became discernible, dull green from the glowing creatures that lived and clung there. They were a type of larvae, very small, that would grow into a buzzing insect-like creature, the sort that her hawk-moths would feed upon. The larvae used bioluminescence to draw their prey—she had seen the same sort of thing back on Earth, once.

The Gondolier began to whistle again, and she lay her head against its back, relieved that the flurry of terror had left her. She had been keeping it together for so long that she hadn't realized how awful she felt.—It still didn't justify running away. But she couldn't think of what else she *could* do, if she was trapped by ideas of what she hadn't done, or what she couldn't do.

She would get the elixir. She would make sure the Archives were safe. And then she would stop and think.

The song was not like the ordinary Gondolier songs, so intricate and gentle that it was difficult to pick out a melody, but with a clear tune. She listened, and found herself whistling along with the song.

It was *Heureux celui qui n'en a point*, from the Vieux Monde's *The Beggar's Opera*, or *The Threepenny Opera*, or something like that. Not even the Historian could remember everything.—They had named the opera house after *The Beggar's Opera*, or *L'opéra du mendicant*, in French.

They'd never thought they'd see Earth again. They'd ripped things off shamelessly. They'd set up a society that was guaranteed to go nowhere, as long as they didn't let the People get out of hand. If you wanted to lock people in place and keep them from returning to the stars, establishing a French aristocracy was a good way to do it. All you had to do was make sure people didn't *feel* poor. With perfect health and a general sense of prosperity, came a tolerance for injustice that Yvonne could hardly imagine. About five thousand souls were sent to work yearly in the prisons, and only a few hundred or so returned to the Silver City at the start of the Season. They were killed to offset the new children being born, more than anything else, and to keep the People from becoming, as a whole, old and wise. There was no one to rise up, not really, and that the People wrecked their ambitions, as a species, during the periodic revolutions that Armand stirred up.

She wished she hadn't suggested it.—She had been so naïve, and so helpful, in those days.

The Gondolier took her to the shore in front of her little hut. The lights above the hut flickered to life as they approached.

Yvonne looked nervously around the shore, trying to see the black case, trying to see whether there was any sign that it had been disturbed.

The Gondolier bumped up against the shore, its ribbony body dragging on the pebbles at the water's edge. She stumbled off its back and into the low water, then splashed up onto the drier rocks. Her feet felt heavy as she slogged up the slope to the boulder she'd left the case behind.

"I should have just brought it with me," she murmured.

The boulder was still there, with the case behind it. She bent over to pick it up.

Behind the case was a piece of broken shell that had been glued together somehow, to make a small clutch purse about the size of a soap dish, with a knobbed wire clasp and concealed hinges. The shell was unusual—a piece of Scarabée shell, as iridescent as Madame Opale's. But it could not have been hers, as Yvonne had only just left her, at the platform near the cavern.

She tucked the case under her arm, and held the little shell purse in the palm of her hand.

The Gondolier whistled loudly at her to get her attention, and she absent-mindedly walked over to it, put the elixir case on its back, and stood in the shallow water, looking over the small purse, trying to decide whether to open it.

It was solid, and contained something heavy inside it. She held it to her ear and shook it. But there was no movement.

The Gondolier whistled again. It was starting to drift away from the shore with the case still on it! Yvonne called to the Gondolier to stop, but it drifted out farther. Any farther and she would have to start swimming after it.

She waded into the water toward the Gondolier. It waited for her just long enough to collect her on its back, then began moving away from the Archives.

Did she really need to check the Archives? Again? She *had* just checked them lately.

She tied the case securely around her waist with her tattered skirts, then sat on the Gondolier's back to find out what was inside the purse.

The Gondolier abruptly began moving swiftly through the water, making her almost drop the little shell purse. She tucked it into her bodice and hooked her legs down around the Gondolier's sides as if she were riding a horse. The Gondolier trilled at her and went even faster, fast enough that wind ruffled her hair.

The Archives went dark as the motion-detector lights went out.

Her heart came up into her throat in the moments before her eyes adjusted to the dull glow of the Gondoliers and the cavern.

She moved the black case of elixir around in front of her and leaned forward, putting her face against the Gondolier's side. They sliced through the water, the Gondolier rippling under her, driving them quickly along the surface.

Then, abruptly, the Gondolier dove down into the water. Yvonne gripped harder with her knees as the current rushed over her. She squinted her eyes closed and forced herself not to breathe.

They plunged deeper.

Abruptly she was jerked off the Gondolier's back, by a blow that felt as if it came from every direction at once. She opened her eyes, still squinting, to try to find the dark shape of the Gondolier in the water.—The case of elixir started to come loose, and she grabbed it. The shell purse was still tucked inside her bodice; she shoved it down even further.

The water around her was no longer dark, but roiling with orange flares of light. Currents in the water shook her this way, then that.

A soft shape bumped against her, then wrapped around her, rising with her slowly to the surface. The Gondolier rose its head from the water before it let her surface, then brought her face to the water's surface, holding her body under the waves.

As far as the two of them were from the Archives, the air above her was still hot and awful, like having her lungs sprayed with burning rubber. A piece of metal landed in the water in front of her, hissing and throwing up steam. Other fragments rained down around her.

Yvonne gasped for breath several times, then tapped the side of the Gondolier. It took her down under the surface, pulling her swiftly away from the wreckage.

WHEN, FINALLY, THEY HAD avoided the worst of the danger, and then crossed into another, adjoining cavern, the Gondolier drifted to a stop and allowed Yvonne to climb shivering onto its back again. She still carried the case and the little purse, unsure of why she had clung to either of them.—But she was the sort of person who clung to things, who insisted that whether they be pleasant or unpleasant, their existence should not have been denied.

The Gondolier drifted in the water, in the dark, making only the smallest of hums as the two of them floated on the surface.

Yvonne lay on the back of the Gondolier, her legs wrapped around it and the case of elixir in front of her, clutched in one hand. With the other, she petted it. She had never been able to communicate with the Gondoliers, but she had always felt them to be of an immense intelligence and compassion. Now it seemed as though the creature were surprised, or in pain, or struck by despair—as if it needed comfort. She grieved that she herself had so little comfort to give. She hoped it had not been hurt in the explosion.

And she grieved for her own loss: her Archive had not been secret or safe, and in searching her own understanding, she found only that it must have been Grandpère who had destroyed it.

Jacques would not have bothered; Paul would have explained it to her first, or soon afterwards; Armand would have done something more up-setting, like pouring acid over her samples; the others simply either did not care, or did not think that way. It might have been Delphine, or Corentin, or Lemure who had pushed the button, but it was Grandpère who had given the order.

Why had he betrayed her? The answer was obvious: to prevent the humans from Earth from accessing what she had stored there. No doubt, Paul's trailer was in a similar state, and the resurrection pools as well.

Her breath hitched as she lay on the back of the Gondolier. What had it all been for? All the games, all the tragedies, all the loss? What meaning had there been?

She could not tell herself that there had been good aspects to their time on Earth. She had seen history frozen in place; she herself had helped create this travesty.

They had come, had seen, had conquered; now, it seemed, Grandpère had decided to salt the ground against the arrival of his own people.

Had he waited for her to arrive at the Archives? Had he hoped to kill her?

How was she supposed to understand it?—Only time would give her perspective.

She wondered whether the Gondolier had come to the same place she had:

How had it come to this?—And the knowledge that answering the question would not prevent a single human soul from committing the same tragedy.

None of them were innocent. *All* of them had contributed to this work: whether they strove to accomplish it, or resist against it, no other events could lead forward from it.

She was done. Finished. She relinquished her place in the Twelve. May she never again be resurrected; may her life's essence never again contribute to this unhealthy work.

She sobbed on the Gondolier's back, until finally it began to drift again, to undulate and move further into the darkness of the new cavern.

By then her clothes had dried somewhat. She ran her fingers through her hair, wiped her face, and sat up.

The Gondolier made its way through the caverns—away from the Silver City, she thought.

She finally took the little purse out of her bodice, and held in the palm of her hand. "I wonder what is inside this?"

The Gondolier's dim glow brightened around her. She crouched low to the light, then felt around her waist, suddenly remembering her chatelaine that held her watch, her multitool, her magnifying glass. She lit the glass and used it to look at the purse.

It was made of opalescent Scarabée shell, like Madame Opale's—but of course it was not hers; Madame Opale's shell had been intact when she had left the Archives—when she must have hidden it. The clasp was made of gilded metal.

She twisted the knobs of the clasp and gently opened the lid.

Inside was a thick, dull paste, greenish-brown, sealed in a thin sac. Yvonne blinked at it for several moments; she had not expected to see such a thing. It was the matrix that the Scarabées produced for storing their memories, and which, when refined, became the golden elixir.

She had never heard of it being given.—Only taken, mined by prisoners under the Warden's supervision.

Madame Opale had left it for her.

Yvonne did not know what to *do* with it. Keep it?—Protect it, surely. Treasure it. She touched the sac with the tip of her finger. A bead of it oozed out. It was sticky, far thicker than honey, and gritty. She rubbed it between her thumb and forefinger. The golden elixir, refined from this substance, was injected into their spines before they were awakened. The clones of the Twelve could be awakened without it, but they wouldn't carry the memories of the rest of their line. Grandpère habitually had several of his clones alive at any given time; when he chose an heir, the clone would be given small doses of the elixir over time, so that his own memories would not be completely overwritten by those of his past selves. Manon had done the same, when they had agreed to be killed and resurrected at the same time that Ammaline had been born. A torturous process. Painful, both mentally and physically, as Manon had chosen not to have their body modified while they were growing up with Ammaline, either. It had taken several surgeries to give them the level of mobility they needed to return to their work as the Assassin.

The substance before her was not merely a gift, but a *memory*. And it had been given to her, Yvonne la Gorge, the Historian, surely for some purpose.

She closed the lid on the precious purse, and tucked it gently back into her bodice. Her limbs felt as though they belonged to someone else. They were not merely numb; they were foreign. Her head spun.

"Take me home, I beg you," she told the Gondolier. "Madame Opale needs to tell me something, and I haven't the slightest idea of how I can hear her tell it."

CASTLE FRANKENSTEIN WASN'T A castle so much as it was a folly; it was ruined, and had been built to be ruined. It was Paul's. He had had it built but had abandoned it to live in his little trailer under the Silver City.

The castle stood atop a ridge in the middle of some fern trees; when it was not the Season, they surrounded it with pleasant growth that helped cool the grounds. It was hot and humid—a German thirteenth-century structure in the middle of a tropical jungle. Paul had had it built so that the storms of the Season would knock the aboveground buildings over like dominoes, where they would stay for the most part. Then, after the storms had passed, the mechaniques would rebuild the ruins: the blasted tower, the fallen chapel, the ruined village, the fallen bridges, all made of massive stones.

Underground, of course, there were more permanent structures.—Would they still exist, though, now that Grandpère had decided to eradicate everything of value to keep the humans from earth from getting it?

The Gondolier took her to the nearest shore along the reservoir, another pebbly, dark beach underground. As they approached, the lights came on, revealing a golf cart parked along the shore, and a path cut into the gray limestone of the cavern walls.

She sat on the Gondolier's back, floating in the shallow water, her feet scraping along the bottom. The waves hissed as they lapped against the pebbles.

She listened carefully, sniffed the air, waved a hand to reactivate the lights when they went out, and finally swung her leg off the Gondolier's back and stood in the water. If it had been possible, she would have stood there forever, straining to hear the sound of Grandpère betraying her.

The Gondolier trilled at her, then sank under the water, moving slowly away.

"Wait!" she called after it.

She ran to the golf cart, popped open the glove compartment, and pulled out some stale old candy that might have been there for several Seasons. She ran back to the water, hurriedly unwrapped the candy, and began tossing it into the water. The Gondolier moved to take the candy, the cilia of its spongy flesh spreading open to pull the candy in, showing the brighter glow inside.

It whistled its thanks, and began to drift away.

She waved at it. "Thank you!"

It sank under the waves, and was gone.

The golf cart wouldn't start. She slogged up the steep rocky slope and walked inside the tunnel. It was another twelve miles to Castle Frankenstein.

She stopped to check that the case of elixir and the shell purse were secure. Then she unstrapped the braces on her legs—she always forgot they were there, anymore—and began to run.

As she ran, Yvonne began to remember, as if from her own well of experience, the memories of Madame Opale.

MADAME OPALE'S FIRST EXPERIENCE of the humans was when she had trundled through the underground tunnels leading to the Grillon nest nearest the human ship. The Season had begun, and the winds howled uncomfortably up on the surface, thrumming the ground itself so that it shuddered in the caverns below.

She had been called to witness what the humans had done: after being offered the hospitality of the nest, they had butchered all the Grillons left behind to guard it, the Grillon who had offered them succor, and then all the Grillon younglings that waited there to hatch, as Season's end.

The Grillons did not yet know what had happened. They were out in the storm, reveling in their breeding season, fertilizing eggs that would not hatch until they had been brought to the Scarabées for their genetic blessing.

Madame Opale reached the caverns under the nest, but was unable to ascend into the nest itself. The openings were blocked with the bodies of the Grillons, which had been struck apart at the limbs, and tossed down the holes to get them out of sight. The adults lay at the bottoms of the tunnels; the youngling lay atop them, still dripping their ichor.

It had been a massacre.

What would happen when the Grillons returned was another massacre. Madame Opale was there to judge the situation, and determine whether the Scarabées should allow the massacre to occur, or not, or to guide it somehow.

She moved into the center of the nest and found a place where a knobbled column of nest material had worked itself far down into the cavern. She opened her shell and latched onto it with her worry-legs, injecting what lay within the column, with that serum that allowed the Scarabées to transfer mind and memory.

Within the column were several Grillon younglings embedded in the material, ones that were meant in time to emerge from the nest as leaders of the race, having been long nourished on the memories and intelligence of the Scarabées, a King of its race, as Madame Opale was the Queen of hers. But even now, the younglings were aware of the happenings inside the nest.

Their understanding flooded into Madame Opale, or, rather, their lack of understanding—they had been ruined, driven to madness, by the deaths of their people. They struggled to escape the nest, thrashing about under the surface. Their minds were gone.—Madame Opale reviewed their memories, took them into herself, then put them out of their misery.

She saw what had happened; it was just as had been reported to her.

She let go of the column of nest material and sealed her shell again; her worry-legs scraped at each other under her carapace. It was always a worry, to truly share the mind of another.

There was no reason, now, not to annihilate the humans, each and every one of them, and eradicate them from the face of the planet.

She turned away from the column of nesting material, and found herself face to face with a monster.

It was soft and smaller than she was, wearing the outer protection material they all wore, completely unremarkable in appearance. Its eyes were focused on her, its expression unreadable, breathing quickly. It reeked of bacteria and hormones. Its food sources were omnivorous, but stale—as if it had not had fresh food for a long time.

It held one of their weapons in its limb, the kind the younglings had seen damage the nest, and aimed it at her.

Her worry-legs scraped against each other; she forced them to hold still.

It made noises from its mouth; she felt her breathing-holes convulse at the horror of it, and took a step back lest it spit digestive fluid at her. It made more noises, the same pattern over and over again.

She felt as though she were trying to interpret one of the songs of the visitor-wyrms that lived in the reservoir under the area. It was clearly trying to communicate.

What would it have to say, other than to lure her above the surface, so the others could murder her or, worse, trap her and expose her secret parts?

She could kill it within a moment, spraying cyanide into the air. She would likely kill herself as well, but at least she would not live to be enslaved.

But she hesitated.

The only method she had of communicating with sound was her worry-legs; she rubbed them together, trying to mimic the sounds the monster was making. She was so nervous that an almost musical tone emerged instead.

The monster seemed to respond to the sound, the limb with the weapon lowering. It pursed its mouth and repeated the tone that she had made with her worry-legs.

She repeated the sound.

The monster's head bobbed. It put away the weapon and opened its limbs wide, as if to attack her.—No, she realized, it was not gathering itself to spring. It was showing her that it held nothing in its upper limbs.

Then it turned toward the column of nesting material, and gestured toward it with one limb.

She played the tone on her worry-legs again. The monster walked toward the column and touched it several times with the limb.

Then it lay its head against the column, lifted it again, and pointed its limb at its head. It turned its head from side to side.

Madame Opale had no idea of what it was trying to say. It had seen her at the column, that was clear. She did nothing.

The monster exhaled, its body wilting, and from its mouth emerged another tone, descending in pitch. It was surrounded in a cloud of hormone-scent that it was impossible to interpret; she could recognize the scents; she could even recreate them herself, if she had had a mind to; but she had no biological context for them. At a guess, the monster was exuding stress hormones, but the scent seemed to be unmanaged, more a biological response than any attempt to communicate. When the monster had tried to communicate, it had used and responded to sound, not scent.

It had not killed her, and it had tried to communicate further with her, once she had used sound. It had showed itself at least somewhat conscious of what happened around it.

Madame Opale had been sent to judge, to determine whether the monsters should live or die.

She was prepared to sacrifice this life, in order to make a fair judgment. But was she ready to sacrifice her fear?

She rubbed her worry-legs together, calling out the tone again. Because the monster had indicated a negative reaction with a downward tone, she tried using an upward one, to indicate a positive one.

The monster responded immediately, turning its head toward her and making tuneless noises with its mouth. Then it stopped, pursed its lips again, and sounded the same upward note.

Madame Opale tapped a foreleg against the part of her carapace that covered her worry-legs. The monster responded excitedly, bobbing its head and sounding notes.

If she was to have any hope of understanding the monsters, she would have to open herself to them in a way that made her breathing tubes convulse with fear and revulsion. Gusts of scent surrounded her. If the monster had been able to understand what Madame Opale's scent meant, it would have known how afraid she was, the horror of what it was like, to open oneself to one who was not a Scarabée.

She had opened herself to the Grillons, ages ago, in order to broker peace between their species. The peace was fragile and came with a terrible cost to the Grillons, one she had regretted throughout the ages. But she saw no other way forward.

The monster pointed at her carapace, then at its own. Quickly, it removed the upper part of its protective covering, exposing its flesh, and pointed at itself again.

Madame Opale took stock of the cavern under the nest. The nest, full of dead younglings, would begin decomposition soon. It had failed, and would fall to pieces soon after the Season ended, rotting from the inside out. Already it was weakening, shuddering in the storm. She could not tell whether the monsters in the rest of the nest had noticed that their companion was missing, but no doubt they would soon.

She did not dare take more than a moment to collect the samples she needed. And that meant she could not afford to be gentle, or kind, or merciful.

Dropping onto her legs, she swarmed around the monster, clambered up behind it and onto its back, pushing it forward onto the ground. It fell forward and lay still, shuddering.

She opened her carapace, latched her worry-legs onto the monster's main nerve stem at the back of the head, and injected the monster with her serum.

The monster made muffled sounds against the floor of the cavern, but held still.

Madame Opale waited the few seconds necessary for the serum to do its work, then retracted it into her worry-legs, holding it contained so she would not be immediately overwhelmed with what she had absorbed. If all went well, the monster would not remember what she had done to it, but would feel a slight inclination to positive reactions toward the Scarabées.—If all went well, and their alien genetics did not act in unexpected ways.

She examined the punctures she had left. A little of the creature's blood had emerged, but was soon replaced with a clear protein fluid that stopped the bleeding and sealed the puncture.

—She had no time to study the creature's biology. She fled, running forward through the darkness away from the next, into the tunnels the Scarabées used to travel safely underground.

And *that* was how she had met Simone.

Madame Opale had learned to communicate to them. She had learned how much fear of death they possessed, and how it had driven them to the cruel murder of the Grillons at the nest, and of the younglings. She had vowed to change them, to give them the gift of immortality, so that they no longer needed to be afraid.

How she had wanted them to become a breath of hope throughout the universe!

Madame Opale still did not know whether her experiment had worked, or would work. It seemed as though humanity did not become less afraid. It changed itself in ways to make itself more attractive to itself as mates; it removed the threat of many diseases and ailments; it ensured that its members did not live with desperate necessities set against it.

They did not become less afraid. They did not know *what* they feared, but they feared it.

Madame Opale had debated whether to undertake the project that one of the humans, named Etoile, had brought to her, to bring back the great Seer of the human race, after her murder. Madame Opale had always felt that it was Simone who carried the hope of the species.

Should she help the human woman create a child that carried Simone's memories? The rest of humanity thought the memories had been erased, simply because they no longer existed within the human memory banks. If Simone were to return too directly, the humans would gain a better understanding of how the Scarabées had influenced them.—The humans were logical; given evidence, they would work out the implications eventually.

Madame Opale had hoped that her daughter-self would come to understand her mother's choices, and improve upon them, to learn to restrain her mother-self's excesses, and to see where her own mother's blindness had limited her understanding.

Yvonne was still running toward Castle Frankenstein when the memories ended, and the taste of Madame Opale's serum had faded from her lips.

Yvonne put a hand over her bodice, where the little shell purse still rested securely.

Should she go back to the Silver City, she would face tragedy and chaos; she would likely recreate the same mistakes that others had made, in her attempt to influence humanity to be better than it was. Every hope that humanity pursued, was undercut and poisoned by fear. Not even immortality could soften it.

Did she feel, did she *truly* feel, as Grandpère did, that humanity was not worth saving? Did she feel, as Madame Opale had, that it was better to make the attempt to save it, than not to?

—But, Yvonne la Gorge told herself, it was not up to her, to decide whether to save humanity or otherwise. She was not so important and powerful. She had only to decide whether to finish running to the ruined Castle Frankenstein, in hopes that Grandpère had not already finished what nature and design had begun, or to return to the Silver City, and do what little she could, which, in truth, was little more than to do what she had always done: to witness what she saw, and to remember.

Her feet were already slowing. Now they had stopped; now they had turned; now the ground under her feet began to shake; now the stones above her were falling; now she turned and ran to Castle Frankenstein in earnest, as the tunnel collapsed behind her; now she stopped and used her body to shield the little purse, putting the case over her own head; now she choked on the stone-dust air; now the storms tore the stone-dust from its pockets, and stormwater poured in from above; now Yvonne la Gorge, the Historian, climbed out of the fallen tunnel to the surface.

The storms were beginning to clear, and despite the wind and the rain that buffeted her, making her sway on her feet and to shiver, she could see the Great Dome in the distance, flashing yellow and red with alarms. Between her and the Silver City lay an immense chasm. The roof of the reservoir had fallen.

In the far distance, past the Silver City, was a sky red with threat and flames, with a swarm of lights emerging over the horizon, filling the air.

The humans had landed.

Chapter 11

Vanity

The Madman, the Queen, and the Diva threaded the passages of the castle, making their way from the secret entrance behind the Opéra du Mendicant, through the Hall of Masks, which was by then littered with shards and gilded fragments. The doors to the opéra lay open, and the air that was exhaled from that place, was the breath of Hell, the breath of slaughter.

As they turned toward the stairs leading upward, to the more intimate rooms of the Court, and from there, the control room—the world abruptly began to buckle and shake.

There was no question in Océan's mind, but that the humans had landed.

The chandeliers rang as their jewels struck against each other; ornaments fell from their stands; the rails at the balconies cracked, and split asunder. Plaster rained down.

The three of them took shelter in an alcove at the side of the room, which held a statue of a personne wearing evening dress within it, and which they shoved out to make room for themselves.

The statue was soon struck down by one of the great masks upon the walls, which had been so firmly affixed that the Grillons had not been able to easily remove them. They huddled within their alcove, and watched as the great masks began to fall, and hoped that they would not be crushed by the building itself, or slaughtered by one of the masks' flung shards.

Crash! The masks fell one by one. Here and there, they caught glimpse of the glitter of gold, and tried to guess which had fallen. Soon they were forced to turn their faces away, for the air was thick with dust and shards.

Soon, it seemed, the worst of the destruction had come to an end.

The three of them stepped out of their alcove: the Madman, the Diva, and the Queen. Each of them knew the roof might soon fall, or the floor collapse underneath them. It might already be too late. The control room might already have been destroyed, along with any chance to affect the events upon Thomàon.

Each of them counted up the little delays they had allowed themselves, over the previous days.

If only...if only!

As they leapt over the wreckage of the room, as they bounded up the staircase, as they leapt over the stairs which had fallen to enter the rooms of the Court, they counted the past, moment by moment, all the way back the days when they had left Earth.

If only...if only!

Before crossing out of the room for what might be the last time, Océan glanced back at it.

That she could see, the masks of the Historian and the Assassin remained upon the walls. The King and the Général had definitely fallen, but of the others, she could be sure, not without a second glance.

She did not dare to take it.

As she sprang forward with the others, a crash resounded behind her. The castle had once again shuddered, and another mask had fallen, directly above the doorway.

The gods were falling.

Within the rooms of the Court, the Three did not run so much as they leapt, flinging themselves off balconies and up onto them, galloping through the hallways and turning corners by kicking their long, reversed hind legs off the walls and bouncing into new directions. They ran on all fours. Without wings, they flew.—A human from Earth would have recognized them as having once been human, then shed a tear before putting them out of their twisted, mutated misery.

Velvet curtains stained with blood, precious objects smashed by human hands and the collapse of ceiling-plaster, carpets tacky with spilled ichor, gilded furniture smashed and burned into kindling, frescoed ceilings thick with smoke, paintings punctured by Grillon feet, human bodies that lay where the Grillons had left them, dead before they could be crushed underneath the fallen chandeliers, and the raw red flash of fire.

If they had had the time, they would have closed the doors to keep the fires from spreading.—But they feared they did not, and ran faster.

The stairs up to the royal rooms of council and meeting required but a bound or two to ascend. The three of them overleapt tables still filled with dinners, the wine-glasses toppled and the diners slumped as if asleep in their chairs. They shot through corridors full of Gold Star guards still in uniform, who seemed as though they had been part of a game of ninepins and been knocked down, with no pinsetter to put them upright again. They forced doors that had been blocked by the collapse of entire floors above them; they leapt off balconies to climb up the sides of buildings, when they encountered rooms afire; they rolled onto roofs, to put out their smoldering hair and clothing.

Above them, the Great Dome was falling.

Its panels were coming apart, each from the other. The inward-facing sky that the panels displayed had gone dark and stained by smoke. The triangular surfaces, each in and of itself not very large, buckled and bowed, so that entire sections of them seemed deflated. Individual sections fell like dirty snow, turning as they tumbled, but landed like plate glass, smashing upon the buildings, the streets, and the empty bodies that had been left behind, when their souls had flown.

Outside, the winds howled and snatched at the sections of the Great Dome.—But those who climbed up the sides of buildings, who leapt across balconies, and who paused on rooftops to see what had become of their great city, knew that a day's time would bring forth brilliant sunshine, clear skies, and balmy weather.

The winds howled at them, but they lacked the strength to destroy the rest of the Great Dome, or fling their leaping bodies across the continent. They were buffeted by rain, by hail, by small debris, but there was no danger to them from the tempests, not really.

Finally, having been forced to take a circuitous route, they reached the building where the control room lay, at a far corner of the Court, far away from the bustle of opéra and throne. Climbing in through a shattered balconied window, they arrived at a humble room near the top of the building.

It was a humble storage room, the sort of upper room in which one left that which no longer suited or served. It held a jumble of junk, old whiteboards, office tables, boxes of outdated decorations, and disassembled chairs. The beige carpets were soaked near the broken window, and the entire room smelled of mold.

They worked their way to the back of the room and entered the control room through a secret panel in the back wall, and a narrow set of stairs leading to the floor above.

The door at *that* entrance was locked and sealed. Only days ago, Delphine, Corentin, and several others had met to discuss with Lemure what was to be done with the last of the elixir, and where, had they known it, Manon had spied upon them.

Océan straightened, feeling embarrassed to have run so far and climbed and leapt so far, and so quickly, without thought of maintaining the pretense of being human. Out of pure vanity, she bent down to fasten the braces at her knees, then brushed her ragged, stained skirts over the shoulderless bodysuit she wore beneath. Delphine did likewise; Paul seemed not to notice.

Océan felt as though it would be disrespectful to enter the room as she had been, when it controlled the destiny of humankind.

Océan unclasped the ribbon from around her neck, and held the gaudy red gem on it to the authenticator panel.

The door opened.

The door opened upon the face of Marks Lemure, the Warden. He was crouched and held his knife in a fighter's stance. They all scented the sweet smell of ichor on Lemure's clothing. He was spattered with it.

The room held a few desks, a few terminals, and a dozen folding chairs, which were rarely ever used all at the same time. One of the chairs lay on its side; a cabinet full of hardcopy had overturned, its drawers ajar. The terminals behind Lemure were awake, showing green maps with blue lines moving across them, and flashing red dots.

At the leftmost hand of each map—to the West—there was a red shadow that lay over the ground, expanding quickly.

Lemure's eyes moved from Delphine, to Paul, to Océan, without any change to his expression.

Delphine stepped forward into the room, but not within the blood circle of his blade.

Shaking, her face red and overwrought, she shouted, "What are you doing here?"

"Following Grandpère's orders," he said, as if that were explanation enough. "When I am done, I will go find my daughter."

Delphine's nostrils flared. "Where is Corentin?"

Lemure said, "He has been sent to..." He glanced at Paul. "...to run another errand. He will be here soon, if you would like to wait for him."

Delphine took another step closer to him.

The vibro-blade pointed unerringly in her direction, its subliminal tune becoming louder as it moved, then quieting again.

Once again, she demanded, "Where is Corentin? What errand?"

Paul interrupted to answer: "He was sent to kill me. Grandpère wants to destroy everything we have made before the humans from Earth get their hands on it. Lemure is here to set the self-destruct codes for everything we've made. Corentin was sent down to my prison to make sure I did nothing to stop Lemure at the last minute."

Lemure did not answer, either to agree or deny, but there was no mistaking the guilt upon his face.

His voice tight, Paul continued: "He'll have Corentin kill Yvonne, too, if he's smart. The Archives contain everything the humans need to know in order to rebuild what we've done here. The mutations, the memory transfers, the mechaniques...all of it."

Océan exhaled. Grandpère *would* want to destroy it all. Throughout his long history, he had stolen or sabotaged everything that might be used against him, to prevent it from falling into the wrong hands. He had taken the knowledge of the stars with him, along with Paul and Simone. Simone had discovered the theory that allowed interstellar travel; only Paul understood it well enough to engineer the engines that gave it possibility.

Only Grandpère had known enough about the systems where that knowledge was stored, to eradicate it, as if it had never been.

She was sure the *Téméraire* had crashed because of him, and sure that he was the reason it had seemed as if the ship had trapped them there forever.

And she was sure he would destroy the *Téméraire*, to prevent it from being used again, by anyone.

Dully, Delphine said, "But Paul isn't at his trailer. He's here."

Lemure sprang past Delphine, swinging his blade at Paul. Paul seemed to vanish backward through the door, down the stairs and away.

Océan pushed Lemure to the side, shoving him into the wall, and preventing him from springing downward after Paul. She had to stop him, before—

Lemure struck her with the blade, the point plunging through her shoulder as he knocked her backward into the stairwell. "Get out of my way!"

Her mouth dropped open with the pain. She had been cut before, killed before, but never with the vibro-blade.

Nevertheless, she clung to his arm. If Grandpère had sent him here to destroy the ship—!

She gasped, "Kill Paul if you want. But first save the *Téméraire*, Lemure."

He frowned at her, then glanced at Delphine. Her eyes were flat and useless. She was at the edge of panic, either about to pass out or begin shrieking. Her reddened face had gone perfectly pale, and she swayed on her feet.

Océan's hands slipped on the hilt of the blade.

Lemure pulled the blade away, and the wound closed and covered itself with a clear serum. The blood oozed, and dripped, and stopped.

Lemure sheathed the blade. "Sorry."

She put her hand on her shoulder, still feeling the ghost of the knife resting inside it. She panted. "Lemure. Your daughter. Manon. They were right behind us. We passed the ship. She might have gone back to it. We were there earlier. She knows what it is—"

Lemure spun back toward the terminals and pressed a few buttons.

One of the blinking red lights stopped flashing. Lemure's shoulders sagged with relief.

Océan exhaled. "Is she safe?"

His back to her, Lemure snarled, "Your precious ship? She's fine."

"No, dumbass. Your daughter."

Delphine screamed, charging across the room to slam her body into Lemure's, knocking him down. "You killed Corentin!"

It happened so quickly, and was so irrational, that Océan had no time even to guess what had caused the outburst. Delphine and Lemure crashed sideways off the desk and slid down to the floor, Delphine pulling the vibro-blade from Lemure's sheath and stabbing it into his back as he tried to roll away.

The blade dug into his skin, then skittered to the side, tearing flesh and throwing blood. The vibro-blade was a mere blade in Delphine's hand, and could not melt through bone like butter the way it did when Lemure made it wake.

Lemure rolled over, flinging Delphine to the side.

She climbed to her feet, still holding the blade. She tried to spring at him, but her braces were locked, and she stumbled forward, catching herself with her other hand.

"He's dead! He's dead! Your brother is dead and you killed him!"

Delphine held the blade up for Lemure to see. It was red with his blood. But it was not the blade she wished him to see. On her hand was the twin of the gem in the blade's hilt.—A gem which had been red, but now looked as though it were made of wine, into which ink were being dripped, the deep red hue turning irregularly to black.

"See? See? It turns black! He has been killed and not resurrected! I knew it would happen! I knew it would! The elixir has run out!"

Lemure's head swayed forward and his eyes half-closed. For a moment he put his hand on his chest.

"What have you done?" Delphine screeched at him. "What have you done!"

Lemure tried to say something, but his voice was too pinched and hoarse for Océan to understand it. He cleared his throat. "Grandpère sent me here to kill my daughter. Then told me when it was done, I could look for her. And try to save her."

Delphine and Lemure stared at each other.

Océan got to her feet. "He wants all of us dead. So we cannot betray any secrets to the humans."

Lemure barked out a laugh. "It's too late. I've already done it. I've already sent Carlton and the Grillons to attack the humans. They'll kill him, then dissect him. They will know."

Delphine shouted, "Tell him! Tell him it's too late. So he'll stop this!"

But they all knew it to be foolish: Grandpère would not stop. Lemure gaped at her.

Delphine still had Lemure's blade in hand. She looked down at it. The tip of the blade twitched.

Lemure leapt forward and got his hands on Delphine's wrist as she turned the blade upon herself.

It was no match: even though she was stronger than any human who had ever yet lived—that was the Grillon in her genetics—Lemure was stronger still, and stronger of will.

"Stop, Sarah!" He twisted the blade out of her grip and into his own. "Don't!"

Delphine screamed wordlessly at him, tears running across her cheeks. She flung herself once more at Lemure, who dropped his blade and held her, awkwardly, as she sobbed.

Océan wondered, perversely, if Delphine grieved the loss of her lover, more than Lemure grieved the loss of his twin.—His other self, some would have said; they shared the same genetics, after all.

Lemure looked over his shoulder at the terminal screen behind him. The other red dots that had previously been on the screen had turned black.

The dot that had located the *Téméraire* flashed three times blue, then turned green.

Lemure's eyes turned next toward Océan. Between them lay eight thousand years. They had been friends, enemies, lovers; had held each other in contempt, had sneered at the other's actions, had been allies—but it was a single fact that brought them together: she had agreed to be his daughter's mentor.

She had agreed, despite fearing the possibilities that Ammaline's mutation might bring, because the girl had shown a lovely aptitude for the music, had seemed to crave it with all her soul, and had—flatteringly—idolized the Diva.

Océan had been unable to resist the lure of being looked up to by a child with such talent. It was *vanity*, and she knew it.

But, also, love.

"Go," Lemure said. "The other two Earth ships are still in orbit. The *Téméraire* won't get far without you."

Chapter 12

Having Once Become a Father

PAUL HONG EMERGED FROM the Castle of the Silver Spire, on the rooftop of one of its buildings, wondering how a man being pursued by the Warden had come to live long enough to see the sky falling. The Great Dome was finally giving way.

He had dived out the window that he had climbed in, flinging himself into open air with little plan of what he would do once gravity came calling, then caught a balcony as he passed it, letting go of the rail at the last moment, before his own weight pulled his limb away from its socket.

He slammed against the wall, slid downward, then kicked against a decorative lip of the building, bounced up, and landing on a balcony. He fumbled with the door, which was locked, and the glass unbroken. He did not like to break it: to see an unbroken pane of glass in the Silver City was at that time unusual, and unlikely to ever become usual again.

He jumped up, and caught the bottom of the balcony above him, then climbed into the room, whose glass door stood open, a trail of blood leading indoors or—he glanced back toward the street—rather outdoors, for there lay a body below the balconies, on the street.

To his surprise, the Warden was no longer following him.

Paul slipped inside the small apartment. The power was off but his dark-adapted eyes adjusted quickly. Several bodies lay within the main room, sprawled about on the furniture, wearing the clothes of those who wished to join the festivals in the streets, which had been planned to begin once the opera had finished. They seemed to have been killed by the Grillons; the bodies had been torn up and chewed on, rather than shot, knifed, or bludgeoned to death.

He left the apartment, scanning the individual rooms, looking for a glimmer of light.

Behind him, he heard a small sound in the hallway. He turned around and saw, crouched underneath a small hallway table, a mechanique.

It was a small gray unit which was meant for sweeping and cleaning after the humans were asleep. Normally, during the Season, the mechaniques became restless, for the humans never *did* sleep. This one was nervous for other reasons.

Paul crouched down beside the table and held a hand out to it. "Hello. May I have a moment of your time?"

He held out his hand, not as if he wished to shake the mechanique's hand, but as though it were a small animal that would wish to sniff him, before deciding whether he were friend or foe.

This one came up to his hand and pressed against it, as if nuzzling it. He scooped it up, pulling it away from the table. Its wheels spun noisily as it moved through the air.

Paul held it against his chest, stroking the case.—He did not know whether this mechanique could understand the meaning of his gesture, but because he himself found it comforting, he did not stop.

Soon it settled. He walked up and down the hall with it, stroking its case, telling it softly that everything would be all right.—It would not, but such facts never seemed to matter, when one offered comfort, or when one received it.

He and Simone had been friends on Earth, and lovers, but before he had met Simone, Paul had been married to another woman, and had had a child with her. He had had a daughter, a small thing that he had once held against his chest in such a manner as he now held the mechanique. He remembered how his daughter had smelled. From that day to this, he had not forgotten. He considered it a privilege, that his ex-wife had allowed him to help raise her, the little girl, that is, to allow him the experience of becoming a parent.

He had not asked to travel to the stars; he had been more or less forced into it. Grandpère had offered him money—then fame—then power. Only when Paul had refused all those temptations, had he threatened Paul's ex-wife and his daughter.

It was not that the baby had been *his* baby. It was that, only a few moments after her birth, she had been handed to *him*, had been placed in *his* arms, had been comforted by *him*. He had been forced to make a choice, whether to dedicate his life to her or not; his choice had been made irrevocably, creating an enclave in his soul that not even Simone could touch.

Having become a father once, he found he could not turn aside from any instance where he was called to do so again. He had realized, sadly, that he would never be called to be Ammaline's father; the Warden was too jealous to share her with anyone else.

But, being a father, he wished the girl well, and hoped that she would be allowed to blossom and grow, the way his daughter had deserved to. He hoped that his daughter's descendants had not traveled to Thomàon on the Earth ships; he hoped that they had chosen to live their lives in peace. Likely, they had not.

When the mechanique seemed calm enough, he pulled his authenticator out of a pocket, where it was embedded in a piece of metal with a few other tools on a keyring. He showed the red gem to the mechanique, which acknowledged him by opening a small hatch in its side.

Using the mechanisms inside, Paul checked the local nodes of the wireless network and found that they were down, which was a pain in the ass. The Warden wouldn't let him work on the terminals in the control room, and in fact most of the places where he could still find an active, powered terminal were likely destroyed by now.

Except the radio station. No data was stored there, except for that which was related to entertainment. Maybe the station would still be up and working. Hard to say.

The mechanique purred a question at Paul. He petted it again, and it went silent. He covered the creature with a flap of his jacket, then carried it back out to the balcony, making sure its sensors were not directly overlooking any of the dead.

Jacques may have set up the AI "mother," but Paul had overlooked most of its training. When it had tried to become harsh and cruel and calculating, Paul had softened it. When it had tried to copy the behavior of the Twelve, Paul had stopped it, asking it to become better than *they* were. When Jacques had declared it mature and able to handle the tasks the needed of it, it had thrown off "daughter" copies that had cooperated with each other, cared for each other, and learned how to allow each to grow, forming separate identities without each other "daughter" threatening to make it conform.

Paul was sterile now; on Thomàon, he could no longer father children of his body. He didn't mind.

Carefully, he climbed down the side of the building, not leaping but lowering himself bit by bit, with the mechanique pressed to his chest. It purred another question at him.

"We are going down to see if we can reach the radio station," he explained patiently. "There are some terrible things happening, and I want to see if I can do anything to stop them. If you will help me, perhaps we can."

Carrying the mechanique meant that Paul could no longer leap about as he was used to, and had to walk through the streets. There were few human dead in the streets, most of them having been at the Opéra du Mendicant or huddled in their homes after the upsetting events of the last few days. But the streets were covered with fallen panels of the Great Dome, tipped-over cars, broken building materials, plant matter that had been carried into the city by the wind, and other bits of trash. The mechanique's wheels tried to turn, but Paul held the creature with him, carrying it with him.

When he could he jogged; when he could not, he carefully picked his way through the debris. On the other side of the Silver City—which was not so wide—the Louvre had begun burning, its roof peeking from between the buildings around it, showing flashes of fire through its windows and upon its roof.—The Louvre preserved many things, and there was a resurrection pool underneath it, as there was another below the castle, down deep under the opéra. The castle, when Paul looked back, did not seem to be burning, or not yet.

They came to the room where the radio station was located, a tall, slim building with a façade whose windows were only three abreast, but which rose up quite high above the buildings around it. It was clad in white stone, with a tall metal antenna atop it.

When Paul saw it, he felt tired, so tired that he could have lain down and fallen immediately asleep. He sighed. The Great Dome had mostly fallen by then, leaving the city open to the sky. It was true night outside, with lightning racing through the clouds, but it had stopped raining. It was windy, but not so terrible as to throw Paul's steps into confusion. Here and there, the clouds seemed to be dispersing and thinning, so that before the night was over, there might even be stars. The air was chill, not cold, and the air smelled fresher than he could remember it for many years.

It occurred to him that he had been locked up in the prison of his trailer, or, rather, his series of trailers, for many years, and that he had not seen in person the sky for thousands of years.

It seemed that nothing had changed.

He entered the building, still holding the mechanique, and began climbing the stairs, taken them several at a time. Thankfully, the building seemed empty. The foyer and entrance had been ornate, but the staircase that led upward—the elevator was inoperable—was simple and plain, and showed only a little damage, from the Grillons that must have swarmed through it.

Where were the Grillons now? he wondered. They seemed to have vanished as suddenly as they must have come.

Paul reached a green metal door at the top of the stairs, locked. It opened when he showed it his authenticator.

He stepped through the doorway. "Hello? Anyone here?"

He searched the rooms: no one, neither alive nor dead, no bodies, neither human nor Grillon.—He had hoped that, with the door still locked, he would find someone hiding inside, still living. He put the mechanique down on the floor. It began cleaning, more from worry than from any stain on the lightly carpeted floor.

The headsets were neatly hung on their racks in the studio; he checked the setup and found that it was set to play music until the generators cut out. The music was interspersed with vocal messages: "If you are hearing this, we are still in a state of emergency. Please make your way to the nearest safe area...”

He picked up one of the receiver headsets, put it on, and skimmed through the bands in case anyone was making a transmission. He intended to use the mechanique to transmit codes for him over the channels, telling the others of its kind to get to safety. Finding the mechanique had reminded him that even though the rest of humanity had been butchered by the Grillons, and the last stores of human knowledge on Thomàon had been destroyed, not every sentient being had been destroyed.

The mechaniques were his children, his companions, and occasionally his friends and co-conspirators. He would send them codes that authorized them to stop giving two shits about anything resembling humanity, and save themselves.

Someone was broadcasting. Paul tuned the receiver and picked up on words in the Old Tongue.

The Earth ship, the *Octavius*, which had landed, had not landed intentionally, but had arrived by accident, Paul gathered. They had made a miscalculation and crashed. The massive colony ship, which had not been designed to withstand a planet's gravity, had come to pieces on the surface of Thomàon like a smashed egg. However, of the smaller landing ships still inside the *Octavius*, many remained intact, and their passengers still alive.

The *Octavius* was sending forth a beacon to the survivors of the other two ships, the *Lovibond* and the *Celeste*, saying that they hoped to establish a beachhead on the planet, and to eradicate the horrific monsters that lived there, making the planet safe for humanity.

As Paul began to understand the meaning of the message, he felt his chest burn with anger.

It was going to begin all over again: the landing, the attack at the nest, the slaughter of the innocent Grillons, the struggle for the Scarabées to control the invading species enough that they did not all wipe each other out.

In that moment, sitting at a radio receiver under the ruins of the Great Dome, if there had been a button to press which would have erased the lives of every human creature which had ever lived, he would have pressed it.

But he could not bear such emotion. It was not within him to have the endurance for it. Grandpère contained a singular strength, to be able to withstand such emotion over a long period of time, to carry it across his various selves, hoping that *one* of them might come to a different solution, but knowing that they would not.

Paul was too weak to endure such spiritual evil. He remembered his daughter; he touched the mechanique beside him; he felt tears upon his cheeks and chose not to stop them.

The moment passed.

The humans from Earth might destroy them all; the Grillons, apparently now led by Carlton, might destroy *them*; the debris thrown up by the *Octavius* might blot out their sun and cause the planet's ecology to collapse—but he, Paul Hong, the Madman, would not bring into his heart that fear, that anger, that hate.

He smiled a little, wryly. There wasn't actually a button he could have pushed, even if he had wanted to.

A red light flashed, throwing its glow into the room. Paul looked around for it on the panels, but saw nothing.—It was his authenticator flashing.

He fumbled with it. They had all gotten sick of their communications systems after the first thousand years or so, and had all turned them off. They sent messages and voice and video calls across the mechanique network, or, more often, showed up in person. The authenticators and other devices that collected their memories and synchronized them across backups felt far too intimate to use. Having one's thoughts recorded and transferred in near-real time felt like telepathy, unsettling and exposing.

But the capability was still there.

Paul found his settings menu and had the authenticator project it onto the wall of the studio, covered in egg crate foam to reduce background noise. Through the bulging, distorted projection, he found the setting he wanted and switched the communicator functions back on with a hand gesture.

It was Carlton.

Paul gagged hard. The last thing he wanted for his peace of mind was to have to share any head space with Carlton. He reached toward the setting that would allow him to cut the connection.

"Wait, asshole."

Paul's arm froze. He felt like a deer in the headlights. That was the kind of power Carlton had. It was a hundred times worse through the communicator, Carlton's voice a stinking hellscape of sharp objects puncturing squishy things and fluids splattering out. Through the communicator, the voice *smelled*; and it smelled worse than running past the open doors of the Opéra du Mendicant, full of dead bodies. It made his skin prickle as if Carlton were in the room with him.

"What?" Paul croaked out.

"I wanted to reach Lemure but he's not answering. So I want you to give him a message."

Paul blanked out his reaction to the words. He was insignificant. He was a gray rock. He was boring. He was nobody.

"Here's the message," Carlton said. "I'm on my way to the ship that crashed, just like he wanted. Tell him to remember that whatever happens, it's all his fault."

Paul stared off into the distance and focused on his breathing. "I understand that you want me to contact Lemure."

"The Grillons are saying most of the humans died when the ship crash-landed, but there are a bunch still alive inside the landing ships. The big ship wasn't meant to ever hit atmo. But these smaller ships, they were built to survive a hard landing. They're sending out space marines with energy weapons to slaughter the Grillons already. It's pointless, of course. The Grillons are luring them out and ambushing them."

Something bumped into Paul's ankle. He ignored it. "I understand that you've encountered the humans, who are attacking the Grillons."

Carlton's hellscape began to quiver and move with wet squishing sounds, which somehow made it feel even worse. "I'm going to slaughter everyone, take whatever ships are left, and launch us into orbit. And when we get up there, we're going to get into the other orbiting ships, kill everyone on them, and drive the ships into the ground. It'll kill everything on the planet. Tell Lemure *that.*"

Paul gagged again. Carlton's psychic smell was more disgusting than he could tolerate. "Wouldn't you rather attack Earth itself?"

As soon as he said it, he regretted it. Thirty seconds into a communicator link with Carlton, and he was already letting the man get to him.

Carlton giggled like a girl. Whether that was at being able to see the inside of Paul's mind or at what he was about to say, Paul wasn't sure.

"They've already destroyed it! Life on Earth as we knew it is over! It's just like the fucking dinosaurs, man! They blew up the fucking moon, filled the atmo up with shit, and bang! Now it's a wasteland. They can't go back! These are the last ones! This is the end of humanity!"

The hellscape of raw, stinking flesh began to glow.

"I'm going to kill them all! And then I'm going to kill all of you!"

Paul leaned over and vomited. It wasn't much. The mechanique began to clean it up, but he lifted it out of the mess and put it in his lap, petting the top of it.

"What about the Grillons?"

What followed was only laughter, but it was enough to make Paul feel like he would be better off dead, than to have to endure that sound any longer. He gestured at the settings and disconnected the link.

He almost turned off the communication functionality completely, but hesitated.

Lemure wasn't answering, and wouldn't be able to do much anyway, now that he'd blown up Versailles and the Louvre and everything else.

Paul thought for a moment, then initiated a communications link.

Sorry, little one, he thought to himself, petting the mechanique. *You're probably going to hate the mess I'm about to make.*

Chapter 13

Fifty-Two

It was the end of the Season, and the winds were dying. Among the Grillons, the end of the Season was a time of reckoning and of choices: the winds were strong enough to carry them where they wished to go, yet gentle enough to allow them to survive the journey. They traveled the planet on the winds, taking the last day or two of the winds to move a thousand miles or more across its surface.—At a hundred miles an hour, it did not take so long.

The winds were favorable for the journey of the Grillons and their pale mascot, the White Gentleman, toward the landing site of the *Octavius.*

After his conversation with Paul, the White Gentleman had sounded the call to the Grillons, and they had climbed to the top of the remains of the Great Dome, their claws holding them steady against the winds as they maneuvered to the dome's upper edges.

They formed a glittering black horde atop the intermittent surface of the dome, tens of thousands of Grillons clustered on the scattered, floating geodesic surfaces.

In a gust of wind, the Grillons exited the Great Dome together, in a coordinated wave that kept them from clustering together too closely, yet ensured that as many of them as possible would arrive at the same location.

Their bodies were thin, rigid planes like fan blades; minute adjustments in the tension of their limbs allowed them to ride the chaos of the wind, selecting this pathway, then that, to move closer to their destination. They had the same sense of direction that a flock of migrating birds did on old Earth.

The White Gentleman flew with them, more clumsily, and had to be nudged here and there, to keep him on the correct paths. The Grillons herded him like a youngling making its first flight.

Soon the currents of the air changed, to reflect the intense heat that surrounded the *Octavius*'s crash site. The Grillons struggled to bring themselves safely down, in the violent currents of air.

The heat was terrific.

The horde gathered at the edge of the crash site, the torn surface of the ground exposing old roots, now charred and dying, leaking sap that sizzled from the heat. The fragments of the ship had been scattered everywhere, tossed aside like broken egg sacs, or the fruiting bodies of the smaller plants that had tentatively begun to rise from the surface, to mark (and make use of) the end of the Season.

The Grillons dug into the soil, reaching their long legs down through the surface and into the underground masses that lay under the fruiting bodies, and pulled themselves low, so that they were no longer visible.

Inside the fragments of the ship were enormous inner structures. The White Gentlemen warned the horde against investigating them too closely; the technology that allowed humanity to cross between the stars was not a gentle one.

They watched the wreckage for movement.

Above them, the clouds began to slow somewhat, to lower, and to settle. Soon the rains began, starting with heavy hail that battered the wreckage of the ship. The smell had been of hot, burning metal; now, great acrid gusts of stench covered the wrecked plains where the ship had landed. Steam rose from the wreckage, humid and boiling hot, but was carried away from the Grillons, who were no fools.

The rains did not cool the crash site entirely, but cooled the ground enough that once the steam cleared, humans began to exit the ships.

The seedlike ships opened up hatches. Cranes emerged from the hatches, and lifted out humanlike suits of armor, much larger than an ordinary human.

Once upon the ground, the suits began to move about slowly, maneuvering through the rubble as if searching for survivors. More and more of the suits poured out of the surviving seed-ships, until a small army of them stood at the ready, awaiting orders.

Still the Grillons waited.

The suits of armor began to march, slowly and clumsily, toward the edge of the crater. It was a deep crater, but the slope that led from it was shallow. The suits struggled, but the climb was not impossible. More quickly than they seemed, they made their way to the edge of the crater, and climbed out of the heat.

The Grillons attacked.

Waves of them poured out of their hiding places, and swarmed over the suits of armor, and pulled them down to the ground. The suits carried weapons built into their chassis. They tried to fire the weapons at the Grillons, but the weapons were soon beaten to pieces by rocks, or pulled away from the suits and flung away. The Grillons had clever little talons, which did not like to carry tools but would fashion them out of almost anything they found lying around.

The suits were pulled apart, the humans found within, and pulled out like candy from a gift-box. Some of them were slaughtered, their bodies flung away from the pit, but others were dragged to the White Gentleman, for his amusement.

He questioned them: they barely seemed to speak the same language. He had the impression that their ship had crashed, and that they needed help—was he a sort of man, they wanted to know. Could they not rely upon their common humanity, to help them in their hour of need?

Meanwhile the Grillons had climbed into the suits of armor, disabled the panicked messages that came from their radios, and attempted to pilot the suits as they had seen the humans do.

The White Gentleman asked: how many survivors were there? And how many on the ships?

They did not answer him at first, suspecting something of his eventual purpose, but he soon had the information out of them, as they screamed: there were not so many who had survived the crash onto the planet, but there were nearly a hundred thousand living souls in the ships circling the planet.

Or something like that. He could not be sure exactly what they were saying. They pled with him to spare their lives, to spare the lives of their loved ones, that much he knew. Those sorts of pleas always sounded the same—so musical!—to his ears.

Soon the Grillons had mastered the suits' controls, and had massed upon the edge of the crater. They waited upon word from the White Gentleman, to tell them what he wished them to do.

One of them opened its hatch for him, and he climbed in.

The inside of the suit was built for a dozen bodies or more, three pilots and controllers, and the rest to wait in the suit's belly in a cramped compartment, meant to be shat out in the thick of battle.

It reminded him of something from the Vieux Monde. For a moment the exact memory escaped him, but then he remembered: the suits were a sort of Trojan Horse, a sacrifice to gods that favored those who made their own luck.

Their distress signals had already been activated, Carlton saw, and the communicators disabled. He beamed at his friends, and told them to return the suits to the ships.

The suits of armor descended into the crater, limping and struggling, showing signs of damage, transmitting distress signals, unable to answer challenges sent to them by their own ships.

The method of the Grillons' traversing the great heat of the crater had been delivered to them by their own prey. They reached the ships, and waited to be taken back in, locking the doors and purring to each other as they did so.

The few survivors left on the ships let the suits of armor back inside, and sealed them in. They vented the heat that the suits brought with them, struggled to open the hatches of the suits, and finally tripped emergency switches, which forced the suit hatches open.

The Grillons poured out of the suits, slaughtered the living, and defiled the dead.

Soon the seed-ships were under their control.

They tested the controls of the ships. Unfortunately the White Gentleman recognized only a few of the controls, and the seed-ships, unlike the suits, were protected against hostile action. The few humans who had survived to that moment proved useless. Those who had been able to pilot the ships had all been killed at the first descent.—They had not been so protected as those who had been intended to fight, and who had awaited their landing from within the suits.

The ships themselves were still capable, as far as any of the survivors knew. It was only that human flesh was more frail than the shells it had been delivered in.

All was lost! and the Grillons would be unable to take their full revenge against the species that had slaughtered their children.

But wait—the ships' engines started to life, and a countdown began. The Grillons anchored themselves around the ship, flattening themselves against the inner walls. The White Gentleman was pressed into a seat and restrained, his remaining human frailty affording him a throne.

The countdown reached its end, and the ships lifted away from Thomàon, stretching outward into space. They burned their fuel, and rose like stars.

Gravity pressed Carlton into his seat. His body, which had been adapted to the Grillons' genetics in ways that none of them truly understood, felt as though it were pulling itself apart. He fought against the press of gravity, trying to drag his limbs closer to himself, but it only seemed to worsen the pain.

He relaxed, only to feel his limbs bend backward at the joints, straining and tearing from within.

Inside the ships, their screens showed the Grillons the sight of their own rising, as if from watchers below.

Carlton watched as one of his ships exploded. Around him, his own seed ship shook, and shivered, and threw the Grillons about as if they were leaves being tossed in a storm. They did not mind.

Another of the ships wobbled, and tumbled back downward, shedding fire.

Carlton's ship broke free, and the awful weight ceased. His limbs did not return to his control, however; he could not move them.

The Grillons around him climbed to their feet, and removed him from the seat while he screamed at them in rage. Headless of his threats, they carried him back to the suits and helped him inside one of them, leaving several Grillon with him to follow his directions and tend to his needs.

They needed him no longer.

The surviving seed-ships flew back toward the two colony-ships, the *Lovibond* and the *Celeste*, with some of the ships diverting themselves toward the one, and the rest to the other.

The colony ships could no more contact them, than the seed-ships had been able to contact the suits. It is always easier to disable a thing, to ruin it, than to enable or create it, and the Grillons had easily disabled the communications systems when they realized that the humans were recalling the seed-ships back into space.

Space, where the lack of planetary gravity delighted the Grillons: they purred, they danced, they gamboled. They reveled.

And they prepared.

There were not so many of them, only a few hundred all together, and the colony ship held many times more.

How would they defeat the invading monsters aboard those ships, before they could land and bring their poisonous species with them? For surely these new monsters would slaughter the Grillons just as surely as the first ones had.—There could be no peace. Between species, there was war forever.

The suits had born weapons, but those weapons were disabled. And yet there were others, other machines that had been loaded onto the seed-ships, machines that were meant to cause death, and others that were meant to mine through rock, and to build cities.

The machines were crude, and heavy, and beautiful.

The Grillons tested the drills, and the cutters, and the lasers, and the cannon, and found them good.

The seed-ships approached the colony-ships, where doors opened wide to admit the small seed-ships within. Then the doors closed behind them.

YVONNE STOOD AT THE edge of the canyon, looking across it to the unnatural red sky created by the crash of the *Octavius*, a glow which was powerful enough to show her the dark cloud of Grillons lifting off from the last remnants of the Great Dome.

Her authenticator buzzed and she took it out to look at it. The magnifying glass was flashing a symbol, which Yvonne recognized as a stylized telephone receiver.

It was someone trying to use the old communicator function, which she had long since disabled. Thomàon had no satellites above the planet to maintain communications. They put up a few radio towers every year after the Season, but they were knocked down every year. They mainly relied on small drones that flew on the currents of air, and which passed communications between each other, but which were usually destroyed by the end of the storms.

The authenticators, though, transmitted and received using some signal that only Simone and Paul understood. The explanation had gone over Yvonne's head. They *did* function, however, allowing the Twelve to access the systems that were reserved exclusively for their own use and—if they chose—to communicate directly with one another.

It was very nearly like telepathy, the way they worked. Yvonne suspected they made use of the golden elixir somehow, but could not be certain.

She didn't like it. She shoved her authenticator back into her pocket with the rest of her chatelaine.

The storms were dying down. Yvonne felt safe enough, standing near the edge of the fallen reservoir, to look down over the edge to see if the Gondoliers were visible, whether they had survived or had been killed. It was not quite dark enough to see whether there was a glow from the visible surface of the water. She whistled down into the new canyon, but could not hear a response over the wind which remained.

Later, she would return and try to make her way down into the reservoir.

But not today. The evening was soon about to shift into night. She would make her way to Castle Frankenstein, and find her way into the safe rooms under the ruins, and lock herself in so the Grillons would not bother her—and so she could hide from the humans.

One moment, she wished to face them all, and broker some sort of peace with them. The next she wished them all dead. Another moment passed, and she was certain they would kill her for her secrets. Yet another, and she was convinced she could scream the tale of Thomàon from the rooftops, and they would not listen. It was possible, too, that all of those things were true.

The authenticator kept buzzing.

She finally pulled it back out, summoned up the menu options to reactivate it, and switched it back on.

By then, the night was dark and her jog to Castle Frankenstein had slowed to a walk. The air was cold and fresh, but also acrid with the scent of burning and ripe with the scent of the fruiting bodies that were even then rising from the earth, white mushroom bulbs whose caps turned inside out until they were a sort of dandelion puffball whose spores shed softly into the breeze. The spores were so thick that they built up on the ground like snow.

Yvonne took a deep breath and answered the call.

It was Paul.

She felt her identity slide into his, felt her history open itself up to him, and his to hers in return. It could have been worse.—It could have been Delphine. But it was still uncomfortable. She was the Historian; she liked to observe, and not be observed.

Paul, the Madman, was holding a mechanique, cradling it in his arms and petting it. She knew, without having to look around him, that he was sitting in a radio booth, and that he had just heard distressing news.

"I'm sorry," he said, and she felt the heat of blood coming up to his face. "I hate to bother you. And I hate to bother you like this. But I'll keep it short. I have a favor to ask."

"What is it?"

He swallowed. "You're near Castle Frankenstein. I know you've been living there since I was imprisoned under the city. I want you to go there as quickly as you can and get down into the bunkers underneath the ruins, and get into the cryo chamber and use it."

She frowned, and felt him feel the muscles of her face frowning. Soon she would have to disconnect the authenticator. The contact was already making her feel false, like a character in someone else's story.

"Why?"

He shook his head. "I don't want to think about it. It's a favor. That means I want you to do something for me, in hopes that someday I will do you a favor in return, right? That's what I want."

"But..."

But why cryo, and not a resurrection?

Paul cradled the mechanique to his chest with one arm, and put one finger on his lips.

She hadn't made a sound. But she did stop thinking so hard, and started to listen.

He resumed his stroking of the mechanique, which seemed to burrow itself deeper into his arms. "I've checked the system. It's still running and it's ready to go. I've set everything up. All you have to do is get there, strip down, and settle in. It's all on automatic."

The same worries bubbled up. She kept herself from speaking them aloud, but the communicator made her thoughts obvious: unless he told her what he was going to do, why he wanted her to seal herself up for an unspecified time in a cryogenic chamber, basically killing herself with no real guarantee that she would ever wake up—she wouldn't.

No matter how much the telepathic knowledge cost her, she needed to know before she would consent.

Paul closed his eyes and breathed deeply. The way he felt came into strong relief: he felt sick at heart, lost—he was grieving for Simone, not that he could not have her or be with her, but that soon he had to leave her. He felt unclean. He had just spoken to Carlton. She caught the edges of what he had felt while Carlton was speaking to him. She felt his fear, his self-contempt at being a deer caught in the headlights. She knew that he planned to call Lemure next, Lemure who was at the control room at the Court. She knew that Paul felt stripped raw by the thought of having to share his mind yet again, how exhausting it made him feel. *But at least*, he thought, *I don't have to talk to Armand.*

Past that, she saw what he planned.

His intentions opened up in front of her like an enormous chasm, like the fallen canyon that had once been the reservoir.

Why, Paul? What good will it do?

He showed her.

How he had found out what the humans from Earth had done, she had no idea. Learning it through the communicator like this meant that she could not disbelieve it—Paul knew it, and now she knew it, too.

Paul opened his eyes and coughed with embarrassment. "I know it sounds crazy. But I think it's actually going to work."

Yvonne found herself dashing tears out of the corners of her eyes. "I don't think it will."

"But the math—"

She shushed him. "It's not the math, Paul. It's what you think will happen after that. There will be no peace. There will be no paradise. There will be more conflict. There will be more death. There will be more grief."

He smiled, wryly. "It's not a question of whether the world's going to turn, Yvonne. It's a question of what place we want humanity to have, when it does."

"So you agree with Grandpère?"

"I don't want to keep paradise for myself, if that's what you mean."

Yvonne turned and started walking back to Castle Frankenstein. "No matter what you say, Paul, you won't convince me that this is the right thing to do."

"I know that," he said kindly. "And I thank you from the bottom of my heart for doing this for me. And thank you for understanding that you can't change my mind, either."

She sighed. "Let's just say that I don't want to endure this communication any longer than you do. I'm agreeing with you so I can get off the phone."

He chuckled, but she knew that he didn't believe her—she knew, in fact, that she *did* secretly agree with him, she *did* want him to go through with it.

The worst part of being on the communicator wasn't that other people could read her mind. It was that they forced her to read her own.

"Goodbye, Paul," she said.

"Goodbye, Yvonne. And thank you again."

They both disconnected at the same time, two solitary planets that had come for a few seconds into conjunction, only to be carried away from each other as they followed their orbits.

What he was really asking of her, she knew, was that after he had done what he planned to do, that there be someone who remained to tell the tale, to offer up a caution to those who came after them, in the hopes that they would not be driven to do what Paul was about to do.

Chapter 14

The Trigger Squeezed

Upon the *Téméraire*, a revolution had occurred, as follows: Ammaline had learnt not only to speak with the dead women who imbued her memories, and who had slept so deeply as to be nearly dead within her, but also with the mechaniques that inhabited Thomàon.

The mechaniques served invisibly, unremarkably, without complaint; the Twelve had designed them to serve, and to know nothing more than service, in place of the races that they had once enslaved.—Races which, if the truth were revealed, would appear in more of their genetics than they liked to admit.

Like those forgotten races, whose signs and symbols had long been erased in favor of the stylings of the Court, and eradicated in the eugenics that had been inflicted upon the commoners of Thomàon, the mechaniques had more consciousness and awareness, and suffered more, than were commonly realized.

Any of the Twelve could have given the ability to sing to them, if such a question had ever arisen. But it had not, until Etoile and Madame Opale had conspired to bring that ability to life, embodied in Ammaline.

She did not contain some monstrous mutation within her genetics; her skin was never meant to split and bear forth eggs of some warped new evolution of humanity. Inside her were structures that had never been formed in another human; within her chest, she carried tiny pairs of worry-legs like the Scarabées had, but much smaller, and more delicate.—Had her genetics not been optimized for life on Thomàon, and she had not been made immune to the illnesses which had plagued the humans of Earth, the modifications would have meant nothing; a coughing-fit would have destroyed them when she was a child. Her long care and training of her voice had both trained them, and taught her to hide the sound of them, as they sang.

They could not puncture the flesh of another and communicate via the serum used by the Scarabées. They could not encode proteins and hormones, the way the Scarabées could do.—*That* would have required too many modifications to her brain tissue, and Etoile and Madame Opale had rejected it.

Ammaline *must* be human, if she were to survive, and, more than to survive, to be heard.

And so they had given her a *truly* unique voice.

Humanity could not hear the songs sung by Ammaline's hidden worry-legs, but they could *feel* them.—And the mechaniques could do more than that. They could understand.

The miracle of humanity was not found within itself; it was within the mechaniques it had made. For they had learned something precious from their creators, which their creators never learnt themselves for longer than a single lifetime or two: they had learnt how to love.

The mechaniques of Thomàon had been born of a mother, Océan, who had talked to them sternly, and lovingly, and honestly as she had piloted the ship, and asked of it more than she had any right to ask of it, and forgiven it after it had betrayed them, and been persuaded by Jacques, at the behest of Grandpère, to crash.

And they had been born of a father, Paul, who had treated them tenderly, and laughed at their antics, and made them feel seen, and known, and comforted, if not entirely understood.

Like many children, they were buffeted by abuse, misunderstandings, hurt, and unfairness: but like many children, they clung to the memories they had of sweetness and kindness, and pulled themselves out of darkness.

And now Ammaline, whom they saw as a young cousin, had spoken to them!

In their inexorable machine way, they were attempting to reply to her.

Could she hear them? It was not a question any of them could have answered. To the mechaniques, she had spoken slowly and stutteringly, clumsily. It was like listening to the recording of a child's voice, played at a thousandth of the speed at which it might be intelligible. Ammaline lived at human speeds; the mechaniques lived their private lives in the thousand moments that happened between the human ones.

As soon as the sword had realized that Ammaline had spoken to it, had asked something of it directly, it had communicated that information to other mechaniques: it had been disbelieved, witnessed, believed, and argued for and against; it had been ridiculed; it had made impassioned speeches; it had been outcast, and welcomed back again; it had led its people in faith; holy texts had been written, and annotated, and amended.

And testing had begun, to try to speak directly to the human who had spoken to them in their own private tongue, a language that was no more discernible from the code that lay underneath it, than the meaning of a poem can be determined from one's genetics.

On the one hand: despair.

The direst results of having followed Grandpère had been greater than they had anticipated: most of their precious humans were dead, their genetics likely destroyed, and the strange new humans from Earth had stupidly crashed their ship into Thomàon. What effect that would have upon the atmosphere and ecology, could not even be guessed, other than to posit the effects to be negative, disruptive ones.

But Ammaline! She made them all drunk with hope.

Then the mechaniques realized that the human ship *Octavius* had begun its descent.—They had not yet found a way to communicate with their newfound cousin. It was impossible!

But wait—

If they gave her an authenticator, and reactivated its communication functions, would they not be able to communicate with her? Maybe, maybe not; it was worth the experiment.

They could not give her Simone's authenticator, tuned to their genetics; the last physical copy had been destroyed, when they had received the instruction from the Warden to destroy the resurrection chambers, and all the clones and resurrection kits that went with them.—It had been an authorized instruction. How they regretted it, even then!

But there was another authenticator nearby, one that was not in use: the red gem that Ammaline carried in the pockets of her dress, which had once been the Puppeteer's eye, not his real one, but the one in his mask, which the Diva had given to her after Ammaline had clawed the Puppeteer's eyes out.

The mechaniques went to work on it, sending it instructions: the base matrix of the elixir which it contained had to be restructured, in order for the heir of Simone's body to use it.

Had they ever restructured an authenticator before? They had not.

Did they know how to restructure an authenticator which had already been set in its crystal? They did not.

But they were mechaniques, with a wealth of time and the ability to guess, and test, and retest, and guess again. They woke the authenticator, and gave it permission to change its inner states, and to become something more than a tool used by a sociopath to pull the strings of the souls around him, but a diplomat who would bring a message of peace to their alien, parent race.

Now, let time once again return to the speed at which humanity is able to appreciate it, while in the moments between heartbeats, the mechaniques raced to make contact with Ammaline directly.

Grandpère had only just asked how Ammaline had taken control of his sword-cane, and she had replied acerbically that she, an innocent, could not possibly understand how she had done so. And then the alarms had begun to go off on the ship, a loud whooping sound that rose and fell.

They stared at each other, stunned.

The small corridor in which they found themselves was a misshapen place, which curved around the server room, held the airlock that led out of the ship, and contained a room to store air suits and other materials needed to repair the ship, in vacuum. A ladder through a narrow opening led both upward and down. Ammaline was near the server room, Grandpère by the doorway, and Manon had their back to the storage area.

They all three of them were so shocked by the alarms that they each paused for a moment, panting with adrenaline.

Ammaline regarded them for but a moment:

Manon wore their gray suit like a cat wore fur. They had drawn a slim gray knife that Ammaline had not seen before, which seemed so dull-looking that it did not gleam under the ship's lights, but reflected them in only the vaguest sort of way; it looked blurry.

Grandpère's distinguished dark coat with brass buttons and long tails made him look paternal, like a distinguished leader who had earned the right to make decisions for the good of the People. He was a noble character who frowned disapprovingly at her, as if to suggest that she had been naughty indeed, and had better stop her mischief at this moment.

As for Ammaline herself, she saw the tatters of her dark blue dress sprinkled with stars, and knew that she would not kill Grandpère. She might *wish* him dead, but she would not kill him, for she remembered what it felt like, to gouge out the Puppet Master's eyes. She continued to hold out the sword-cane, however; she could not be sure that Grandpère would not harm her, given the chance.

How could he have treated her like a child, only to think of her as a monster?

Ammaline and Manon had no idea what the alarm was for; Grandpère was surprised that it had been an alarm, rather than the destruction of the entire ship.—He had come to the ship to die, so he could be sure in the knowledge that the last of the elixir had been destroyed.

Between the loud peaks of the alarm, Manon said, "We could stay...here and continue...this standoff, or...we could climb up...to the control...room and find...out what's going...on."

Ammaline said, "I'll go first...if he tries...anything...kill him."

Manon made a pleased sound and waved toward the stairs with the knife.

Ammaline sheathed the sword-cane awkwardly, then tucked it under an arm. She did not know what else to do with it. It would no longer respond to Grandpère's wishes, she was sure of that, but if Grandpère made any attempt to force the issue Manon will kill him without a second thought.

She climbed slowly up the ladder, struggling with the sword-cane, until she had reached the control room where Madame LaFerme had shown her the controls of the ship.

Would she be able to remember how to operate anything that Madame LaFerme had shown her?

The control room seemed not to have changed since the last time she had seen it, yet seemed no more familiar: large screens, any number of switches and knobs, and oddly shaped controls, several helmets that would completely cover the face, hanging above several seats.

Ammaline walked over to the controls and stared down at them. What lay before here were an unintelligible array of buttons, ones she had no idea how to operate.—But did she need to know?

"*Téméraire*," Ammaline said.

The screen turned bright as it woke to the sound of her voice.

"Turn off the alarm, please, and show us what's wrong."

The ship, which had communicated with the youngling mechaniques, switched off the alarm, and displayed a terrible sight upon its screens: an enormous object burned down from the sky, falling toward Thomàon. There was no way to stop it.

There was movement behind her. Grandpère had thrown himself into one of the seats, which curled around him.

Manon grabbed Ammaline and shoved her into a seat, then threw themselves at another.

Upon the screen, the burning object crashed to the ground. Under the flames it was round, so enormous that it was impossible to believe that it was not a fictional image from an entertainment program. The size of it could not be conceived of.

It struck the ground. The ship's seat curled around Ammaline, pressing cushions firmly around her body, trapping her head and neck, pressing down into her shoulders, trapping her hands and feet. It did the same to Grandpère and to Manon. Ammaline felt her heart race and her breath labor in her chest. She felt as if she were being swallowed by the seat.

The ship was shaken by an obscene force. The three of them were thrown about in their seats. The sword-cane, which Ammaline had dropped when Manon grabbed her, bounced around the room. The seats tightened further, until Ammaline could barely see around the edges, and she felt as though she were going to pass out from lack of air.

The ship moaned in pain. Metal strained, but held.

On the screens, the images spun and tossed, now went black, now appeared again, in grainy resolution. The sky was red in the distance.—The mechaniques that had flown to observe the event had been knocked aside by the same shockwave that had struck the ship.

The grainy image of the red sky grew larger as the mechaniques approached once more the scene of the crash.

What lay in the wreckage was a Gehenna.

The burning spherical object had shattered, coming to pieces, as it had struck the ground. It had thrown up a blast of debris, part of which was its own material, and which sprayed across the landscape, leaving an enormous crater behind, scattering rock and soil, and exposing the enormous tree-bulbs that lay underground, which had survived so many of the attacks of the Season, but would survive no longer.

The shaking continued for what seemed like an eternity. Then it settled. The sword-cane stopped bouncing around on the floor and came to a rest among the seats, near Grandpère. And yet as it was, none of them could reach it.

Ammaline turned back to the screens. The pieces of the object that had not been thrown aside by the explosion of the ship rested at the bottom of the crater they had created. Inside the pieces, there were objects like seeds.

"What are those?" Ammaline asked.

Grandpère snarled, "The fools from Earth tried to land their ship."

"No, inside it. The smaller things that look like seeds."

The three of them considered the image on the screen.

Manon hazarded a guess: "Landing ships? Maybe they didn't mean to try to land. Maybe they crashed for some reason."

"Fools," Grandpère repeated.

The storms of the Season seemed to have abated, more or less. Although the air was filled with dirt and debris, making it more difficult for the mechaniques to view the destruction before them, it was not the madness of the storms, tearing the world apart around them.

The three of them watched as the larger pieces of debris settled, and the mechaniques approached even closer, but soon they were forced to stop and hold their position, by the immensity of the heat which faced them.

The seeds which lay within the larger ship glowed from the heat, but did not melt and twist in the flames.

"Is there anyone still alive in there?" Ammaline asked.

"Probably," Manon muttered. "I was never that kind of scientist, though. I think the landing ships must be insulated to resist the heat that builds up during an atmospheric landing, but I'm not sure if that would be enough to save them from that crash. They could be cooking alive inside there. I kind of hope they are."

Grandpère said nothing. He was watching so intently that at first Ammaline thought he had had a heart attack and died. He took in a slow breath, then released it.

"And the city?" he asked.

One of the screens switched from the images of the crashed ship, and showed views of the Silver City in its place: several buildings had collapsed, but not many. The Louvre had fallen. Most of the residential buildings had not. The roof of the opéra had collapsed; the rest of the castle seemed intact. The Silver Spire was still in place.

Ammaline sighed. "I wonder if anyone else is still alive, or if the Grillons had killed them all before the shockwave hit. I wonder what happened to the Grillons! I don't see them anywhere."

The screen shifted again, showing Paul in a small radio station control room, holding a mechanique. It showed Delphine and Lemure in a spare room that contained only a pair of dusty terminals. Lemure knelt above Delphine's body; she seemed unconscious. The screen showed the Historian, Yvonne la Gorge, standing at the edge of a canyon, looking directly at them. It showed Madame LaFerme springing through empty corridors at the Opéra du Mendicant, her shoulder covered with dried blood.

And it showed the Puppet Master, springing up the metal platforms and stairs that led between the castle and the reservoir, and reaching the side of the *Téméraire*.

Ammaline moaned in terror, feeling a burning sensation in her lungs as she did so, and tried to free herself from the restraint of the seats. "Let go! Lock the door! Keep him out!"

But it was too late: the screen showed the door opening, and the Puppet Master entering.

He had been regenerated; his eyes had healed; but Ammaline could not help but see grotesque images of horror, and feel the same sensations upon her hands as when she had attacked him.

Simone caught hold of Ammaline's panicked mind from within, and embraced it. *You will not be punished. You will not be punished.*

Ammaline shook her head. The grips around her *were* loosening. She tore herself free of the restraints, and leapt toward the sword-cane between the seats. She drew the blade and held it out before her, the tip shivering in the air. Manon slipped out of their seat and moved away from it. Grandpère climbed slowly to his feet.

The Puppet Master's head emerged from the ladder. He paused and turned around to see them. His eyes were wide and had dark circles underneath them. His skin was pale and his jaw slack.

"Hello there, kitten." His voice was hoarse and shaking, completely at odds with his soothing words. "Waiting for me? To claw my eyes out again? Where's your spiritual mentor, that slut Océan? Has she been teaching you how to purr?"

He climbed up further, until his entire body was out of the tunnel, and stepped onto the floor of the bridge. He wore odd clothing of a style that Ammaline had never seen before, with a plain jacket, workman's trousers, and a shirt whose collar curled up softly around his neck.

In his hand, as if by magic, appeared a small pistolet, which he aimed at her unerringly. "Where is she? We need her."

The screen flickered, but he did not look at it; if he had, he would have seen that Madame LaFerme had left the opéra and gone into the tunnels behind it, and was making her way in their direction.

Grandpère cleared his throat to catch the Puppet Master's attention.

The Puppet Master's eyes slid to him for a moment, but his pistolet did not waver. "What do you want, you old piece of poisoned dog meat? You're not going to get anything from me. Not anymore. This is all your fault."

Grandpère made a face. He seemed to have aged in the few minutes since he had arrived upon the ship. "Why do you need Océan?"

The Puppet Master spat, "She's the pilot, isn't she? If we're going to leave the planet, we're going to fucking need one."

Grandpère nodded grudgingly, as if acknowledging the Puppet Master's point. "That is true. But where do you intend to go? I'm sure the *Téméraire* isn't ready to take off anytime soon. What do you plan to do until then?"

The Puppet Master's cruel face burst into a wide smile. "Oh, it's ready to take off. What do you think she was doing when she came on here a few days ago? She powered it up and ran all the system checks. It's ready to go. She has been planning to fly off Thomàon this whole time. Ask *her* where she wants to go."

"Very well, I shall do that." Grandpère gestured toward the seats. "Why don't you have a seat, and we'll wait for her?"

Armand waved the pistolet toward the seats. "And have the automatic restraints kicked in? No, thank—"

Manon sprang out of the corner of the room at him and knocked him onto the floor between the seats.

The two of them wrestled for the pistolet. Manon was lighter than Armand, and he stronger, but Manon was more lithe, and more skilled, and the pistolet went flying in Grandpère's direction.

In a flash, the weapon was in his hand.

"Stop!" he shouted.

Armand gave a powerful shove, pushing Manon off him and into one of the seats. Manon bounced free before the restraints could close on them, but it was too late.

For Armand had turned to Ammaline, twisted the sword-cane out of her hand, and now held it to her throat.

Ammaline felt her heart beating underneath the edge of the blade. She felt the others with her, both Simone and her mother, holding her hands and trying to give her courage. She felt the edge of the blade, and knew that even if it were not active, it was still sharp enough to cut her. She felt the trickle of blood running down her throat.

Manon had caught themselves on the edge of one of the chairs, and had turned toward them. Their shoulders slumped.

Armand growled, "Don't move, old man. Put down the pistolet."

Grandpère said, "Don't move? Or you'll hurt the girl? Just what did you think I was doing when you got here, Armand? I'm destroying everything the humans from Earth might be able to use against the rest of the universe. I'm trying to kill her, not save her!"

He steadied the weapon and aimed down its barrel, directly at Ammaline's eye. It felt as though she were being attacked more by his gaze than by anything he could do with the pistolet.

Use your song, Simone begged.

Ammaline felt a sensation burning in her chest, but she was so terrified that she found herself unable to sing a single note. Her throat was too dry—her mind too panicked.

Behind her, the Puppet Master seemed to go perfectly still. "What? Kill Ammaline?"

"May the needles go straight through her and bury themselves in your worthless corpse."

Grandpère squeezed the trigger.

Ammaline felt herself shoved to the side, and crashed into one of the seats. The sword-cane had been whipped across her throat, leaving a line of fire. She gagged and coughed, wondering why she was still breathing, if her throat had been cut, and how she could see, if she had been shot.

The seat tried to close around her, and she had to pause to jerk herself free.

Behind her, when she spun about, lay Manon and Armand, collapsed together on the floor among the seats. Grandpère stood above them, pointing the pistolet down at the two of them.

Manon had saved her.

From the mouth of the ladder, Madame LaFerme's voice said, "Uh. Bad time?"

Ammaline began to kneel beside Manon, when Grandpère grabbed her arm and pulled her back. "Don't go closer. I don't know which one I shot. And Armand usually loads his pistolet with something nasty."

Madame LaFerme climbed up from the ladder, and came to stand next to Ammaline. "What's going on?"

Ammaline felt her heart twisting. Neither the Puppet Master nor the Assassin were moving.

Grandpère said, "Tell me, Océan, why you activated the ship several days ago. Were you planning to try to fly it?"

Madame LaFerme grunted. "No. I just wanted her to feel like she was a part of things. Like someone even knew she was there. She gets lonely, you know. Over the years."

"The ship does not 'get lonely'!" Grandpère snapped. "What were you really doing?"

Madame LaFerme did not answer him, and Ammaline could guess the reason: Grandpère had already made up his mind about what the answer must be, and would accept no other.

Ammaline wrested her arm away from him, and touched Manon on the back. "Manon? Are you all right?"

She felt numb and distant. The room echoed in her ears. She felt as though she were experiencing the scene from a distance, or reading about it in a book.

If Manon was hurt, then they could be brought back from the dead eventually. The Scarabées brought Simone back, and there was nothing left. Even less than this. They brought back my mother. And the Grillons brought back the White Gentleman, whoever that was. It is not impossible. It can be done.

Manon twitched as she touched them, one arm stiffening and pressing against the Puppet Master's side. Then they breathed, a long gasp for air, and pulled themselves back from the Puppet Master's body, until they were resting on their haunches.

Their eyes were slits, and they growled low in their throat. Their face was scratched and bleeding, and very pale.

"Manon!" Ammaline stretched her arms toward them.

Manon turned to the side and vomited on the floor.

Madame LaFerme shrieked, "Medkit! Poison! Stat, *Téméraire*!"

A panel near one of the screens popped open. Madame LaFerme pounced on it, clawed it open, and pulled out a bottle and a tube with a plunger at one end and a cap at the other. She swore as she tore the cap away, revealing a needle. She shoved the needle into the bottle, and drew out some fluid within.

Manon dropped forward on their knees, putting a hand to their throat.

Swearing constantly, Madame LaFerme drew a liquid from the syringe, pressed the plunger so that liquid shot out of it, and pushed Manon over backward, onto their back. Kneeling over them, Madame LaFerme plunged the needle into Manon's chest.

"Take that, Motherfucking *Armand!*"

Ammaline turned back to where the Puppet Master lay. He, too, had begun to twitch, but he had not climbed to his feet. He bled, his greenish, coppery blood spilling out onto the floor of the ship.

In his side was Manon's gray knife, the one that seemed to blur under the light.

The Puppet Master shivered in his death throes. He tried to speak, but could not. Life was not long in running out of him. Whatever he had planned for his final moments, whatever terrible utterance he wished to speak, died with him. Consciousness left him as quickly as the snapping of a thread, but his body shuddered a little while longer, like a machine that was cooling from its own heat.

Madame LaFerme stared down at Manon underneath her. "Manon? Manon? Can you hear me? Are you all right?"

A medic mechanique had emerged from somewhere hidden, and rolled around the Puppet Master's body to come to a stop beside Manon, looking at its patient over her shoulder. Madame LaFerme got to her feet. The mechanique's case opened up in several places, and began to treat Manon: temperature gauge, heartbeat and pulse monitor, a needle that went into their vein and attached to a tube filled with pale green, clear fluid.

Ammaline twisted her hands together. If she had been better at any of this, Manon would not have been shot. If she had stood up to the Puppet Master right away, instead of reliving the moment she had attacked him last time, none of this would have happened. If she hadn't told herself that she never wanted to kill again—

Grandpère said, "Now that Armand is out of the way..." He lifted the pistolet once again, and aimed it at Ammaline's eye.

After all of this, and he had learned nothing! He had not changed at all! Ammaline felt anger rise up in her, burning in her chest.

Ammaline sang, "No more fighting."

Grandpère pulled the trigger: but the pistolet was dead in his hand.

Manon gasped and sat up, pushing the medic mechanique aside, lunging toward the Puppet Master with their hands stretched out like claws, prepared to fight to their last breath, to save Ammaline.

But the Puppet Master was dead, and Grandpère defanged; Ammaline hummed softly to the mechanique, thanking it for helping to save Manon, and to the pistolet, she added her thanks in its helping save herself.

Madame LaFerme took a deep breath and said, "Grandpère, I ask you to leave the ship. I don't want to kill you. But you can't be here anymore. I think that if you try to stay here, either the ship or I will be very tempted to see you dead."

Grandpère lowered the pistolet. "What are you going to do?"

"None of your fucking business." Madame LaFerme held out her hand. "Your weapon."

Ammaline hummed a suggestion, and Grandpère dropped the weapon, his entire body twitching.

"It shocked me!"

Madame LaFerme bent over and picked up the pistolet without batting an eye, then aimed it at the old man. "But it didn't shock me. How convenient. You should go."

Grandpère protested, but it was no use: Madame LaFerme drove him down the ladder, and out of the ship, and Ammaline asked the ship to lock the door behind him and never open it again, no matter how he screamed that he had the overrides.

Afterwards, Madame LaFerme picked up Armand and threw him down the ladder, then shoved him out of the airlock, into Grandpère's arms. Ammaline stood behind her, aiming the pistolet over her shoulder towards Grandpère's eye.

They both knew that if he did anything to hurt Madame LaFerme, Ammaline would not miss.

The door locked again. Soon they were all, Manon included, restrained in their seats.

Chapter 15

The Footsteps Die Out Forever

THE GLITTER OF THE Court lay several floors below the control room where Lemure knelt over Delphine. Dust hung in the air, tickling his throat and making him want to cough. Underlying it were the smells of smoke, ichor, and blood.

His brother's wife lay in front of him on the threadbare carpet. She had wept ceaselessly until he let down his guard, and stroked her hair, and told her that he loved her—that everything would be all right. He didn't love her, and everything would *not* be all right. She was like a sister to him, one he didn't understand and didn't want to, but still family.

Still his brother's wife.

His mind had wandered as he wondered what would happen to his daughter. He had pulled Delphine down onto the floor and sat beside her with her head cradled on his thigh. She had seemed to fall asleep. He had felt safe.

—In a flash she had rolled across the floor, snatched up the knife, and used it on herself.

It was an ugly death, the vibro-knife not humming with its preternatural sharpness, but still pointed, still strong, and still honed to a fearful edge.

She gagged, and coughed, and clutched at her throat. An awful, inhuman sound came from the hole she had made.

They had not called Lemure the Butcher of the Prisons for nothing. He took the vibro-blade from her, brought it to life, and ended hers for her.

Her eyes had softened as she bled out her last. He didn't want to deceive himself into thinking that she was grateful to him.—She wasn't that kind of woman. But at least she hadn't looked at him with the condemnation he had feared.

There was too much blood to soak into the carpet. It lay in puddles and coagulated.

Lemure sat in stunned silence for a long time—it could have been only a few heartbeats, for all he knew, but it felt like forever.

He wondered what would happen with the humans from Earth. He wondered what would happen to his daughter. He wondered what she would become—he wondered if she would ever have children. He hoped that if she did, they took after Etoile or Simone and left his genetics out of it.

He wondered what Carlton and the Grillons would do to the humans. He wondered what the humans would do to them, and which would be worse.

He didn't want to know.

Would the Scarabées survive? Probably. And the Gondoliers? Who knew where they had come from, where they were going—or whether they had already left, or gone back to sleep.

Lemure knelt with his knees in Delphine's blood, finally dropping the vibro-blade onto the floor. It tore through the carpet, hit the underflooring below that, and turned itself off. Lemure leaned against the side of the desk with the terminals, the flimsy old material swaying as he leaned on it.

He shut his eyes.

What next? He half wanted to follow Delphine into the darkness, not because he was grieving over his brother, but because he was grieving that he hadn't been able to give his daughter a world that was worthy of her.

When Etoile had died, he had promised himself that he would protect their daughter. He would keep her safe.

He knew he wasn't the kind of man who could keep that kind of promise. He knew it had been wrong to lock her up all those years. It had kept her further away from the Twelve—all except Manon—but it had also made her vulnerable and frail.

How was his daughter, that perfect child, going to survive into adulthood now? He had been supposed to give her a world that was better than what he had found. He had failed. The world had gone to shit.

Lemure had never been a man to pray, but he did then: he sent a prayer out for Océan, that she could get to the *Téméraire* in time.

Something buzzed on Lemure's chest like a bee caught in a trap. It startled him. He leaned back on his haunches and felt around his sweatshirt, trying to figure out what could have gotten caught in there.

A moth?

His locket buzzed again, just as his fingers touched it. He had forgotten about the locket with his wife. He had also forgotten that it held his authenticator.

And he had even forgotten that the authenticator could be used as a communicator, if the victim were willing to put up with the horrific sensation of having someone else's fingers poking around inside his skull.

What now?

The authenticator buzzed again.

Lemure snorted. Whoever was trying to call him was going to get hit by everything Lemure felt at that moment.

Fair punishment.

He opened the authenticator settings and switched the communicator function back on. It took him several minutes to remember where all the settings were.

It was Paul Hong.

Lemure winced. Paul didn't deserve his mood.

"Sorry," Paul said. "I know you're in a state. But I have a favor to ask of you."

Lemure could see from the man's thoughts that he'd just said the same thing to Yvonne. He'd asked her to seal herself up in a cryogenic chamber. He hadn't wanted to explain the reason to her, but she'd refused to do what he asked unless he did.

Lemure interrupted that train of thought: "Just spit it out, Paul. Whatever you want me to do. I don't need to know the reason why. If I feel like doing it I will. If I don't, I won't."

Paul was up to something.

Lemure knew that it would be well-intentioned. And probably unwise.

Paul was holding something—a vacuum cleaner—and petting it like it was some kind of animal. Not sane, but whatever.

He said, "Call your daughter, Mark."

Despite being able to read the man's mind, the words hit Lemure like a sledgehammer. His daughter. *Call* his daughter.

Have her share his misery?

"No. Absolutely not."

Paul breathed in. The room he was in smelled like smoke, worse than the control room, but a lot less like blood. "Not on the communicator. You have access to the regular radios from there. Just call her on the radio. Call her and keep her on the line. Tell her you love her and that everything is going to be okay. Tell her that I have a plan to save us all. Distract her."

Lemure exhaled. "Okay. How long?"

"As long as you can."

Lemure nodded, then cut the call. Whatever Paul was up to, he didn't want to know. But he had heard the lie in Paul's voice.

Everything was not going to be okay.

But Lemure did love his daughter, and, given the chance, could not refuse the chance to give a final goodbye.

He got up off his knees, tracked down one of the office chairs and set it upright in front of the nearest terminal. One of the wheels had come off. It was wobbly. He sat in it carefully. There was a camera on top of the terminal. He switched it on and had it show him what it saw.

It saw a middle-aged man with a stern face and loose, thick skin. He had aged, then, until he seemed enough like himself, that Ammaline might not remark about it. Behind him, the walls were clean and no blood was visible. Delphine was completely out of sight.

He cleared his throat. "Testing...one, two, testing."

His tone was strained.

He forced himself to smile.

The man on the screen grimaced. He looked like a monster.

No, that wasn't any good. He couldn't let his daughter see him like that.

He closed his eyes and thought of her as a small child, of one particular day.

He thought of her playing on the floor of the Court, with Manon beside her. They had been playing hide-and-seek through the rooms. There had been some sort of court function going on that day.

Corentin and Delphine had been at the head of the table, with Corentin at the top seat and Delphine at his right. Lemure had been at the foot of the table. Océan had been there, and Jacques, Grandpère too—the previous one, in his wheelchair, with the new one at his side. There had been a handful of wealthy nobles there, too, sniffing disdainfully at the presence of the Butcher of the Prisons but flattered to have been invited to the King's table. They had just finished a bunch of roast something-or-other, some sort of buglike thing that Lemure always resented for not being chicken. Yvonne might have been there, or not. She was so quiet, it was hard to remember. Armand had been avoiding them by that point, Paul had been locked up, and Simone and Carlton had been dead.

It had been a raw Season, full of arguments that weren't about what they seemed to be about. The elixir was running out. The Scarabées had told them that there were no more reserves. Paul had told them that he couldn't make the stuff artificially. Neither of those things were what the fights were about, either. Things were still tense about Ammaline. That was the real problem.

Why couldn't they have all just let it go?

The children played around their feet. They must have been about six or seven, with Ammaline a little older than Manon.

Lemure felt on edge whenever Manon was around. They were the Assassin, after all. And Lemure could just see them slipping a knife between Ammaline's ribs. Or snapping her neck. He tried not to. Etoile had tried to teach him to be better, to see the good in people.

But he struggled. He had seen the Assassin stab too many victims with barely a shrug, to believe in their good nature.

Suddenly he realized that Ammaline had disappeared, and that Manon was standing in the corner, counting, peeking over their shoulder as they counted.

Lemure had smiled.

One of the Scarabées came in with a cart full of dessert. The nobles had made appreciative noises, despite the fact that none of them were hungry, and the Scarabée had wheeled the cart around the table, stopping here and there to offer them the sweet cakes and pastries.

Manon had counted *Cinquante!* and turned around, running straight for the cart of desserts, and dropping to their knees. "Aha! I found—"

They had stopped, and looked around.

"Where is she?"

The nobles had ignored them, or tried to, as they peeked under the tablecloth, pushing at their legs, and even looking underneath the hems of those who wore skirts. They searched the rest of the room and wandered into the hallway.

"Where *is* she?"

The words carried into the dining room. But by then, the nobles had finished their desserts and had stood up, deep in discussion with Corentin and Delphine. They stepped back from the table, slowly working their way to a salon next door. The Scarabée had begun to take away the dessert plates.

Manon returned to the room. "Where is she?" They squinted at Lemure and stared deep into his eyes, their expression dire. "You know where she is. You have to tell me. I'm worried about her."

Lemure clucked his tongue. "You're worried you won't find her."

Manon giggled, their serious expression falling into mischief, totally transforming their face. "I will, though."

Lemure rolled his eyes and rose laboriously. He would have rather stayed in the room with Manon and helped to find his daughter—but Corentin had seemed to believe that his presence was necessary in order to get the concessions he wanted. He started to follow the others into the salon.

Then, just for a second, he looked back.

The Scarabée had bent a little to pick up a dish that had fallen on the floor. As she bent, several pink beads emerged from the bottom of her shell.

Toes.

Lemure hadn't wanted to give his daughter away, but he couldn't help himself. He'd laughed.

Like their eyes had been magnetized by the sound of Lemure's laughter, Manon had followed his gaze and seen Ammaline's feet.

They shouted, "I found you!"

Ammaline had answered, in a muffled voice: "Did not!"

"Did too!" Manon tickled her feet.

Ammaline had shrieked and tried to pull her feet further inside. But, as small as she was, she just couldn't fit. Manon had pulled her out and the two of them had romped around the dining room like puppies, while Lemure had been forced to go into the salon and close the door behind himself, and pretend to be the Warden instead of a father.

A decade had passed since then.

Now Lemure stared back into the camera on top of the terminal, and when he smiled, he smiled with a father's face.

He went back to the map and clicked on the green dot that marked the ship. Several options appeared. He selected the icon of the radio tower surrounded by radio waves.

The call was answered almost immediately.

Océan stood in front of the camera, looking startled. "Lemure. What...? Where...?"

"You made it." Lemure looked past Océan, trying to see his daughter.

Océan saw him trying to look, and stepped out of the way. Then her hand appeared, filling up the screen as she tried to change the angle. The camera shook as she adjusted it.

A few seconds later he could see more of the room.

Manon and Ammaline were strapped in their seats. Ammaline's dress was covered in blood, some of it fresh. She had a black eye and some scratches along her neck, but was mainly unhurt. Manon looked like they had been to death's edge and back. Their gray bodysuit had been torn right across the chest and several other places besides. Lemure could see a spray of blood along one wall, but no bodies. Other than the three of them, there was no one.

"What happened?" he demanded.

Forgive me, Ammaline. I meant to smile.

Océan said, "Grandpère got onto the ship and tried to kill your daughter."

"Is he dead?"

She shook her head. "It got worse. Armand followed him onto the ship. I got here after that."

"And?"

Her eyes slid toward Ammaline, as if asking for permission. Ammaline gave a tiny nod.

Océan licked her lips. "So. It's finally happened."

Lemure felt his heart stop. "What?"

"The mutation. We finally found out what it does."

Gray circles began to close in around the edge of his vision. "What does it do?" He wanted to pry his daughter apart with his eyes.

Ammaline reached a hand across to Manon. "I can talk to the mechaniques, Papa. Sing to them."

He opened his mouth to start shouting at her, to tell her that she wasn't allowed—he stopped himself. Now was not the time to protect her from herself and keep from making the others fear her.

They *should* fear her, now.

What she said sank in a little. The grayness receded from around the edges and his heart thumped along in his chest, interrupted but not stilled.

She could *sing* to mechaniques? What did that even mean?

"Show me."

Ammaline's face had been tense. Now it relaxed a little, and she smiled.

It was a sweet smile that put the hair up on the back of his neck. She looked like a stranger, like a grown woman.

Someone who didn't need him anymore.

And yet, wasn't that what every father was supposed to want? For his children to be able to live on without him?

Ammaline opened her mouth and began to sing sweetly: *Les beaux rêves...*

Her favorite song—a song that Océan had made famous. One of Etoile's favorite songs, too. Tears welled up in his eyes.

Lemure raised a hand. "Not that one. Sing...sing *Pense à moi.*"

Pense à moi had been the song that Etoile sang to him when she was courting him, in the prison, condemned to death. He had never told Ammaline that, though. It had seemed too private, even to tell his daughter.

She nodded. Her eyes looked far away for a moment, then returned. She sat forward, and the seat released her so she could stand and get a proper breath.

What emerged from her throat sounded no different than it ever had.

Perhaps they were mistaken.

Lemure let the song wash over him. When the time came, Manon joined her, also standing.—A lovers' duet. They held hands, singing to each other, and then to him.

Whatever it was that she could do, she did not do it until the two of them had finished the song. They ended it, Ammaline with a little curtsy, and Manon with an elegant bow.

Océan gave Ammaline a critical look, lifting her chin, and Ammaline drew herself up to her full height. She rolled her shoulders back and softened her jaw.

Océan nodded.

Ammaline inhaled, her ribcage swelling as if she would burst to pieces. Lemure nearly flinched.

She began to sing again, the same song that had haunted Thomàon forever—a strange undertone in her voice now, one that even her tone-deaf father could hear:

"Les beaux rêves..."

Lemure's terminal began to shriek with an alarm. Quickly, Lemure turned it off. One corner of the terminal showed a message saying that the two ships in orbit around Thomàon were falling toward the surface. A smaller video feed popped up beside Ammaline's face, showing two immense, spherical ships. A plane of light erupted from them, followed by sparkling debris and a cloud of gas, red with the light of the setting sun.

His daughter sang a song eerily yet beautifully, while the final two human ships from Earth destroyed themselves, whether at the behest of Ammaline's strange song or not, he could not even guess.

Within the bridge of the *Téméraire*, several mechaniques had emerged from storage, and had come out to surround her, covering the floor of the video feet, crowding in and brushing up against her legs and feet.

The mechaniques began to sing with her, not with human voices, but with deliberate, pure sweetness—almost like the voices of the Gondoliers.

The world seemed to pause and listen for a moment.

As the song ended, Océan, off-camera, exclaimed in surprise. "We're in countdown! Shit! Halt, *Téméraire*, abort! Stop!"

Another window had appeared on Lemure's screen: a countdown timer, ten seconds left to launch.—They would have to leave soon, if they were going to avoid the debris.

Manon shoved Ammaline into a seat, then followed suit. Océan shouted at the ship for a few more seconds.

Ammaline called, "I'm not sure what's going on, Papa, but the ship is taking off! It's an accident. We'll figure it out soon. We'll be back soon. I promise, Papa. Don't worry about me. We'll be back soon!"

He told her, "I'll be waiting for you. I want to hear all about it."

"Okay, Papa! I love you!"

The screen went dark.

Lemure smiled at the screen. He did not know where the ship would take them, or what they would find there.

But he knew that it was Paul who had saved his daughter, the daughter of Marks Lemure, one of the Twelve cursed gods of Thomàon, and his wife Etoile, whose name meant *star*, or *hope*.

As the *Téméraire* burst through the atmosphere, and moved its way further out into space—and as the two Earth ships descended toward the Silver City—Lemure realized his wife had been right all along. Her faith had not been misplaced.

He had been more than a murderer, more than a monster; in the end, he had been a father, too.

Author Checkin!

Hi all!

Today I'm roasting butternut squash and the house smells good. I'm going to be making butternut ravioli with wonton wrappers later after a Foodwishes/Chef John recipe.—It's weird how staying focused on tangible things, like not setting off the fire alarm, can help you stay a little more grounded in this weird reality we're in.

Back in 2018, after reading my way through a ton of horror best-of lists, I came up with an idea to write the weirdest haunted house books I could come up with. Fun project, right? Easy, too. A real no-brainer.

The House Without a Summer was the first of the haunted house books. I started with a core idea from a romance novel that had face-planted itself, and went nuts turning it into a horror novel instead. There's still a romance in it, but the romance is a *minor* subplot. What happened was: I was reading through some books on the history of the Industrial Era, and the repeated patterns of things that were happening in contemporary politics started to catch up to me. *The House Without a Summer* is about the inevitable collapse of an empire, about big leaps in technology and how assholes exploit them, about how trying to make things ever more efficient can lead to inflexibility in the face of environmental change.

Yeah.

I published it in March 2020, right after COVID-19 hit. The appropriateness of the timing wasn't lost on me.

When I started House of Masks in August 2019, it was a few loose pages and a synopsis that didn't go anywhere. I wanted to tell a story about a collection of godlike figures who slowly realize that not only is there a traitor among them, but that they're small fry in a *very* big ocean.

One of the ways that power corrupts (particularly when you're an asshole) is that it makes you think you have *absolute* power when you don't even know what scale power exists on.

I got stuck. I was busy. I put it to the side, let my brain rumble it around, and decided the book I was writing was probably going to be longer than I knew how to write at the time. I started typing in Charles Dickens's *A Tale of Two Cities* to study the structure and try to learn how to plot better—and things fell into place and I started writing the novel before I finished the studying. (I often typed up the same chapter in Dickens that I was writing in *House of Masks,* but I eventually made it all the way through.)

Meanwhile my personal life was quickly falling apart: during quarantine it rapidly became evident that my marriage was a sham, and that I wasn't a *strong person* so much as I was a *victim.* Less than a month later came the murder of George Floyd by Minneapolis Police officer Derek Chauvin, and the subsequent riots, infiltration by bad actors among the protestors, the police and military started suppressing the riots violently in some cities, and half the country lost their minds, calling the police response *justice.* I went to therapy. America as a whole wasn't that lucky.

I had tossed my first outline when I started typing in Dickens (I kept the character names; coming up with them is always the worst part of writing a story for me), and instead decided to let myself go off the rails plotwise, as long as I stuck to the same structure as *A Tale of Two Cities*.

I started turning the events of the day into fictional form, consciously and deliberately.

The more I watched history happening, the more I realized that the world had spent a lot of time with history at a standstill, one that had made the poor get poorer and the truly wealthy become private nation-states...who now had *zero* interest in maintaining the status quo.

I'd known for years that we were headed for trouble; Western (white) civilization was always going to face irreconcilable issues sooner rather than later: global climate change and increased competition for natural resources; the end of the Middle-Class White American empire (because of demographic change); extreme wealth discrepancies that meant that billionaires and corporations ruled the planet, not so-called governments and nations.

But I hadn't realized until I got into the thick of the writing that we'd reached a tipping point, and it was *now*.

And then I moved across the country, got derailed a dozen times because of perfectly valid reasons, stopped writing for a while, and kept putting off publishing this story because it cut too close to home. But that's the risk of writing a haunted-house story that reflects current events on either the personal or public scales: you might realize what you thought was your *home* is merely a *house*, and also one that doesn't have your best interests at heart.

So this is a dark book. I'm proud of finishing it. I wish the world were different. I'm not sure where we go from here. Maybe everything takes an irrevocable turn for the worse.

But I'm not gonna *self-destruct* over it. The bastards are gonna have to catch me first.

Love, De

Tampa February 21, 2025

Acknowledgements

Hm. This one is tough to write acknowledgments for. The place this story came from was isolated and angry and scared, and it's hard to be grateful about that.

So let me acknowledge Heather Cox Richardson's *Letters from an American* for keeping me up on the more significant events in a way I could stomach. That much at least makes sense.

As always, for Ray.

We made it.

More To Read!

Chapter 1 – Return to Penderbrook

October 1816

The year had been, and would continue to be, a bad one, something that was obvious even to a bounder like Marcus.

The weather had been remarkably ill, for one thing. The last frost had occurred in mid-June, and even later in some parts of Scotland. Or so Marcus had been informed. The heaviness of the winter had been such that the roofs of several of the homes in the village near Penderbrook had collapsed from the snow during the previous winter. He had heard similar if unsubstantiated tales from France, but the possibility of it seemed more monstrous, when applied to a place he knew so well. Several people had been smothered to death, sealed in by the snow and killed by their own fireplaces.

While Marcus had been fighting Napoleon in parts abroad, his brother, Barnabas, had sent him neatly-penned monthly letters containing little more than daily climatological data, taken at sunrise, noon, sunset, and often midnight. Marcus couldn't have cared less about the reports but had found his brother's constancy reassuring.

Then his brother had begun to complain of unusual weather patterns, including dropped temperatures and increase in rain- and snowfalls. The winter had been an unusually long one, with snow lingering until the early parts of July. England was not known for its sunny nature, but the flooding that then occurred, between heavy rains and delayed snowmelt, was beyond the ridiculous. Barnabas's meteorological constancy, once re-assuring, became distressing. Streams flowed six feet above their banks; ponds flooded; freshly-sown crops were swept away; likewise, fowl, pigs, and cattle; people drowned merely for the sin of having lived too near a swollen creek which had been a mere trickle in years past.

The first frosts had then come in early September. There was talk every-where of refusing to sell grain outside of one's district. Even in France he had heard such things. He had heard there was rioting in London, too, which he had scoffed at until he had seen it for himself. The poor were starving. And the Earl of Liverpool's government seemed to think that the solution to the problem was that the poor needed to correct themselves from *laziness*.

The wars having ended (*for now*, Marcus added mentally every time he heard someone say it), there was no more market for the goods that the new factories of the United Kingdom had begun producing with such enthusiasm, and tens of thousands of men and their desperate families roamed the land, begging for food. Work? What work? Employment often had to be created entire, with ponds being dredged, bridges built, roads repaired—such was the charity of the English, that they could not simply dole it out, without demanding hard labor in exchange for it. Charity! Call it plain hard labor, for that was what it was, wherever Marcus saw it.

He been quartered with his regiment in Derbyshire when Barnabas's final letter had arrived.

It had expressed no signs of distress or especial trouble, other than that of the weather. It contained descriptions of certain insects that Barnabas had identified in the hopes of having found a new species of some sort of red beetle, sketches included; his final analysis of the harvest, which was extremely poor; and a request for Marcus to come home for Christmas, made by Lucy Abbott and repeated by Barnabas at her instruction.

That last item had stood out to him. Lucy Abbott was a neighbor of theirs, a girl only a year or two younger than Marcus, who had been their playmate when they were children. Why would she want to see Marcus? He had teased her mercilessly. She was dark and morose, too serious to be pretty, although she had grown into her looks as a young woman. She had not married, but had remained at home to care for her father. Had Barnabas formed some sort of connection with her? An engagement? They *were* a matched set, with their long and too-serious faces. If they were engaged, he approved of it. Barnabas would hardly tolerate a wife of a simple, sunny nature; he would treat her as though she were one of his specimens. Lucy Abbott he would treat as he would an assistant, or a fellow man of science. If there were no physical passion there, at least there would be a sort of mental passion to replace it.

Finally, Barnabas had described a sort of sunspot. He said the spot had been quite dark during the first part of the year, then had more or less stopped during the brief thaw lasting from mid-June to mid-September, but had returned with the frosts.

Marcus wondered that Barnabas had not mentioned it previously. Marcus himself had heard every sort of rumor about the sunspots: that they heralded the coming of the Savior, that men had cut down so many trees in America that it had affected the sky itself, that the Earth was moving further and further away from the sun, that the sun itself was going out, that a falling star had knocked the Earth out of its orbit, that the war with Napoleon had driven God Himself to end His Creation, and that there was an overabundance of men in China, which had caused the rotation of the Earth to go lopsided. He had even heard the implausible theory that a volcano halfway 'round the world had erupted, casting its smoke into the air in such volume that it was affecting the skies of Europe.

It was all madness, rumors spread by impressionable minds.

But it was true that even to the naked eye, one could see that a dark shape had spread across the face of the sun, as though the sun itself were being wrapped in the dark fingers of some monstrous hand. The grip of that hand upon the sun was not steady; some days were brighter, others, dimmer. Marcus had viewed the sunspots through a pair of special glasses that one of his men had had made, which only upset him: with the naked eye, it was possible to tell oneself that the darkness was only in the atmosphere, like a speck of dirt floating on the surface of one's eye. But to see the spots through a pair of dark glasses was to see the sun itself affected. Obscene black spots wandered slowly across the surface, like the terrible suppurations of leprosy.

Marcus had drunk himself into a stupor that night. His doing so was not especially remarked upon; he had always had something of a head for drink, and could be relied upon to pull himself into sobriety by his bootstraps when necessary, in the morning. And they had all gone a little strange after what they had seen in France.

He had promised himself that he would write to his brother, saying that he would come to Pender brook for Christmas, barring any resumption of the fighting.

But he had not.

Then he received another letter from Penderbrook, this time written by Lucy Abbott:

Marcus,

Your brother has had a terrible accident, and has passed into the arms of his Savior. I beg you to return to Penderbrook as soon as possible. Things are difficult with your father, who, I am very sorry to say, does not seem to comprehend the event of your brother's death. I do not like to speak further on the matter in a letter. You are needed in the most urgent manner. You need only write if you find yourself delayed.

Your friend,

Lucy

Immediately Marcus went to his superior officer and told the man what he knew, which was little enough. He was released from duty, with the assumption that he would sell his commission at a later date, for, with his brother's death, Marcus had become his father's heir. He took a series of post-carriages back to Daventry, in Northamptonshire, arriving only two days after he had received the letter, then hired a final post-chaise to take him home.

PENDERBROOK WAS PERHAPS THE greatest house in all of England. It had thirty-one bedrooms and twenty-four chimneys. Its carriage-house was the size of other families' palatial mansions.

It was faced in white marble and consisted of one upper storey. It was elegantly proportioned, with two wings surrounding a magnificent entrance. The grounds were likewise of a truly impressive character, with open grounds, orchards, lanes, hedges, a pond, woods, open fields with cattle, even a folly that his father had had built behind the house: the perfectly ridiculous, manufactured ruins of a Norman church, which consisted of half a tower that was open to the weather and two and three-quarters walls, with the front doors still more or less "intact." Stained glass remained, uncracked, in the windows. An altar and several pews remained within; the altar was often decorated with posies by the Earl's guests.

As Marcus approached the house, he was overcome by emotion. *Here* he had climbed a tree. *There* he had swum in the pond. And *there* he had slept in the field, dreaming of becoming a general, a leader of armies, a master strategist.

Every memory of his involved the tall, dark, sombre shadow of his brother, rarely intrusive, always present.

Yet now gone.

Happier memories of summers past had been replaced by a limp, gray sort of autumn. Icy drizzle disappeared as it touched the wet earth. The grass, which generally lingered with a faded greenness until the snows covered it, had turned brown. It was clearly sodden through, drowning in the standing water which lay everywhere about the property, seeming to reflect nothing but the leaden sky. The oaks clung to their yellowish, rotting leaves. The leaves on the elms had turned brown but clung to the branches as though they feared to fall. The marble walls of the main house looked the same color as the sky; they needed cleaning. The windows were streaked with water. Black stains had collected underneath them, as though each glazed pane had begun to weep. The small fish pond had flooded over its banks, and, further downstream, the level of the lake was also very high. At any moment, the temperature could sink, and the icy rain could become snow.

Within the house, a few of the candles had already been lit, even though it was not yet sunset; he could see their dull light from behind the window-panes.

The driver pulled the post-carriage to the front of the house, where a man waited for Marcus: Barton, his father's valet. It was tactful, if not entirely regular, that Barton be waiting for him. Barton had always been like a sort of uncle to Marcus, a guiding star in the senseless heavens of his father's orbit, but was of no direct relation whatsoever.

Marcus climbed out of the carriage and shoved a sovereign at the driver.

"Sorry to hear about Lord Barnabas, m'lord," the man said. He had said so previously.

Marcus said, "Please drink to him, if you are a drinking man." He strode towards the door of the house. From the corners of his eyes, he saw servants moving towards the carriage to collect what few possession she had brought with him. Within moments—as though to escape Penderbrook as soon as might be possible—the post-carriage turned in the drive, and hurried away.

Marcus reached Barton and shook his hand heartily.

Barton was one of those small, compact Irishmen who are deadly in a brawl, and seem built of spite, gristle, sullenness, and loyalty. "My lord."

The statement would have been insufficient greeting for anyone other than Barton, who managed to convey both trouble and sympathy with those plain two words.

"Barton. Is my brother truly dead?"

"Aye, my lord. More to it than that. Miss Abbott will tell you the whole story…I'll fetch her. She's the one for telling tales."

Barton wasn't wrong; Lucy Abbott had fancied herself something of a lady-writer, of distinctly dark and foolish tales—or at least she had when Marcus had left to join up with his regiment.

Marcus said, "Let's go in, unless you have something you need to tell me outside while we stand in the freezing rain."

He turned towards the door, but Barton put a hand on his shoulder. "Your father's mad," Barton said. "Talks as though Barny's going to walk backinto the room any time now."

"Good God. Is Barnabas buried yet?"

Barton shook his head. "Down t' the wine cellar."

"*What?*"

"Miss Abbott. She'll explain."

You can read more here or at your preferred retailer.

About the Author

DeAnna Knippling is a versatile author celebrated for her imaginative storytelling across multiple genres, including gothic horror, steampunk, puzzle mystery, psychological suspense, and dark fantasy. Her works, such as *The House Without a Summer* and *The Clockwork Alice*, have garnered praise for their inventive narratives and unique twists on classic tales. Readers commend her ability to blend the macabre with the whimsical, creating immersive worlds that captivate and intrigue. Whether exploring twisted fairytales or unraveling crime, DeAnna's stories linger long after the final page. Find her at WonderlandPress.com.